Further praise for *Let the Great World Spin*

'A glorious, thumping tale of intersecting lives, told in language which all but sings'   Kamila Shamsie, *Guardian* Books of the year

'Lives collide dramatically in this beautifully written New York novel'
                                                    Financial Times Books of the Year

'A lyrical cycloramic high-low portrait of New York City in its days of burning . . . a masterful chorus of voices'
                        Richard Price, author of *Lush Life* and writer on *The Wire*

'Wonderful . . . McCann himself is a writer who doesn't fear high-wire acts . . . He is that rare species in contemporary fiction: a literary writer who is an exceptional storyteller. This novel never trumpets itself as a metropolitan kaleidoscope, but prefers the quiet intimacy of personal suffering'   Douglas Kennedy, *Independent*

'A bravura performance by McCann: a subtle allegory of 9/11'
                                                    Times Literary Supplement

'McCann has spun a mad, bad and seductive world of his own, riding life's subtle fluctuations like a master tightrope walker'   *Metro*

'The first great 9/11 novel . . . It is a pre-9/11 novel that delivers the sense that so many of the 9/11 novels have missed: We are all dancing on the wire of history, and even on solid ground we breathe the thinnest of air'
                                                    Esquire

'Stunning . . . [an] elegiac glimpse of hope . . . It's a novel rooted firmly in time and place. It vividly captures New York at its worst and best. But it transcends all that. In the end, it's a novel about families – the ones we're born into and the ones we make for ourselves'   *USA Today*

'McCann has a sympathetic talent for character and a flair for the lyric'
Guardian

'It is a mark of the novel's soaring and largely fulfilled ambition that McCann just keeps rolling out new people, deftly linking each to the next, as his story moves toward its surprising and deeply affecting conclusion . . . *Let the Great World Spin* is an emotional tour de force. It is a heartbreaking book, but not a depressing one'
New York Times

'Spins with a dizzying array of characters'
Image

'Mesmerizing . . . weaves a portrait of a city and a moment, dizzyingly satisfying to read and difficult to put down'
Seattle Times

'With a series of spare, gorgeously wrought vignettes, Colum McCann brings 1970s New York to life . . . And as always, McCann's heart-stoppingly simple descriptions wow'
Entertainment Weekly

'The Great New York Novel. With echoes of Wolfe, Doctorow, and DeLillo, Colum McCann's mesmerizing *Let the Great World Spin* is a prophetic portrait of New York City in the summer of 1974 . . . One of the year's best novels'
Daily Beast

'[McCann] both resurrects and redeems the horrors of September 11, creating a metaphorical landscape of human endurance in the face of unspeakable tragedy . . . This is McCann's gift, finding grace in grief and magic in the mundane'
San Francisco Chronicle

'A shimmering, shattering novel. In McCann's wise and elegiac novel of origins and consequences, each of his finely drawn, unexpectedly connected characters balances above an abyss, evincing great courage with every step'
Booklist

LET THE GREAT WORLD SPIN

COLUM MCCANN, born in Dublin, Ireland,
is the author of five novels and two collections
of stories. He has won numerous international
literary awards. *Zoli*, *Dancer* and *This Side of
Brightness* were international bestsellers and
his fiction has been published in over thirty
languages. He lives in New York.

ALSO BY COLUM McCANN

Zoli

Dancer

Everything in This Country Must

This Side of Brightness

Songdogs

Fishing the Sloe-Black River

LET THE GREAT
WORLD SPIN

COLUM McCANN

BLOOMSBURY
LONDON · BERLIN · NEW YORK · SYDNEY

First published in Great Britain 2009

This paperback edition published 2010

Copyright © 2009 by Colum McCann

The moral right of the author has been asserted

Bloomsbury Publishing, London, Berlin and New York

36 Soho Square, London W1D 3QY

A CIP catalogue record for this book is available from the British Library

ISBN 978 1 4088 1092 7
10 9 8 7 6 5 4 3

Printed in Great Britain by Clays Ltd, St Ives plc

FSC
Mixed Sources
Product group from well-managed
forests and other controlled sources
Cert no. SGS - COC - 2061
www.fsc.org
© 1996 Forest Stewardship Council

www.bloomsbury.com/colummccann

For John, Frank, and Jim.
And, of course, Allison.

"*All the lives we could live, all the people we will never know, never will be, they are everywhere. That is what the world is.*"

—Aleksandar Hemon,
THE LAZARUS PROJECT

CONTENTS

LET THE GREAT
WORLD SPIN

Those who saw him hushed. On Church Street. Liberty. Cortlandt. West Street. Fulton. Vesey. It was a silence that heard itself, awful and beautiful. Some thought at first that it must have been a trick of the light, something to do with the weather, an accident of shadowfall. Others figured it might be the perfect city joke—stand around and point upward, until people gathered, tilted their heads, nodded, affirmed, until all were staring upward at nothing at all, like waiting for the end of a Lenny Bruce gag. But the longer they watched, the surer they were. He stood at the very edge of the building, shaped dark against the gray of the morning. A window washer maybe. Or a construction worker. Or a jumper.

Up there, at the height of a hundred and ten stories, utterly still, a dark toy against the cloudy sky.

He could only be seen at certain angles so that the watchers had to pause at street corners, find a gap between buildings, or meander from the shadows to get a view unobstructed by cornicework, gargoyles, balustrades, roof edges. None of them had yet made sense of the line strung at his feet from one tower to the other. Rather, it was the man-shape that held them there, their necks craned, torn between the promise of doom and the disappointment of the ordinary.

It was the dilemma of the watchers: they didn't want to wait around for nothing at all, some idiot standing on the precipice of the towers, but they didn't want to miss the moment either, if he slipped, or got arrested, or dove, arms stretched.

Around the watchers, the city still made its everyday noises. Car horns. Garbage trucks. Ferry whistles. The thrum of the subway. The M22 bus pulled in against the sidewalk, braked, sighed down into a pothole. A flying chocolate wrapper touched against a fire hydrant. Taxi doors slammed. Bits of trash sparred in the darkest reaches of the alleyways. Sneakers found their sweetspots. The leather of briefcases rubbed against trouserlegs. A few umbrella tips clinked against the pavement. Revolving doors pushed quarters of conversation out into the street.

But the watchers could have taken all the sounds and smashed them down into a single noise and still they wouldn't have heard much at all: even when they cursed, it was done quietly, reverently.

They found themselves in small groups together beside the traffic lights on the corner of Church and Dey; gathered under the awning of Sam's barbershop; in the doorway of Charlie's Audio; a tight little theater of men and women against the railings of St. Paul's Chapel; elbowing for space at the windows of the Woolworth Building. Lawyers. Elevator operators. Doctors. Cleaners. Prep chefs. Diamond merchants. Fish sellers. Sad-jeaned whores. All of them reassured by the presence of one another. Stenographers. Traders. Deliveryboys. Sandwichboard men. Cardsharks. Con Ed. Ma Bell. Wall Street. A locksmith in his van on the corner of Dey and Broadway. A bike messenger lounging against a lamppost on West. A red-faced rummy out looking for an early-morning pour.

From the Staten Island Ferry they glimpsed him. From the meatpacking warehouses on the West Side. From the new high-rises in Battery Park. From the breakfast carts down on Broadway. From the plaza below. From the towers themselves.

Sure, there were some who ignored the fuss, who didn't want to be bothered. It was seven forty-seven in the morning and they were too jacked up for anything but a desk, a pen, a telephone. Up they came from the subway stations, from limousines, off city buses, crossing the street at a clip, refusing the prospect of a gawk. Another day, another dolor. But as they passed the little clumps of commotion they began to slow down. Some stopped altogether, shrugged, turned nonchalantly, walked to the corner, bumped up against the watchers, went to the tips of their toes, gazed over the crowd, and then introduced themselves with a *Wow* or a *Gee-whiz* or a *Jesus H. Christ*.

The man above remained rigid, and yet his mystery was mobile. He stood beyond the railing of the observation deck of the south tower—at any moment he might just take off.

Below him, a single pigeon swooped down from the top floor of the Federal Office Building, as if anticipating the fall. The movement caught the eyes of some watchers and they followed the gray flap against the small of the standing man. The bird shot from one eave to another, and it was then the watchers noticed that they had been joined by others at the windows of offices, where blinds were being lifted and a few glass panes labored upward. All that could be seen was a pair of elbows or the end of a shirtsleeve, or an arm garter, but then it was joined by a head, or an odd-looking pair of hands above it, lifting the frame even higher. In the windows of nearby skyscrapers, figures came to look out—men in shirtsleeves and women in bright blouses, wavering in the glass like funhouse apparitions.

Higher still, a weather helicopter executed a dipping turn over the Hudson—a curtsy to the fact that the summer day was going to be cloudy and cool anyway—and the rotors beat a rhythm over the warehouses of the West Side. At first the helicopter looked lopsided in its advance, and a small side window was slid open as if the machine were looking for air. A lens appeared in the open window. It caught a brief flash of light. After a moment the helicopter corrected beautifully and spun across the expanse.

Some cops on the West Side Highway switched on their misery lights, swerved fast off the exit ramps, making the morning all the more magnetic.

A charge entered the air all around the watchers and—now that the day had been made official by sirens—there was a chatter among them, their balance set on edge, their calm fading, and they turned to one another and began to speculate, would he jump, would he fall, would he tiptoe along the ledge, did he work there, was he solitary, was he a decoy, was he wearing a uniform, did anyone have binoculars? Perfect strangers touched one another on the elbows. Swearwords went between them, and whispers that there'd been a botched robbery, that he was some sort of cat burglar, that he'd taken hostages, he was an Arab, a Jew, a Cypriot, an IRA man, that he was really just a publicity stunt, a corporate scam, *Drink more Coca-Cola, Eat more Fritos, Smoke more Parliaments, Spray more Lysol, Love more Jesus.* Or that he was a protester and he was going to hang a slogan, he would slide it from the towerledge, leave it there to flutter in the breeze, like some giant piece of sky laundry—NIXON OUT NOW! REMEMBER 'NAM, SAM! INDEPENDENCE FOR INDOCHINA!—and then someone said that maybe he was a hang glider or a parachutist, and all the others laughed, but they were perplexed by the cable at his feet, and the rumors began again, a collision of curse and whisper, augmented by an increase in sirens, which got their hearts pumping even more, and the helicopter found a purchase near the west side of the towers, while down in the foyer of the World Trade Center the cops were sprinting across the marble floor, and the undercovers were whipping out badges from beneath their shirts, and the fire trucks were pulling into the plaza, and the redblue dazzled the glass, and a flatbed truck arrived with a cherry picker, its fat wheels bouncing over the curb, and someone laughed as the picker kiltered sideways, the driver looking up, as if the basket might reach all that sad huge way, and the security guards were shouting into their walkie-talkies, and the whole August morning was blown wide open, and the watchers stood rooted, there was no going anywhere for a while, the voices rose to a crescendo, all sorts of accents, a babel, until a small redheaded man in the Home Title Guarantee Company on Church Street lifted the sash of his office window, placed his elbows on the sill, took a deep breath, leaned out, and roared into the distance: Do it, asshole!

There was a dip before the laughter, a second before it sank in among the watchers, a reverence for the man's irreverence, because secretly that's what so many of them felt—Do it, for chrissake! Do it!—and then a torrent of chatter was released, a call-and-response, and it seemed to ripple all the way from the windowsill down to the sidewalk and along the cracked pavement to the corner of Fulton, down the block along Broadway, where it zigzagged down John, hooked around to Nassau, and went on, a domino line of laughter, but with an edge to it, a longing, an awe, and many of the watchers realized with a shiver that no matter what they said, they really wanted to witness a great fall, see someone arc downward all that distance, to disappear from the sight line, flail, smash to the ground, and give the Wednesday an electricity, a meaning, that all they needed to become a family was one millisecond of slippage, while the others—those who wanted him to stay, to hold the line, to become the brink, but no farther—felt viable now with disgust for the shouters: they wanted the man to save himself, step backward into the arms of the cops instead of the sky.

They were jazzed now.

Pumped.

The lines were drawn.

Do it, asshole!

Don't do it!

Way above there was a movement. In the dark clothing his every twitch counted. He folded over, a half-thing, bent, as if examining his shoes, like a pencil mark, most of which had been erased. The posture of a diver. And then they saw it. The watchers stood, silent. Even those who had wanted the man to jump felt the air knocked out. They drew back and moaned.

A body was sailing out into the middle of the air.

He was gone. He'd done it. Some blessed themselves. Closed their eyes. Waited for the thump. The body twirled and caught and flipped, thrown around by the wind.

Then a shout sounded across the watchers, a woman's voice: God, oh God, it's a shirt, it's just a shirt.

It was falling, falling, falling, yes, a sweatshirt, fluttering, and then their eyes left the clothing in midair, because high above the man had unfolded upward from his crouch, and a new hush settled over the cops above and the watchers below, a rush of emotion rippling among them, because the man had arisen from the bend holding a long thin bar in his hands, jiggling it, testing its weight, bobbing it up and down in the air, a long black bar, so pliable that the ends swayed, and his gaze was fixed on the far tower, still wrapped in scaffolding, like a wounded thing waiting to be reached, and now the cable at his feet made sense to everyone, and whatever else it was there would be no chance they could pull away now, no morning coffee, no conference room cigarette, no nonchalant carpet shuffle; the waiting had been made magical, and they watched as he lifted one dark-slippered foot, like a man about to enter warm gray water.

The watchers below pulled in their breath all at once. The air felt suddenly shared. The man above was a word they seemed to know, though they had not heard it before.

Out he went.

BOOK ONE

ONE OF THE MANY THINGS my brother, Corrigan, and I loved about our mother was that she was a fine musician. She kept a small radio on top of the Steinway in the living room of our house in Dublin and on Sunday afternoons, after scanning whatever stations we could find, Radio Éireann or BBC, she raised the lacquered wing of the piano, spread her dress out at the wooden stool, and tried to copy the piece through from memory: jazz riffs and Irish ballads and, if we found the right station, old Hoagy Carmichael tunes. Our mother played with a natural touch, even though she suffered from a hand which she had broken many times. We never knew the origin of the break: it was something left in silence. When she finished playing she would lightly rub the back of her wrist. I used to think of the notes still trilling through the bones, as if they could skip from one to the other, over the breakage. I can still after all these years sit in the museum of those afternoons and recall the light spilling across the carpet. At times our mother put her arms around us both, and then guided our hands so we could clang down hard on the keys.

It is not fashionable anymore, I suppose, to have a regard for one's mother in the way my brother and I had then, in the mid-1950s, when the noise outside the window was mostly wind and sea chime. One looks for the chink in the armor, the leg of the piano stool shorter than the other, the sadness that would detach us from her, but the truth is we enjoyed each other, all three of us, and never so evidently as those Sundays when the rain fell gray over Dublin Bay and the squalls blew fresh against the windowpane.

Our house in Sandymount looked out to the bay. We had a short driveway full of weeds, a square of lawn, a black ironwork fence. If we crossed the road we could stand on the curved seawall and look a good distance across the bay. A bunch of palm trees grew at the end of the road. They stood, smaller and more stunted than palms elsewhere, but exotic nonetheless, as if invited to come watch the Dublin rain. Corrigan sat on the wall, banging his heels and looking over the flat strand to the water. I should have known even then that the sea was written in him, that there would be some sort of leaving. The tide crept in and the water swelled at his feet. In the evenings he walked up the road past the Martello Tower to the abandoned public baths, where he balanced on top of the seawall, arms held wide.

On weekend mornings we strolled with our mother, ankle-deep in the low tide, and looked back to see the row of houses, the coastline, and the little scarves of smoke coming up from the chimneys. Two enormous red and white towers broke the horizon to the east, but the rest was a gentle curve, with gulls on the air, the mail boats out of Dun Laoghaire, the scud of clouds on the horizon. When the tide was out, the stretch of sand was corrugated and sometimes it was possible to walk a quarter-mile among isolated waterpools and bits of old refuse, long shaver shells, bedstead pipes.

Dublin Bay was a slow heaving thing, like the city it horseshoed, but it could turn without warning. Every now and then the water smashed up against the wall in a storm. The sea, having arrived, stayed. Salt crusted the windows of our house. The knocker on the door was rusted red.

When the weather blew foul, we sat on the stairs, Corrigan and I. Our father, a physicist, had left us years before. A check, postmarked in London, arrived through the letter box once a week. Never a note, just a check, drawn on a bank in Oxford. It spun in the air as it fell. We ran to bring it to our mother. She slipped the envelope under a flowerpot on the kitchen windowsill and the next day it was gone. Nothing more was ever said.

The only other sign of our father was a wardrobe full of his old suits and trousers in our mother's bedroom. Corrigan drew the door open. In the darkness we sat with our backs against the rough wooden panels and slipped our feet in our father's shoes, let his sleeves touch our ears, felt the cold of his cuff buttons. Our mother found us one afternoon, dressed in his gray suits, the sleeves rolled up and the trousers held in place with elastic bands. We were marching around in his oversize brogues when she came and froze in the doorway, the room so quiet we could hear the radiator tick.

"Well," she said, as she knelt to the ground in front of us. Her face spread out in a grin that seemed to pain her. "Come here." She kissed us both on the cheek, tapped our bottoms. "Now run along." We slipped out of our father's old clothes, left them puddled on the floor.

Later that night we heard the clang of the coat hangers as she hung and rehung the suits.

Over the years there were the usual tantrums and bloody noses and broken rocking-horse heads, and our mother had to deal with the whispers of the neighbors, sometimes even the attentions of local widowers, but for the most part things stretched comfortably in front of us: calm, open, a sweep of sandy gray.

Corrigan and I shared a bedroom that looked out to the water. Quietly it happened, I still don't recall how: he, the younger one by two years, took control of the top bunk. He slept on his stomach with a view out the window to the dark, reciting his prayers—he called them his slumber verses—in quick, sharp rhythms. They were his own incantations, mostly indecipherable to me, with odd little cackles of laughter and long sighs. The closer he got to sleep the more rhythmic the prayers got, a sort of jazz, though sometimes in the middle of it all I could hear him curse, and they'd be lifted away from the sacred. I knew the Catholic hit parade—the Our Father, the Hail Mary—but that was all. I was a raw, quiet child, and God was already a bore to me. I kicked the bottom of Corrigan's bed and he fell silent awhile, but then started up again. Sometimes I woke in the morning and he was alongside me, arm draped over my shoulder, his chest rising and falling as he whispered his prayers.

I'd turn to him. "Ah, Jesus, Corr, shut up."

My brother was light-skinned, dark-haired, blue-eyed. He was the type of child everyone smiled at. He could look at you and draw you out.

People fell for him. On the street, women ruffled his hair. Workingmen punched him gently on the shoulder. He had no idea that his presence sustained people, made them happy, drew out their improbable yearnings—he just plowed along, oblivious.

I woke one night, when I was eleven, to a cold blast of air moving over me. I stumbled to the window but it was closed. I reached for the light and the room burned quickly yellow. A shape was bent over in the middle of the room.

"Corr?"

The weather still rolled off his body. His cheeks were red. A little damp mist lay on his hair. He smelled of cigarettes. He put a finger to his lips for hush and climbed back up the wooden ladder.

"Go to sleep," he whispered from above. The smell of tobacco still lingered in the air.

In the morning he jumped down from the bed, wearing his heavy anorak over his pajamas. Shivering, he opened the window and tapped the sand from his shoes off the sill, into the garden below.

"Where'd you go?"

"Just along by the water," he said.

"Were you smoking?"

He looked away, rubbed his arms warm. "No."

"You're not supposed to smoke, y'know."

"I didn't smoke," he said.

Later that morning our mother walked us to school, our leather satchels slung over our shoulders. An icy breeze cut along the streets. Down by the school gates she went to one knee, put her arms around us, adjusted our scarves, and kissed us, one after the other. When she stood to leave, her gaze was caught by something on the other side of the road, by the railings of the church: a dark form wrapped in a large red blanket. The man raised a hand in salute. Corrigan waved back.

There were plenty of old drunks around Ringsend, but my mother seemed taken by the sight, and for a moment it struck me that there might be some secret there.

"Who's that, Mum?" I asked.

"Run along," she said. "We'll sort it out after school."

My brother walked beside me, silent.

"Who is it, Corrie?" I thumped him. "Who is it?"

He disappeared towards his classroom.

All day I sat at my wooden desk, gnawing my pencil, wondering—visions of a forgotten uncle, or our father somehow returned, broken. Nothing, in those days, was beyond the realm of the possible. The clock was at the rear of the room but there was an old freckled mirror over the classroom sink and, at the right angle, I could watch the hands go backwards. When the bell struck I was out the gate, but Corrigan took the long road back, short, mincing steps through the housing estates, past the palm trees, along the seawall.

There was a soft brown paper package waiting for Corrigan on the top bunk. I shoved it at him. He shrugged and ran his finger along the twine, pulled it tentatively. Inside was another blanket, a soft blue Foxford. He unfolded it, let it fall lengthwise, looked up at our mother, and nodded.

She touched his face with the back of her fingers and said: "Never again, understand?"

Nothing else was mentioned, until two years later he gave that blanket away too, to another homeless drunk, on another freezing night, up by the canal on one of his late-night walks, when he tiptoed down the stairs and went out into the dark. It was a simple equation to him—others needed the blankets more than he, and he was prepared to take the punishment if it came his way. It was my earliest suggestion of what my brother would become, and what I'd later see among the cast-offs of New York—the whores, the hustlers, the hopeless—all of those who were hanging on to him like he was some bright hallelujah in the shitbox of what the world really was.

—

CORRIGAN STARTED GETTING drunk young—twelve or thirteen years old—once a week, on Friday afternoons after school. He'd run from the gates in Blackrock towards the bus stop, his school tie off, his blazer bundled, while I stayed behind in the school fields, playing rugby. I could see him hop on the 45 or the 7A, his silhouette moving towards the backseat of the bus as it pulled away.

Corrigan liked those places where light was drained. The docklands. The flophouses. The corners where the cobbles were broken. He often sat with the drunks in Frenchman's Lane and Spencer Row. He brought a bottle with him, handed it around. If it came back to him he drank with a flourish, wiping the back of his hand across his mouth as if he were a practiced drunk. Anyone could tell he wasn't a real drinker—he didn't search it out, and drank from the bottle only when it came his way. I suppose he thought he was fitting in. He got laughed at by the more vicious drunks but he didn't care. They were using him, of course. He was just another snotnose trying on the poorman shoes, but he had a few pennies in his pockets and was always prepared to give them up—they sent him to the off-license for bottles, or to the corner shop for loose cigarettes.

Some days he came home not wearing any socks. Other times he was shirtless and ran up the stairs before our mother caught him. He brushed his teeth and washed his face and came down, fully dressed, a little starry-eyed, not quite drunk enough to get caught.

"Where were you?"

"God's work."

"And is God's work not looking after your mother?" She adjusted his shirt collar as he sat down to dinner.

After a while with the down-and-outs he began to fit in, slipped into the background, melted in among them. He walked with them to the flophouse on Rutland Street and sat slumped up against the wall. Corrigan listened to their stories: long, rambling tales that seemed rooted in a different Ireland altogether. It was an apprenticeship for him: he crept in on their poverty as if he wanted to own it. He drank. He smoked. He never mentioned our father, not to me or anyone else. But he was there, our gone father, I could tell. Corrigan would either drown him in sherry or spit him away like a fleck of tobacco from his tongue.

The week he turned fourteen my mother sent me to pick him up: he'd been gone all day and she'd baked a cake for him. An evening drizzle fell over Dublin. A horsecart went past, the light from its dynamo shining. I watched it clop away down the street, the pinpoint of light spreading. I hated the city at times like that—it had no desire to get out from under its grayness. I walked on past the bed-and-breakfast houses, the antique shops, the candle makers, the suppliers of liturgical medals. The flophouse was marked by a black gate, ironwork sharpened to points. I went to the back, where the bins were kept. Rain dripped from a broken pipe. I stepped over a pile of crates and cardboard boxes, shouting his name. When I found him, he was so drunk that he couldn't stand. I grabbed his arm. "Hi," he said, smiling. He fell against the wall and cut his hand. He stood staring at his palm. The blood ran down his wrist. One of the younger drunks—a teddy boy in a red T-shirt—spat at him. It was the only time I ever saw Corrigan throw a punch. It missed completely but blood from his hand flew, and I knew—even while I watched it—that it was a moment I would never forget, Corrigan swinging in midair, droplets of his blood spraying the wall.

"I'm a pacifist," he said, slurring his words.

I walked him all the way along the Liffey, past the coal ships and into Ringsend, where I washed him with water from the old hand pump on Irishtown Road. He took my face in his hands. "Thank you, thank you." He began to cry as we got to Beach Road, which led towards our house. A deep dark had fallen over the sea. Rain dripped from the roadside palms. I hauled him back from the sand. "I'm soft," he said. He wiped his sleeve across his eyes, lit a cigarette, coughed until he threw up.

At the gate of the house, he looked up to the light in our mother's bedroom. "Is she awake?"

He minced his steps up the driveway but once inside he charged up the stairs, ran into her arms. She smelled the drink and tobacco off him, of course, but didn't say anything. She ran a bath for him, sat outside the door. Silent at first, she let her feet stretch across the landing, then laid her head against the doorjamb and sighed: it was as if she too were in a bath, stretching out towards days yet to be remembered.

He put on his clothes, stepped out into the landing, and she toweled his hair dry.

"You won't drink again, will you, love?"

He shook his head no.

"A curfew on Fridays. Home by five. You hear me?"

"Fair enough."

"Promise me now."

"Cross my heart and hope to die."

His eyes were bloodshot.

She kissed his hair and held him close. "There's a cake downstairs for you, love."

Corrigan took two weeks off from his Friday jaunts, but soon began to meet the drunks again. It was a ritual he couldn't give up. The down-and-outs needed him, or at least wanted him—he was, to them, a mad, impossible angel. He still drank with them, but only on special days. Mostly he was sober. He had this idea that the men were really looking for some type of Eden and that when they drank they returned to it, but, on getting there, they weren't able to stay. He didn't try to convince them to stop. That wasn't his way.

It might've been easy for me not to like Corrigan, my younger brother who sparked people alive, but there was something about him that made dislike difficult. His theme was happiness—what it is and what it might not have been, where he might find it and where it might have disappeared.

I was nineteen, and Corrigan was seventeen, when our mother died. A short, quick struggle with kidney cancer. The last thing she told us was to take care to close the curtains so the light didn't fade the living room carpet.

She was taken to St. Vincent's Hospital on the first day of summer. The ambulance left wet tracks along the sea road. Corrigan cycled furiously after it. She was put in a long ward full of sick patients. We got her a private room and filled it with flowers. We took turns sitting at her bedside, combing her hair, long and brittle to the touch. Clumps of it came out in the comb. For the first time ever she had a jilted air about her: her body was betraying her. The bedside ashtray filled with hair. I clung to the idea that if we kept her long gray strands we could get back to the way we once were. It was all I could manage. She lasted three months, then passed on a September day when everything seemed split open with sunlight.

We sat in the room waiting for the nurses to appear and take her body away. Corrigan was in the middle of a long prayer when a shadow appeared in the hospital doorway.

"Hello, boys."

Our father had an English accent on his grief. I hadn't seen him since I was three years old. A stringpiece of light fell on him. He was pale and hunched. There was a smattering of hair across his scalp, but his eyes were a pellucid blue. He took off his hat and put it to his chest. "Sorry, lads."

I went across to shake his hand. It startled me that I was taller than him. He gripped my shoulder and squeezed.

Corrigan remained silent, in the corner.

"Shake my hand, son," our father said.

"How did you know she was sick?"

"Go on, now, shake my hand like a man."

"Tell me how you knew."

"Are you going to shake my hand or not?"

"Who told you?"

He rocked back and forth on his heels. "Is that any way to treat your father?"

Corrigan turned his back and laid a kiss on our mother's cold brow, left without saying a word. The door closed with a snap. A cage of shadow crossed the bed. I went to the window and saw him yank his bicycle away from a pipe. He rode through the flowerbeds and his shirt flapped as he merged into the traffic on Merrion Road.

My father pulled up a chair and sat beside her, touched her forearm through the sheets.

"When she didn't cash the checks," he said to me.

"Pardon me?"

"That's when I knew she was sick," he said. "When she didn't cash the checks."

A sliver of cold moved down my chest.

"I'm only telling you the truth," he said. "If you can't stand the truth, don't ask for it."

Our father came to sleep in our house that night. He carried a small suitcase with a black mourning suit and a pair of polished shoes. Corrigan stopped him as he made his way up the stairs. "Where d'you think you're going?" Our father gripped the banister. His hands were liver-spotted and I could see him trembling in his pause. "That's not your room," said Corrigan. Our father tottered on the stairs. He took another step up. "Don't," said my brother. His voice was clear, full, confident. Our father stood stunned. He climbed one more step and then turned, descended, looked around, lost.

"My own sons," he said.

We made a bed for him on a sofa in the living room, but even then Corrigan refused to stay under the same roof: he went walking in the direction of the city center, and I wondered what alley he might be found in later that night, what fist he might walk into, whose bottle he might climb down inside.

The morning of the funeral, I heard our father shouting Corrigan's first name. "John, John Andrew." A door slammed. Another. And then a long silence. I lay back against the pillow, allowed the quiet to surround me. Footsteps on the stairs. The creak at the top step. The noises were full of mystery. Corrigan rumbled through the downstairs cupboards and slammed the front door.

When I went to the window I saw a line of well-dressed men on the strand, right outside our house. They were wearing our father's old suits and hats and scarves. One had tucked a red handkerchief in the breast pocket of the black suit. Another carried a pair of polished shoes in his hand. Corrigan went among them, a little lopsided, his hand jammed down into his trouser pocket, where he was holding a bottle. He was shirtless and wild-looking. A head of uncombed hair. His arms and neck were brown, but the rest of his body was pale. He grinned and waved at my father standing now at the front door, barefoot, stunned, watching a dozen copies of himself out walking the tidal sands.

A couple of women I recognized from the charity lines at the flophouses were sauntering along the mucky sand in my mother's old summer dresses, celebrating their new clothes.

—

CORRIGAN TOLD ME once that Christ was quite easy to understand. He went where He was supposed to go. He stayed where He was needed. He took little or nothing along, a pair of sandals, a bit of a shirt, a few odds and ends to stave off the loneliness. He never rejected the world. If He had rejected it, He would have been rejecting mystery. And if He rejected mystery, He would have been rejecting faith.

What Corrigan wanted was a fully believable God, one you could find in the grime of the everyday. The comfort he got from the hard, cold truth—the filth, the war, the poverty—was that life could be capable of small beauties. He wasn't interested in the glorious tales of the afterlife or the notions of a honey-soaked heaven. To him that was a dressing room for hell. Rather he consoled himself with the fact that, in the real world, when he looked closely into the darkness he might find the presence of a light, damaged and bruised, but a little light all the same. He wanted, quite simply, for the world to be a better place, and he was in the habit of hoping for it. Out of that came some sort of triumph that went beyond theological proof, a cause for optimism against all the evidence.

"Someday the meek might actually want it," he said.

After our mother died, we sold the house. Our father took half the money. Corrigan gave his portion away. He lived off the charity of others and began studying the work of Francis of Assisi. For hours on end he would walk the city, reading. He made himself sandals out of some scrap leather and wore wild-colored socks underneath. He became a staple on the streets of Dublin in the mid-sixties, with stringy hair and carpenter pants, books tucked under his arm. He had a long, shambling stride. He went around penniless, coatless, shirtless. Every August, on the anniversary of Hiroshima, he locked himself to the gates of the Parliament on Kildare Street, a quiet vigil for one night, no photos, no journalists, just him and his cardboard box spread out on the ground.

When he was nineteen he began studying with the Jesuits at Emo College. Mass in the early dawn. Hours of theological study. Afternoon walks through the fields. Night walks along the Barrow River, beseeching his God out under the stars. The morning prayers, the noontime prayers, the evening prayers, the complines. The glorias, the psalms, the gospel readings. They gave a rigor to his faith, it staked him to a purpose. Still, the hills of Laois couldn't hold him. He couldn't be an ordinary priest—it wasn't the life for him; he was ill defined for it, he needed more space for his doubt. He left the novitiate and went to Brussels, where he joined a group of young monks who took their vows of chastity, poverty, obedience. He lived in a small flat in the center of the city. Grew his hair out. Kept his head in books: Augustine, Eckhart, Massignon, Charles de Foucauld. It was a life of ordinary labor, friendship, solidarity. He drove a fruit truck for a local cooperative and organized a labor union for a small group of workers. In his work he wore no religious garments, or collars, carried no Bible, and preferred to stay quiet, even around the brothers of his own Order.

Few of the people who came across him ever knew of his religious ties and, even in those places where he spent the longest, he was seldom known for his beliefs—instead, people looked at him with a fondness for another era, when time seemed slower, less complicated. Even the worst of what men did to one another didn't dampen Corrigan's beliefs. He might have been naïve, but he didn't care; he said he'd rather die with his heart on his sleeve than end up another cynic.

The only furniture he owned was his oak-wood prayer kneeler and his bookshelves. The shelves were lined with a number of religious poets, radicals mostly, and some liberation theologians. He had long angled for a posting somewhere in the Third World but couldn't get one. Brussels was too ordinary for him. He wanted somewhere with a rougher plot. He spent a while in the slums of Naples, working with the poor in the Spanish Quarter, but then was shipped off to New York in the early seventies. He disliked the idea, bucked against it, thought New York too mannered, too antiseptic, but had no sway with those higher up in his Order—he had to go where he was sent.

He boarded a plane with a suitcase full of books, his kneeler, and a Bible.

—

I HAD DROPPED OUT of university and spent the best part of my late twenties in a basement flat on Raglan Road, catching the tail end of the hippie years. Like most things Irish, I was a couple of years too late. I drifted into my thirties, found a desk job, but still wanted the old reckless life.

I had never really followed what happened up north. Sometimes it seemed like an entirely foreign land, but in the spring of '74 the violence came south.

I went to the Dandelion Market one Friday evening to buy some marijuana, an occasional habit. It was one of the few places where Dublin hummed: African beads, lava lamps, incense. I bought half an ounce of Moroccan hash at a stall for secondhand records. I was walking along South Leinster Street into Kildare Street when the air shook. Everything went yellow for an instant, a perfect flash, then white. I was knocked through the air, against a fence. I woke, panic all around. Shards of glass. An exhaust pipe. A steering wheel rolling in the street. The wheel flopped, exhausted, and all was strangely still until the sirens rang out, as if already mourning. A woman went by with her dress torn neck to hem, as if designed to show off her chest wound. A man stooped to help me up. We ran together a few yards, then parted. I was stumbling around the corner towards Molesworth Street when a Garda stopped me and pointed to a few spots of blood on my shirt. I fainted. When I woke in hospital they told me I'd lost a little flesh at the lobe of my right ear when I'd been slammed back against the spear of a railing. A fleur-de-lis. Such fine irony. The tip of my ear left behind on the street. The rest of me was intact, even my hearing.

At the hospital the police went through my pockets to look for identification. I was arrested for possession and brought to the courthouse, where the judge took pity and said it was a wrongful search, gave me a lecture, and sent me on my way. I went straight to a travel agency on Dawson Street, bought my ticket out.

I came through John F. Kennedy Airport in a long necklace and an Afghan coat, carrying a torn copy of *Howl*. The customs men sniggered. The cloth latch on my rucksack snapped when I tried to put it together again.

I stood looking around for Corrigan—he had promised, in a postcard, that he'd meet me. It was eighty-seven degrees in the shade. The heat hit me with the force of an ax. The waiting area pulsed. Families roamed about, pushing past one another to get at flight information. Taxi drivers had a shiny menace to them. No sign of my brother anywhere. I sat on my rucksack for an hour until a policeman with a billy club prodded me and knocked the book out of my hands.

I boarded a bus amid the swelter and noise. Later on the subway I loitered beneath the whirling fan. A black woman stood beside me, fanning herself with a magazine. Ovals of sweat at her underarms. I had never seen a black woman so close before, her skin so dark it was almost blue. I wanted to touch it, just press her forearm with my finger. She caught my eye and pulled her blouse tight: "Whatcha lookin' at?"

"Ireland," I blurted. "I'm Irish."

A moment later she glanced at me again. "No kiddin'," she said. She got off at 125th Street, where the train screeched to a halt.

It was nightfall by the time I reached the Bronx. I stepped out of the station to the late heat. Gray brick and billboards. A rhythmic sound came from a radio player. A kid in a sleeveless shirt spun on a piece of cardboard, his shoulder somehow a fulcrum for his whole body. A loosening of contour. No limits. Hands to the ground, his feet whipped out a long extended circle. He went low and suddenly spun on his head, then arced backwards, unsprung, and hopped into the air, darkness moving.

Some gypsy cabs idled on the Concourse. Old white men in wide hats. I flung my rucksack into the boot of a giant black car.

"Ants in their pants, man," said the driver as he leaned over the seat. "You think that kid's gonna go anywhere? After spinning on his goddamn head?"

I gave him Corrigan's address on a slip of paper. He grunted something about power steering, said they never had it in 'Nam.

After half an hour we pulled sharply into the curve. We had been driving in elaborate circles. "Twelve bucks, bud." No point in arguing. I threw the money over the seat, got out, grabbed my rucksack. The driver of the cab pulled off before I got a chance to close the boot. I clutched my copy of *Howl* to my chest. *I saw the best minds of my generation.* The lid of the taxi bounced and slammed shut when the driver turned sharply by the traffic lights and away.

On one side was a row of high-rise tenements behind a chain-link fence. Parts of the fence were topped with razor wire. On the other, the expressway: the light-streak of cars zipping above. Below, by the underpass, a long line of women. Cars and trucks were pulling into the shadows. The women struck poses. They wore hotpants and bikini tops and swimsuits, a bizarre city beach. An angled arm, in the shadowlight, reached the top of the expressway. A stiletto climbed to the top of a barbed-wire fence. A leg stretched half the length of a city block.

Nightbirds flew out from under the highway girders, momentarily intent on the sky, but then swooped back into hiding.

A woman emerged from under the girdings. She wore a fur coat open at the shoulders and spread her knee-high boots wide. A car went by and she threw open the coat. Underneath she wore nothing at all. The car beeped and sped off. She screamed after it, started walking my way, carrying what looked like a parasol.

I scanned the balconies of the high-rises for any sign of Corrigan. The street lights flickered. A plastic bag tumbled. Some shoes were strung on the high telegraph wire.

"Hey, honey."

"I'm broke," I said without turning around. The hooker spat thickly at my feet and raised the pink parasol over her head.

"Asshole," she said as she walked past.

She stood on the lit side of the street and waited underneath the parasol. Every time a car went past she lowered and raised it, making herself into a little planet of light and dark.

I carried my rucksack towards the projects with as much nonchalance as I could. Heroin needles lay along the inside of the fence, among the weeds. Someone had spray-painted the sign near the entrance to the flats. A few old men sat outside the lobby, fanning themselves in the heat. They looked ruined and decrepit, the sort of men who'd soon turn into empty chairs. One of them reached for the slip of paper with my brother's address written on it, shook his head, sagged back.

A kid ran past, a metallic sound coming from him, a tinny bounce. He disappeared into the darkness of a stairwell. The smell of fresh paint drifted from him.

I turned the corner to another corner: it was all corners.

Corrigan's place was in a gray block of flats. The fifth floor of twenty. A little sticker by the doorbell: PEACE AND JUSTICE in a crown of thorns. Five locks on the doorframe. None of them worked. I pushed the door open. It swung and banged. A little bit of white plaster fell from the wall. I called his name. The place was bare but for a torn sofa, a low table, a simple wooden crucifix over the single wooden bed. His prayer kneeler faced against the wall. Books lay on the floor, open, as if speaking to one another: Thomas Merton, Rubem Alves, Dorothy Day.

I stepped over to the sofa, exhausted.

I woke later to the parasol hooker slamming through the doorway. She stood mopping her brow, then threw her handbag on the sofa beside me. "Oops, sorry, honey," she said. I turned my face so she wouldn't recognize me. She walked across the room, hitching off her fur coat as she went, naked but for her boots. She stopped a moment, looked in a long slice of broken mirror propped against the wall. Her calf muscles were smooth and curved. She hitched the flesh of her bottom, sighed, then stretched and rubbed her nipples full. "Goddamn," she said. The sound of running water came from the bathroom.

The hooker emerged with her lipstick bright and a new clack in her step. The sharp smell of perfume filled the air. She blew me a kiss, waved the parasol, left.

It happened five or six times in a row. The turn of the door handle. The ping of stilettos on the bare floorboards. A different hooker each time. One even leaned down and let her long thin breasts hang in my face. "College boy," she said like an offer. I shook my head and she said curtly: "I thought so." She turned at the door and smiled. "There'll be lawyers in heaven before you see somethin' so good again."

She went down the corridor, laughing.

In the bathroom was a small metal rubbish can. Tampons and sad polyps of used condoms wrapped in tissue.

Corrigan woke me later that night. I had no idea what time it was. He wore the same type of thin shirt he had for years: black, collarless, long-sleeved, with wooden buttons. He was thin, as if the sheer volume of the poor had worn him wayward to his old self. His hair was shoulder length and he had grown out his sideburns, a little punch of gray already at his temples. His face was cut slightly, and his right eye bruised. He looked older than thirty-one.

"Beautiful world you're living in, Corrigan."

"Did you bring tea?"

"What happened you? Your cheek? It's cut."

"Tell me you at least brought a few tea bags, brother?"

I opened the rucksack. Five boxes of his favorite. He kissed my forehead. His lips were dry. His stubble stung.

"Who beat you up, Corr?"

"Don't worry about me—let me see you."

He reached up and touched my right ear, where the tip of the lobe was gone.

"You all right?"

"It's a memento, I suppose. You still a pacifist?"

"Still," he said with a grin.

"You've got nice friends."

"They just need to use the bathroom. They're not allowed turn tricks. They weren't turning tricks in here, were they?"

"They were naked, Corrigan."

"No they weren't."

"I'm telling you, man, they were naked."

"They don't like cumbersome clothes," he said with a little laugh. He palmed my shoulder, pushed me back on the couch. "Anyway, they must've been wearing shoes. It's New York. You have to have good stilettos."

He put the kettle on, lined up the cups.

"My very serious brother," he said, but his chuckle died away as he turned the flame on the stove high. "Look, man, they're desperate. I just want to give them a little spot that they can call their own. Get out of the heat. Splash some water on their faces." His back was turned. I was reminded of how, years before, he had drifted away from one of our afternoon strolls and got surrounded by the tide—Corrigan, isolated on a sandbar, tangled in light, voices from the shore drifting over him, calling his name. The kettle whistled, louder now and shrill. Even from the back he looked like he'd been knocked around. I said his name, once, twice. On the third time he snapped to, turned, smiled. It was almost the same as when he'd been a child—he looked up, waved, and returned waist-high through the water.

"On your own here, Corr?"

"Just for a while."

"No Brothers? No others with you?"

"Oh, I'm getting to know the immemorial feelings," he said. "The hunger, the thirst, being tired at the end of the day. I've started wondering if God's around when I wake up in the middle of the night."

He seemed to be talking to a point over my shoulder. His eyes were deep and pouchy. "That's what I like about God. You get to know Him by His occasional absence."

"You all right, Corr?"

"Never better."

"So who beat you up?"

He looked away. "I had a run-in with one of the pimps."

"Why?"

"Because."

"Because why, man?"

"Because he claimed I was taking up their time. Guy calls himself Birdhouse. Only got one good eye. Go figure. In he came, knocked on the door, said hello, called me brother this, brother that, real nice and polite, even hung his hat on the doorknob. Sat down on the sofa and looked up at the crucifix. Said he had a real appreciation for the holy life. Then produced a length of lead pipe that he'd ripped from the toilet. Imagine that. He'd been sitting there all that time, just letting my bathroom flood."

He shrugged.

"But they still come around," he said. "The girls. I don't encourage it, really. I mean, what are they going to do? Pee on the street? It's not much. Just a little gesture. A place they can use. A tinkling shop."

He arranged the tea and a plate of biscuits, went to his prayer kneeler—a simple piece of wood that he tucked behind him to support his body as he knelt—and gave his thanks to God for the biscuits, the tea, the appearance of his brother.

He was still praying when the door swung hard and in marched three hookers. "Ooh, snowing in here," cooed the parasol hooker as she stood under the fan. "Hi, I'm Tillie." The heat oozed from her: little droplets of sweat on her forehead. She dropped her parasol on the table, looked at me with a half-grin. She was made up to be seen from a distance: she wore huge sunglasses with rose-colored rims and sparkly eye makeup. Another girl kissed Corrigan on the cheek, then started primping in the broken slice of mirror. The tallest, in a white tissue minidress, sat down beside me. She looked half Mexican, half black. She was taut and lithe: she could have been walking down a runway. "Hi," she said, grinning. "I'm Jazzlyn. You can call me Jazz."

She was very young—seventeen or eighteen—with one green eye, one brown. Her cheekbones were pulled even higher by a line of makeup. She reached across, lifted Corrigan's teacup, blew it cool, left a smudge of lipstick on the rim.

"I don't know why you don't put ice in this shit, Corrie," she said.

"Don't like it," said Corrigan.

"If you wanna be American you gotta put ice in it."

The parasol hooker giggled then as if Jazzlyn had just said something fabulously rude. It was like they had a code going between them. I edged away, but Jazzlyn leaned across and picked a piece of lint off my shoulder. Her breath was sweet. I turned again to Corrigan.

"Did you get him arrested?"

My brother looked confused: "Who?" he said.

"The bloke who beat you up?"

"Arrested for what?"

"Are you serious?"

"Why would I get him arrested?"

"Did someone beat you up again, honey?" said the parasol hooker. She was staring at her fingers. She bit a long edge of fingernail from her thumb, examined the little slice. She scraped the fingernail paint off with her teeth, and flicked the slice of nail towards me from off her extended finger. I stared at her. She flashed a white grin. "I can't stand it when I get beaten up," she said.

"Jesus," I muttered to the window.

"Enough," said Corrigan.

"They always leave marks, don't they?" said Jazzlyn.

"Okay, Jazz, enough, okay?"

"Once, this guy, this asshole, this quadruple motherfucker, he used a telephone book on me. You want to know something about the telephone book? Lots of names and not one of them leaves a mark."

Jazzlyn stood up and removed her loose blouse. She wore a neon-yellow bikini underneath. "He hit me here and here and here."

"Okay, Jazz, time to go."

"I bet you could find your own name here."

"Jazzlyn!"

She stood and sighed. "Your brother's cute," she said to me. She buttoned her blouse. "We love him like chocolate. We love him like nicotine. Isn't that right, Corrie? We love you like nicotine. Tillie's got a crush on him. Ain't you, Tillie? Tillie, you listening?"

The parasol hooker stepped away from the mirror. She touched the edge of her mouth where the lipstick smeared. "Too old to be an acrobat, too young to die," she said.

Jazzlyn was fumbling under the table with a small glassine package. Corrigan leaned across and touched her hand. "Not here, you know you can't do that in here." She rolled her eyes, sighed, and dropped a needle in her handbag.

The door bounced on its hinges. All of them blew kisses, even Jazzlyn, with her back turned. She looked like some failed sunflower, her arm curving backwards as she went.

"Poor Jazz."

"What a mess."

"Well, at least she's trying."

"Trying? She's a mess. They all are."

"Ah, no, they're good people," Corrigan said. "They just don't know what it is they're doing. Or what's being done to them. It's about fear. You know? They're all throbbing with fear. We all are."

He drank the tea without cleaning the lipstick off the rim.

"Bits of it floating in the air," he said. "It's like dust. You walk about and don't see it, don't notice it, but it's there and it's all coming down, covering everything. You're breathing it in. You touch it. You drink it. You eat it. But it's so fine you don't notice it. But you're covered in it. It's everywhere. What I mean is, we're afraid. Just stand still for an instant and there it is, this fear, covering our faces and tongues. If we stopped to take account of it, we'd just fall into despair. But we can't stop. We've got to keep going."

"For what?"

"I don't know—that's my problem."

"What are you into here, Corr?"

"I suppose I have to put flesh on my words, y'know. But sometimes that's my dilemma too, man. I'm supposed to be a man of God but I hardly ever mention Him to anyone. Not to the girls, even. I keep these thoughts to myself. For my own peace of mind. The ease of my conscience. If I started thinking them out loud all the time I think I'd go mad. But God listens back. Most of the time. He does."

He drained the teacup and cleaned the rim with the flap of his shirt.

"But these girls, man. Sometimes I think they're better believers than me. At least they're open to the faith of a rolled-down window."

Corrigan turned the teacup upside down onto his palm, balanced it there.

"You missed the funeral," I said.

A little dribble of tea sat in his palm. He brought his hand to his mouth and tongued it.

Our father had died a few months before. In the middle of his university classroom, a lecture about quarks. Elementary particles. He had insisted on finishing his class while a pain shot down his left arm. *Three quarks for Muster Mark.* Thank you, class. Safe home. Good night. Bye-bye. I was hardly devastated, but I had left Corrigan dozens of messages, and even got through to the Bronx police, but they said there was nothing they could do.

In the graveyard I had kept turning, hoping to see him coming up the narrow laneway, maybe even in one of our father's old suits, but he never appeared.

"Not too many people there," I said. "Small English churchyard. A man cutting the grass. Didn't turn the engine off for the service."

He kept tilting the teacup on his hand, as if trying to get the last drops out.

"What scriptures did they use?" he said finally.

"I can't remember. Sorry. Why?"

"Doesn't matter."

"What would you have used, Corr?"

"Oh, I don't know, really. Something Old Testament, maybe. Something primal."

"Like what, Corr?"

"Not sure exactly."

"Go on, tell me."

"I don't know!" he shouted. "Okay? I don't fucking know!"

The curse stunned me. The shame flushed him red. He lowered his gaze, scrubbed the cup with the flap of his shirt. The sound of it made a high, unusual squeak and I knew then that there'd be no more talk about our father. He had closed that path down, quick and hard, made a border; do not cross here. It pleased me a little to think that he had a flaw and that it went so deep that he couldn't deal with it. Corrigan wanted other people's pain. He didn't want to deal with his own. I felt a pulse of shame too, for thinking that way.

The silence of brothers.

He tucked the prayer kneeler at the back of his knees, like a wooden cushion, and he began mumbling.

When he stood he said: "Sorry for cursing."

"Yeah, me too."

At the window, he absently pulled the cord of the blinds open and shut. Down below, a woman by the underpass screamed. He parted the window blind again, with two fingers.

"Sounds like Jazz," he said.

The orange streetlight from the window latticed him as he crossed the floor at a clip.

—

HOURS AND HOURS of insanity and escape. The projects were a victim of theft and wind. The downdrafts made their own weather. Plastic bags caught on the gusts of summer wind. Old domino players sat in the courtyard, playing underneath the flying litter. The sound of the plastic bags was like rifle fire. If you watched the rubbish for a while you could tell the exact shape of the wind. Perhaps in a way it was alluring, like little else around it: whole, bright, slapping curlicues and large figure eights, helixes and whorls and corkscrews. Sometimes a bit of plastic caught against a pipe or touched the top of the chain-link fence and backed away gracelessly, like it had been warned. The handles came together and the bag collapsed. There were no tree branches to be caught on. One boy from a neighboring flat stuck a lineless fishing pole out the window but he didn't catch any. The bags often stayed up in one place, as if they were contemplating the whole gray scene, and then they would take a sudden dip, a polite curtsy, and away.

I'd fooled myself into thinking I'd some poems in me while I was in Dublin. It was like hanging old clothes out to dry. Everyone in Dublin was a poet, maybe even the bombers who'd treated us to their afternoon of delight.

I'd been in the South Bronx a week. It was so humid, some nights, we had to shoulder the door closed. Kids on the tenth floor aimed television sets at the housing cops who patrolled below. Air mail. The police came in, clubbing. Shots rang out from the rooftop. On the radio there was a song about the revolution being ghettoized. Arson on the streets. It was a city with its fingers in the garbage, a city that ate off dirty dishes. I had to get out. The plan was to look for a job, get my own little place, maybe work on a play, or get a job on a paper somewhere. There were ads in the circulars for bartenders and waiters, but I didn't want to go that way, all flat hats and micks in shirtsleeves. I found a gig as a telemarketer but I needed a dedicated phone line in Corrigan's apartment, and it was impossible to get a technician to visit the housing complex: this was not the America I had expected.

Corrigan wrote out a list of things for me to see, Chumley's bar in the Village, the Brooklyn Bridge, Central Park by day. But I had little money to speak of. I went to the window and watched the plot of the days unfold. The rubbish accused me. Already the smell rose up to the fifth-floor windows.

Corrigan worked as part of his Order's ethic, made a few bob by driving a van for some old folk in the local nursing home. The bumper was tied with rusted wire. The windows were plastered with his peace stickers. The front headlights hung loose in the grille. He was gone most of the day, in charge of the ones that were infirm. What was ordeal for others was grace for him. He picked them up in the late morning in the nursing home on Cypress Avenue—mostly Irish, Italian, one old Jewish man, nicknamed Albee, in a gray suit and skullcap. "Short for Albert," he said, "but if you call me Albert I'll kick your ass." I sat in with them a few afternoons, men and women—most of them white—who could have been folded up just like their wheelchairs. Corrigan drove at a snail's pace so as not to bounce them around. "You drive like a pussy," said Albee from the backseat. Corrigan laid his head against the steering wheel and laughed, but kept his foot on the brake.

Cars behind us beeped. A hellish ruckus of horns. The air was stifled with ruin. "Move it, man, move it!" Albee shouted. "Move the goddamn van!"

Corrigan took his foot off the brake and slowly guided the van around to the playground at St. Mary's, where he wheeled the old folk out into whatever bits of shade he could find. "Fresh air," he said. The men sat rooted like Larkin poems. The old women looked shaken, heads nodding in the breeze, watching the playground. It was mostly black or Hispanic kids, zooming down the slides or swinging on the monkey bars.

Albee managed to wheel himself into the corner, where he took out sheets of paper. He bent over them and said not another word, scratching on the paper with a pencil. I hunkered down beside him.

"What you doing there, friend?"

"None of your goddamn business."

"Chess, is it?"

"You play?"

"Right on."

"You rated?"

"Rated?"

"Oh, get the fuck outta here—you're a pussy too."

Corrigan winked at me from the edge of the playground. This was his world and he plainly loved it.

Lunch had been made for them in the old folks' home, but Corrigan went across the road to the local bodega to buy them extra potato crisps, cigarettes, a cold beer for Albee. A yellow awning. A bubblegum machine sat triple-chained to the shutters. A dustbin was overturned at the corner. There had been a garbage strike earlier that spring and still it wasn't all cleaned up. Rats ran along the street gutters. Young men in sleeveless tops stood malevolently in the doorways. They knew Corrigan, it seemed, and as he disappeared inside he gave them a series of elaborate hand-shakes. He spent a long time inside and came out clutching large brown paper bags. One of the hoodlums back-slapped him, grabbed his hand, drew him close.

"How d'you do that?" I asked. "How d'you get them to talk to you?"

"Why wouldn't they?"

"It just seems, I don't know, they're tough, y'know."

"Far as they're concerned, I'm just a square."

"You're not worried? You know, a gun, or something, a switchblade?"

"Why would I be?"

Together we loaded the old folk up in the van. He revved the engine and drove to the church. There had been a vote among the old folk, the church as opposed to the synagogue. It was daubed in graffiti—whites, yellows, reds, silvers. TAGS 173. GRACO 76. The stained-glass windows had been broken with small stones. Even the cross on top was tagged. "The living temple," said Corrigan. The elderly Jewish man refused to get out. He sat, head down, saying nothing, skipping through the notes in his book. Corrigan opened the back of the van and slipped him an extra beer over the seat.

"He's all right, our Albee," said Corrigan as he strolled away from the back of the van. "All he does is work on those chess problems all day long. Used to be a grandmaster or something. Came from Hungary, found himself in the Bronx. He sends his games off in the post somewhere. Does about twenty games all at once. He can play blindfolded. It's the only thing that keeps him going."

He helped the others out of the van and we wheeled them one by one towards the entrance. "Let's walk the plank." There were a series of bro-ken steps at the front but Corrigan had stashed two long pieces of wood around the side, near the sacristy. He laid the planks parallel to each other and guided the chairs up. The wood lifted in the air with the weight of the wheelchairs, and for a moment they looked like they were bound for the sky. Corrigan pushed them forward and the planks slapped back down. He had the look of a man at ease. A shine in the corners of his eyes. You could see the gone boy in him, the nine-year-old back in Sandy-mount.

He left the old folk waiting by the holy-water font, until they were all lined up, ready to go.

"My favorite moment of the day, this," he said. He crossed over into the cool dark of the church, rolled them to whatever spot they wanted, some in the rear pews, some to the sides.

An old Irish woman was brought up to the very front, where she wrapped and rewrapped her rosary beads. She had a mane of white hair, blood in the corner of her eyes, an otherworldly stare. "Meet Sheila," said Corrigan. She could hardly speak anymore, barely able to make a sound. A cabaret singer, she had lost most of her voice to throat cancer. She had been born in Galway but emigrated just after the First World War. She was Corrigan's favorite and he stayed near her, said the formal prayers alongside her: a decade of the Rosary. She had no idea, I'm sure, about his religious ties, but there was an energy about her in that church she didn't have elsewhere. She and Corrigan, it was like they were praying together for a good rain.

When we got out into the street again, Albee was dozing in the van, a bit of spittle on his chin. "Goddamn it," he muttered when the engine rumbled into life. "Pair of pussies, the two of ya."

Corrigan pulled into the nursing home in the late afternoon, then dropped me off in front of the housing project. He had another job to do, he said; there was someone he had to see.

"It's a little project I'm working on," he said, over his shoulder. "Nothing to worry about. I'll see you later."

He climbed in and touched something in the glove box of his van before he took off. "Don't wait up for me," he called. I watched him go, hand out the window, waving. He was holding something back, I knew.

It was pitch black when I saw him finally arriving back down among the whores alongside the Major Deegan. He gave out iced coffee from a giant silver canister that he kept in the back of the van. The girls gathered around him as he spooned ice into their cups. Jazzlyn wore a one-piece neon swimsuit. She tugged the back, snapped the elastic, edged close to him, gave the hint of a belly dance against his hip. She was tall, exotic, so very young she seemed to flutter. Playfully, she pushed him backwards. Corrigan ran a circle around her, high-stepping. A scream of laughter. She ran off when she heard a car horn blow. Around Corrigan's feet lay a row of empty paper coffee cups.

Later he came back upstairs, thin, dark-eyed, exhausted.

"How was your meeting?"

"Oh, grand, yeah," he said. "No problem."

"Out tripping the light fantastic?"

"Ah, yeah, the Copacabana, you know me."

He collapsed on the bed but was up early in the morning to a quick mug of tea. No food in the house. Just tea and sugar and milk. He said his prayers, and then touched the crucifix as he went towards the door once more.

"Down to the girls again?"

He looked at his feet. "I suppose so."

"You think they really need you, Corr?"

"Don't know," he said. "I hope so."

The door swung on its hinges.

I've never been interested in calling out the moral brigade. Not my place. Not my job. Each to his own. You get what you create. Corrigan had his reasons. But these women disturbed me. They were light-years removed from anything I'd ever known. The high of their eyes. Their heroin sway. Their swimsuits. Some of them had needle marks at the back of their knees. They were more than foreign to me.

Down in the courtyard, I walked the long way around the projects, following the broken lines in the concrete, just to avoid them.

A few days later a gentle knock sounded on the door. An older man with a single suitcase. Another monk from the Order. Corrigan rushed to embrace him. "Brother Norbert." He had come from Switzerland. Norbert's sad brown eyes gladdened me. He looked around the apartment, swallowed deeply, said something about the Lord Jesus and a place of deep shelter. On his second day Norbert was robbed in the lift at gunpoint. He said he had gladly given them everything, even his passport. There was a shine like pride in his eyes. The Swiss man sat in serious prayer for two solid days, not leaving the apartment. Corrigan stayed down on the streets most of the time. Norbert was too formal and correct for him. "It's like he's got a toothache and he wants God to cure it," said Corrigan.

Norbert refused the couch, lay on the floor. He balked each time the door opened and the hookers came in. Jazzlyn sat in his lap, ran his fingers on the rim of his ear, messed with his orthopedic shoes, hid them behind the couch. She told him that she could be his princess. He blushed until he almost wept. Later, when she was gone, his prayers became high-pitched and frantic. "The Beloved Life was spared, but not the pain, the Beloved Life was spared but not the pain." He broke down in tears. Corrigan was able to get Norbert's passport back and he drove him out to the airport in the brown van to get a flight to Geneva. Together they prayed and then Corrigan dispatched him. He looked at me as if he expected me to be leaving also.

"I don't know who these people are," he said. "They're my brothers, but I don't really know who they are. I've failed them."

"You should leave this hole, Corr."

"Why would I leave? My life's here."

"Find somewhere with a bit of sunshine. You and me together. I've been thinking about California or somewhere like that."

"I'm called here."

"You could be called anywhere."

"This is where I am."

"How did you get his passport back?"

"Oh, I just asked around."

"He was robbed at gunpoint, Corr."

"I know."

"You're going to get hurt."

"Oh, give me a break."

I went to the chair by the window and watched the large tractor-trailers pulling up under the highway. The girls jostled to get at them. A single neon sign blinked in the distance: an advertisement for oatmeal.

"The edge of the world here," said Corrigan.

"You could do something back home. In Ireland. Up north. Belfast. Something for us. Your own people."

"I could, yeah."

"Or shake up some campesinos in Brazil or something."

"Yeah."

"So why stay here?"

He smiled. Something had gone wild in his eyes. I couldn't tell what it was. He put his hands up close to the ceiling fan, as if he were about to thrust them in there, right up into the whirling blades, leave his hands there, watch them get mangled.

—

IN THE RAW OF mornings the girls stretched in a line along the block, though daylight thinned them out. After his morning matins, Corrigan went down to the corner deli to buy *The Catholic Worker*. Through the underpass, across the road, under the awning. Old men in their undershirts sat at the door, pigeons working bread crumbs at their feet. Corrigan came out carrying the paper tucked under his arm. I could see him as he crossed back, framed through the concrete eye of the underpass. Out of the shadows, he passed the hookers and they called to him in their singsong. It hit the scale on about three different notes. Corr—i-gan. Cor—rig-gan. Caw-rig-gun.

He passed through the gauntlet. Jazzlyn stood chatting with him, her thumb hooked under the strap of her swimsuit. She looked like an old-time cop in the wrong body, snapping the thin, lime-colored straps against her breasts. She leaned close to him again, her bare skin almost touching his lapel. He did not recoil. She was getting a charge from it all, I could tell. The lean of her young body. The hard snap of the strap. Her nipple against the fabric. Her head tilting closer and closer to him.

As cars passed, she turned to watch them, and her morning shadow lengthened. It was like she wanted to be everywhere, all at once. She leaned closer still and whispered in my brother's ear. He nodded, turned, and went back towards the deli, came out carrying a can of Coke. Jazzlyn clapped her hands in delight, took it from him, pulled the ring off, sauntered away. A row of eighteen-wheelers was parked along the expressway. She propped her leg on the silver grille and sipped from the can, then suddenly threw the drink on the ground and climbed up into the truck.

Halfway in the door, she was already removing her swimsuit. Corrigan turned away. The cola lay in a black puddle in the gutter beneath her.

It happened times in a row, Jazzlyn asking him for a can of Coke, then throwing it to the ground when she found a mark.

I thought I should go down to her, negotiate a price, and treat myself to whatever trick it was she was able for, grab the back of her hair, bring her face close to mine, that sweet breath, curse her, spit on her, for wringing out my brother's charity.

"Hey, leave the door open for them, will ya?" he said to me after he came home. I had taken to closing the locks in the afternoon, even though they pounded on the door.

"Why don't they piss in their own houses, Corrigan?"

"Because they don't have houses. They have apartments."

"Why don't they piss in their own apartments then?"

"Because they've got families. Mothers and fathers and brothers and sons and daughters. They don't want their families to see them dressed like that."

"They've got kids?"

"Sure."

"Jazz, she got kids?"

"Two," he said.

"Oh, man."

"Tillie's her mother."

I turned on him. I knew how it sounded. Step into that river, you don't step out—no return. It came out in a torrent, how disgusting they were, sucking on his blood, all of them, leaving him thin, dry, helpless, taking the life out of him, leeches, worse than leeches, bedbugs that crawled from the wallpaper; he was a fool—all his religiosity, all his pious horseshit, it came down to nothing, the world is vicious and that's what it amounts to, and hope is nothing more or less than what you can see with your own bare eyes.

He pulled at a small thread on the sleeve of his shirt, but I caught his elbow.

"Don't give me your shit about the Lord upholding all that fall and raising up all that be bowed down. The Lord's too big to fit in their miniskirts. Guess what, brother? Look at them. Look out the window. No amount of sympathy is ever going to change it. Why don't you cop on? You're just placating your conscience, that's all. God comes along and sanctifies your guilt."

His lips broke open a little. I waited but still he did not speak. We were so close together I could see his tongue move behind his teeth, flicking up and down like something nervous. His eyes were fixed and intent.

"Grow up, brother. Pack your bags, go somewhere you matter. They deserve nothing. They're not Magdalenes. You're just a bum among them. You're looking for the poor man within? Why don't you humble yourself at the feet of the rich for once? Or does your God just love use-less people?"

I could see the small, oblong reflection of the white door in his pupils, and I kept thinking that one of his hookers, one of his holy failures, was going to walk in and I'd see her reflection in the flicker.

"Why don't you embarrass the rich with some of your charity? Go sit on a rich woman's step and bring her to God? Tell me this—if the poor really are the living image of Jesus, why are they so fucking miserable? Tell me that, Corrigan. Why are they standing out there, displaying their misery to the rest of the world? I want to know. It's just vanity, isn't it? Love thy neighbor as thyself. It's rubbish. You listening? Why don't you take all those hookers of yours and have them go sing in the choir? The Church of the High Vision. Why don't you have them sit in the front pews? I mean, there you go on your knees to all the tramps and the lep-ers and the cripples and dopeheads. Why don't they do something? Be-cause they want nothing but to suck you dry, that's why."

Exhausted, I laid my head against the windowsill.

I kept waiting for him to give me some sort of bitter benediction—something about being weak towards the strengthless, strong against the powerful, there is no peace save in Jesus, freedom is given, not received, some catch-all to soothe me, but instead he let it all wash over him. His face did not betray a thing. He scratched the inside of his arm and nod-ded.

"Just leave the door open," he said.

He went down the stairwell, footsteps echoing, around the edge of the courtyard, disappeared into the grayness.

I ran down the slick steps of the apartment building. Huge swirls of fat graffiti on the walls. The drift of hash smoke. Broken glass on the bot-tom steps. Smells of piss and puke. Through the courtyard. A man held a pit bull on a training rope. He was teaching it to bite. The dog snapped at his arm: there were huge metal bracelets strapped across the man's wrists. The snarls rolled across the yard. Corrigan was backing up his brown van, which he'd parked on the side of the road. I slapped the win-dows. He didn't turn. I suppose I thought I might knock some sense into him, but after a moment the van was out of sight.

Over my shoulder the dog was snapping again at the man's arm, but the man was staring at me, like I was the one trying to rip his wrists. A half-smile crawled over his face, malevolent and pure. I thought: *Nigger*. I couldn't help it, but that's what I thought: *Nigger*.

This place would ruin me: how did Corrigan stand it?

I wandered the neighborhood, hands down deep in my pockets, not on the pavement, but at the edge of parked cars, an altered perspective. Taxis brushed by, close to my hip. The wind blew the smell of the subways up through the traffic. A hard, musty waft.

I went to the church on St. Ann's. Up the broken steps, into the vestibule, past the holy-water font, into the dark. I was half expecting to see him there, head bowed, praying, but no.

Small red electric candles could be lit at the back of the church. I dropped a quarter inside and heard the deep rattle against the emptiness. My father's ancient voice in my ear: *If you don't want the truth, don't ask for it.*

Corrigan came home to the apartment late that night. I left the door unlocked but he came in with a screwdriver anyway, began to take all the screws from the chains and locks. "Job to do." He was lethargic and his eyes were rolling around in his head and I should have known then, but I didn't recognize it. He knelt on the floor, eye-level with the doorknob. The underside of his sandals were worn down. The sole had faded away, a little bubble of flat rubber. His carpenter pants were tied around his waist with a length of cord. They wouldn't have stayed up on his hips otherwise. The long-sleeved shirt he wore was tight to his body and the bones of his ribcage were like some odd musical instrument.

He worked intently but he was using a flathead screwdriver for a Phillips head bolt and he had to prop the screwdriver sideways and angle it into the grooves.

I had already packed my bag and was ready to go, find a room, get a bartending job, anything, just get out of there. I pulled the couch into the center of the room under the ceiling fan, folded my arms, waited. The blades couldn't cut through the heat. For the first time ever I noticed that Corrigan had a bald spot beginning in the back of his hair. I wanted to make some crack about it being a monkish thing but there was nothing between us anymore, no words or glances. He toiled away at the locks. A couple of screws fell on the floor. I watched the beads of sweat come down the back of his neck.

He rolled up his sleeve absentmindedly, and then I knew.

—

IF YOU THINK YOU know all the secrets, you think you know all the cures. I suppose it wasn't too much of a surprise to me that Corrigan was scoring heroin: he had always done what the least of them had done. It was the perverse mantra of what he believed. He wanted to hear his own footsteps to prove that he trod the ground. There was no getting away from it. It was what he had done in Dublin too, though a different quarry of recklessness. He was standing on the little ledge of reality he had left, but it seemed to me that he wasn't getting high, just getting level. He had an affinity with pain. If he couldn't cure it, he took it on. He was shooting smack because he couldn't stand the thought of others being left alone with the same terror.

He left his sleeve rolled up for an hour or so while he dealt with the locks. The bruises inside his arm were a deep blue. When he was finished, the door didn't even click closed, just swung on the hinges.

"There," he said.

He went into the bathroom, where I was sure I could hear him strapping an elastic band around his arm. He came out, long-sleeved again.

"Now leave the friggin' door alone," he said.

He fell soundlessly into bed. I was sure I wouldn't sleep, but I woke to the usual thrum of the Deegan. The outside world was dependable. Engine noise and tire song. Huge metal sheets had been laid over some potholes. They boomed deeply when a truck ran over them.

It was an easy enough choice to stay: it wasn't as if Corrigan was ever going to ask me to leave. I was up and shaved early in the morning to accompany him on his rounds. I stirred him from the blankets. He had a faint nosebleed and the blood was dark against his stubble. He turned away. "Put on the tea, will you?" When he stretched, he touched the wooden crucifix on the wall. It swung back and forth on its nail. There was a light patch where the paint was not discolored. The faint imprint of the cross. He reached up to steady it, muttered something about God being ready to move sideways.

"Leaving today?" he asked.

The rucksack was packed on the floor.

"I was thinking I'd stay a couple more days."

"No problem, brother."

He combed his hair in the fragment of broken mirror, sprayed on some deodorant. At least he was keeping up pretenses. We took the lift instead of the stairs.

"A miracle," said Corrigan as the door sighed open, and the little moons of light shone on the inside panel. "It's working."

Outside, we crossed the small patch of grass in front of the projects, among the broken bottles. All of a sudden, being around him felt right for the first time in years. That old dream of purpose. I knew what I had to do—bring him on the long walk back towards a sensible life.

Among the early-morning hookers I felt strangely charmed. Corr-gan. Corr-i-gun. Corry—gan. It was, after all, my last name too. It was a strange taking of ease. Their bodies did not embarrass me as much as when I'd watched them from afar. Coyly, they covered their breasts with their arms. One had dyed her hair a bright red. Another wore sparkling silver eyeliner. Jazzlyn, in her neon swimsuit, positioned the strap over her nipples. She took a deep drag on her cigarette and exhaled smoke in expert streams from nose and mouth. Her skin shone. In another life she could have been aristocratic. Her eyes went to the ground as if she was looking to find something she had dropped. I felt a softening for her, a desire.

They kept up a wavery pitch of banter. My brother gazed across at me and grinned. It was like Corrigan whispering in my ear to give his approval to all I couldn't understand.

A few cars cruised past. "Get outta here," said Tillie. "We got business to accomplish." She said it like it was a stock exchange transaction. She nodded to Jazzlyn. Corrigan pulled me into the shadows.

"They all use smack?" I said.

"Some of them, yeah."

"Nasty stuff."

"The world tries them, then shows them a little joy."

"Who gets it for them? The smack?"

"No idea," he said as he took a small silver pocket watch out from his carpenter pants. "Why?"

"Just wondering."

The cars rumbled above us. He slapped my shoulder. We drove to the nursing home. A young nurse was waiting on the steps. She stood up and waved brightly as the van pulled in. She looked South American—

small and beautiful with a clout of black hair and dark eyes. Something fierce shot in the air between them. He loosened around her, his body more pliable. He put his hand on the small of her back, and they both disappeared inside the electronic door.

In the glove box of the van I looked for evidence: needles, packets, drug paraphernalia, anything. It was empty except for a well-worn Bible. In the inside flap Corrigan had written scattered notes to himself: *The wish to make desire null. To be idle in the face of nature. Pursue them and beg for forgiveness. Resistance is at the heart of peace.* When he was a boy he had seldom even folded down the pages of his Bible—he had always kept it pristine. Now the days were stacked up against him. The writing was spidery and he had underlined passages in deep-black ink. I recalled the myth that I had once heard as a university student—thirty-six hidden saints in the world, all of them doing the work of humble men, carpenters, cobblers, shepherds. They bore the sorrows of the earth and they had a line of communication with God, all except one, the hidden saint, who was forgotten. The forgotten one was left to struggle on his own, with no line of communication to that which he so hugely needed. Corrigan had lost his line with God: he bore the sorrows on his own, the story of stories.

I watched as the short nurse negotiated the ramp with the wheelchairs. She had a tattoo at the base of her ankle. It crossed my mind that she might be the one supplying him heroin, but she looked so cheerful in the hot slanting sun.

"Adelita," she said, extending her hand out to me through the van window. "Corrigan's told me all about you."

"Hey, get your carcass out here and help us," my brother said from the side of the van.

He was straining to get the old Galway woman through the door. The veins in his neck pulsed. Sheila was just a rag doll of a thing. I had a sudden recollection of our mother at the piano. Corrigan breathed heavily as he heaved her inside, arranged a series of straps around the woman's body.

"We have to talk," I said to him.

"Yeah, whatever, let's just get these people in the van."

He and the nurse glanced at each other across the rim of the seats. She had a little bead of sweat around the top of her lip and she wiped it away with the short sleeve of her uniform. As we drove off, she leaned against the ramp and lit a cigarette.

"The lovely Adelita," he said as he turned the corner.

"That's not what I want to talk about."

"Well, it's all I want to talk about," he said. He flicked a look in the rearview mirror and said: "Right, Sheila?" He did a fake drum roll on the steering wheel.

He was back to his old singsong self. I wondered if perhaps he had shot up while inside the nursing home: from what little I knew of addiction, anything at all could happen. But he was bright and cheery and didn't have many of the hallmarks of heroin, or at least the ones I imagined. He drove with one arm out the window, the breeze blowing back his hair.

"You're a mystery, you are."

"Nothing mysterious at all, brother."

Albee piped up from the backseat: "Pussy."

"Shaddup," said Corrigan with a grin, his accent tinged a little by the Bronx. All he cared about was the moment he was in, the absolute now. When we had fought as children, he used to stand and take the blows— our fights had lasted as long as I punched him. It would be easy to thump him now, fling him back against the van door, rifle his pockets, take out the packets of poison that were ruining him.

"We should make a visit back, Corr."

"Yeah," he said absently.

"I mean to Sandymount. Just for a week or two."

"Isn't the house sold?"

"Yeah, but we could find somewhere to stay."

"The palm trees," he said, half smiling. "Strangest sight in Dublin. I try to tell people about them, but they just don't believe me."

"Would you go back?"

"Sometime, maybe. I might bring some people with me," he said.

"Sure."

He flicked a look in the rearview mirror. I couldn't imagine that he wanted to bring the old woman back to Ireland, but I was ready to let Corrigan have whatever space he needed.

At the park he wheeled them into the shadows by the wall. It was a bright day, sunny and close. Albee took out his sheaf of papers, mutter-

ing the moves to himself as he worked on his chess problems. Every time
he made a good move he let the brake go on his wheelchair and rocked
himself back and forth in joy. Sheila wore a wide-brimmed straw hat over
her long white hair. Corrigan dabbed his handkerchief on her brow. She
scratched out some sounds from her throat. She had that emigrant's sadness—she would never go back to her old country—it was gone in more
senses than one—but she was forever gazing homewards anyway.

Some kids nearby had turned on a fire hydrant and were dancing in
the spray. One of them had taken a kitchen tray and was using it as a surfboard. The water skimmed him along by the monkey bars, where he fell
headlong, laughing, into the fence. Others clamored to use the tray. Corrigan moved over to the fence and pressed his hands against the wire di-
amonds. Beyond him, farther, some basketball players, sweat-soaked,
driving towards the netless basket.

It seemed for a moment that Corrigan was right, that there was something here, something to be recognized and rescued, some joy. I wanted
to tell him that I was beginning to understand it, or at least get an inkling,
but he called out to me and said he was running across to the bodega.

"Watch Sheila for a while, will you?" he said. "Her hat's tilted. Don't
let her get sunburned."

A gang of youths in bandannas and tight jeans hung out in front of
the bodega. They lit one another's cigarettes importantly. They gave Corrigan the usual handslaps, then disappeared inside with him. I knew it. I
could feel it welling up in me. I jogged across, my heart thumping in my
cheap linen shirt. I stepped past the litter piled up outside the shop,
liquor bottles, torn wrappers. A row of goldfish bowls sat in the window,
the thin orange bodies spinning in aimless circles. A bell sounded. Inside, Motown came over the stereo. A couple of kids, dripping wet from
the fire hydrant, stood by the ice cream vault. The older ones, in their red
bandannas, were down by the beer fridges. Corrigan was at the counter,
a pint of milk in his hand. He looked up, not the least bit disturbed. "I
thought you were watching Sheila."

"Is that what you thought?"

I expected some shove, a packet of heroin into his pocket, some clandestine transaction across the counter, another handslap with the gang,
but there was nothing. "Just put it on my tab," said Corrigan to the
shopowner, and he tapped one of the fishbowls on the way out.

The shop doorbell rang.

"They sell smack there too?" I asked as we crossed through the traffic to the park.

"You and your smack," he said.

"Are you sure, Corr?"

"Am I sure of what?"

"You tell me, brother. You're looking rough. One look in the mirror."

"You're kidding me, right?" He reared back and laughed. "Me?" he said. "Shooting smack?"

We reached the fence.

"I wouldn't touch that stuff with a barge pole," he said. His hands tightened around the wire, the tip of his knuckles white. "With all respects to heaven, I like it here."

He turned to look at the short row of wheelchairs set out along the fence. Something remained fresh about him, young, even. When he was sixteen Corrigan had written, in the inside of a cigarette packet, that all the proper gospel of the world could be written in the inside of a cigarette packet—it was that simple, you could do unto others what you'd have them do unto you, but at that time he hadn't figured on other complications.

"You ever have the feeling there's a stray something or other inside you?" he said. "You don't know what it is, like a ball, or a stone, could be iron or cotton or grass or anything, but it's inside you. It's not a fire or a rage or anything. Just a big ball. And there's no way to get at it?" He cut himself short, looked away, tapped the left side of his chest. "Well, here it is. Right here."

We seldom know what we're hearing when we hear something for the first time, but one thing is certain: we hear it as we will never hear it again. We return to the moment to experience it, I suppose, but we can never really find it, only its memory, the faintest imprint of what it really was, what it meant.

"You're having me on, right?"

"Wish I was," he said.

"Come on now . . ."

"You don't believe me?"

"Jazzlyn?" I asked, floored. "You haven't fallen for that hooker, have you?"

He laughed heartily but it was a laugh that ran away. His eyes shot across the playground, and he ran his fingers along the fence.

"No," he said, "no, not Jazzlyn, no."

—

CORRIGAN DROVE ME through the South Bronx under the flamed-up sky. The sunset was the color of muscle, pink and striated gray. Arson. The owners of the buildings, he said, were running insurance scams. Whole streets of tenements and warehouses abandoned to smolder.

Gangs of kids hung out on the street corners. Traffic lights were stuck on permanent red. At fire hydrants there were huge puddles of stagnant water. A building on Willis had half collapsed into the street. A couple of wild dogs picked their way through the ruin. A burned neon sign stood upright. Fire trucks went by, and a couple of cop cars trailed each other for comfort. Every now and then a figure emerged from the shadows, homeless men pushing shopping trolleys piled high with copper wire. They looked like men on a westward-ho, shoving their wagons across the nightlands of America.

"Who are they?"

"They ransack the building, pull the guts of the walls out, and then they sell the copper wire," he said. "They get a dime a pound or something."

Corrigan pulled the van up outside a series of tenements that were abandoned but untouched by fire, yanked the gearshift on the steering column down into park.

A haze hung over the street. You could hardly see the top of the street lamps. Warning tape had been fixed over the doorways but the doors behind them had been kicked in. He drew his feet up onto the seat, so that his sandals were nestled close to his crotch. He lit a cigarette and brought it right down to the dregs, threw the butt out the window.

"Thing is, I have a mild case of a thing called TTP or something," he said finally. "I started getting these bruises all over. Here and here. It's worst on my legs. They're splotchy. About a year or so ago. At first I didn't really think anything of it, honest. I had a bit of a fever. A few dizzy spells.

"And then I was in the nursing home in February. Helping them move some furniture from the first floor to the third. Stuff too big to fit in the elevator. And it was hot as hell in there. They keep the heat turned up for all the old ones. You can't imagine how hot, especially in the stairwell there, where the pipes were. Like Dante had furnished the place. Rough work. So I took off my shirt. Down to my string vest. You know how many years it's been since I've been down to a string vest? And I was halfway up the stairs with a few lads, when one of them points to me, my arms and shoulders, and says that I must have been in some sort of fight. Truth is, I had been in a fight. The pimps were giving me a hard time for letting the girls use the bathroom. I'd been knocked around a little. Had some stitches over my eye. One of them wore cowboy boots and roughed me up good. But I didn't give it a second thought until we got the furniture up on the third floor and Adelita was there, directing the traffic. 'Put this here. Put that there.' We heaved this big desk into a corner. And the lads were still giving me a hard time about being the only white bloke who still gets in fights in the neighborhood. Like I'm some throwback. Like I'm some Big Jack Doyle, you know. They're all joking: 'Come on Corrigan, let's dance, man, let's rumble!' They say they ought to bring me to Zaire, I'm such a fighter. They don't know I'm in the Order. Nobody knows. Not then anyway, they didn't. And Adelita came over and just pushed her finger down hard on one of the bruises and she said something like, 'You've got TTP.' And I made some crack about DDT and she said, 'No, I think it could be TTP.' It turns out she's studying at night. She wants to do medicine. She was a nurse in Guatemala in a couple of fancy hospitals. Always wanted to be a doctor, even went to university and all, but the war kicked in, and she got all caught up in it. Lost her husband. So she nurses here. They won't take her credentials. She's got two kids. They've got American accents now. Anyway she says something about low platelet counts and bleeding into the tissues and that I've got to get it seen to. She surprised me, brother."

Corrigan rolled down the window of the van and sprinkled some tobacco on a thin piece of paper, lit up.

"So, fair enough, I get it seen to. And she's bang on. I have this thing they don't know much about. It's idiopathic, you know, they don't know what causes it. But they say it's serious enough, you can get real sick from it. I mean, you gotta eventually get the treatment or you can die. And so I go home at night and I call on God in the dark, and I say, 'Thanks, God, another thing to worry about.' But the thing is, God's there this time, brother. He's there. In plain sight. It would be easier if He wasn't there. I could pretend I was searching for Him. But no, He's there, the son of a gun. He's telling me all the logical things about being sick and getting over it and dealing with it and looking at the world in a new way, the way He does, the way He should talk to you, the Body, the Soul, the sacrament of being alone, being furious with an aim, using it for the greater good. Opening yourself to the promise. But, see, this logical God, I don't like him all that much. Even His voice, He's got this voice that I just can't, I don't know, I can't like. I can understand it, but I don't necessarily like it. He's out of my range. But that's no problem. Plenty of times I haven't liked Him. It's good to be at a disturbance with God. Plenty of fine people have been in my place and worse.

"I figure being sick is old news anyway and dying's even older than that. What's fatal is the big hollow echo every time I tried Him out. See, I just felt hollow every time I tried talking with Him. I gave it everything, brother. My proper confession, you know, about maintaining faith and all. I talked with Father Marek there in St. Ann's. A good priest. We struggled together, him and I. Hours on end. And with Him too, with God, at all hours of the day. Used to be, though, that the arguments with Him stirred the depths of my heart. I wept in His presence. But He kept coming back at me with all His pure logic. Still, I knew it would pass. I knew I'd get over it. I wasn't even thinking about Adelita then. She wasn't even on my mind. It was losing God. The prospect of losing that. The rational part of me knew it was me—I mean, I was just talking to myself. I was obstructing Him. But being rational about it didn't cure it. You meet a rational God and you say, Well, okay, that's not my cup of tea right now, Heavenly Father, I'll come back at a better time.

"You know, when you're young, God sweeps you up. He holds you there. The real snag is to stay there and to know how to fall. All those days when you can't hold on any longer. When you tumble. The test is being able to climb up again. That's what I'm looking for. But I wasn't getting up. I wasn't able.

"So, anyway, I'm in the nursing home one Friday afternoon and Adelita was sitting in the stock room, going through the bottles of cough mixture. And I just sat down on the low ladder and was chatting away with her. She was asking me if I was getting treatment in the hospital and I find myself lying, flat-out lying, saying, Yes, of course, everything's fine, not a bother on me. 'That's good,' she said, 'because you really need to be looking after yourself.' Then she stepped over beside me, pulled up a chair, and started rubbing the inside of my arm. She said that I had to keep the blood flowing. She pushed her fingers into my arm here. And it was like she put her hands down deep in the earth. That's how it felt. I got goosebumps, my blood moving under her fingers. My other hand gripped the side of the ladder. And there was a voice inside me saying, 'Strengthen yourself against this, this is a test, be ready, be ready.' But it's the same voice I don't like. I'm looking behind the veil of it and all I see is this woman, it's a catastrophe, I'm descending, sinking like a hopeless swimmer. And I'm saying, God don't allow this to happen. Don't let it. She was tapping the inside of my arm with her fingernail, just flicking it. I closed my eyes. Please don't allow this. Please. But it was so pleasant. So so very pleasant. I wanted to keep my eyes closed and pry them open at the same time. No words for it, brother. I couldn't stand it. I got up and stormed out of the place. Stumbled out into the van.

"I think I drove all night. I just kept going. Following the white lines. I got snared up on bridges. Had no idea where I was going. Soon enough the lights of the city were fading. I figured I was out somewhere way upstate, but it was the island, man, Long Island. I thought I was going west, across some great open land, where I'd work everything out, but I wasn't, I was actually heading east along this big highway. And I just kept going. Driving and driving. Cars zipping by me. I had to keep muttering to myself and lighting matches, smelling the sulfur, to keep awake. Trying to pray. To make two plus two equal five. And then the highway ended, middle of nowhere, it seemed like, and I just followed a smaller road. Out through farmland and past these isolated houses, little pinpoints of light. Montauk. I'd never been there before. The dark got thicker, no lights at all. And it turned into this little one-laner. That's what takes you to the end of this country, man, a tiny little potholed road that ends up at a lighthouse. And I thought: 'This is right, this is where I'll find Him.'

"I got out and stepped in among the dunes, along the beach. I walked about and screamed at Him, under the clouds. Not a star shining anywhere. No response. You'd expect a bit of moon at least. Something. Anything. Not even a boat. It was like everything had deserted me. And I could still feel her touch there, on the inside of my arm. Like it was deep and there was something growing there. And I'm out in the middle of an endless beach with a lighthouse twirling behind me. Thinking stupid things. The way you do. I'll move away. I'll give it all up. I'll leave the Order, I'll go back to Ireland, find a different poverty. But nothing made sense. The end of the country, man, but there was no revelation.

"After a while I gathered myself into that silence and finally I sat down in the sand and said to myself, 'Well, maybe it will only make me better for Him in the long run, I have to fight this, battle it, use it for my own advantage, it's a sign.' I resigned myself to it. That which doesn't break you, blah blah blah. I was running a fever but I left the beach, got back in the van and calmed myself down, and said good-bye to the lighthouse, the water, the east, and said it will be fine, nothing holy is free, and I drove all the way back to the flat, parked the van, fell into the lift, and closed the door. I actually fell asleep in the lift. Only woke up when it started moving. Found myself staring at the face of some frightened black woman. I scared her. I locked myself in for two days. Waiting for the bandages to blacken, y'know, that sort of thing. Waiting for it to blow over. And I bolted the chain. Can you believe that? I bolted the door shut. So much for the crap I gave you, brother, about the locks."

He chuckled a little and a spray of headlight went across his face from the far side of the boulevard.

"The girls thought I was dead. They were banging on the door, wanting to use the facilities. And I didn't reply. I just lay there, trying to pray for some sign of gentle mercy. But I kept seeing Adelita in my mind. Eyes closed, eyes open, it didn't matter. Things I shouldn't have been thinking of. Her neck. The back of her neck. Her clavicle. The side of her face in a slice of light. There she was, taking me in. And I wanted to scream at her, No, no, no, you're just pure lust, and I've made a pact with God to fight lust, please just let me be, please just go. But she's still standing there, smiling, understanding. And I'd whisper to her again: Please go. But I knew it wasn't lust, it was so much more than lust. I was looking for a simple answer, the sort we give to children, you know. And I kept thinking that we were all children once, maybe I could return. That's what echoed in my head. Go back to being a child. Sprint along the strand there. Up past the tower. Run along the wall. I wanted that sort of joy. Make it simple again. I was trying, really trying, to pray, get rid of my lust, return to the good, rediscover that innocence. Circles of circles. And when you go around in circles, brother, the world is very big, but if you plow straight ahead it's small enough. I wanted to fall along the spokes to the center of the circle, where there was no movement. I can't explain it, man. It was like I was staring at the ceiling, waiting for the sky. All this banging was still going on outside the door. Then hours of silence.

"At one time I heard Jazzlyn, you know, that voice of hers, like she just swallowed the Bronx, man, leaning in against the keyhole and screaming: 'Okay! To hell with you, you dumbass cracker!' It's the only time I laughed. If only she knew. 'To hell with you, you dumbass cracker, I'll piss somewheres else!'

"Then they actually got the Guards in to bash down the door. And they come rushing in, flashing badges, guns drawn. They stop and stare. Looking at me, lying on the couch, the Bible over my face. And one cop is saying, 'What's going on here, man? What the hell is this? He's not dead. He smells bad, but he's not dead.' I'm just lying there and I swipe the Book off my face and cover my eyes with my forearm. And Jazz comes charging in behind them, saying, 'I gotta go, I gotta go.' Then comes Tillie with her pink parasol. Then both of them came out and started shouting. 'How come you keep the door locked, Corrie? Asshole! That's mean and unusual punishment. That's the honkypox, man!' The Guards were standing there, open-mouthed. They couldn't believe what was going on. One of them was wrapping a piece of gum tight around his finger. He kept winding it, like he wanted to strangle me. I'm sure they were thinking that they'd done this for nothing, for a bunch of working girls who just wanted to pee. They were not happy at all. Not at all. They wanted to give me a citation for wasting their time, but they couldn't dream up anything. I said maybe they should give me one for losing my faith and then they thought I was really off my rocker. One of them said to me, 'Look at this shithole—get a life, man!' And it was just so simple, the way he said it, the young Guard, right in my face: 'Get a life, man!' He kicked over the flowerpot as he went out the door.

"Tillie and Angie and Jazzlyn and the girls threw a 'not-dead' party for me. They even bought me a cake. One candle. I had to blow it out. I was going to take it as a sign. But there were no signs. I went back down the nursing home and that night I asked Adelita if she'd mind just moving the blood around a little—that's the way I said it, 'Move the blood around a little, would you?' She gave me that big cheerful smile and said that she was busy on her rounds, maybe she'd get to it later. I sat there, trembling with God, all my sorrows, bound up inside. And sure enough she came back a short while later. It was all very simple. I just stared at the dark of her hair. Couldn't look in her eyes. She was rubbing my shoulder and the small of my back and even my calf muscles. I kept hoping maybe somebody would come in the door and find us, make a big stink, but nobody did. And I kissed her. And she kissed me back. I mean, how many men can say they'd rather be nowhere else in the world? That's how I felt. That moment. That I wanted nothing but the here and now, and nowhere else. On earth as it is in heaven. That one moment. And then after a few days I started going to her house."

"She's got three kids, you said."

"Two. And a husband who got killed down in Guatemala. Fighting. For, I don't know, Carlos Arana Osorio or someone. A fascist of some sort. She hated him, the husband—she got caught up in this marriage young—and still she's got his picture on the bookcase. For the kids to know that he exists, existed, that they had a father. We just sit there and he's looking out at us. She doesn't talk about him. He's got this hard stare. I sit in her kitchen and she cooks a little and I move the food around on the plate and we chat and then she rubs my shoulders while her kids are in the other room, watching cartoons. She knows I'm in the Order, knows the celibacy rules, everything. I told her. She says that if it doesn't matter to me then it doesn't matter to her. She's the loveliest person I've ever known. I can't stand it. I can't deal with it. I sit there and it's like these blades turning in my stomach. The voice I go home to is not the voice I ever heard before. I can't lay a hand on the old one. He's gone. I find myself stretching out at night, trying to grab a hold of it but He's not there. All I get is sleeplessness and disgust. Call it what you like. Call it joy, even. How can I pray with this inside me? How can I do what I'm supposed to do? I don't even judge myself by my actions. I judge myself by what's in my heart. And it's rotten because it wants to own things, but it's not rotten because it's the most content I've ever been, and it's the most content she's ever been too, sitting there, together. We're happy. And I keep wondering if we're supposed to be happy. I haven't slept with her, brother. At least not . . . We've thought about it, yes, but, I mean . . ."

He faded off.

"You know my vows. You know what they mean. I used to think there was no other man in me, no other person, just me, the devoted one. That I was alone and strong, that my vows were everything, and I wasn't tempted. And I've turned it over and over in my mind. What happens if this? What happens if that? And maybe it's not even a matter of losing faith. I stand in the mess of myself. It's against everything I've ever been, and suddenly just watching it all disappear, and then also lying to her, even about my treatment."

"What's this sickness mean? This TTP stuff?"

"It means I've just got to get better."

"How?"

"I have to get treatment. Plasma replacement and that sort of thing. I will."

"Painful?"

"Pain's nothing. Pain's what you give, not what you get."

He took out the slim pack of rolling papers and sprinkled the tobacco along the curved edge of a paper.

"And her? Adelita? What're you going to do?"

He worked the grains over, looked out the window.

"Her kids are out of school for the summer. They're running around. Lots of time on their hands. Used to be that I went over with the excuse that I was helping them with their homework. But it's summer, so there's no more homework. Guess what. I'm still going over. And no real excuse except the truth—I want to see her. And we just sit there, Adelita and me. I have to come up with other excuses for myself. Oh, they need someone to help clean up the rubbish in front of the apartment. She really needs to get that toaster fixed. She needs time to study her medical books. Anything. Except I can't pretend that I can give them a catechism lesson because they're Lutheran, man, Lutherans! From Guatemala. Just my luck, man! I find the only non-Catholic woman in Central America. Brilliant. She's a believer, though. She's got a heart, huge and kind. She really does. She tells me these stories about where she grew up. I go to her house every chance I get. I want to. I need to. That's where I've been disappearing all these afternoons. I guess I wanted to keep it hidden from everyone.

"And all the time I'm sitting there, in her house, thinking that this is the one place I shouldn't be. And I wonder what's going to be left over when I extricate myself from the mess. Then her kids come in from outside and jump on the sofa and watch TV and spill yogurt all over the cushions. Her youngest, Eliana, she's five, she drifts in trailing a blanket along the floor and grabs my hand and brings me into the living room. I'm bouncing her up and down on my knee, and they're beautiful kids, both of them. Jacobo's just turned seven. I sit there thinking about how much courage it takes to live an ordinary life. At the end of *Tom and Jerry,* or *I Love Lucy,* or *The Brady Bunch,* whatever dose of irony you want, I say to myself, That's okay—this is real, this is something I can handle, I'm just sitting here, I'm not doing anything bad. And then I leave because I can't accept the brokenness."

"So, leave the Order."

He knitted his hands together.

"Or leave her."

The whites of his knuckles.

"I can't do either," he said. "And I can't do both."

He studied the lit end of his cigarette.

"You know what's funny?" he said. "On Sundays I still feel the old urges, the residual feelings. That's when the guilt hits most. I walk along, the Our Father in my mind. Over and over again. To cut the edge off the guilt. Isn't that ridiculous?"

A car pulled up slowly behind us and a sharp light shone through the back window. The red and blue lights flicked on, but no siren. We waited in silence for the cops to get out of the car, but they hit the megaphone: "Move on, faggots, move it!"

Corrigan gave a pinch of a smile as he pulled the gearshift down into drive.

"You know, I have a dream every night that I'm running my lips down along her spine, like a skiff down a river."

He eased the van out into the street and said nothing more until he pulled in near the projects, where his hookers were. Instead of walking in among them, he waved them off and brought me across the street to where a yellow light pulsed on the corner. "What I need to do is get drunk." He pushed open the door of a little bar, arm around my shoulder.

"Straight as a good fence the last ten years, now look at me."

He sat at the counter, raised two fingers, ordered a couple of beers.

There are moments we return to, now and always. Family is like water— it has a memory of what it once filled, always trying to get back to the original stream. I was on the bottom bunk again, listening to his slumber verses. The flap of our childhood letter box opened. Opening the door to the spray of sea.

"You ask me if I'm using heroin, man?" He was laughing, but looking out the bar window at the rafters of the highway. "It's worse than that, brother, much worse."

—

IT WAS LIKE ALL the clocks agreed and the fridge was humming and the sirens outside sounded out like flutes. He had talked her free. Just mentioning her was enough for him: he became new.

For the next couple of days they saw each other as much as they could—in the nursing home mainly, where she changed her shift just to be with him. But Adelita also came to the apartment, knocked on the door, uncorked a bottle of wine, and sat across the table. She wore a ring on her right hand, twirling it absently. There was a grace and a toughness about her, entwined. They needed me there. I was hardly allowed to stand up from the table. "Sit down, sit down." I was still the safe border between them. They weren't ready to fully let go. Some propriety held them back, but they looked as if they wanted to leave some of their good sense behind, at least for a while.

She was the sort of woman who became more beautiful the more you watched her: the dark hair, almost blue in the light, the curve of her neck, a mole by her left eye, a perfect blemish.

I suppose, as the nights wore on, my presence made them feel that they had to entertain someone, that they were in it together, that they were more properly alone by being together.

She spoke softly to Corrigan, as if to get him to lean closer. He would look at her as if it were quite possible he wasn't ever going to see her again. Sometimes she just sat there with her head upon his shoulder. She gazed past me. Outside, the fires of the Bronx. To them it could have been sunlight through the girders. I dragged my chair across the floor.

"Sit down, sit down."

Adelita had a wild side that Corrigan liked but couldn't bring himself to grin about. One night she wore a wide white off-the-shoulder blouse and orange hot pants. The blouse was modest, but the pants were tight to her thighs. We drank a little cheap wine, and Adelita was whooped up a little. She gathered her shirt and knotted it at the front, showing the brown of her stomach, stretched slightly from children. The small dip of her belly button. Corrigan was embarrassed by the cling of the pants. "Look at you, Adie," he said, his cheeks flushing. But instead of asking her to unknot the blouse and cover herself up, he made a theater of giving her one of his own shirts to wear over her outfit. As if it were the tender thing to do. He draped it around her shoulders, kissed her cheek. It was one of his old black collarless shirts, past her thighs, almost down to her knees. He hitched it on her shoulders, half afraid that he was being a prude, the other half rocked by the sheer immensity of what was happening to him.

Adelita paraded around the apartment, doing a slight hula-hoop movement.

"I'm ready now for heaven," she said, tugging the shirt lower still.

"Take her, Lord," said Corrigan.

They laughed, but there was something in that, like Corrigan wanted his life to make sense again, that he had fallen from grace, all he had now was his old recklessness and temptation, and he wasn't sure he could handle it. He looked up as if the answer might be written on the ceiling. What might happen if she tumbled short of his dreams? How much might he hate his God if he left her behind? How might he detest himself if he stuck to his Lord?

He walked her home, holding hands in the dark. When he returned to the apartment, many hours later, he hung the shirt on the edge of the mirror. "Orange hot pants," he said. "Can you believe it?"

We sat, hunched over the bottle.

"You know what you should do?" said Corrigan. "Come work at the nursing home."

"Need a bodyguard, is that it?"

He smiled, but I knew what he was saying. *Come help me, I'm still that hopeless swimmer.* He wanted someone from the past around in order to make sure that it wasn't all just a colossal illusion. He couldn't just be an observer: he had to get some message through. It had to make sense, if even just for me. But I got a job in Queens instead, in one of the shamrock bars I dreaded. A low ceiling. Eight stools along the formica counter. Sawdust on the floor. Pouring pale draft beer and putting my own dimes in the jukebox so I wouldn't have to hear the same old tunes over and over. Instead of Tommy Makem, the Clancy Brothers, and Donovan, I tried some Tom Waits instead. The single-minded drinkers groaned.

I figured I might write a play set in a bar, as if it had never been done before, as if it were some sort of revolutionary act, so I listened to my countrymen and wrote notes. Theirs was a loneliness pasted upon loneliness. It struck me that distant cities are designed precisely so you can know where you came from. We bring home with us when we leave. Sometimes it becomes more acute for the fact of having left. My accent deepened. I took on different rhythms. I pretended I was from Carlow. Most of the customers were from Kerry and Limerick. One was a lawyer, a tall, fat sandy-haired man. He lorded it over the others by buying them drinks. They clinked glasses with him and called him a "motherfucking ambulance chaser" when he went to the bathroom. It was not a series of words they would have used at home—motherfucking ambulance chasers weren't big in the old country—but they said it as often as they could. With great hilarity they injected it into songs when the lawyer left. One of the songs had an ambulance chaser going over the Cork and Kerry mountains. Another had an ambulance chaser in the green fields of France.

The place grew busier as the night went on. I poured the drinks and emptied the tip jar.

I was still staying with Corrigan. He spent a few evenings at Adelita's place, but he never told me a word about them. I wanted to know if he'd finally been with a woman but he simply shook his head, wouldn't say, couldn't say. He was still in the Order after all. His vows still shackled him.

There was a night in early August when I dragged myself back on the subway, but couldn't find a cab on the Concourse. I didn't like the idea of walking back to Corrigan's place at that hour. There had been beatings and random murders in the Bronx. Being held up was close to ritual. And being white was a bad idea. It was time to get a room of my own somewhere else, maybe the Village or the East Side of Manhattan. I stuck my hands in my jeans, felt the rolled-up wad of money from the bar. I had just begun walking when a whistle sounded from the other side of the Concourse. Tillie was pulling up the strap on her swimsuit. She had been kicked out of a car and her knees were scraped raw.

"Sugarplum," she shouted as she stumbled towards me with her handbag waving above her head. She had lost her parasol. She put her arm in the crook of mine. "Whosoever brought me here is going to have to take me home."

It was, I knew, a line from Rumi. I stood, stunned. "What's the big deal?" she shrugged. She dragged me on. Her husband, she said, had studied Persian poetry.

"Husband?"

I stopped on the street and gaped at her. Once, as a teenager, I had examined a piece of my skin on a glass slide, staring at it through a microscope: an amplitude of ridged canals striving beneath my eye, all pure surprise.

My intense disgust—so remarkable on other days—in that single moment turned into an awe for the fact that Tillie didn't care at all. She jiggled her breasts and told me to get a grip. It was her ex-husband anyway. Yes, he had studied Persian poetry. Big fucking deal. He used to get a suite at the Sherry-Netherlands, she said. I assumed she was high. The world seemed to grow smaller around her, shrunken to the size of her eyes, painted purple and dark with eye shadow. I suddenly wanted to kiss her. My own wild, yea-saying overburst of American joy. I leaned towards her and she laughed, pushed me away.

A long pimped-up Ford Falcon pulled up at the curb and, without turning, Tillie said: "He already paid, man."

We continued up the street, arm in arm. Under the Deegan she nestled her head against my chest. "Didn't you, honey?" she said. "You already paid for the goodies?" She was rubbing her hand against me and it felt good. There's no other way to say it. That's how it felt. Good.

"Call me SweetCakes," she said in an accent that loitered around her.

"You're related to Jazzlyn, aren't you?"

"What about it?"

"You're her mother, right?"

"Shut up and pay me," she said, touching the side of my face. Moments later there was the surprising condolence of her warm breath against my neck.

—

THE RAID BEGAN in the early morning, a Tuesday in August. Still dark. The cops lined up the paddy wagons in the streetlight shadows near the overpass. The girls didn't seem to care half as much as Corrigan did. One or two dropped their handbags and ran towards the intersections, arms flailing, but there were more paddy wagons waiting there, doors open. The police tightened the handcuffs and herded the girls into the well of the dark vehicles. Only then could we hear any shouting—they leaned out, looking for their lipstick or their sunglasses or their stilettos. "Hey, I dropped my keyring!" said Jazzlyn. She was being helped into the wagon by her mother. Tillie was calm, as if it happened all the time, just another rising sun. She caught my eye, gave half a wink.

On the street, the cops sipped their coffees, smoked their cigarettes, shrugged. They called the girls by their names and nicknames. Foxy. Angie. Daisy. Raf. SweetCakes. Sugarpie. They knew the girls well and the crackdown was as lethargic as the day. The girls must have heard the rumor of it beforehand, and they had gotten rid of their needles and any other drug paraphernalia, dropped them down into the gutter. There'd been raids before, but never so complete a sweep.

"I want to know what's happening to them," said Corrigan, going cop to cop. "Where are they going?" He spun on his heels. "What are you arresting them for?"

"Stargazing," said a cop, bashing into Corrigan's shoulder.

I watched a long pink boa scarf get caught up in the wheels of a patrol car. It wrapped the wheelbase as if in affection, and bits of tufted pink spun in the air.

Corrigan took down a series of badge numbers. A tall female cop plucked the notebook out of his hand and shredded it slowly in front of him. "Look, you dumb Mick, they'll be back soon, okay?"

"Where're you taking them?"

"What's it to you, buddy?"

"Where are you bringing them? Which station house?"

"Step back. Over there. Now."

"Under what statute?" said Corrigan.

"Under the statute that I'll kick your ass if you don't."

"All I want is an answer."

"The answer's seven," the female cop said, staring Corrigan down. "The answer's always seven. Get it?"

"No I don't."

"What are you, man, some sort of fruit or something?"

One of the sergeants swaggered up and shouted: "Somebody take care of Mr. Lovey-Dovey here." Corrigan was pushed to the side of the road and told to stand on the curb. "We'll lock you up if you say another word."

I guided him aside. His face was red and his fists tightened. Veins thrummed at his temple. A new splotch had appeared on his neck. "Take it easy, okay, Corr? We'll sort it out later. They'll be better off in a station anyway. It's not as if you actually like them being here."

"That's not the point."

"Oh, Jesus, come on," I said. "Just trust me. We'll get to them later."

The paddy wagons bounced down off the curbs and all but one of the squad cars followed behind. A few onlookers gathered in clumps. Some kids rode their bicycles in circles around the empty space as if they'd found themselves a brand-new playground. Corrigan went to pick up a keyring from the gutter. It was a cheap little glass thing with a picture of a child in the center. Flipped over, there was a picture of another child.

"That's the reason," said Corrigan, thrusting the keyring towards me. "They're Jazz's kids."

Whosoever brought me here is going to have to take me home. Tillie had charged me fifteen dollars for our little tryst, patted me on the back, then said I represented the Irish quite well, a grand dollop of irony in her voice. *Call me SweetCakes.* She flicked the ten-dollar bill and said she knew some Khalil Gibran too—she would quote a bit or two if I wanted. "Next time," I said. She'd riffled through her handbag. "Are you interested in a little horse?" she asked as she buttoned me up. She said she could get some from Angie. "Not my style," I said. She giggled and leaned closer to me. "Your style?" she said. She put her hand on my hip, laughed again. "Your style!" There was a sickening moment when I thought she had pickpocketed all my tips, but she hadn't; she just tightened my belt and slapped me on the arse.

I was glad that I hadn't gone with her daughter. I felt almost virtuous, as if I hadn't been tempted at all. Tillie's smell had lingered with me for a couple of days and it returned again now that she had been taken off and arrested.

"She's a grandmother?"

"I told you that," said Corrigan. He stormed towards the last remaining cop car, brandishing Jazz's key chain. "What're you going to do about this?" he shouted. "You going to get someone to look after her kids? Is that what you're going to do? Who's going to look after her kids? Are you going to leave them there on the street? You're arresting her mother and her!"

"Mister," the cop said, "one more word from you—"

I pulled Corrigan's elbow hard and dragged him back through the projects. For a moment the buildings seemed more sinister without the hookers outside: the territory was transformed, none of the old totems anymore.

The lift was broken again. Corrigan wheezed up the stairs. Inside, he began dialing all the community groups he knew, looking for a lawyer, and a babysitter for Jazzlyn's kids. "I don't even know where they've gone," he screamed into the phone. "They wouldn't tell me. Last time, the lockups were full and they got sent down to Manhattan."

Another phone call. He turned away from me, cupped his hand around the receiver.

"Adelita?" he said.

His grip deepened around the phone as he whispered. He had spent the previous few afternoons with her, at her house, and each time he came home he was the same: roaming the room, pulling at the buttons on his shirt, muttering to himself, trying to read his Bible, looking for something that might justify himself, or maybe looking for a word to leave him even further tortured, a pain that would leave him again on edge. That, and a happiness too, an energy. I wasn't sure what to tell him anymore. Give in to the despondency. Find a new posting. Forget her. Move on. At least with the hookers he didn't have time to juggle notions of love and loss—down on the street it was pure take and take. But with Adelita it was different—she wasn't pushing any greed or climax. *This is my body, it has been given up for you.*

Later, around noon, I found Corrigan in the bathroom, shaving in front of the mirror. He had been down to the Bronx county courthouse, where most of the hookers had already been released on time served. But there were outstanding warrants in Manhattan for Tillie and Jazzlyn. They had pulled some robbery together, turned on a trick. The case was old. Still, they were both going to be transported downtown. He pulled on a crisp black shirt and dark trousers, went to the mirror again, pasted his long hair back with water. "Well, well," he said. He took a small scissors to his hair and lopped off about four inches. His fringe went in three smooth snips.

"I'm going to go down to help them," he said.

"Where?"

"The parthenon of justice."

He looked older, more worn. With his haircut, the bald spot was more pronounced.

"They call it the Tombs. They'll be arraigned in Centre Street. Listen, I need you to take my shift in the nursing home. I talked with Adelita. She already knows."

"Me? What am I going to do with them?"

"I don't know. Take them to the beach or something."

"I have a job in Queens."

"Do it for me, brother, will you, please? I'll give you a shout later on." He turned at the door. "And look after Adelita for me too, will you?"

"Sure."

"Promise me."

"Yeah, I will—now, go."

Outside I could hear the sounds of the children following Corrigan down the stairs, laughing. It was only when the apartment had fallen into full silence did I remember that he had taken the brown van with him.

At a rental joint down in Hunts Point, I used the very last of my tips to make a deposit on a van. "Air-conditioning," said the clerk with an idiotic grin. It was like he was explaining science. He had his badge name pasted over his heart. "Don't run it too hard, it's brand new."

It was one of those days when the summer seemed to have fallen into place, not too warm, cloudy, a tranquilized sun high in the sky. On the radio a DJ played Marvin Gaye. I maneuvered around a low-slung Cadillac and onto the highway.

Adelita was waiting by the ramp of the home. She had brought her children to work—two dark beauties. The younger one tugged at her uniform and Adelita went down to eye level with her, kissed the child's eyelids. Adelita's hair was tied back with a long colorful scarf and her face shone.

I understood perfectly, then, what Corrigan knew: she had an interior order, and for all her toughness there was a beauty that rose easily to the surface.

She smiled at the idea that we should try the beach. She said it was ambitious but impossible—no insurance, and it was against the rules. Her kids screamed beside her, tugged on her uniform, grabbed her wrist. "No, *m'ijo*," she said sharply to her son, and we went through the routine of loading all the wheelchairs and jamming the kids between the seats. Litter was pinned against the railings of the park. We pulled the van in under the shade of a building. "Oh, what the hell," said Adelita. She slid across into the driver's seat. I rounded the back of the van. Albee was looking out at me, and he mouthed a word with a grin. No need to ask. Adelita beeped the horn and pulled the van out into a light summer traffic. The children cheered as we merged onto the highway. In the distance, Manhattan was like something made out of play boxes.

We found ourselves snared in the Long Island traffic. Songs came from the back, the old folk teaching the kids bits and pieces of songs they couldn't really conjure. "Raindrops Keep Fallin' on My Head." "When the Saints Go Marching In." "You Should Never Shove Your Granny off the Bus."

At the beach, Adelita's kids tore down to the waterfront while we lined the wheelchairs up in the shade of the van. The van shadow grew smaller as the sun arced. Albee dropped the suspenders from his shirt and opened up his shirt buttons. His arms and neck were extraordinarily tanned but beneath the shirt his skin was translucent white. It was like watching a sculpture of two different colors, as if he were designing his body for a game of chess. "Your brother likes those hookers, huh?" he said. "You ask me, they're a bunch of rip-off artists." He said nothing more, just stared out at the sea.

Sheila sat with her eyes closed, smiling, her straw hat tilted down over her eyes. An old Italian whose name I didn't know—a dapper man in perfectly pressed trousers—dented and redented his hat upon his knee and sighed. Shoes were taken off. Ankles exposed. The waves crashed along the shore and the day slipped from us, sand between our fingers.

Radios, beach umbrellas, the burn of salt air.

Adelita walked down to the waterfront, where her children were kicking happily in the low surf. She drew attention like a draft of wind. Men watched her wherever she went, the slender curve of her body against the white uniform. She sat on the sand beside me with her knees pressed against her breasts. She shifted and her skirt rose slightly: a red welt on the ankle near where her tattoo was.

"Thanks for renting the van."

"Yeah, no problem."

"You didn't have to do it."

"No big deal."

"It runs in the family?"

"Corrigan's going to pay me back," I said.

A bridge lay between us, composed almost entirely of my brother. She shaded her dark eyes and looked down towards the water, as if Corrigan might have been in the surf alongside her children, not in some dark courthouse arguing a series of hopeless causes.

"He will be down there for days, trying to get them out," she said. "It's happened before. Sometimes I think they would be better off if they learned their lesson. People get locked up for less."

I was warming up to her, but wanted to push her, to see how far she'd go for him.

"Then he'd have nowhere to go, would he?" I asked. "At night. Nowhere to work."

"Maybe, maybe not."

"He'd have to go to you, then, wouldn't he?"

"Yes, maybe," she said, and a little shadow of anger went across her face. "Why you ask me this?"

"I'm just saying."

"I don't know what you're saying," she said.

"Just don't string him along."

"I'm not stringing him along," she said. "Why would I want to, as you say, string him along? ¿Por qué? Me dice que eso."

Her accent had sharpened: the Spanish had an edge to it. She let the sand drift between her fingers and looked at me like it was the first time she'd seen me, but the silence calmed her and finally she said: "I don't really know what to do. God is cruel, no?"

"Corrigan's one is, that's for sure. I don't know about yours."

"Mine is right beside his."

The kids were throwing a frisbee at each other in the surf. They leaped at the flying disc and landed in the water and splashed.

"I'm terrified, you know," she said. "I like him so much. Too much. He doesn't know what he's going to do, you understand? And I don't want to stand in his way."

"I know what I'd do. If I were him."

"But you're not, are you?" she said.

She turned away and whistled at the children and they came trudging up the sand. Their bodies were brown and supple. Adelita pulled Eliana close and softly blew sand off her ear. Somehow, for whatever reason, I could see Corrigan in both of them. It was like he had already entered them by osmosis. Jacobo climbed in her lap too. Adelita nipped his ear with her teeth and he squealed in delight.

She had safely surrounded herself with the children and I wondered if it was the same thing she did with Corrigan, reeling him in close enough and then shielding herself, gathering the many and making it too much. For a moment I hated her and the complications that she had brought to my brother's life, and I felt a strange fondness for the hookers who had taken him away, to some police station, down to the very dregs, some terrible cell with iron bars and stale bread and filthy toilets. Maybe he was even in the cells alongside them. Maybe he got himself arrested just so he could be near them. It wouldn't have surprised me.

He was at the origin of things and I now had a meaning for my brother—he was a crack of light under the door, and yet the door was shut to him. Only bits and pieces of him would leak out and he would end up barricaded behind that which he had penetrated. Maybe it was entirely his own fault. Maybe he welcomed the complications: he had created them purely because he needed them to survive.

I knew then that it would only end badly, her and Corrigan, these children. Someone or other was going to get torn asunder. And yet why shouldn't they fall in love, if even just for a short while? Why shouldn't Corrigan live his life in the body that was hurting him, giving up in places? Why shouldn't he have a moment of release from this God of his? It was a torture shop for him, worrying about the world, having to deal with intricacies when what he really wanted was to be ordinary and do the simple thing.

Yet nothing was simple, certainly not simplification. Poverty, chastity, obedience—he had spent his life in fealty to them, but was unarmed when they turned against him.

I watched Adelita as she loosened an elastic band from her daughter's hair. She tapped her on the bottom and sent her along the beach. The waves broke far out.

"What did your husband do?" I asked.

"He was in the army."

"Do you miss him?"

She stared at me.

"Time doesn't cure everything," she said, looking away along the strand, "but it cures a lot. I live here now. This is my place. I won't go back. If that's what you're asking me, I won't go back."

It was a look that suggested she was part of a mystery she wouldn't let go of. He was hers now. She had made her declaration. There could indeed be no going back. I recalled Corrigan when he was a boy, when everything was pure and definite, when he walked along the strand in Dublin, marveling at the roughness of a shell, or the noise of a low-flying plane, or the eave of a church, the bits and pieces of what he thought was assured around him, written in the inside of that cigarette box.

—

OUR MOTHER USED to like to use a gambit in the telling of her stories: "Once upon a time and long ago, in fact so long ago that I couldn't have been there, and if I had been there, I could not be here, but I am here, and I wasn't there, but I'll tell you anyway: Once upon a time and long ago . . ." whereupon she would launch into a story of her own creation, fables that sent my brother and me to different places, and we would wake in the morning wondering if we had dreamed different parts of the same dream, or if we had duplicated each other, or if in some strange world our dreams had overlapped and switched places with each other, something I would have done easily after I heard about Corrigan's smash into the guardrail: *Teach me, brother, how to live.*

We have all heard of these things before. The love letter arriving as the teacup falls. The guitar striking up as the last breath sounds out. I don't attribute it to God or to sentiment. Perhaps it's chance. Or perhaps chance is just another way to try to convince ourselves that we are valuable.

Yet the plain fact of the matter is that it happened and there was nothing we could do to stop it—Corrigan at the wheel of the van, having spent all day down in the Tombs and the courtrooms of lower Manhattan, driving north up along the FDR, with Jazzlyn beside him in the passenger seat, her yellow high heels and her neon swimsuit, her choker tight around her neck, and Tillie had been locked away on a robbery charge, she had taken the rap, and my brother was giving Jazzlyn a lift back to her kids, who were more than keyrings, more than a flip in the air, and they were going fast along the East River, hemmed in by the buildings and the shadows, when Corrigan went to change lanes, maybe he hit the indicator, maybe he didn't, maybe he was dizzy or tired or out of sorts, maybe he'd gotten some medicine that slowed him or fogged his vision, maybe he tapped the brake, maybe he cut it too hard, maybe he was gently humming a bit of a tune, who knows, but it was said that he was clipped in the rear by a fancy car, some old antique, nobody saw the driver, a gold vehicle going about its everyday applause of itself, it caught the back end of his van, nudged it slightly, but it sent Corrigan into a spin across all three lanes, like some big brown dancing thing, elegant for a split second, and I think now of Corrigan gripping the steering wheel, frightened, his eyes large and tender, while Jazzlyn beside him screamed, and her body tightened, her neck tensed, it all flashing in front of her—her short vicious life—and the van skidded on the dry roadway, hit a car, hit a newspaper truck, and then smashed headlong into the guardrail at the edge of the highway, and Jazzlyn went head-first through the windshield, no safety belt, a body already on the way to heaven, and Corrigan was smashed back by the steering wheel, which caught his chest and shattered his breastbone, his head rebounding off the spidery glass, bloody, and then he was whipped back into the seat with such force that the metal frame of the seat shattered, a thousand pounds of moving steel, the van still spinning from one side of the road to the other, and Jazzlyn's body, only barely dressed, made a flying arc through the air, fifty or sixty miles per hour, and she smashed in a crumpled heap by the guardrail, one foot bent in the air as if stepping upwards, or wanting to step upwards, and the only thing of hers they found later in the van was a yellow stiletto, with a Bible sitting canted right beside it, having fallen out of the glove compartment, one on top of the other and both of them littered with glass, and Corrigan, still breathing, was bounced around and smashed sideways so that he finished up with his body twisted down in the dark well by the accelerator and the brake, and the engine whirled as if it still wanted to go fast and be stopped at the same time, all of Corrigan's weight on both of the pedals.

They were sure he was dead at first, and he was loaded in a meat wagon with Jazzlyn. A cough of blood alerted a paramedic. He was taken to a hospital on the East Side.

Who knows where we were, driving back, in another part of the city, on a ramp, in a traffic jam, at a toll booth—does it matter? There was a little bubble of blood at my brother's mouth. We drove on, singing quietly, while the kids in the back seats dozed. Albee had solved a problem for himself. He called it a mutual checkmate. My brother was scooped into an ambulance. There was nothing we could have done to save him. No words that would have brought him back. It had been a summer of sirens. His was another. The lights spun. They took him to Metropolitan Hospital, the emergency room. Sprinted him down through the pale-green corridors. Blood on the floor behind them. Two thin tracks from the back trolley wheels. Mayhem all around. I dropped Adelita and her children outside the tiny clapboard house where they lived. She turned and looked over her shoulder at me, waved. She smiled. She was his. She would suit him. She was all right. He would find his God with her. My brother was wheeled into the triage room. Shouts and whispers. An oxygen mask over his face. Chest ripped open. A collapsed lung. One-inch tubes inserted to keep him breathing. A nurse with a manual blood-pressure cuff. I sat at the wheel of the van and watched as the lights went on in Adelita's house. I saw her shape against the light curtains until heavier ones were drawn across. I started the engine. They held him in traction with counterweights above the bed. A single breathing machine by his bed. The floor so skiddy with blood that the interns had to wipe their feet.

I drove on, oblivious. The Bronx streets were potholed. The orange and gray of arson. Some kids were dancing on the corners. Their bodies in flux. Like they had discovered something entirely new about themselves, shaking it through like a sort of faith. They cleared the room while they took X-rays. I pulled in under the bridge where I had spent most of my summer. A few girls were scattered around that night—the ones who had missed the raid. Some swallows scissored out from underneath the rafters. Seeding the sky. They didn't call out to me. My brother, in Metropolitan Hospital, still breathing. I was supposed to work in Queens, but I crossed the road instead. I had no idea what was happening. The blood swelling in his lungs. Towards the tiny bar. The jukebox blared. The Four Tops. Intravenous lines. Martha and the Vandellas. Oxygen masks. Jimi Hendrix. The doctors did not wear gloves. They stabilized him. Gave him a shot of morphine. Shot it right into his muscle. Wondered about the bruises on the inside of his arm. Took him for a junkie at first. The word was he'd come in with a dead hooker. They found a religious medal in the pocket of his pants. I left the bar and crossed the late-night boulevard, half drunk.

A woman called out to me. It wasn't Tillie. I didn't turn. Darkness. In the courtyard some kids were high and playing basketball without a ball. Everyone working towards repair. The single lights of the heart machine beeping. A nurse leaned into him. He was whispering something. What last words? *Make this world dark. Release me. Give me love, Lord, but not just yet.* They lifted his mask. I got to the fifth floor of the projects. The stairs exhausted me. Corrigan lay in the hospital room, in the cramped space of his own prayer. I leaned against the apartment door. Someone had tried to pry open the gold lock on the telephone. Some books lay scattered on the floor. There was nothing to take. Perhaps he drifted in and out, in and out, in and out. Tests going to see how much blood he had lost. In and out. In and out. The knock came on the door at two in the morning. Not many knocked. I shouted for them to come in. She pushed the door slowly. My brother's heart machine at a slow canter. In and out. She held a tube of lipstick. That I recall. Not a girl I knew. Jazzlyn has been in a crash, she said. Maybe her friend. Not a hooker. Almost casually. With half a shrug. The lipstick going across her mouth. A vivid red slash. My brother's heart machine blipping. The line like water. Not returning to any original place. I burst out through the door. Through the graffiti. The city wore it now, the swirls, the whorls. Fumes of the fresh.

I stopped at Adelita's house. Oh, Jesus, she said. The shock in her eyes. She pulled a jacket over her nightgown. I'm bringing my kids, she said. She bundled them into my arms. The taxi sped, flashing its lights. At the hospital, her children sat in the waiting room. Drawing with crayons. On newspaper. We ran to find Corrigan. Oh, she said. Oh. Oh, God. Doors swinging open everywhere. Closing again. The lights fluorescent above us. Corrigan lay in a small monkish cell. A doctor closed the door on us. I'm a nurse, said Adelita. Please, please, let me see him, I have to see him. The doctor turned with a shrug. Oh, God. Oh. We pulled two very simple wooden chairs up by his bed. Teach me who I might be. Teach me what I can become. Teach me.

The doctor came in, clipboard to his chest. He spoke, quietly, of internal injuries. A whole new language of trauma. The electrocardiogram beeped. Adelita leaned down to him. He was saying something in his morphine haze. He had seen something beautiful, he whispered. She kissed his brow. Her hand on his wrist. Heart monitor flickering. What's he saying? I asked her. Outside, the clack of wheels down the corridor. The screams. The sobs. The odd laughter of interns. Corrigan whispered something to her again, the blood bubbling at his mouth. I touched her forearm. What's he saying? Nonsense, she said, he's talking nonsense. He's hallucinating. Her ear to his mouth now. Does he want a priest? Is that what he wants? She turned to me. He says he saw something beautiful. Does he want a priest? I shouted. Corrigan was lifting his head slightly again. Adelita leaned down to him. Her reigning calmness. She was softly crying. Oh, she said, his forehead's cold. His forehead's very cold.

FROM OUTSIDE, THE SOUNDS OF PARK AVENUE. Quiet. Ordered. Controlled. Still, the nerves jangle in her. Soon she will receive the women. The prospect ties a small knot at the base of her spine. She brings her hands to her elbows, hugs her forearms. The wind ruffles the light curtains at the window. Alençon lace. Handmade, tatted, with silk trimmings. Never much for French lace. She would have preferred an ordinary fabric, a light voile. The lace was Solomon's idea, long ago. The stuff of marriage. The good glue. He brought her breakfast this morning, on the three-handled tray. Croissant, lightly glazed. Chamomile tea. A little slice of lemon on the side. He even lay down on the bed in his suit and touched her hair. Kissed her before he left. Solomon, wise Solomon, briefcase in hand, off downtown. The slight waddle in his step. The clack of his polished shoes on the marble floor. His low-growled good-bye. Not mean, just throaty. Sometimes it strikes her—there is my husband. There he goes. Same way he's been going for thirty-one years. And then a sort of silence interrupted. The drifting sounds, the snap of the lock, the dim bell, the elevator boy—*G'morning Mr. Soderberg!*—the whine of the door, the clank of machinery, the soft murmur of descent, the clanging stop at the lobby below, the roundelay of the cables rising.

She pulls the curtains back and peeps out the window once more, catches sight of the flap end of Solomon's gray suit as he disappears into a taxi. The little bald head dips. The slam of yellow. Into the traffic and away.

He does not even know about the visitors—she will tell him sometime, but not yet, no harm. Perhaps this evening. At dinner. Candle and wine. *Guess what, Sol.* As he settles in the chair, fork poised. *Guess what.* A slight sigh from him. *Just tell me, Claire, honey—I've had a long day.*

Nimble out of her nightdress. Her body in the full-length mirror. A little pale and puckered, but she can still stretch out of it. She yawns, hands high in the air. Tall, still thin, jet-black hair, a single streak of badger gray from the temple. Fifty-two years old. She passes a damp cloth over her hair and brushes it with a wooden comb. Turns her head sideways and presses the hair lengthwise against her palm. Tangled at the split ends. Time for a trim. She cleans out the comb and dumps the strands in the foot-flip garbage can. They say the hair of the dead still grows. Takes on a life of its own. Down there with all the other detritus, tissues, tubes of lipstick, toothpaste tops, allergy pills, eyeliner, heart medicine, youth, nail clippings, dental floss, aspirin, grief.

But how is it that the gray hairs are never the ones to come out? In her twenties she had hated the badger streak when it appeared overnight, dyed it, hid it, chopped it. Now it defines her, the elegant swift ray of gray, sideways from the temple.

A road in my hair. Do not overtake.

Things to do. Hurryhurry. Toilet. Toothbrush rub. A light swish of makeup. Some blush. A little eyeliner and a lipstick dab. Never one to fuss with makeup. At the dresser she pauses. Bra and panties in simple beige. Her favorite dress. Aqua and green silkscreen, with a shellfish motif. A-line. Sleeveless. Just above the knee. Bows on the slits. Zip behind. Fashionable and feminist at the same time. Not too fancy or showoffy, but contemporary, modest, good.

She hitches the hem a little higher. Extends her foot. Legs that glisten, said Solomon years ago. She told him once he made love like a hanged man, erect but dead. A joke she had heard at a Richard Pryor concert. She had sneaked in alone, using a friend's press pass. A one-off. Found the concert neither too risqué nor boring. But Solomon pouted for a week— three days at the joke, four days because she went to the concert at all. *Women's lib,* he said. *Burn your bra, lose your marbles.* Small, sweet man.

Devoted to good wine and martinis. The last little peninsula of hair on his head. Needs sunscreen in summertime. Freckles on his dome. Boyhood summers still around his eyes. When they met at Yale he had an overhang of hair, fair and thick over his eye. In Hartford as junior counsel he would walk along the narrow paths with Wallace Stevens, of all people, both men in sleeveless shirts. *It did not give of bird or bush, Like nothing else in Tennessee.* Home to her, they would make love on the four-poster bed. They lay on the sheets and he would try to recite poems in her ear. He could seldom recall the lines. Still, it was a sensual wonder, his lips against the tip of her ear, the side of her neck, down to her clavicle, the glow of enthusiasm about him. The bed broke one night from their hijinks. Nowadays it is not often, but often enough, and she still reaches up to hold the back of his hair. Not so woody anymore. The end of the stem where the fruit once was. The thugs in court are quiet until they're sentenced, then the anvil comes down and they scream and shout and thrash, call him filthy names. She no longer goes downtown with him to the dark wood-paneled room to observe—why endure the abuse? *Hey, Kojak! Who loves ya, baby?* In chambers there is a photograph of her, beachside, with Joshua, just a boy, both leaning together, mother and son, heads touching, the dunes behind them endless and grassy.

She feels a little murmur at her ribcage, a swell of air. Joshua. Not a name for a boy in uniform.

The necklace with a phantom hand. Sometimes it happens. She gets a little rush of blood to the throat. A clawing at her windpipe. As if someone is squeezing her, a momentary restriction. She turns to the mirror, sideways, then front, sideways again. The amethyst? The bangles? The small leather necklace Joshua gave her when he was nine? He had drawn a red ribbon on the brown wrapping. In crayon. *Here, Mommy,* he said, then ran away and hid. She wore it for years, around the house mostly. Had to sew it back together twice. But not now, not today, no. She tucks it back in the drawer. Too much. A necklace is too dressy anyway. She dithers at her reflection. Oil crisis, hostage crisis, necklace crisis. I'd rather be deep-solving algorithms. That was her specialty. College days. One of only three women in the math department. She got mistaken for the secretary as she walked the corridors. Had to go along with eyes downcast. A woman of two shoes. Knew the floor very well. The intricacies of tile. Where the baseboards broke.

We find, as in old jewelry, the gone days of our lives.

Earrings, then? Earrings. A pair of tiny seashells bought in Mystic two summers ago. She slides the small silver bar into the piercing. Turns to the mirror. Odd to see the strain of her neck. Not mine. Not that neck. Fifty-two years in that same skin. She extends her chin and her skin tightens. Vain, but better. The earrings against her dress. Seashell with seashell. She sells. By the shore. She drops them in the jewelry box and scatter-searches through. Casts a look at the dresser clock.

Quick quick.

Almost time.

She has been to four houses over the past eight months. All of them simple, clean, ordinary, lovely. Staten Island, the Bronx, two on the Lower East Side. Never any fuss. Just a gathering of mothers. That's all. But they were drop-jawed at her address when she finally told them. She had managed to avoid it for a while, but then they went to Gloria's apartment in the Bronx. A row of projects. She had never seen anything like it before. Scorch marks on the doorways. The smell of boric acid in the hall. Needles in the elevator. She was terrified. She went up to the eleventh floor. A metal door with five locks. When she rapped, the door vibrated on its hinges. But inside the apartment sparkled. Two huge chandeliers hanging from the ceiling, cheap but charming. The light chased the place free of shadows. The other women were already there—they smiled at her from the deep, pouchy sofa. They air-kissed, all of them, and the morning drifted smoothly. They even forgot where they were. Gloria bustled around, changing coasters, swapping napkins, cracking the windows for smokers, then showed them her sons' room. She had lost three boys, imagine—three!—poor Gloria. The photo albums were thick with memory: hairstyles, running meets, graduations. The baseball trophies were passed around the room. It was a lovely morning, all in all, and it drifted, drifted, drifted. And then the clock on top of the radiator clicked to noon and the talk came around to the next time. *Well, Claire, you're up next.* She felt like her mouth was made of chalk. Almost swallowed it as she spoke. Like an apology. Looking at Gloria all the time. *Well, I'm on Park at Seventy-sixth.* Silence, then. *You get the six.* She had rehearsed that. And then she said: *Train.* And then: *The subway.* And then: *Top floor.* None of it came out right, how she said it, like the words didn't quite fit on her tongue. *You live on Park?* said Jacqueline. Another silence. *That's nice,* said Gloria, a dab of light on her lips where she licked them, as if there were something to be removed there. And Marcia, the designer from Staten Island, clapped her hands together. *Tea with the Queen!* she said, joking, no harm meant, really, but still it pulsed, a brief wound.

Claire had told them, at the first meeting, that she lived on the East Side, that was all, but they must have known, even though she wore long pants and sneakers, no jewelry at all, must have intuited anyway, that it was the *Upper* East Side, and then Janet, the blonde, leaned forward and piped up: *Oh, we didn't know you lived up there.*

Up there. As if it were somewhere to climb. As if they would have to ascend to it. Ropes and helmets and carabiners.

She had actually felt faint. Like there was air in the back of her legs. Like she might be trying to show off. Rubbing their noses in it. Her whole body swayed. She stammered. *I grew up in Florida. It's very small, really. The plumbing is shocking. The roof's a mess.* She was about to say that she didn't have help—not *servants,* she would never have said *servants*—when Gloria, dearest Gloria, said: *Hell's bells, Park Avenue, I've only ever been there for Monopoly!* And they had all laughed. Reared back and just flat-out laughed. It gave her a chance to sip water. Squeeze out a smile. Take a breath. They couldn't wait. *Park Avenue! Jeepers creepers, isn't that the purple one?* Well, it wasn't the purple one. The purple one was Park Place, but Claire didn't say a word, why show off? They left together, all except Gloria, of course. Gloria waved from the eleventh-floor window, her patterned dress against the window bars across her chest. She looked so lost and lovely up there. It was the time of the garbage strike. Rats out by the trash. Streetwalkers by the underpass. In hot pants and halters, even in the snow flurries. Sheltering from the cold. Running out to the trucks when they passed. Clouds of white breath coming from them. Terrible cartoon bubbles. Claire wanted to dash back upstairs and bring Gloria with her, take her away from the horrific mess. But there was no going back to the eleventh floor. What could she say? Come, Gloria, pass go, collect two hundred, get out of jail free.

They had walked to the subway in a close group, four white women, their handbags held just a little too tightly. Might have been mistaken for social workers. All of them neatly dressed, but not overdone. They waited for the train in a smiling silence. Janet nervously tapped her shoe. Marcia fixed her mascara in a small mirror. Jacqueline swept back her long red hair. The train came, a wash of color, big curvy whirls, and in they got. It was one of those carriages covered head to toe in graffiti. Even the windows were blotted out. Hardly a moving Picasso. They were the only white women in the car. Not that she minded getting the subway. She just wouldn't tell them that it was only her second time. But nobody looked sideways at them, or said a rotten word. She got out at Sixty-eighth just so she could walk, get some air, be alone. She strolled up the avenue, wondering why she had ever gotten together with them in the first place. They were all so different, so little in common. But, still, she liked them all, she really did. Gloria especially. She had nothing against anyone— why would she? She hated that manner of talk. In Florida, her father had once said at dinner: *I like Negroes, yessir, I think everyone should own one.* She had stormed from the table and stayed in her room for two days. Her dinner was slid in under the door. Well, not slid under. Handed around the doorknob. Seventeen and about to go off to college. *Tell Daddy I'm not coming out until he apologizes.* And he did. Clomped up the curving staircase. Held her in his big round southern arms and called her modern.

Modern. Like a fixture. A painting. A Miró.

But it's only an apartment anyway. An apartment. Nothing more. Silverware and china and windows and trim and kitchenware. Only that. Nothing else. Homespun. Ordinary enough. What more could it be? Nothing. Let me tell you, Gloria, the walls between us are quite thin. One cry and they all come tumbling down. Empty mail slots. Nobody writes to me. The co-op board is a nightmare. Pet hair in the laundry machines. Doorman downstairs in his white gloves and creased trousers and epaulets, but just a little secret between you and me: he doesn't use deodorant.

A quick shiver splits through her: the doorman.

Wonder, will he question them too much? Who is it today? Melvyn, is it? The new one? Wednesday. Melvyn, yes. If he mistakes them for the help? If he shows them to the service elevator? Must call down and tell him. Earrings! Yes. Earrings. Quick now. In the bottom of the box, an old pair, simple silver studs, seldom worn. The bar a little rusty, but no matter. She wets each stem in her mouth. Catches sight of herself in the mirror again. The shell-patterned dress, the shoulder-length hair, the badger streak. She was mistaken once for the mother of a young intellectual seen on television, talking of photography, the moment of capture, the defiant art. She too had a badger streak. *Photographs keep the dead alive,* the girl had said. Not true. So much more than photographs. So much more.

Eyes a little glassy already. Not good. Buck up, Claire. She reaches for the tissues beyond the glass figurines on the dresser, dries her eyes. Runs to the inner hallway, picks up the ancient handset.

—Melvyn?

She buzzes again. Maybe outside smoking.

—Melvyn?!

—Yes, Mrs. Soderberg?

His voice calm, even. Welsh or Scottish—she's never asked.

—I have some friends dining with me this morning.

—Yes, ma'am.

—I mean, they're coming for breakfast.

—Yes, Mrs. Soderberg.

She runs her fingers along the dark wainscoting of the corridor. *Dining?* Did I really say *dining?* How could I say *dining?*

—You'll make sure they're welcome?

—Of course, ma'am.

—Four of them.

—Yes, Mrs. Soderberg.

Breathing into the handset. That fuzz of red mustache above his lip. Should have asked where he was from when he first started working. Rude not to.

—Anything else, ma'am?

Ruder to ask now.

—Melvyn? The correct elevator.

—Of course, ma'am.

—Thank you.

She leans her head against the cool of the wall. She shouldn't have said anything at all about a correct or incorrect elevator. A *bushe,* Solomon would have said. Melvyn'll be down there, paralyzed, and then he'll put them in the wrong one. *The elevator there to your right, ladies. In you go.* She feels a flush of shame to her cheeks. But she used the word *dining,* didn't she? He'll hardly mistake that. *Dining* for breakfast. Oh, my.

The overexamined life, Claire, it's not worth living.

She allows herself a smile and goes back along the corridor to the living room. Flowers in place. Sun bouncing off the white furniture. The Miró print above the couch. The ashtrays placed at strategic points. Hope they won't smoke inside. Solomon hates smoking. But they all smoke, even her. It's the smell that gets to him. The afterburn. Ah, well. Maybe she'll join them anyway, puff away, that little chimney, that small holo-caust. Terrible word. Never heard it as a child. She was raised Presbyte-rian. A small scandal when she married. Her father's booming voice. *He's a what? A yoohoo? From New England?* And poor Solomon, hands clasped behind his back, staring out the window, adjusting his tie, staying quiet, enduring the abuse. But they still took Joshua to Florida, to the shores of Lochloosa Lake, every summer. Walking through the mango groves, all three holding hands, Joshua in the middle, one two three weeeeee.

It was there in the mansion that Joshua learned to play the piano. Five years old. He sat on the wooden stool, slid his fingers up and down the keys. When they got back to the city they arranged lessons in the base-ment of the Whitney. Recitals in a bow tie. His little blue blazer with gold buttons. Hair parted to the left. He used to love to press the gold pedal with his foot. Said he wanted to drive the piano all the way home. Vroom vroom. They bought him a Steinway for his birthday and at the age of eight he was playing Chopin before dinnertime. Cocktails in hand, they settled on the couch and listened.

Good days, they come around the oddest corners.

She grabs her hidden cigarettes from under the lid of the piano chair and walks to the rear of the apartment, swings open the heavy back door. Used to be the maid's entrance. Long ago, when there was such a thing: maids and entrances. Up the rear stairs. She is the only one in the build-ing who ever uses the roof. Shoves open the fire door. No alarm. The blast of heat from the dark rooftop. The co-op board has been trying for years to put a deck up on the roof but Solomon complained. Doesn't want foot-steps above him. Nor smokers. A stickler for that. Hates the smell. Solomon. Good, sweet man. Even in his straitjacket.

She stands in the doorway and drags deep, tosses a little cloud of smoke to the sky. The benefit of a top-floor. She refuses to call it a pent-house. Something leering about that. Something glossy and magazine-y. She has arranged a little row of flowerpots on the black tarmac of the roof, in the shade of the wall. More trouble than they're worth sometimes, but she likes to greet them in the mornings. Floribundas and a couple of straggly hybrid teas.

She bends down to the row of pots. A little yellow spot on the leaves. Struggling through the summer. She taps the ash at her feet. A pleasant breeze from the east. The whiff of the river. The television suggested yesterday a slight chance of rain. No sign. A few clouds, that's all. How is it they fill, the clouds? Such a small miracle, rain. *It rains on the living and the dead, Mama, only the dead have better umbrellas.* Perhaps we will drag our chairs up here, all four of us, no, five, and raise our faces to the sun. In the summer quiet. Just be. Joshua liked the Beatles, used to listen to them in his room, you could hear the noise even through the big headphones he loved. *Let it be.* Silly song, really. You let it be, it returns. There's the truth. You let it be, it drags you to the ground. You let it be, it crawls up your walls.

She pulls again on the cigarette and looks over the wall. A momentary vertigo. The creek of yellow taxis along the street, the crawl of green in the median of the avenue, the saplings just planted.

Nothing much happening on Park. Everyone gone to their summer homes. Solomon, dead against. City boy. Likes his late hours. Even in summertime. His kiss this morning made me feel good. And his cologne smell. Same as Joshua's. Oh, the day Joshua first shaved! Oh, the day! Covered himself in foam. So very careful with the razor. Made an avenue through the cheek, but nicked himself on the neck. Tore off a tiny piece of his Daddy's *Wall Street Journal.* Licked it and pasted it to the wound. The business page clotting his blood. Walked around with the paper on his neck for an hour. He had to wet it to get it off. She had stood at the bathroom door, smiling. My big tall boy, shaving. Long ago, long ago. The simple things come back to us. They rest for a moment by our ribcages then suddenly reach in and twist our hearts a notch backward.

No newspapers big enough to paste him back together in Saigon.

She takes another long haul, lets the smoke settle in her lungs—she has heard somewhere that cigarettes are good for grief. One long drag and you forget how to cry. The body too busy dealing with the poison. No wonder they gave them out free to the soliders. Lucky Strikes.

She spies a black woman on the corner, turning away. Tall and bosom-burdened. Wearing a flowery dress. Perhaps Gloria. But all alone. A housekeeper, probably. You never know. She would love to run downstairs and go to the corner and scoop her up, Gloria, her favorite of them all, gather her in her arms, bring her back, sit her down, make her coffee, talk and laugh and whisper and belong with her, just belong. That's all she wants. Our little club. Our little interruption. Dearest Gloria. Up there in her high-rise every night and day. How in the world did she live in such a place? The chainlink fences. The whirling litter. The terrible stench. All those young girls outside selling their bodies. Looking like they would fall on their backs and use their spines as mattresses. And the fires in the sky—they should call it Dresden and be finished with it.

Perhaps she could hire Gloria. Bring her in. Odd jobs around the house. The bits and pieces. They could sit at the kitchen table together and while away the days, make a secret gin and tonic or two, and let the hours just drift, her and Gloria, at ease, at joy, yes, Gloria, in excelsis deo.

Down on the street, the woman turns the corner and away.

Claire stamps out the cigarette and totters back toward the roof door. A little dizzy. The world shifted sideways for an instant. Down the stairs, head spinning. Joshua never smoked. Maybe on his way to heaven he asked for one. Here's my thumb and here's my leg and here's my throat and here's my heart and here's one lung and, hey, let's bring them all together for a final Lucky Strike.

Back inside, through the maid's entrance, she hears the clock in the living room striking time.

To the kitchen.

Woozy, now. Take a breath.

Who needs a master's degree to boil water?

She steps unsurely along the corridor and back to the kitchen. Marble countertop, gold-handled cabinets, lots of white machinery. The others had made a rule early on in their coffee mornings: the visitors are the ones to bring the bagels, muffins, cheese Danish, fruit, cookies, crullers. The host makes the tea and coffee. A nice balance that way. She had thought about ordering a whole tray of goodies from William Greenberg's up on Madison, rainbow cookies and pecan rings and challahs and croissants, but that would be oneupmanship, womanship, whatever.

She turns the flame under the water high. A little universe of bubble and burn. Good French roast. Instant satisfaction. Tell that to the Viet Cong.

A row of tea bags on the counter. Five saucers. Five cups. Five spoons.

Perhaps the cow-shaped creamer for a touch of humor. No, too much. Too whimsical. But can I not laugh in front of them? Didn't Dr. Tonnemann tell me to laugh?

Go ahead, please, laugh.

Laugh, Claire. Let it out.

A good doctor. He would not let her take pills. Try each day just to laugh a little bit, it's a good medicine, he said. Pills were a second option. I should have taken them. No. Better off to try laughing. Die laughing.

Yes, move wild laughter in the throat of death. A good doctor, yes. Could even quote Shakespeare. Move wild laughter indeed.

Joshua had written her a letter once about water buffalo. He was amazed by them. Their beauty. He saw a squadron once tossing grenades by a river. All merrily laughing. Throat of death indeed. When the water buffalo were finished, he said, the soldiers shot the brightly colored birds out of the trees. Imagine if they had to count that too. *You can count the dead, but you can't count the cost. We've got no math for heaven, Mama. Everything else can be measured.* She had turned that letter over and over in her mind. A logic in every living thing. The patterns you get in flowers. In people. In water buffalo. In the air. He hated the war but got asked to go while out in California at PARC. Got asked politely, of all things. The president wanted to know how many dead there were. Lyndon B. couldn't figure it out. Every day the advisers came to him with their facts and figures and laid them down on his desk. Army dead. Navy dead. Marine dead. Civilian dead. Diplomatic dead. MASH dead. Delta dead. Seabee dead. National Guard dead. But the numbers didn't compute. Someone was messing up somewhere. All the reporters and TV channels were breathing down LBJ's neck and he needed the proper information. He could help put a man on the Moon, but he couldn't count the body bags. Send a satellite spinning, but he couldn't figure out how many crosses to go into the ground. A crack computer unit. The Geek Squad. Quick initiation. Serve your nation. Get your hair cut. *My country, 'tis of thee, we've got technology.* Only the best and brighest came. From Stanford. MIT. University of Utah. U.C. Davis. His friends from PARC. The ones who were developing the dream of the ARPANET. Kitted up and sent off. White men, all. There were other systems also—how much sugar was used, how much oil, how many bullets, how many cigarettes, how many cans of corned beef, but Joshua's beat was the dead.

Serve your country, Josh. If you can write a program that plays chess you surely can tell us how many are falling to the gooks. Give me all your ones and zeros, heroes. Show us how to count the fragged.

They could hardly find uniforms small enough at the shoulders or long enough at the legs for him. He stepped onto the plane, trouser legs at half-mast. I should have known then. Should have just called him back. But on he went. The plane took off and went small against the sky. A barracks was already built out in Tan Son Nhut. At the air force base. A small brass band was there to meet them, he said. Cinder block and desks of pressure-treated wood. A room full of PDP-10's and Honeywells. They walked inside and the place hummed for them. A candy store, he said.

She wanted to tell him so much, on the tarmac, the day he left. The world is run by brutal men and the surest proof is their armies. If they ask you to stand still, you should dance. If they ask you to burn the flag, wave it. If they ask you to murder, re-create. Theorem, anti-theorem, corollary, anti-corollary. Underline it twice. It's all there in the numbers. Listen to your mother. Listen to me, Joshua. Look me in the eyes. I have something to tell you.

But he stood, buzz-haired and red-cheeked, in front of her, and she said nothing.

Say something to him. That shine to his cheeks. Say something. Tell him. Tell him. But she just smiled. Solomon pressed a Star of David into his hands and turned away and said: *Be brave.* She kissed his forehead good-bye. She noticed the way the back of his uniform creased and un-creased in perfect symmetry, and she knew, she just knew, the moment she saw him go, that she was seeing him go forever. *Hello, Central, give me heaven, I think my Joshua is there.*

Can't indulge this heartsickness. No. Spoon the coffee out and line the tea bags up. Imagine endurance. There's a logic to that. Imagine and hang on.

How is it being dead, son, and would I like it?

Oh. The buzzer. Oh. Oh. Spoon clang to the floor. Oh. Stepping quickly along the corridor. Return and pick up the spoon. Everything neat now, neat, yes. Give me back his living body, Mr. Nixon, and we will not quarrel. Take this corpse, all fifty-two years of it, swap it; I won't regret it, I won't complain. Just give him back to us all sewn up and handsome.

Control yourself, Claire.

I shall not fall apart.

No.

Quick now. Doorwise. At the buzzer. Her mind, she knows, needs a quick dip in water. A momentary cold swell, like those little buckets outside a Catholic church. Dip in and be healed.

—Yes?

—Your visitors, Mrs. Soderberg.

—Oh. Yes. Send them up.

Too harsh? Too quick? Should have said, Wonderful. Great. With a big swell to my voice. Instead of *Send them up*. Not even *please*. Like hired hands. Plumbers, decorators, soldiers. She engages the button to listen in. Curious thing, the old intercoms. Faint static and buzz and some laughter and door close.

—The elevator's straight ahead, ladies.

Well, at least there's that. At least he didn't show them to the service elevator. At least they're in the warm mahogany box. No, not that. The elevator.

The faint mumble of voices. All of them together. They must have met up beforehand. Prearranged. Hadn't thought of that. Hadn't let it cross my mind. Wish they hadn't.

Talked about me, maybe. Needs a doctor. Awful gray streak in her hair. Husband's a judge. Wears implausible sneakers. Struggles to smile. Lives in a penthouse but calls it *upstairs*. Is terribly nervous. Thinks she's one of the gals, but she's really a snob. Is likely to break down.

How to greet? Handshake? Air kiss? Smile? The first time around they had hugged good-bye, all of them, in Staten Island, at the doorstep, with the taxi beeping, her eyes streaked with tears, arms around one another, all of us happy, at Marcia's house, when Janet pointed to a yellow balloon caught in the treetops: *Oh, let's meet again soon!* And Gloria had squeezed her arm. They had touched cheeks. *Our boys, you think they knew each other, Claire? You think they were friends?*

War. The disgusting proximity of it. Its body odor. Its breath on her neck all this time, two years now since pullout, three, two a half, five million, does it matter? Nothing's over. The cream becomes the milk. The first star at morning is the last one at night. Did she think they were friends? *Well, they could have been, Gloria, they certainly could have been.*

Vietnam was as good a place to start as any. Yes indeed. Dr. King had a dream and it would not be gassed on the shores of Saigon. When the good doctor was shot, she sent a thousand dollars in twenty-dollar bills to his church in Atlanta. Her father raved and roared. Called it guilt money. She didn't care. There was plenty to be guilty for. She was modern, yes. She should have sent her whole inheritance. *I like fathers; I just think everyone should disown one.* Like it or not, Daddy, it goes to Dr. King, and what do you think of your niggers and kikes now?

Oh. The mezuzah on the door. Oh. Forgot about that. She touches it, stands in front of it. Just tall enough to obscure it. The top of her head. The clang of the elevator. Why the shame? But it's not shame, not really, is it? What is there possibly to be ashamed of? Solomon insisted on it years ago. That's all. For his own mother. To make her comfortable when she visited. To make her happy. And what's wrong with that? It did make her happy. Isn't that enough? I have nothing to apologize for. I have scuttled around all morning with my lips puckered, afraid to breathe. Swallowed a bag of air. I should have been a pair of ragged claws. What is it the young ones say? Get a grip. Hang on. Ropes and helmets and carabiners.

What was it I never said to Josh?

She can see the numbers as they rise. A bustle from the elevator shaft and a loud chatter. They are comfortable already. Wish I had met them earlier, in some coffee shop. But here they are, here they come.

What was it?

—Hello, she says, hello hello hello, Marcia! Jacqueline! Look at you! Come in, oh, I love your shoes, Janet, this way, this way. Gloria! Oh, hi, oh, look, please, come in, it's lovely to see you.

The only thing you need to know about war, son, is: Don't go.

—

IT WAS AS IF SHE could travel through the electricity to see him. She could look at any electronic thing—television, radio, Solomon's shaver—and could find herself there, journeying along the raw voltage. Most of all it was the fridge. She would wake in the middle of the night and wander through the apartment into the kitchen and lean against the freezer. She would open the door then and blast herself with cool. What she liked about it was that the light wouldn't come on. She could go from warm to cold in an instant and she could remain in the darkness and not wake Solomon. No sound, just a soft plop of the rubber-edged opening, and then a rush of cold over her body, and she could gaze past the wires, the cathodes, the transistors, the hand-set switches, through the ether, and she could see him, all of a sudden she was in the very same room, right beside him, she could reach out and lay her hand on his forearm, console him, where he sat under the fluorescents, amid the long rows of desks and mattresses, working.

She had inklings, intuitions about how it all worked. She was no slouch. She had her degree. But how was it, she wondered, that machines could count the dead better than humans? How was it that the punch cards knew? How did a series of tubes and wires know the difference between the living and the dead?

He sent her letters. He called himself a hacker. It felt like a word to chop down trees. But all it meant was that he programmed the machines. He created the language that tripped the switches. A thousand microscopic gates fell in an instant. She thought of it as opening up a field. One gate led to another, and another, over the hill, and soon he was on a river and away, rafting down the wires. He said that just being at a computer made him so giddy that he felt he was sliding down the banisters, and she wondered what banisters he meant, because there had been no banisters in his childhood, but she accepted it, and she saw him there, in the hills around Saigon, sliding down the banisters toward a concrete basement in a cinder-block building, stepping to his desk, punching the buttons alive. The crisp cursor flicking in front of his eyes. The furrow of his brow. His fierce scan through the printouts. His laughter at a joke as it rippled along the row of desks. The breakthroughs. The breakdowns. The plates of food on the floor. The Rolaids strewn on the desks. The web of wires. The whirl of switches. The purr of fans. It got so hot in the room, he said, that they would have to step out every half an hour. Outside, they kept a water hose to cool down. Back at their consoles they would be dry within seconds. They called each other Mac. Mac this, Mac that. Their favorite word. Machine-aided cognition. Men against computers. Multi-access cognition. Maniacs and clowns. Must ask coyly. Might add colostomy bag.

Everything they did centered around their machines, he said. They divided, linked, nested, chained, deleted. Rerouted switches. Cracked passwords. Changed memory boards. It was a sort of black magic. They knew the inner mysteries of each and every computer. They stayed inside all day. Working with hunches, failures, intangibles. If they needed sleep they just slid in under the desk, too tired to dream.

The Death Hack was his core project. He had to go through the files, key all the names in, add the men up as numbers. Group them, stamp them, file them, code them, write them. The problem was not even so much the dying as the overlap in the deaths. The ones who had the same names—the Smiths and the Rodriguezes and the Sullivans and the Johnsons. Fathers with the same names as their sons. The dead uncles with the exact initials as the dead nephews. The ones who went AWOL. The split missions. The misreported. The mistakes. The secret squadrons, the flotillas, the task forces, the reconnaissance crews. The ones who got married in little rural villages. The ones who stayed deep in the jungle. Who could account for them? But he fit them into his program as best he could. Created a space for them so that they became a sort of alive. He put his head down, worked it, asked no questions. It was, he said, the patriotic thing to do. What he liked most was the moment of creation, when he solved what nobody else could solve, when the solution was clean and elegant.

It was easy enough to write a program that would collate the dead, he said, but what he really wanted was to write a program that could make sense of the dying. That was the deep future. One day the computers would bring all the great minds together. Thirty, forty, a hundred years from now. If we don't blow one another asunder first.

We're at the cusp of human knowledge here, Mama, he said. He wrote about the dream of widely separated facilities sharing special resources. Of messages that were able to go back and forth. Of remote systems that could be manipulated through the telephone lines. Of computers that were capable of repairing their own malfunctions. Of protocols and bulk erasers and teletype printouts and memory and RAM and maxing out the Honeywell and fooling around on the prototype Alto that had been sent across. He described circuit boards like some people described icicles. He said that the Eskimos had sixty-four words for snow but that didn't surprise him; he thought they should have more—why not? It was about the deepest sort of beauty, the product of the human mind being stamped onto a piece of silicon that you might one day cart around in your briefcase. A poem in a rock. A theorem in a slice of stone.

The programmers were the artisans of the future. Human knowledge is power, Mama. The only limits are in our minds. He said there was nothing that a computer couldn't do, even the most complicated problems, find the value of pi, the root of all language, the most distant star. It was crazy how small the world truly was. It was a matter of opening up to it. What you want is your machine to speak back to you, Mama. It almost has to be human. You have to think of it that way. It's like a Walt Whitman poem: you can put in it everything you want.

She sat by the fridge and read his letters and smoothed his hair and told him it was time to go to sleep, that he should eat something, he should change his clothes, that he really needed to look after himself. She wanted to make sure he wasn't fading away. Once, during a blackout, she sat against the kitchen cabinets and wept: she couldn't get through to him. She stuck a lead pencil into the wall socket and waited. When the electricity came on the pencil jumped in her fingers. She was aware of how it might look—a woman at a fridge, opening and closing the door—but it was a solace, and not something Solomon would suspect. She could pretend that she was cooking, or getting a glass of milk, or waiting for meat to thaw.

Solomon didn't talk about the war. Silence was his way out. He chatted instead about his court cases, the insane litany of the city, the murders, the rapes, the cons, the hustles, the stabbings, the robberies. But not the war. Only the protesters came in his range—he thought them weak, guileless, cowardly. Gave them the stiffest sentences he could. Six months for pouring blood on the draft board files. Eight months for smashing the windows of the Times Square recruiting office. She wanted to march and protest, to meet all the hippies and yippies and skippies in Union Square, Tompkins Square Park, to carry a banner for the Catonsville Nine. But she just couldn't bring herself to do it. We must support our boy, said Solomon. Our sweet little tow-headed one. Who slept between us not so many years ago, curled against us. Who played train sets on the Oriental rug. Who outgrew his blue blazer. Who knew fish fork, salad fork, dinner fork, the broad tines of life.

And then, from nowhere, blackout, all blackout, ever blackout.

Johsua became code.

Written into his own numbers.

She lay two months in bed. Hardly moving. Solomon wanted to hire a nurse, but she refused. She said she would snap out of it. But the word was not *snap*, more like *slide*. A word Joshua had liked. I will slide out. She began to walk around the house, through the dining room, around the living room, past the breakfast nook, toward the fridge again. She put Joshua's photo front and center. She leaned against it and talked to him. And the fridge collected things that he might have liked. Simple things. She cut them out and pasted them on. Computer articles. Photos of circuit boards. A picture of a new building at PARC. A newspaper article about a graphics hack. The menu from Ray's Famous. An ad from *The Village Voice*.

It struck her that her fridge was beginning to look hairy. The phrase almost made her smile. My hairy fridge.

And then one evening, the little clips fluttered to the floor and she leaned down and read it again. LOOKING FOR MOTHERS TO TALK TO. NAM VETS. P.O. BOX 667. She had never really thought of him as a veteran, or having been in Vietnam—he was a computer operator, had gone to Asia. But the ad made her fingers tingle. She brought it to the kitchen counter, sat down, quickly wrote a reply in pencil, then went over it with ink, stole quietly out the door, slunk into the elevator. She could have mailed it right downstairs in the lobby, but she didn't want to; she ran outside to Park Avenue, middle of the night, in a snowstorm, the doorman stunned to see her going out the door in her nightdress, slippers on: *Mrs. Soderberg, are you okay?*

Can't stop now. Letter in hand. Mother seeks bones of son. Found in blown-up café in foreign land.

She ran down to Lexington to the mailbox on Seventy-fourth. The white breath leaving her for the air. Toes wet with snow. She knew that if she didn't send it right then, she never would. The doorman nodded shyly when she came back in, cast a quick flick of his eyes to her breasts. *'Night, Mrs. Soderberg,* he said. Oh, she wanted to kiss him right then and there. On the forehead. A thanks for peeping. It made her feel good. Thrilled her, to be honest. The cloth stretched tight across her chest, the outline of everything showing, the benefit of cold, a single snowflake melting down along the very front of her throat. Any other time she would have thought it crass. But there, in her nightdress, in the warmth of the elevator, she was thankful. There was a lightness about her that night. She cleaned the front of the fridge of everything but his photo-

graph. Made it simple again. Gave it a haircut of sorts. Thought of her letter winding its way through the postal system, eventually to find another
like her. Who would it be, and what would they look like, and would they
be tender, and would they be kind? That's all she wanted: for them to be
kind.

That night she climbed in and snuggled against the soft warmth of
Solomon. Touched him on the low of the back. *Sol. Solly. Solhoney. Wake
up.* He turned to say that her feet were cold. *Warm me up then, Solly.* He
propped himself on his elbow and leaned across.

And afterward she went to sleep. For the first time in ages. She had almost forgotten what it meant to wake. She opened her eyes beside him in
the morning and nudged him again, ran her fingers on the curve of his
shoulder. *Geez,* he said with a grin, *what is it, honey, my birthday?*

——

IN THEY COME. Cautiously dressed, all except Jacqueline, who has a deep
plunge to her Laura Ashley print. Marcia just behind her, all flushed and
feathery. Like she's just flown through a window and needs to bash at the
walls. Not even a glance at the mezuzah on the door. Thank heavens for
that. No explanations. Janet, with her head down. A touch from Gloria on
the wrist and a deep wide smile. They rush along the corridor with Marcia at the front now, a bakery box in her hand. Past Joshua's door. Past her
own bedroom. Past the painting of Solomon on the wall, eighteen years
younger and a good deal more hair. Into the living room. Straight to the
couch.

Marcia places the box on the coffee table, sits back against the deep
white cushions and fans herself. Maybe it's just hot flashes, or perhaps
she got caught up in the subway. But, no, she's all aflutter, and the others
know something is up.

At least, she thinks, they didn't meet beforehand. Didn't come up with
a Park Avenue strategy. *Do not pass go, do not collect two hundred.* She pulls
up the ottoman and circles the chairs, guides Gloria onto the sofa by the
arm. Gloria, with flowers in her hand, still clutching them. It would be
rude to take them, but they'll need some water soon.

—Oh, God, says Marcia.

—Are you all right?

—What is it?

Gathered around her as if at a campfire, all of them, leaning in, eager for outrage.

—You won't believe it.

Marcia's face is flushed red, with little beads of sweat at her brow. She breathes as if all the oxygen is gone, as if they are at some great height. Ropes and helmets and carabiners indeed.

—What? says Janet.

—Did someone hurt you?

Marcia's chest yammering up and down, a gold-plated bear falling against her chestbone.

—Man in the air!

—What?

—A man in the air, walking.

—Mercy, says Gloria.

Claire considers a moment the notion that Marcia might be a tad drunk, or even high—who knows these days; she might have munched on some mushrooms for breakfast, or downed a little vodka—but she looks perfectly sober, if a little flushed, no redness to the eyes, no slurring.

—Downtown.

Drunk or not, she is thankful for Marcia and this little blip of hysteria. It has guided them all so quickly into the apartment. A minimum of fuss. No need for all those niceties, the oohs and the ahhs, the embarrassments, what fabulous curtains, and isn't that a nice fireplace, and yes, I'll have two sugars with mine, and oh, it's very cozy, really, Claire, very cozy, what a lovely vase, and, Lord above, is that your husband on the wall? All the planning in the world could not have ushered them in so smoothly, without a single hiccup.

She should do something, she knows, to let them know they're welcome. Hand Marcia a handkerchief. Get her a tall, cool glass of water. Take the flowers from Gloria's hands. Open up the bakery boxes and spread them out. Compliment the bagels. Something, anything. But they are stuck on the swell of Marcia now, watching the rise and fall of her chest.

—Glass of water, Marcia?

—Yes, please. Oh, yes.

—A man where?

The voices fading. Silly of me. Into the kitchen, quickquick. She doesn't want to miss a word. The soft murmur of conversation from the living room. To the freezer. The ice tray. Should have put in fresh trays this morning. Never thought of it. She bangs them on the marble counter. Three, four cubes. A few shards spread out across the counter. Old ice. Hazy at the center. One cube slips across the counter as if to release itself, falls on the floor. Should I? She glances toward the living room and picks the cube off the floor. In one smooth motion she's across to the sink. Allows the tap to run a second, washes the cube, fills the glass. She should slice some lemon and would in normal circumstances, but instead she's out of the kitchen and into the living room and across the carpet, with the water.

—Here you go.

—Oh, lovely. Thanks.

And a smile from Janet, of all people.

—But the ferry boat was full, you see, says Marcia.

She's a little hurt that Marcia didn't wait for her to begin, but no matter. The ferry from Staten Island, no doubt.

—And I was standing right at the very front.

Claire dries her hand on the hip of her dress and wonders now where it is she should sit. Should she go right to the heart of the matter, onto the sofa? But that might be a bit much, a bit forward, right beside Marcia, who has all the eye-gaze. And yet to stand on the outside might be noticed too, as if she's not part of them, trying to be separate. Then again, she needs to be mobile, not hem herself in with the coffee table, she has to be able to get up and make refreshments, spread the breakfast out, take orders, make everyone feel at home. Instant or ground? Sugar or not?

She smiles at Gloria and edges across toward her, lifts the belted ashtray off the arm of the chair, places it on the table with a soft rattle, and sits down, feels the thick of Gloria's hand on her back, a reassurance.

—Go on, please, go on. Sorry.

—And I was a little too late to watch the sunrise, but I thought I'd stand up there anyway. It's pretty. The city. At that hour. I don't know if you've ever seen it but it's pretty. And I was just daydreaming, really, when I looked up and I saw a helicopter in the air and, well, you all know me and helicopters.

They know indeed, and it makes the air somber a moment but Marcia doesn't seem to notice, and she coughs for a pause, a fraction of silence, respect, really.

—So I'm watching this helicopter and it's hanging in the air, almost like it's doing a double take. Up there, but not very well. Suspended, like. But rocking back and forth.

—Landsakes.

—And I'm thinking about how Mike Junior would hang a much better turn than that, how he'd handle the craft so much better, I mean he was the Evel Knievel of helicopters, his sergeant said so. And I thought maybe there's something wrong with it, you know? I had that dread. You know, hanging there.

—Oh, no, says Jacqueline.

—I couldn't hear the engine so I didn't really know. And then, suddenly, behind the helicopter, I saw this little flyspeck. No bigger than an insect, I swear to you. But it's a man.

—A man?

—Like an angel? says Gloria.

—A flyman?

—What sort of man?

—Flying?

—Where?

—I just got the heebie-jeebies.

—It's a guy, says Marcia, on a tightrope. I mean, I didn't know it right away, I didn't figure it out just like that, but what it is, there's a guy on a tightrope.

—Where?

—Shh, shh, says Janet.

—Up there. Between the towers. A million miles up. We could just about see him.

—What's he doing?

—Tightroping!

—A funambulist.

—What?

—Oh, my God.

—Does he fall?

—Shh.

—Oh, don't tell me he falls.

—Shh!

—Please don't tell me he falls.

—Shh already, says Janet to Jacqueline.

—So I tapped the shoulder of this young guy beside me. One of those ponytailed ones. And he's like, What, lady? Like he's real annoyed that I disturbed his little standing sleep or dream or whatever it is he's doing at the front of the boat. And I said, Look. And he said, What?

—Mercy.

—And I pointed it out, the little flyman, and then he said a bad word, you'll excuse me, Claire, in your house, I'm sorry, but he said, Fuck.

And Claire wants to say: Well, I'd say fuck too, if I were me. I'd say it backward and forward and around the block, fuck this and fuck that and fuck it all once, twice, three times. But all she does is smile at Marcia and give her what she hopes is a nod that understands that it's absolutely no problem to say fuck, on Park Avenue, on a Wednesday, at a coffee morning, in fact it's probably the best thing to say, given the circumstances, maybe they should all say it in unison, make a singsong out of it.

—And then, says Marcia, everyone around us started looking up and before I knew it even the captain of the ferry was out and he had binoculars with him and he said, That guy's on a tightrope.

—For real?

—Now you can only imagine. The whole deck, full of people. Their early commute. Shoulder to shoulder. And someone's walking a tightrope. Between those new buildings, the World Towery thingymajigs.

—Trade.

—Center.

—Oh, those?

—Listen to me.

—Those monstrosities, says Claire.

—And then this young guy, with the ponytail . . .

—The fuck guy? says Janet with a half-giggle.

—Yes. Well, he starts saying that he's sure, stocksure, five hundred and fifty percent, that it's a projection, that someone is projecting it up on the sky, and maybe it's a giant white sheet, and the image is coming from the helicopter, it's being beamed across from some sort of camera or other, he had all the technical terms.

—A projection?

—Like a TV thing? says Jacqueline.

—Circus, maybe.

—And I tell him that they can't do that from a helicopter. And he looks at me, like, Yeah, lady. And I say it to him again: They can't do that. And he says, And what do you know about helicopters, lady?

—Never!

—And I tell him I know a hell of a lot about 'copters, actually.

And she does. Marcia knows a hell of a hell of a hell of a lot about her helicopters, her hell of helicopters.

She has told them, in her own house, on Staten Island, that Mike Junior had been on his third tour of duty, routine fly mission over the coast at Qui Nhon, bringing cigars to some general or other in a Huey with the 57th Medical Detachment—cigars, can you imagine? and why the hell were the medevacs flying cigars?—and it was a good helicopter, top speed of ninety knots, she said. The figures had trilled off her tongue. It had something wrong with the steering column, she had said, and had gone into detail about the engine and the gearing ratio and the length of the two-bladed metal tail rotor, when what really mattered, all that truly mattered, was that Mike Junior had clipped the top of a goalpost, of all things, a soccer goalpost, only six feet off the ground—and who in the world plays soccer in Vietnam?—which sent the whirligig spinning and he landed awkwardly, sideways, and he smashed his head awkwardly, broke his neck, no flames, even, just a freak fall, the helicopter still intact; she had played it over in her mind a million times, and that was it, and Marcia woke at night dreaming of an army general opening and reopening the cigar boxes, finding bits and pieces of her son inside.

She knows her helicopters, yes she does, and more's the pity.

—So, anyway, I told him he should mind his own damn business.

—Indeed, says Gloria.

—And sure enough the captain of the ferry, looking through his binoculars, he says to everyone, That's no projection.

—That's right.

—And all I could think of, was, Maybe that's my boy and he's come to say hello.

—Oh, no.

—Oh.

—Lord.

A deep swell in her heart for Marcia.

—Man in the air.

—Imagine.

—Very brave.

—Exactly. That's why I thought of Mike Junior.

—Of course.

—And did he fall? says Jacqueline.

—Shh, shh, says Janet. Let her speak.

—I'm just asking.

—So the captain swings the ferry out so we can get a better look and then brings the boat into dock. You know, it bumped against the river wall. I couldn't see anything from there. The wrong angle. Our view was blocked. The north tower, south tower, I don't know which, but we couldn't see what was happening. And I didn't even say another word to the guy with the ponytail. I just turned on my heels. I was the very first person off. I wanted to run and see my boy.

—Of course, says Janet. There, there.

—Shh, says Jacqueline.

The room tight now. One turn of the screw and the whole thing could explode. Janet stares across at Jacqueline, who flicks her long red hair, as if tossing off a fly, even a flyman, and Claire looks back and forth between them, anticipating an overturned table, a broken vase. And she thinks, I should do something, say something, hit the release valve, the escape button, and she reaches across to Gloria to take the flowers from her, petunias, lovely petunias, gorgeous green stalks, neatly clipped at the bottom.

—I should put these in water.

—Yes, yes, says Marcia, relieved.

—Back in a jiffy.

—Hurry, Claire.

—Be right back.

The correct thing to do. Absolutely, positively. She tiptoes to the kitchen and stops at the louvered door. Too much farther in and she won't be able to hear. How silly to say I'd put them in water. Should have delayed somehow, bought more time. She leans against the door slats, straining to hear.

— . . . so I'm running in those old mazy side streets. Past the auction houses and cheap electronic joints and fabric stores and tenements. You'd think you'd be able to see the big buildings from there. I mean, they're huge.

—One hundred stories.

—A hundred ten.

—Shh.

—But they're not in view. I get glimpses of them but they're not the right angle. I was trying to take the most direct route. I should have just gone along the water. But I'm running, running. That's my boy up there and he's come to say hello.

Everyone silent, even Janet.

—I kept darting around corners, thinking I'd get a better view. Ducking this way and that. Looking up all the time. But I can't see them, the helicopter or the walker. I haven't run so fast since junior high. I mean, my boobs were bouncing.

—Marcia!

—Most days I forget I have them anymore.

—Ain't my dilemma, says Gloria, hitching her chest.

There is a swell of laughter around the room and, at the moment of levity, Claire moves back across the carpet, still holding Gloria's flowers, but nobody notices. The laughter ripples around, a reconciliation song, circling them all, making a little victory lap, and settles right back down at Marcia's feet.

—And then I stopped running, says Marcia.

Claire settles on the arm of the sofa again. No matter that she didn't take care of the flowers. No matter that there's no water reboiling. No matter that there's no vase in her hands. She leans forward with the rest of them.

Marcia has a tiny quiver in her lip now, a little tremble of portent.

—I just stopped cold, says Marcia. Dead smack in the middle of the street. I almost got run over by a garbage truck. And I just stood there, hands on my knees, eyes on the ground, breathing heavy. And you know why? I'll tell you why.

Pausing again.

All of them leaning forward.

—Because I didn't want to know if the poor boy fell.

—Ah-huh, says Gloria.

—I just didn't want to hear him dead.

—I hear you, ah-huh.

Gloria's voice, as if she's at a church service. The rest of them nodding slowly while the clock on the mantelpiece ticks.

—I couldn't stand the mere thought of it.

—No, ma'am.

—And if he didn't fall . . .

—If he didn't, no . . . ?

—I didn't want to know.

—Ah-huhn, you got it.

—'Cause somehow, if he stayed up there, or if he came down safe, it didn't matter. So I stopped and turned around and got on the subway and came up here without even so much as a second glance.

—Say gospel.

—Because if he was alive it couldn't possibly be Mike Junior.

All of it like a slam in the chest. So immediate. At all of their coffee mornings, it had always been distant, belonging to another day, the talk, the memory, the recall, the stories, a distant land, but this was now and real, and the worst thing was that they didn't know the walker's fate, didn't know if he had jumped or had fallen or had got down safely, or if he was still up there on his little stroll, or if he was there at all, if it was just a story, or a projection, indeed, or if she had made it all up for effect—they had no idea—maybe the man wanted to kill himself, or maybe the helicopter had a hook around him to catch him if he fell, or maybe there was a clip around the wire to catch him, or maybe maybe maybe there was another maybe, maybe.

Claire stands, a little shaky at the knees. Disoriented. The voices around her a blur now. She is aware of her feet on the deep carpet. The clock moving but not sounding anymore.

—I think I'll put these in water now, she says.

—

HE WOULD WRITE letters to her about the wheel wars late at night. Four in the morning at his terminal under the white fluorescents, cutting code, when sometimes a message flashed up. Most of the intrusions were from members of his own squad, linked in a couple of desks away, working on other programs, the tallies of war, and it was just a thing to pass the time, to hack another man's code, to test his strength, find his vulnerability. Harmless, really, Joshua said.

Charlie and the Viet Cong didn't have any computers. They weren't going to sneak in past the cathode tubes and transistors. But the phone lines were linked up back to PARC and Washington, D.C., and some universities, so it was possible, every now and then, for a single slider—he called them sliders, she had no idea why—to come in from somewhere else and cause havoc, and once or twice they blindsided him. Maybe he was working on an overlap line, he said, or a code for the disappeared. And he would be in the zone. He would feel, yes, like he was sliding down the banisters. It was about speed and raw power. The world was at ease and full of simplicity. He was a test pilot of a new frontier. Anything was possible. It could even have been jazz, one chord to the next. All fingertips. He could stretch his fingers and a new chord was suddenly there. And then without warning it would begin disappearing in front of his eyes. *I want a cookie!* Or: *Repeat after me, Bye-Bye Blackbird.* Or: *Watch me smile.* He said it was like being Beethoven after scribbling the Ninth. He'd be out on a nice stroll in the countryside and suddenly all the sheet music was blowing away in the wind. He sat rooted to the chair and stared at his machine. The small blipping cursor ate away what he'd been doing. His code got munched. No way to stop it. All that dread rose in his throat. He watched it as it climbed over the hills and disappeared into the sunset. *Come back, come back, come back, I haven't heard you yet.*

How strange to think that there was someone else at the other end of the wires. It was like a burglar breaking into his house and trying on his slippers. Worse than that. *Someone getting into my skin, Mama, taking over my memory.* Crawling right inside him, up his spinal cord, inside his head, deep into the cranium, walking over his synapses, into his brain cells. She could imagine him leaning forward, his mouth almost to the screen, static on his lips. *Who are you?* He could feel the intruders beneath his fingertips. Thumbs drumming on his spine. Forefingers at his neck. He knew they were American, the intruders, but he saw them as Vietnamese—he had to—gave them a brown slant to their eyes. It was him and his machine against the other machine. *Right, okay, now, well done, you got me, but now I'm going to crush you.* And then he would step right into the fray.

And she would go to the fridge and read his letters and sometimes she would open the freezer section and allow it all to cool him down. *It's all right, honey, you'll get it back.*

And he did. Joshua always got it back. He would phone her at odd hours, when he was elated, when he had won one of the wheel wars. Long, looping calls that had an echo to them. Didn't cost him a cent, he said. The squad had a switchboard with multiline capability. He said he had tapped into the lines, routed them down through the army recruiting number just for fun. It was just a system, he said, and it was there to be exploited. *I'm okay, Mama, it's not so bad, they treat us fine, tell Dad they even have kosher here.* She listened intently to the voice. When the elation wore off, he sounded tired, distant even, a new language creeping in. *Look, I'm cool, Mama, don't freak out.* Since when did he say *freak?* He had always been careful with language. Wrapped it up in a tight Park Avenue crispness. Nothing loose or nasal about it at all. But now the language was coarser and his accent had stretched. *I'm gonna go with the flow but it seems I'm driving another man's hearse, Mama.*

Was he taking care of himself? Did he have enough food? Did he keep his clothes clean? Was he losing weight? Everything reminded her. She even once put an extra plate out on the dinner table just for Joshua. Solomon said nothing about it. That and her fridge, her little idiosyncrasies.

She tried not to fret when his letters started to slacken. He wouldn't call for a day or two. Or three in a row. She would sit staring at the phone, willing it to ring. When she stood, the floorboards gave out a little groan. He was busy, he said. There had been a new development in electronic postings. There were more nodes on the electronic net. He said it was like a magic blackboard. The world was bigger and smaller both. Someone had hacked in to chew away parts of their program. It was a dogfight, a boxing match, a medieval joust. *I'm in the front line, Mama, I'm in the trenches.* Someday, he said, the machines would revolutionize the world. He was helping other programmers. They logged on at the consoles and stayed on. There was a battle going on with the peace protesters, who were trying to break into their machines. But it was not machines that were evil, he said, but the minds of the top brass behind them. A machine could be no more evil than a violin, or a camera, or a pencil. What the intruders didn't understand is that they were coming in at the wrong place. It was not the technology that they needed to attack, but the human mind, the way it failed, how it fell short.

She recognized a new depth in him, a candor. The war was about vanity, he said. It was about old men who couldn't look in the mirror anymore and so they sent the young out to die. War was a get-together of the vain. They wanted it simple—hate your enemy, know nothing of him. It was, he claimed, the most un-American of wars, no idealism behind it, only about defeat. There were over forty thousand to account for now in his Death Hack, and the numbers kept growing. Sometimes he would print the names out. He could unfurl them up and down the stairs. He sometimes wished that someone would hack his program from outside, chew it up, spit it all back out, give life again to all those boys, the Smiths and the Sullivans and the Rodriguez brothers, these fathers and cousins and nephews, and then he'd have to do a program for Charlie, a whole new alphabet of dying, Ngo, Ho, Phan, Nguyen—wouldn't that be a chore?

—You okay, Claire?

A touch on her elbow. Gloria.

—Help?

—Excuse me?

—You want help with those?

—Oh, no. I mean, yes. Thanks.

Gloria. Gloria. Such a sweet round face. Dark eyes, moist, almost. A lived-in face. A generosity to it. But a little perturbed. Looking at me. Looking at her. Caught in the act. Daydreaming. *Help?* She almost thought for a second that Gloria wanted to *be* the help. Presumptuous. Two seventy-five an hour, Gloria. Clean the dishes. Mop the floor. Weep for our boys. A chore indeed.

She reaches high into the top cupboard and pulls out the Waterford glass. Intricate cut. Distant men do that. There are some that aren't savages. Yes, that'll do nicely. She hands it to Gloria, who smiles, fills it.

—You know what you should do, Claire?

—What?

—Put sugar in the bottom. It keeps the flowers longer.

She has never heard that before. But it makes sense. Sugar. To keep them alive. Fill up our boys with sugar. Charlie and His Chocolate Factory. And who was it called the Vietnamese *Charlie* anyway? Where did it come from? Some radiospeak, probably. Charlie Delta Epsilon. Incoming, incoming, incoming.

—Even better if you clip the bottom of them first, says Gloria.

Gloria takes the flowers out and spreads them on the dish rack, takes a small knife from the kitchen counter and lops off a tiny segment of each, sweeps the stems into the palm of her hand, twelve little green things.

—Amazing, really, isn't it?

—What's that?

—The man in the air.

Claire leans against the counter. Takes a deep breath. Her mind whirling. She is not sure, not sure at all. A nagging discontent about him too. Something about his appearance sitting heavy, bewildering.

—Amazing, she says. Yes. Amazing.

But what is it about the notion that she doesn't like? Amazing, indeed, yes. And an attempt at beauty. The intersection of a man with the city, the abruptly reformed, the newly appropriated public space, the city as art. Walk up there and make it new. Making it a different space. But something else in it still rankles. She wishes not to feel this way, but she can't shake it, the thought of the man perched there, angel or devil. But what's wrong with believing in an angel, or a devil, why shouldn't Marcia be allowed to feel that way, why wouldn't every man in the air appear to be her son? Why shouldn't Mike Junior appear on the wire? What is wrong with that? Why shouldn't Marcia be allowed to freeze it there, her boy returned?

Yet still a sourness.

—Anything else, Claire?

—No, no, we're perfect.

—Right-y-o, then. All set.

Gloria smiles and hoists the vase, goes to the louvered door, pushes it open with her generous bulk.

—I'll be right out, says Claire.

The door swings back shut.

She arranges the last of the cups, saucers, spoons. Stacks them neatly. What is it? The walking man? Something vulgar about the whole thing. Or maybe not vulgar. Something cheap. Or maybe not quite cheap. She doesn't quite know what it is. To think this way, how petty. Downright selfish. She knows full well that she has the whole morning to do what they have done on other mornings—bring out the photos, show them the piano Joshua used to play, open the scrapbooks, take them all down to his room, show them his shelf of books, pick him out from the yearbook. That's what they have always done, in Gloria's, Marcia's, Jacqueline's, even Janet's, especially Janet's, where they were shown a slide show and later they all cried over a broken-spined copy of *Casey at the Bat*.

Her hands wide on the kitchen counter. Fingers splayed. Pressing down.

Joshua. Is that what rankles her? That they haven't yet said his name? That he hasn't yet figured into the morning's chatter? That they've ignored him so far, but no, it's not that, but what is it?

Enough. Enough. Lift the tray. Don't blow it now. So nice. That smile from Gloria. The beautiful flowers.

Out.

Now.

Go.

She steps into the living room and stops, frozen. They are gone, all of them, gone. She almost drops the tray. The rattle of the spoons as they slide against the edge. Not a single one there, not even Gloria. How can it be? How did they disappear so suddenly? Like a bad childhood joke, as if they might spring out of the closets any moment, or pop up from behind the sofa, a row of carnival faces to throw water balloons at.

It is, for an instant, as if she has dreamed them into being. That they have come to her, unasked, and then they have stolen away.

She lays the tray down on the table. The teapot slides and a little bubble of tea spurts out. The handbags are there and a single cigarette still burns in the ashtray.

It is then that she hears the voices, and she chides herself. Of course. How silly of me. The bang of the back door and then the upper roof door in the wind. She must have left it open, they must have felt the breeze.

Down along the corridor. The shapes beyond the upper doorway. She climbs the final few steps, joins them on the roof, all of them leaning out over the wall, looking south. Nothing to see, of course, just a haze and the cupola at the top of the New York General Building.

—No sign of him?

She knows of course that there could not be, even on the clearest of days, but it is nice to have the women turn to her in unison and shake their heads, no.

—We can try the radio, she says, sliding in behind them. It might be on a news report.

—Good idea, says Jacqueline.

—Oh, no, says Janet. I'd rather not.

—Me neither, says Marcia.

—Probably won't be on the news.

—Not yet, anyway.

—I don't think so.

They remain a moment, looking south, as if they might still be able to conjure him up.

—Coffee, ladies? A little tea?

—Lord, says Gloria with a wink, I thought you'd never ask.

—A nibble of something, yes.

—Calm our nerves?

—Yes, yes.

—Okay, Marcia?

—Downstairs?

—Mercy, yes. It's hotter than a July bride up here.

The women guide Marcia back down the inside stairs, through the maid's door, into the living room once more, with Janet on one arm, Jacqueline on the other, Gloria behind.

In the armchair ashtray, the cigarette has burned down to the quick, like a man about to break and fall. Claire puts it out. She watches as the women scrunch up tight on the sofa, arms around one another. Enough chairs? How could she have made such a mistake? Should she bring out the beanbag chair from Joshua's room? Put it on the floor so that her body can spread itself out in his old impression?

This walking man, she can't shake him. The bubble of discontent in her mind. She is being ungenerous, she knows, but she just can't get rid of it. What if he hits somebody down below? She has heard that at night there are whole colonies of birds that fly into the World Trade Center buildings, their glass reflection. The bash and fall. Will the walker thump with them?

Snap to. Enough.

Pull your mind together. Pick up all the feathers. Guide them gently back into the air.

—The bagels are in the bag there, Claire. And there's doughnuts too.

—Lovely. Thanks.

The small niceties.

—Dearest Lord, look at those!

—Oh, my word.

—I'm fat enough.

—Oh, stop. I only wish I had your figure.

—Take it and run, says Gloria. Bet it spills over!

—No, no, you have a lovely figure. Fabulous.

—Come on!

—I must say, truly.

And a hush around the room for the little white lie. A pullback from the food. They glance at one another. An unfolding of seconds. A siren outside the window. The static broken and thoughts taking shape in their minds, like water in a pitcher.

—So, says Janet, reaching for a bagel. Not to be morbid or any-thing . . .

—Janet!

— . . . I don't want to be morbid . . .

—Janet McIniff . . . !

— . . . but you think he fell?

—Ohmigod! Who gave you the sledgehammer?

—Sledgehammer? I just heard the siren and I—

—It's okay, says Marcia. I'm okay. Really. Don't worry about me.

—My God! says Jacqueline.

—I'm just asking.

—Really, no, says Marcia. I'm kinda wondering the same myself.

—Oh my God, says Jacqueline, the words stretched out now as if on elastic. I can't believe you just said that.

Claire wishes now to be removed and off somewhere distant, some beach, some riverbank, some deep swell of happiness, some Joshua place, some little hidden moment, a touch of Solomon's hand.

Sitting here, absent from them. Letting them close the circle.

Maybe, yes, it's just pure selfishness. They did not notice the mezuzah on the door, the painting of Solomon, didn't mention a single thing about the apartment, just launched right in and began. They even walked up to the rooftop without asking. Maybe that's just the way they do it, or maybe they're blinded by the paintings, the silverware, the carpets. Surely there were other well-heeled boys packed off to war. Not all of them had flat feet. Maybe she should meet other women, more of her own. But more of her own what? Death, the greatest democracy of them all. The world's oldest complaint. Happens to us all. Rich and poor. Fat and thin. Fathers and daughters. Mothers and sons. She feels a pang, a return. *Dear Mother, this is just to say that I have arrived safely,* the first began. And then at the end he was writing, *Mama, this place is a nothing place, take all the places and give me nothing instead.* Oh. Oh. Read all the letters of the world, love letters or hate letters or joy letters, and stack them up against the single one hundred and thirty-seven that my son wrote to me, place them end to end, Whitman and Wilde and Wittgenstein and whoever else, it doesn't matter—there's no comparison. All the things he used to say! All the things he could remember! All that he put his finger upon!

That's what sons do: write to their mothers about recall, tell themselves about the past until they come to realize that they *are* the past.

But no, not past, not him, not ever.

Forget the letters. Let our machines fight. You hear me? Let them go at it. Let them stare each other down the wires.

Leave the boys at home.

Leave my boy at home. Gloria's too. And Marcia's. Let him walk a tightrope if he wants. Let him become an angel. And Jacqueline's. And Wilma's. Not Wilma, no. There was never a Wilma. Janet. Probably a Wilma too. Maybe a thousand Wilmas all over the country.

Just give my boy back to me. That's all I want. Give him back. Hand him over. Right now. Let him open the door and run past the mezuzah and let him clang down here at the piano. Repair all the pretty faces of the young. No cries, no shrieks, no bleats. Bring them back here now. Why shouldn't all our sons be in the room all at once? Collapse all the boundaries. Why shouldn't they sit together? Berets on their knees. Their slight embarrassment. Their creased uniforms. You fought for our country, why not celebrate on Park Avenue? Coffee or tea, boys? A spoonful of sugar helps the medicine go down.

All this talk of freedom. Nonsense, really. Freedom can't be given, it must be received.

I will not take this jar of ashes.

Do you hear me?

This jar of ashes is not what my son is.

—What's that now, Claire?

And it's as if she is rising again from a daydream. She has been watching them, their moving mouths, their mobile faces, but not hearing anything they've been saying, some sort of argument about the walking man, about whether the tightrope was attached or not, and she had drifted from it. Attached to what? His shoe? The helicopter? The sky? She folds and refolds her fingers into one another, hears the crack of them as they pull apart.

You need more calcium in your bones, the good doctor Tonnemann said. Calcium indeed. Drink more milk, your children won't go missing.

—Are you okay, dear? says Gloria.

—Oh, I'm fine, she says, just a little daydreamy.

—I know the feeling.

—I get that way too sometimes, says Jacqueline.

—Me too, says Janet.

—First thing every morning, says Gloria, I start to dream. Can't do it at night. I used to dream all the time. Now I can only dream in daytime.

—You should take something for it, says Janet.

Claire cannot recall what she has said—has she embarrassed them, said something silly, out of order? That comment from Janet, as if she should be on meds. Or was that aimed at Gloria? Here, take a hundred pills, it will cure your grief. No. She has never wanted that. She wants to break it like a fever. But what is it that she said? Something about the tightrope man? Did she say it aloud? That he was vulgar somehow? Something about ashes? Or fashion? Or wires?

—What is it, Claire?

—I'm just thinking about that poor man, she says.

She wants to kick herself for saying it, for bringing him up again. Just when she felt that they could be getting away, that the morning could get back on track again, that she could tell them about Joshua and how he used to come home from school and eat tomato sandwiches, his favorite, or how he never squeezed the toothpaste properly, or how he always put two socks into one shoe, or a playground story, or a piano riff, anything, just to give the morning its balance, but, no, she has shunted it sideways again and brought it back around.

—What man? says Gloria.

—Oh, the man who came here, she says suddenly.

—Who's that?

She picks a bagel from the sunflower bowl. Looks up at the women. She pauses a moment, slices through the thick bread, pulls the rest of the bagel apart with her fingers.

—You mean the tightrope man was here?

—No, no.

—What man, Claire?

She reaches across and pours tea. The steam rises. She forgot to put out the slices of lemon. Another failure.

—The man who told me.

—What man?

—The man who told you what, Claire?

—You know. That man.

And then a sort of deep understanding. She sees it in their faces. Quieter than rain. Quieter than leaves.

—Uh huhn, says Gloria.

And then a loosening over the faces of the others.

—Mine was Thursday.

—Mike Junior's was Monday.

—My Clarence was Monday as well. Jason was Saturday. And Brandon was a Tuesday.

—I got a lousy telegram. Thirteen minutes past six. July twelfth. For Pete.

For Pete. For Pete's sake.

They all fall in line and it feels right, it's what she wants to say; she holds the bagel at her mouth but she will not eat; she has brought them back on track, they are returning to old mornings, together, they will not move from this, this is what she wants, and yes, they are comfortable, and even Gloria reaches out now for one of the doughtnuts, glazed and white, and takes a small, polite nibble and nods at Claire, as if to say: *Go ahead, tell us.*

—We got the call from downstairs. Solomon and I. We were sitting having dinner. All the lights were off. He's Jewish, you see . . .

Glad to get that one out of the way.

— . . . and he had candles everywhere. He's not strict, but sometimes he likes little rituals. He calls me his little honeybee sometimes. It started from an argument when he called me a WASP. Can you believe that?

All of it coming out from her, like grateful air from her lungs. Smiles all around, befuddled, yet silence all the same.

—And I opened the door. It was a sergeant. He was very deferent. I mean, nice to me. I knew right away, just from the look on his face. Like one of those novelty masks. One of those cheap plastic ones. His face frozen inside it. Hard brown eyes and a broad mustache. I said, Come in. And he took off his hat. One of those hairstyles, short, parted down the middle. A little shock of white along his scalp. He sat right there.

She nods over at Gloria and wishes she hadn't said that, but there's no taking it back.

Gloria wipes at the seat as if trying to get the stain of the man off. A little sliver of doughnut icing remains.

—Everything was so pure I thought I was standing in a painting.

—Yes, yes.

—He kept playing with his hat on his knee.

—Mine did too.

—Shh.

—And then he just said, Your son is passed, ma'am. And I was thinking, Passed? Passed where? What do you mean, Sergeant, he's passed? He didn't tell me of any exam.

—Mercy.

—I was smiling at him. I couldn't make my face do anything else.

—Well, I just flat-out wept, says Janet.

—Shh, says Jacqueline.

—I felt like there was rushing steam going up inside me, right up my spine. I could feel it hissing in my brain.

—Exactly.

—And then I just said, Yes. That's all I said. Smiling still. The steam hissing and burning. I said, Yes, Sergeant. And thank you.

—Mercy.

—He finished his tea.

All of them looking at their cups.

—And I brought him to the door. And that was it.

—Yes.

—And Solomon took him down in the elevator. And I've never told anyone that story. Afterward my face hurt, I smiled so much. Isn't that terrible?

—No, no.

—Of course not.

—It feels like I've waited my whole life to tell that story.

—Oh, Claire.

—I just can't believe that I smiled.

She knows that she has not told certain things about it, that the intercom had buzzed, that the doorman had stuttered, that the wait was a stunned one, that the sound of his knocking was like that against a coffin lid, that he took off his hat and said ma'am and then sir, and that they had said, Come in, come in, that the sergeant had never seen the like of the apartment before—it was obvious just from the way he looked at the furniture that he was nervous but thrilled too.

In another time he might have found it all glamorous, Park Avenue, fancy art, candles, rituals. She had watched him as he caught a mirror glance of himself, but he turned away from his own reflection and she might have even liked him then, the way he coughed into the hollow of his rounded hand, the gentleness of it. He held his hand at his mouth and he was like a magician about to pull out a sad scarf. He looked around, as if about to leave, as if there might be all sorts of exits, but she sat him down again. She went to the kitchen and brought a slice of fruitcake for him to eat. To ease the tension. He ate it with a little flick of guilt in his eyes. The little crumbs on the floor. She could hardly bring herself to vacuum them up afterward.

Solomon wanted to know what had happened. The sergeant said that he wasn't at liberty, but Solomon pressed and said, *None of us are at liberty, are we, really? I mean, when you think about it, Sergeant, none of us are free.* And the hat went bouncing on the military knee again. *Tell me,* said Solomon, and there was a tremble in his voice then. *Tell me or get out of my home.*

The sergeant coughed into a closed fist. A liar's gesture. They were still collecting the details, the sergeant said, but Joshua had been at a café. Sitting inside. They had been warned, all the personnel, about the cafés. He was with a group of officers. They had been to a club the night before. Must have been just blowing off steam. She couldn't imagine that, but she didn't say anything—her Joshua at a club? It was impossible, but she let it slide, yes, that was the word, *slide*. It was early morning, the sergeant said, Saigon time. Bright blue skies. Four grenades rolled in at their feet. He died a hero, the sergeant said. Solomon was the one who coughed at that. *You don't die a fucking hero, man.* She had never heard Solomon curse like that before, not to a stranger. The sergeant arranged his hat on his knee. Like his leg might be the thing now that needed to tell the story. Glancing up at the prints above the couch. Miró, Miró, on the wall, who's the deadest of them all?

He pulled his breath in. His throat looked corrugated. *I'm very sorry for your loss,* he said again.

When he had gone, when the night was silent, they had stood there in the room, Solomon and Claire, looking at each other, and he had said they would not crack, which they hadn't, which she wouldn't, no, they wouldn't blame each other, they wouldn't grow bitter, they'd get through it, survive, they would not allow it to become a rift between them.

—And all the time I was just smiling, see.

—You poor thing.

—That's awful.

—But it's understandable, Claire, it really is.

—Do you think so?

—It's okay. Really.

—I just smiled so much, she says.

—I smiled too, Claire.

—You did?

—That's what you do, you keep back the tears, gospel.

And then she knows now what it is about the walking man. It strikes her deep and hard and shivery. It has nothing to do with angels or devils. Nothing to do with art, or the reformed, or the intersection of a man with a vector, man beyond nature. None of that.

He was up there out of a sort of loneliness. What his mind was, what his body was: a sort of loneliness. With no thought at all for death.

Death by drowning, death by snakebite, death by mortar, death by bullet wound, death by wooden stake, death by tunnel rat, death by bazooka, death by poison arrow, death by pipe bomb, death by piranha, death by food poisoning, death by Kalashnikov, death by RPG, death by best friend, death by syphilis, death by sorrow, death by hypothermia, death by quicksand, death by tracer, death by thrombosis, death by water torture, death by trip wire, death by pool cue, death by Russian roulette, death by punji trap, death by opiate, death by machete, death by motorbike, death by firing squad, death by gangrene, death by foot-sore, death by palsy, death by memory loss, death by claymore, death by scorpion, death by crack-up, death by Agent Orange, death by rent boy, death by harpoon, death by nightstick, death by immolation, death by crocodile, death by electrocution, death by mercury, death by strangula-tion, death by bowie knife, death by mescaline, death by mushroom, death by lysergic acid, death by jeep smash, death by grenade trap, death by boredom, death by heartache, death by sniper, death by paper cuts, death by whoreknife, death by poker game, death by numbers, death by bureaucracy, death by carelessness, death by delay, death by avoidance, death by appeasement, death by mathematics, death by car-bon copy, death by eraser, death by filing error, death by penstroke, death by suppression, death by authority, death by isolation, death by incarceration, death by fratricide, death by suicide, death by genocide, death by Kennedy, death by LBJ, death by Nixon, death by Kissinger, death by Uncle Sam, death by Charlie, death by signature, death by si-lence, death by natural causes.

A stupid, endless menu of death.

But death by tightrope?

Death by performance?

That's what it amounted to. So flagrant with his body. Making it cheap. The puppetry of it all. His little Charlie Chaplin walk, coming in like a hack on her morning. How dare he do that with his own body? Throwing his life in everyone's face? Making her own son's so cheap? Yes, he has intruded on her coffee morning like a hack on her code. With his hijinks above the city. Coffee and cookies and a man out there walk-ing in the sky, munching away what should have been.

—You know what? she says, leaning into the circle of ladies.

—What?

She pauses a moment, wondering what she should say. A tremble running deep through her body.

—I like you all so much.

She is looking at Gloria when she says it, but she means it to them all, she genuinely means it. A little catch in her throat. She scans the row of faces. Gentleness and courtesy. All of them smiling at her. Come, ladies. Come. Let us while away our morning now. Let it slide. Let us forget walking men. Let us leave them high in the air. Let us sip our coffee and be thankful. Simple as that. Let's pull back the curtains and allow light through. Let this be the first of many more. No one else will intrude. We have our boys. They are brought together. Even here. On Park Avenue. We hurt, and have one another for the healing.

She reaches for the teapot, her hands trembling. The odd sounds in the room, the lack of quiet, the rustle of bagel bags, and the peeling back of muffin wrappers.

She takes her cup and drains it. Dabs her knuckle at the side of her mouth.

Gloria's flowers on the table, already opening. Janet picking a crumb off her plate. Jacqueline with her knee going up and down, in rhythm. Marcia looking off into space. That's my boy up there and he's come to say hello.

Claire stands, not shaky at all, not one bit, not now.

—Come, she says, come. Let's go see Joshua's room.

A FEAR OF LOVE

Bᴇɪɴɢ ɪɴsɪᴅᴇ ᴛʜᴇ ᴄᴀʀ, when it clipped the back of the van, was like being in a body we didn't know. The picture we refuse to see of ourselves. That is not me, that must be somebody else.

In any other circumstance we might have ended up at the side of the road, swapping license numbers, maybe haggling over a few dollars, even going immediately to a body shop to get the damage repaired, but it didn't turn out that way. It was the gentlest tap. A small screech of the tires. We figured afterward that the driver must have had his foot on the brake, or his rear lights weren't working, or maybe he had been riding the brake all along—in the sunlight we didn't see the shine. The van was big and lazy. The rear fender was tied with wire and string. I recall seeing it like one of those old horses from my youth, a lumbering, impatient animal grown stubborn to being slapped on the rump. It was the back wheels that went first. The driver tried to correct. His elbow pulled in from the window. The van went sideways right, which is when he tried to correct again, but he pulled too hard and we felt the second jolt, like bumper cars at a fair, except we weren't in a spin—our car was steady and straight.

Blaine had just lit a joint. It smoldered on the rim of an empty Coke can that sat between us. He had barely smoked any, one or two drags, when the van spun out, brown and horsey: the peace decals on the rear glass, the dented side panels, the windows left slightly ajar. On and on and on it spun.

There is something that happens to the mind in moments of terror. Perhaps we figure it's the last we'll ever have and we record it for the rest of our long journey. We take perfect snapshots, an album to despair over. We trim the edges and place them in plastic. We tuck the scrapbook away to take out in our ruined times.

The driver had a handsome face and his hair was peppered toward gray. There were deep, dark bags under his eyes. He was unshaven and he wore a shirt ambitiously undone at the neck, the sort of man who might have been calm at most times, but the wheel was sliding through his hands now and his mouth open wide. He looked down at us from the height of the van as if he might be freezing our faces in memory too. His mouth stretched into a further *O* and his eyes widened. I wonder now how he saw me, my fringed dress, my curved beads, my hair cut flapper-style, my eyeliner royal blue, my eyes bleary with lack of sleep.

There were canvases in our backseat. We had tried to flog them at Max's Kansas City the night before, but we had failed. Paintings that nobody wanted. Still, we had carefully arranged them so they wouldn't get scratched. We had even placed bits of styrofoam between them to keep them from rubbing one another.

If only we had been so careful with ourselves.

Blaine was thirty-two. I was twenty-eight. We were two years married. Our car, an antique 1927 Pontiac Landau, gold with silver paneling, was almost older than both of us put together. We had installed an eight-track that was hidden under the dashboard. We played twenties jazz. The music filtered out over the East River. There was so much cocaine still pumping through our bodies even at that hour that we felt there was still some promise.

The van spun farther. It was almost front-on. On the passenger side, all I could see was a pair of bare feet propped up on the dashboard. Untangling in slow motion. The bottoms of her feet were so white at the edges and so dark in their hollows that they could only have belonged to a black woman. She untucked at the ankles. The spin was slow enough. I could just see the top of her frame. She was calm. As if ready to accept. Her hair was pulled back tight off her face and bright baubles of jewelry bounced at her neck. If I hadn't seen her again, moments later, after she was thrown through the windshield, I might have thought she was naked, given the angle I was looking from. Younger than me, a beauty. Her eyes traveled across mine as if asking, What are you doing, you tan blond bitch in your billowy blouse and your fancy Cotton Club car?

She was gone just as quickly. The van went into a wider spin and our car kept on going straight. We passed them. The road opened like a split peach. I recall hearing the first crunch behind us, another car hitting the van, then the clatter of a grille that fell to the ground, and later on, when we went back over it all in our minds, Blaine and I, we reheard the impact of the newspaper truck as it sent them into the guardrail, a big boxy truck with the driver's door open and the radio blaring. It hit with brute force. There never would have been a way out for them.

Blaine looked over his shoulder and then floored it for an instant until I shouted at him to stop, please stop, please. Nothing more uncluttered than these moments. Our lives in perfect clarity. You must get out. Take responsibility. Walk back to the crash. Give the girl mouth-to-mouth. Hold her bleeding head. Whisper in her ear. Warm the whites of her feet. Run to a phone. Save the crushed man.

Blaine pulled over to the side of the FDR and we stepped out. The caw of gulls from the river, breasting the wind. The dapple of light on the water. The surging currents, their spinning motions. Blaine shaded his eyes in the sunlight. He looked like an ancient explorer. A few cars had stopped in the middle of the road and the newspaper truck had come to a sideways halt, but it wasn't one of those enormous wrecks that you sometimes hear about in rock songs, all blood and fracture and American highway; rather, it was calm with only small sprinklings of jeweled glass across the lanes, a few bundles of newspapers in a havoc on the ground, distant from the body of the young girl, who was expressing herself in a patch of blooming blood. The engine roared and steam poured out of the van. The driver's foot must still have been on the pedal. It whined incessantly, at its highest pitch. Some doors were opening in the stalled cars behind and already some other drivers were leaning on their horns, the chorus of New York, impatient to get going again, the fuck-you shrill. We were alone, two hundred yards ahead of the clamor. The road was perfectly dry but with patches of puddled heat. Sunlight through the girdings. Gulls out over the water.

I looked across at Blaine. He wore his worsted jacket and his bow tie. He looked ridiculous and sad, his hair flopping down over his eyes, all of him frozen to the past.

—Tell me that didn't happen, he said.

The moment he turned to check the front of the car I recall thinking that we'd never survive it, not so much the crash, or even the death of the young girl—she was so obviously dead, in a bloodied heap on the road—or the man who was slapped against the steering wheel, almost certainly ruined, his chest jammed up against the dashboard, but the fact that Blaine went around to check on the damage that was done to our car, the smashed headlight, the crumpled fender, like our years together, something broken, while behind us we could hear the sirens already on their way, and he let out a little groan of despair, and I knew it was for the car, and our unsold canvases, and what would happen to us shortly, and I said to him: Come on, let's go, quick, get in, Blaine, quick, get a move on.

———

IN '73 BLAINE AND I had swapped our lives in the Village for another life altogether, and we went to live in a cabin in upstate New York. We had been almost a year off the drugs, even a few months off the booze, until the night before the accident. Just a one-night blowout. We'd slept in that morning, in the Chelsea Hotel, and we were returning to the old Grandma notion of sitting on the porch swing and watching the poison disappear from our bodies.

On the way home, silence was all we had. We ducked off the FDR, drove north, over the Willis Avenue Bridge, into the Bronx, off the highway, along the two-lane road, by the lake, down the dirt track toward home. The cabin was an hour and a half from New York City. It was set back in a grove of trees on the edge of a second, smaller lake. A pond, really. Lily pads and river plants. The cabin had been built fifty years before, in the 1920s, out of red cedar. No electricity. Water from a spring well. A woodstove, a rickety outhouse, a gravity-fed shower, a hut we used for a garage. Raspberry bushes grew up and around the back windows. You could lift the sashes to birdsong. The wind made the reeds gossip.

It was the type of place where you could easily learn to forget that we had just seen a girl killed in a highway smash, perhaps a man too—we didn't know.

Evening was falling when we pulled up. The sun touched the top of the trees. We saw a belted kingfisher bashing a fish upon the dock. It ate its prey and then we sat watching its wheeling flight away—something so beautiful about it. I stepped out and along the dock. Blaine took out the paintings from the backseat, propped them against the side of the hut, pulled open the huge wooden doors where we kept the Pontiac. He parked the car and locked the hut with a padlock and then swept the car tracks with a broom. Halfway through the sweeping, he looked up and gave me a wave that was also a half-shrug, and he set to sweeping again. After a while, there was no sign that we had even left the cabin.

The night was cool. A chill had silenced the insects.

Blaine sat beside me on the dock, kicked off his shoes, dangled his feet out over the water, fished in the pockets of his pleated trousers. The burned-out shadows of his eyes. He still had a three-quarter-full bag of cocaine from the night before. Forty or fifty dollars' worth. He opened it and shoved the long thin padlock key into the coke, scooped up some powder. He cupped his hands around the key and held it to my nostril. I shook my head no.

—Just a hit, he said. Take the edge off.

It was the first snort since the night before—what we used to call the cure, the healer, the turpentine, the thing that cleaned our brushes. It kicked hard and burned straight through to the back of my throat. Like wading into snow-shocked water. He dipped into the bag and took three long snorts for himself, reared his head back, shook himself side to side, let out a long sigh, put his arm around my shoulder. I could almost smell the crash on my clothes, like I'd just crumpled my fender, sent myself spinning, about to smash into the guardrail.

—Wasn't our fault, babe, he said.

—She was so young.

—Not our fault, sweetie, you hear me?

—Did you see her on the ground?

—I'm telling you, said Blaine, the idiot hit his brakes. Did you see him? I mean, his brake lights weren't even working. Nothing I could do. I mean, shit, what was I supposed to do? He was driving like an idiot.

—Her feet were so white. The bottoms of them.

—Bad luck's a trip I don't go on, babe.

—Jesus, Blaine, there was blood everywhere.

—You've gotta forget it.

—She was just lying there.

—You didn't see a goddamn thing. You listening to me? We saw nothing.

—We're driving a '27 Pontiac. You think nobody saw us?

—Wasn't our fault, he said again. Just forget it. What could we do? He hit his goddamn brakes. I'm telling you, he was driving that thing like it was a goddamn boat.

—D'you think he's dead too? The driver? You think he's dead?

—Take a hit, honey.

—What?

—You gotta forget it happened, nothing happened, not a goddamn thing.

He stuffed the small plastic bag into the inside of his jacket pocket and stuck his fingers under the shoulder of his vest. We had both been wearing old-fashioned clothes for the better part of a year. It was part of our back-to-the-twenties kick. It seemed so ridiculous now. Bit players in a bad theater. There'd been two other New York artists, Brett and Delaney, who had gone back to the forties, living the lifestyle and the clothes, and they had made a killing from it, became famous, had even hit the *New York Times* style pages.

We had gone further than Brett and Delaney, had moved out of the city, kept our prize car—our only concession—and had lived without electricity, read books from another era, finished our paintings in the style of the time, hid ourselves away, saw ourselves as reclusive, cutting-edge, academic. At our core, even we knew we weren't being original. In Max's the night before—pumped up on ourselves—we had been stopped by the bouncers, who didn't recognize who we were. They wouldn't let us into the back room. A waitress pulled a curtain tight. She took pleasure in her refusal. None of our old friends were around. We spun backward, went up to the bar, the canvases in our arms. Blaine bought a bag of coke from the bartender, the only one to compliment our work. He leaned across the counter and gazed at the canvases, ten seconds, at most. Wow, he said. Wow. That'll be sixty bucks, man. Wow. If you want some Panama Red, man, I got that too. Some Cheeba Cheeba. Wow. Just say the word. Wow.

—Get rid of the coke, I said to Blaine. Just throw it in the water.

—Later, babe.

—Throw it away, please.

—Later, sweetie, okay? I'm chomping now. I mean, that guy, come on! He couldn't drive. I mean what type of fucking idiot hits the brakes in the middle of the FDR? And you see her? She wasn't even wearing any clothes. I mean, maybe she was blowing him or something. I bet that's it. She was sucking him off.

—She was in a pool of blood, Blaine.

—Not my fault.

—She was all smashed up. And that guy. He was just lying there against the steering wheel.

—You were the one told me to leave the scene. You're the one said, Let's go. Don't forget it, you're the one, you made the decision!

I slapped him once across the face, surprised at how hard it stung my hand. I rose from the dock. The wooden boards creaked. The dock was old and useless, jutting out into the pond like a taunt. I walked over the hard mud, toward the cabin. Up on the porch, I pushed open the door, stood in the middle of the room. It smelled so musty inside. Like months of bad cooking.

This is not my life. These are not my cobwebs. This is not the darkness I was designed for.

We had been happy, Blaine and me, in the cabin over the past year. We had chased the drugs from our bodies. Rose each morning clear-headed. Worked and painted. Carved out a life in the quiet. That was gone now. It was just an accident, I told myself. We had done the right thing. Sure, we'd left the scene, but maybe they would have searched us, discovered the coke, the weed, maybe they would have set Blaine up, or found out my family name, put it all over the newspapers.

I looked out the window. A thin stream of moonlight skidded on the water. The stars above were little pinpoints of light. The longer I looked the more they seemed like claw marks. Blaine was still on the dock, but stretched out lengthwise, almost a seal shape, cold and black, as if ready to slip away off the dock.

I made my way through the dark to the kerosene lamp. Matches on the table. I flicked the lamp alive. Turned the mirror around. I didn't want to see my face. The cocaine was still pumping through me. I turned the lamp higher and felt its heat rise. A bead of sweat at my brow. I left the dress in a puddled heap, stepped to the bed. I fell against the soft mattress, lay facedown, naked, under the sheets.

I could still see her. Most of all it was the bottoms of her feet, I had no idea why, I could see them there, against the dark of the tarmac. What is it that had made them so very white? An old song came back to me, my late grandfather singing about feet of clay. I buried my face further in the pillow.

The latch on the door clicked. I lay still and trembling—it seemed possible to do both at once. Blaine's footsteps sounded across the floor. His breathing was shallow. I could hear his shoes being tossed near the stove. He turned the kerosene lamp down. The wick whispered. The edges of the world got a little darker. The flame trembled and righted itself.

—Lara, he said. Sweetie.

—What is it?

—Look, I didn't mean to shout. Really.

He came to the bed and bent down over me. I could feel his breath against my neck. It felt cool, like the other side of a pillow. I've got something for us, he said. He pulled the sheet down to my thighs. I could feel the cocaine being sprinkled on my back. It was what we had done together years ago. I did not move. His chin in the hollow at my low back. The bristle where he hadn't shaved. His arm draped against my ribcage and his mouth at the center of my spine. I felt the run of his face down along the back of my body and the very touch of his lips, aloof and rootless. He sprinkled the powder again, a rough line that he licked with his tongue.

He was rampant now and had pulled the sheet fully off me. We hadn't made love in a few days, not even in the Chelsea Hotel. He turned me over and told me not to sweat, that it would make the cocaine clump.

—Sorry, he said again, sprinkling the coke low on my stomach. I shouldn't have shouted like that.

I pulled him down by the hair. Beyond his shoulder the faint knots in the ceiling wood looked like keyholes.

Blaine whispered in my ear: Sorry, sorry, sorry.

—

WE HAD ORIGINALLY made our money in New York City, Blaine and me. In the late sixties he had directed four black-and-white art films. His most famous film, *Antioch,* was a portrait of an old building being demolished on the waterfront. Beautiful, patient shots of cranes and juggernauts and swinging headache balls caught on sixteen-millimeter. It anticipated much of the art that came behind it—light filtering in through smashed warehouse walls, window frames lying over puddles, new architectural spaces created by fracture. The film was bought by a well-known collector. Afterward Blaine published an essay on the onanism of moviemakers: films, he said, created a form of life to which life had to aspire, a desire for themselves only. The essay itself finished in midsentence. It was published in an obscure art journal, but it did get him noticed in the circles where he wanted to be seen. He was a dynamo of ambition. Another film, *Calypso,* had Blaine eating breakfast on the roof of the Clock Tower Building as the clock behind him slowly ticked. On each of the clock hands he had pasted photographs of Vietnam, the second hand holding a burning monk going around and around the face.

The films were all the rage for a while. The phone rang incessantly. Parties were thrown. Art dealers tried to doorstep us. *Vogue* profiled him. Their photographer had him dress in nothing but a long strategic scarf. We lapped up the praise, but if you stand in the same river for too long, even the banks will trickle past you. He got a Guggenheim but after a while most of the money was going toward our habits. Coke, speed, Valium, black beauties, sensimilla, 'ludes, Tuinals, Benzedrine: whatever we could find. Blaine and I spent whole weeks in the city hardly sleeping. We moved among the loud-mouthed sinners of the Village. Hardcore parties, where we walked through the pulsing music and lost each other for an hour, two hours, three hours, on end. It didn't bother us when we found the other in someone else's arms: we laughed and went on. Sex parties. Swap parties. Speed parties. We inhaled poppers and gorged on champagne. This is happiness, we screamed at each other across the floor.

A fashion designer made me a purple dress with yellow buttons made from amphetamines. Blaine bit the buttons off one by one as we danced. The more stoned he got, the more open my dress fell.

We were coming in at exits and going out at entrances. Nighttime wasn't just a dark thing anymore; it had actually acquired the light of morning—it seemed nothing to think of night as having a sunrise in it, or a noontime alarm. We used to drive all the way up to Park Avenue just to laugh at the bleary-eyed doormen. We caught early movies in the

Times Square grind houses. *Two-Trouser Sister. Panty Raid. Girls on Fire.* We greeted sunrises on the tar beaches of Manhattan's rooftops. We picked our friends up from the psych ward at Bellevue and drove them straight to Trader Vic's.

Everything was fabulous, even our breakdowns.

There had been a tic in my left eye. I tried to ignore it but it felt like one of Blaine's clock hands, moving time around my face. I had been lovely once, Lara Liveman, midwestern girl, blond child of privilege, my father the owner of an automobile empire, my mother a Norwegian model. I am not afraid to say it—I'd had enough beauty to get taxi drivers fighting. But I could feel the late nights draining me. My teeth were turning a tinge darker from too much Benzedrine. My eyes were dull. Sometimes it seemed that they were even taking my hair color. An odd sensation, the life disappearing through the follicles, a sort of tingling.

Instead of working on my own art, I went to the hairdresser, twice, three times a week. Twenty-five dollars a time. I tipped her another fifteen and walked down the avenue, crying. I would get back to painting again. I was sure of it. All I needed was another day. Another hour.

The less work we did, the more valuable we thought we had become. I had been working toward abstract urban landscapes. A few collectors had been hovering at the edges. I just needed to find the stamina to finish. But instead of my studio, I stepped from the sunlight in Union Square into the comfortable dark of Max's. All the bouncers knew me. A cocktail was placed on the table: a Manhattan first, washed down with a White Russian. I was airborne within minutes. I wandered around, chatted, flirted, laughed. Rock stars in the back room and artists in the front. Men in the women's bathroom. Women in the men's, smoking, talking, kissing, fucking. Trays of hash brownies carried around. Men snorting lines of coke through the carcasses of pens. Time was in jeopardy when I was at Max's. People wore their watches with the faces turned against their skin. By the time dinner rolled around it could have been the next day. Sometimes it was three days later when I finally got out. The light hit my eyes when I opened the door onto Park Avenue South and Seventeenth Street. Occasionally Blaine was with me, more often he wasn't, and there were times, quite honestly, I wasn't sure.

The parties rolled on like rain. Down in the Village, the door of our dealer, Billy Lee, was always open. He was a tall, thin, handsome man. He had a set of dice that we used for sex games. There was a joke around that people came and went in Billy's place, but mostly they came. His apartment was littered with stolen prescription pads, each script in triplicate with an individual BNDD number. He had stolen them from doctors' offices on the Upper East Side; he used to go along the ground-floor offices on Park and Madison, kick the air conditioners in, and then crawl through the open window. We knew a doctor on the Lower East Side who would write the prescriptions. Billy was popping twenty pills a day. He said sometimes his heart felt as if it wrapped itself around his tongue. He had a thing for the waitresses at Max's. The only one who eluded him was a blonde named Debbie. Sometimes I substituted for whichever waitress didn't make it. Billy recited passages from *Finnegans Wake* in my ear. *The father of fornicationists.* He had learned twenty pages by heart. It sounded like a sort of jazz. Later I could hear his voice ringing in my ear.

In Blaine's and my apartment, there were a few citations for loud music, once an arrest for possession, but it was a police raid that finally stalled us. A crashing through the door. The cops swarming around the place. *Get to your feet.* One of them bashed my ankle with a nightstick. I was too scared to scream. It was no ordinary raid. Billy was lifted from our couch, kicked to the floor, strip-searched in front of us. He was taken away in cuffs, part of a Federal Bureau of Narcotics sting. We got away with a warning: they were watching us, they said.

Blaine and I crawled around the city looking for a bump. Nobody we knew was selling. Max's was closed for the night. The tough-eyed queers on Little West Twelfth Street wouldn't let us into their clubs. There was a haze over Manhattan. We bought a bag on Houston but it turned out to be baking soda. We still stuffed it up our noses in case there was a small remnant of coke. We walked to the Bowery among the plainsong drunks and got smashed against a grocery store grate and robbed at knifepoint by three Filipino kids in lettered jackets.

We ended up in the doorway of an East Side pharmacy. *Look what we've done to ourselves,* said Blaine. Blood all over his shirt front. I couldn't stop my eye from pulsing. I lay there, the wet of the ground seeping into my bones. Not even enough desire to weep.

An early-morning greaseball threw a quarter at our feet. *E pluribus unum.*

It was one of those moments from which I knew there would be no

return. There comes a point when, tired of losing, you decide to stop fail-
ing yourself, or at least to try, or to send up the final flare, one last chance.
We sold the loft we owned in SoHo and bought the log cabin so far upstate that it would be a long walk back to Max's ever again.

What Blaine had wanted was a year or two, maybe more, in the sticks.
No distraction. To return to the moment of radical innocence. To paint. To
stretch canvas. To find the point of originality. It wasn't a hippie idea. Both
of us had always hated the hippies, their flowers, their poems, their one
idea. We were the furthest thing from the hippies. We were the edge, the
definers. We developed our idea to live in the twenties, a Scott and Zelda
going clean. We kept our antique car, even got it refurbished, the seats re-
upholstered, the dashboard buffed. I cut my hair flapper-style. We loaded
up on provisions: eggs, flour, milk, sugar, salt, honey, oregano, chili, and
racks of cured meat that we hung from a nail in the ceiling. We wiped away
the cobwebs and filled the cupboards with rice, grain, jams, marshmal-
lows—we believed we'd eventually be that clean. Blaine had decided it was
time to go back to canvas, to paint in the style of Thomas Benton, or John
Steuart Curry. He wanted that moment of purity, regionalism. He was sick
of the colleagues he'd gone to Cornell with, the Smithsons and the Turleys
and the Matta-Clarks. They had done as much as they possibly could, he
said, there was no going further for them. Their spiral jetties and split
houses and pilfered garbage cans were passé.

Me too—I'd decided that I wanted the pulse of the trees in my work,
the journey of grass, some dirt. I thought I might be able to capture water
in some new and startling way.

We had painted the new landscapes separately—the pond, the kingfisher, the silence, the moon perched on the saddle of the trees, the
slashes of redwings among the leaves. We had kicked the drugs. We had
made love. It all went so well, so very very well, until our trip back to Manhattan.

—

A BLUE DAWN stretched in the room. Blaine lay like a stranded thing, all
the way across the bed. Impossible to wake. Grinding his teeth in his
sleep. A thinness to him, his cheekbones too pronounced, but he was not
unhandsome: there were times he still reminded me of a polo player.

I left him in bed and went out onto the porch. It was just before sunrise and already the heat had burned the night rain off the grass. A light wind riffled across the surface of the lake. I could hear the faintest sounds of traffic from the highway a few miles away, a low gurgle.

A single jet stream cut across the sky, like a line of disappearing coke.

My head was pounding, my throat dry. It took a moment to realize that the previous two days had actually occurred: our trip to Manhattan, the humiliation at Max's, the car crash, a night of sex. What had been a quiet life had gotten its noise again.

I looked over at the hut where Blaine had hidden the Pontiac. We had forgotten the paintings. Left them out in the rain. We hadn't even covered them in plastic. They sat, ruined, leaning against the side of the hut, by some old wagon wheels. I bent down and flicked through. A whole year's work. The water and paint had bled down into the grass. The frames would soon warp. Fabulous irony. All the wasted work. The cutting of canvas. The pulling of hair from brushes. The months and months spent painting.

You clip a van, you watch your life fade away.

I let Blaine be, didn't tell him, spent the whole day avoiding him. I walked in the woods, around the lake, out onto the dirt roads. Gather all around the things that you love, I thought, and prepare to lose them. I sat, pulling the roots of vines off trees: it felt like the only valuable thing I could do. That night I went to bed while Blaine stared out over the water, licking the very last of the coke from the inside of the plastic baggie.

The following morning, with the paintings still out by the garage, I walked toward town. At a certain stage every single thing can be a sign. Halfway down the road a group of starlings flew up from a pile of discarded car batteries.

—

THE TROPHY DINER was at the end of Main Street, in the shadow of the bell-tower church. A row of pickup trucks stood outside with empty gun racks in their windows. A few station wagons were parked on the church grounds. Weeds had cracked through the pavement at the door. The bell clanged. The locals on the swivel seats turned to check me out. More of them than usual. Baseball caps and cigarettes. They turned quickly away again, huddled and chatting. It didn't bother me. They never had much time for me anyway.

I smiled across at the waitress but she didn't gesture back. I took one of the red booths under a painting of ducks in flight. Some sugar packets, straws, and napkins were scattered on the table. I wiped the formica top clean, made a structure out of toothpicks.

The men along the stools were loud and charged up but I couldn't make out what they were saying. There was a momentary panic that they somehow knew of the accident, but it seemed beyond the bounds of logic.

Calm down. Sit. Eat breakfast. Watch the world slide by.

The waitress finally came and slid the menu across the table, placed a coffee in front of me without even asking. She usually wore her weariness like an autograph, but there was something jumped-up about her as she hurried back to the counter and settled in once more among the men.

There were small drip marks on the white coffee mug where it hadn't been washed properly. I scrubbed it with a paper napkin. On the floor beneath me there was a newspaper, folded over and egg-stained. *The New York Times*. I hadn't read a paper in almost a year. In the cabin we had a radio with a crank arm that we had to wind up if we wanted to listen to the outside world. I kicked the paper under the far side of the booth. The prospect of news was nothing in the face of the accident and the paintings we had lost as a result. A full year's work gone. I wondered what might happen when Blaine found out. I could see him rising from bed, tousled, shirtless, scratching himself, the male crotch adjust, walking outside and looking over at the hut, shaking himself awake, running through the long grass, which would rebound behind him.

He didn't have much of a temper—one of the things I still loved about him—but I could foresee the cabin strewn with bits and pieces of the smashed frames.

You want to arrest the clocks, stop everything for half a second, give yourself a chance to do it over again, rewind the life, uncrash the car, run it backward, have her lift miraculously back into the windshield, unshatter the glass, go about your day untouched, some old, lost sweet-tasting time.

But there it was again, the girl's spreading bloodstain.

I tried to catch the waitress's eye. She was leaning on her elbows on the counter, chatting with the men. Something about their urgency trilled through the room. I coughed loudly and smiled across at her again. She sighed as if to say that she'd be there, for God's sake, don't push me. She rounded the counter, but stopped once more, in the middle of the floor, laughed at some intimate joke.

One of the men had unfolded his paper. Nixon's face on the front page rolled briefly before me. All slicked back and rehearsed and gluttonous. I had always hated Nixon, not just for obvious reasons, but it seemed to me that he had learned not only to destroy what was left behind, but also to poison what was to come. My father had part-owned a car company in Detroit and the whole enormity of our family wealth had disappeared in the past few years. It wasn't that I wanted the inheritance—I didn't, not at all—but I could see my youth receding in front of me, those good moments when my father had carried me on his shoulders and tickled my underarms and even tucked me in bed, kissed my cheek, those days gone now, made increasingly distant by change.

—What's going on?

My voice as casual as possible. The waitress with her pen poised over her writing pad.

—You didn't hear? Nixon's gone.

—Shot?

—Hell, no. Resigned.

—Today?

—No, tomorrow, honey. Next week. Christmas.

—'Scuse me?

She tapped her pen against the sharp of her chin.

—Whaddaya want?

I stammered an order for a western omelet and sipped from the water in the hard plastic glass.

A quickshot image across my mind. Before I met Blaine—before the drugs and the art and the Village—I had been in love with a boy from Dearborn. He'd volunteered for Vietnam, came home with the thousand-yard stare and a piece of bullet lodged perfectly in his spine. In his wheelchair he stunned me by campaigning for Nixon in '68, going around the inner city, still giving his approval to all he couldn't understand. We had broken up over the campaign. I thought I knew what Vietnam was—we would leave it all rubble and bloodsoak. The repeated lies become history, but they don't necessarily become the truth. He had swallowed them all, even plastered his wheelchair with stickers. NIXON LOVES JESUS. He went door to door, spreading rumors about Hubert Humphrey. He even bought me a little chain with a Republican elephant. I had worn it to please him, to give him back his legs, but it was like the firelight had faded on the inside of his eyelids and his mind was punched away in a little drawer. I still wondered what might have happened if I had stayed with him and learned to praise ignorance. He had written to me that he had seen Blaine's Clock Tower film and it had made him laugh so hard he had fallen out of his chair, he couldn't get up, now he was crawling, was it possible to help him up? At the end of the letter he said, *Fuck you, you heartless bitch, you rolled up my heart and squeezed it dry.* Still, when I recalled him I would always see him waiting for me under the silver high school bleachers with a smile on his face and thirty-two perfect shining white teeth.

The mind makes its shotgun leaps: punch them away, yes, in a drawer.

I saw the girl from the crash again, her face appearing over his shoulder. It was not the whites of her feet this time. She was full and pretty. No eye shadow, no makeup, no pretense. She was smiling at me and asking me why I had driven away, did I not want to talk to her, why didn't I stop, come, come, please, did I not want to see the piece of metal that had ripped open her spine, and how about the pavement she had caressed at fifty miles per hour?

—You all right? asked the waitress, sliding the plate of food across the table.

—Fine, yeah.

She peered into the full cup and said: Something wrong?

—Just not in the mood.

She looked at me like I was quite possibly alien. No coffee? Call the House of Un-American Activities.

Hell with you, I thought. Leave me be. Go back to your unwashed cups.

I sat silently and smiled at her. The omelet was wet and runny. I took a single bite and could feel the grease unsettling my stomach. I bent down and extended my foot under the table, pulled in yesterday's newspaper, lifted it up. It was open to an article about a man who had walked on a tightrope between the World Trade Center towers. He had, it seemed, scoped out the building for six years and had finally not just walked, but danced, across, even lay down on the cable. He said that if he saw oranges he wanted to juggle them, if he saw skyscrapers he wanted to walk between them. I wondered what he might do if he walked into the diner and found the scattered pieces of me, lying around, too many of them to juggle.

I flicked through the rest of the pages. Some Cyprus, some water treatment, a murder in Brooklyn, but mostly Nixon and Ford and Watergate. I didn't know much about the scandal. It was not something Blaine and I had followed: establishment politics at its coldest. Another sort of napalm, descending at home. I was happy to see Nixon resign, but it would hardly usher in a revolution. Nothing much more would happen than Ford might have a hundred days and then he too would put in an order for more bombs. It seemed to me that nothing much good had happened since the day Sirhan Sirhan had pulled the malevolent trigger. The idyll was over. Freedom was a word that everyone mentioned but none of us knew. There wasn't much left for anyone to die for, except the right to remain peculiar.

In the paper there was no mention of a crash on the FDR Drive, not even a little paragraph buried below the fold.

But there she was, still looking at me. It wasn't the driver who struck me at all—I didn't know why—it was still her, only her. I was wading up through the shadows toward her and the car engine was still whining and she was haloed in bits of broken glass. How great are you, God? Save her. Pick her up off the pavement and dust the glass from her hair. Wash the fake blood off the ground. Save her here and now, put her mangled body back together again.

I had a headache. My mind reeling. I could almost feel myself swaying in the booth. Maybe it was the drugs flushing out of my body. I picked up a piece of toast and just held it at my lips, but even the smell of the butter nauseated me.

Out the window I saw an antique car with whitewall tires pull up against the curb. It took me a moment to realize it wasn't a hallucination, something cinematic hauled from memory. The door opened and a shoe hit the ground. Blaine climbed out and shielded his eyes. It was almost the exact same gesture as on the highway two days before. He was wearing a lumber shirt and jeans. No old-fashioned clothes. He looked like he belonged upstate. He flicked the hair back from his eyes. As he crossed the road, the small-town traffic paused for him. Hands deep in his pockets, he strolled along the windows of the diner and threw me a smile. There was a puzzling jaunt in his step, walking with his upper body cocked back a notch. He looked like an adman, all patently false. I could see him, suddenly, in a seersucker suit. He smiled again. Perhaps he had heard about Nixon. More likely he hadn't yet seen the paintings, ruined beyond repair.

The bell sounded on the door and I saw him wave across to the waitress and nod to the men. He had a palette knife sticking out of his shirt pocket.

—You look pale, honey.

—Nixon resigned, I said.

He smiled broadly as he leaned over the table and kissed me.

—Big swinging Dickey. Guess what? I found the paintings.

I shuddered.

—They're far out, he said.

—What?

—They got left out in the rain the other night.

—I saw that.

—Utterly changed.

—I'm sorry.

—You're sorry?

—Yeah, I'm sorry, Blaine, I'm sorry.

—Whoa, whoa.

—Whoa what, Blaine?

—Don't you see? he said. You give it a different ending. It becomes new. You can't see that?

I turned my face up to his, looked him square in the eye, and said, No, I didn't see. I couldn't see anything, not a goddamn thing.

—That girl was killed, I said.

—Oh, Christ. Not that again.

—Again? It was the day before yesterday, Blaine.

—How many times am I gonna have to tell you? Not our fault. Lighten up. And keep your fucking voice down, Lara, in here, for crying out loud.

He reached across and took my hand, his eyes narrow and intent: Not our fault, not our fault, not our fault.

It wasn't as if he'd been speeding, he said, or had had an intention to go rear-end some asshole who couldn't drive. Things happen. Things collide.

He speared a piece of my omelet. He held the fork out and half pointed it at me. He lowered his eyes, ate the food, chewed it slowly.

—I've just discovered something and you're not listening.

It was like he wanted to prod me with a dumb joke.

—A moment of satori, he said.

—Is it about her?

—You have to stop, Lara. You have to pull yourself together. Listen to me.

—About Nixon?

—No, it's not about Nixon. Fuck Nixon. History will take care of Nixon. Listen to me, please. You're acting crazy.

—There was a dead girl.

—Enough already. Lighten the fuck up.

—He might be dead too, the guy.

—Shut. The. Fuck. It was just a tap, that's all, nothing else. His brake lights weren't working.

Just then the waitress came over and Blaine released my hand. He ordered himself a Trophy special with eggs, extra bacon, and venison sausage. The waitress backed away and he smiled at her, watched her go, the sway of her.

—Look, he said, it's about time. When you think about it. They're about time.

—What's about time?

—The paintings. They're a comment on time.

—Oh, Jesus, Blaine.

There was a shine in his eyes unlike any I'd seen in quite a while. He sliced open some packets of sugar, dumped them in his coffee. Some extra grains spilled out on the table.

—Listen. We made our twenties paintings, right? And we lived in that time, right? There's a mastery there, I mean, they were steady-keeled, the paintings, you said so yourself. And they referred back to that time, right?

They maintained their formal manners. A stylistic armor about them, right? Even a monotony. They happened on purpose. We cultivated them. But did you see what the weather did to them?

—I saw, yeah.

—Well, I went out there this morning and the damn things floored me. But then I started looking through them. And they were beautiful and ruined. Don't you see?

—No.

—What happens if we make a series of paintings and we leave them out in the weather? We allow the present to work on the past. We could do something radical here. Do the formal paintings in the style of the past and have the present destroy them. You let the weather become the imaginative force. The real world works on your art. So you give it a new ending. And then you reinterpret it. It's perfect, dig?

—The girl died, Blaine.

—Give it over.

—No, I won't give it over.

He threw up his hands and then slammed them down on the table. The solitary sugar grains jumped. Some men at the counter turned and flicked a look at us.

—Oh, fuck, he said. There's no use talking to you.

His breakfast came and he ate it sullenly. He kept looking up at me, like I might suddenly change, become the beauty he had once married, but his eyes were blue and hateful. He ate the sausage with a sort of savagery, stabbed at it as if it angered him, this thing once alive. A little bit of egg stuck at the side of his mouth where he hadn't shaved properly. He tried to talk of his new project, that a man could find meaning anywhere. His voice buzzed like a trapped fly. His desire for surety, for meaning. He needed me as part of his patterns. I felt the urge to tell Blaine that I had in fact spent my whole life really loving the Nixon boy in the wheelchair, and that it had all been pabulum since then, and juvenile, and useless, and tiresome, all of our art, all our projects, all our failures, it was just pure cast-off, and none of it mattered, but instead I just sat there, saying nothing, listening to the faint hum of voices from the counter, and the rattle of the forks against the plates.

—We're finished here, he said.

Blaine snapped his fingers and the waitress came running. He left an extravagant tip and we stepped outside into the sunlight.

Blaine tipped a pair of giant sunglasses over his eyes, extended his stride, and walked toward the garage at the end of Main Street. I followed a couple of paces behind. He didn't turn, didn't wait.

—Hey, man, can you get a special order? he said to a pair of legs that were extended from underneath a car.

The mechanic wheeled himself out, stared upward, blinked.

—What can I get you, bud?

—A replacement headlight for a 1927 Pontiac. And a front fender.

—A what?

—Can you get them or not?

—This is America, chief.

—Get them, then.

—It takes time, man. And money.

—No problem, said Blaine. I got both.

The mechanic picked at his teeth, then grinned. He labored over toward a cluttered desk: files and pencil shavings and pinup calendar girls. Blaine's hands were shaking, but he didn't care; he was caught up on himself now and what he would do with his paintings once the car was fixed. As soon as the light and the fender could get repaired the whole matter would be forgotten and then he'd work. I had no idea how long this new obsession might last for him—an hour, another year, a lifetime?

—You coming? said Blaine as we stepped out of the garage.

—I'd rather walk.

—We should film this, he said. Y'know, how this new series gets painted and all. All from the very beginning. Make a document of it, don't you think?

———

A ROW OF SMOKERS stood out in front of Metropolitan Hospital on Ninety-eighth and First Avenue. Each looked like his last cigarette, ashen and ready to fall. Through the swinging doors, the receiving room was full to capacity. Another cloud of smoke inside. Patches of blood on the floor. Junkies strung out along the benches. It was the type of hospital that looked like it needed a hospital.

I walked through the gauntlet. It was the fifth receiving room I had visited, and I had begun to think that perhaps both the driver and the young woman had been killed on impact and were taken immediately to a morgue.

A security guard pointed me toward an information booth. A window was cut into the wall of an unmarked room at the end of the corridor. A stout woman sat framed by it. From a distance it looked as if she sat in a television set. Her eyeglasses dangled at her neck. I sidled up to the window and whispered about a man and woman who might have been brought in from a crash on Wednesday afternoon.

—Oh, you're a relative? she said, not even glancing up at me.

—Yes, I stammered. A cousin.

—You're here for his things?

—His what?

She gave me a quick once-over.

—His things?

—Yes.

—You'll have to sign for them.

Within fifteen minutes I found myself standing with a box of the late John A. Corrigan's possessions. They consisted of a pair of black trousers that had been slit up the side with hospital scissors, a black shirt, a stained white undershirt, underwear, and socks in a plastic bag, a religious medal, a pair of dark sneakers with the soles worn through, his driver's license, a ticket for parking illegally on John Street at 7:44 A.M. on Wednesday, August 7, a packet of rolling tobacco, some papers, a few dollars, and, oddly, a key chain with a picture of two young black children on it. There was also a baby-pink lighter, which seemed at odds with all the other things. I didn't want the box. I had taken it out of embarrassment, out of a sense of duty to my lie, an obligation to save face, and perhaps even to save my hide. I had begun to think that perhaps leaving the scene of the crime was manslaughter, or at least some sort of felony, and now there was a second crime, hardly momentous, but it sickened me. I wanted to leave the box on the steps of the hospital and run away from myself. I had set all these events in motion and all they got for me was a handful of a dead man's things. I was clearly out of my depth. Now it was time to go home, but I had taken on this man's bloodstained baggage. I stared at the license. He looked younger than my freeze-frame memory had made him. A pair of oddly frightened eyes, looking way beyond the camera.

—And the girl?

—She was D.O.A., said the woman like it was a traffic signal.

She looked up at me and adjusted her glasses on her nose.

—Anything else?

—No thanks, I stammered.

The only things I could really jigsaw together was that John A. Corrigan—born January 15, 1943, five foot ten, 156 pounds, blue eyes—was probably the father of two young black children in the Bronx. Perhaps he had been married to the girl who was thrown through the windshield. Maybe the girls in the key chain were his daughters, grown now. Or perhaps it was something clandestine, as Blaine had said, he could've been having an affair with the dead woman.

A photocopy of some medical information was folded at the bottom of the box: his sign-out chart. The scrawl was almost indecipherable. *Cardiac tamponade. Clindamycin, 300 mg.* I was for a moment out on the highway again. The fender touched the back of his van and I was spinning now in his big brown van. Walls, water, guardrails.

The scent of his shirt rose up as I walked out into the fresh air. I had the odd desire to distribute his tobacco to the smokers hanging around outside.

A crowd of Puerto Rican kids were hanging around in front of the Pontiac. They wore colored sneakers and wide flares and had cigarette packets shoved under their T-shirt sleeves. They could smell my nerves as I sidled through. A tall, thin boy reached over my shoulder and pulled out the plastic bag of Corrigan's underwear, gave a fake shriek, dropped them to the ground. The others laughed a pack laugh. I bent down to pick up the bag but felt a brush of a hand against my breast.

I drew myself as tall as I possibly could and stared in the boy's eyes.

—Don't you dare.

I felt so much older than my twenty-eight years, as if I'd taken on decades in the last few days. He backed off two paces.

—Only looking.

—Well, don't.

—Gimme a ride.

—Pontiac! shouted one boy. Poor Old Nigger Thinks It's A Cadillac!

—Gimme one, lady.

More giggles.

Over his shoulder I could see a hospital security guard making his way toward us. He wore a kufi and loped as he came across, talking into a radio. The kids scattered and ran down the street, whooping.

—You all right, ma'am? said the security guard.

I was fumbling with the keys at the door of the car. I kept thinking the guard was going to walk around the front and see the smashed headlight and put two and two together, but he just guided me out into the traffic. In the rearview mirror I saw him picking up the plastic bag of underwear I'd left on the pavement. He held them in the air a moment and then shrugged, threw them in the garbage can at the side of the road.

I turned the corner toward Second Avenue, weeping.

I had gone to the city ostensibly to buy a newfangled video camera for Blaine, to record the journey of his new paintings. But the only stores I knew were way down on Fourteenth Street, near my old neighborhood. Who was it said that you can't go home anymore? I found myself driving to the West Side of the city instead. Out to a little parking area in River-side Park, along by the water. The cardboard box sat in the passenger seat beside me. An unknown man's life. I had never done anything like this before. My intent had entered the world and become combustible. It had been given to me far too easily, just a simple signature and a thank-you. I thought about dropping it all in the Hudson, but there are certain things we just cannot bring ourselves to do. I stared at his photograph again. It was not he who had led me here, but the girl. I still knew nothing about her. It made no sense. What was I going to do? Practice a new form of resurrection?

I got out of the car and fished in a nearby garbage can for a newspaper and scanned through it to see if I could find any death notices or an obituary. There was one, an editorial, for Nixon's America, but none for a young black girl caught in a hit-and-run.

I screwed up my courage and drove to the Bronx, toward the address on the license. Entire blocks of abandoned lots. Cyclone fences topped with shredded plastic bags. Stunted catalpa trees bent by the wind. Auto-body shops. New and used. The smell of burning rubber and brick. On a half-wall someone had written: DANTE HAS ALREADY DISAPPEARED.

It took ages to find the place. There were a couple of police cars out under the Major Deegan. Two of the cops had a box of doughnuts sitting on the dashboard between them, like a third-rate TV show. They stared at me, open-mouthed, when I pulled up the car alongside them. I had lost all sense of fear. If they wanted to arrest me for a hit-and-run, then go ahead.

—This is a rough neighborhood, ma'am, one of them said in a New York nasal. Car like that's going to raise a few eyebrows.

—What can we do for you, ma'am? said the other.

—Maybe not call me ma'am?

—Feisty, huh?

—What you want, lady? Nothing but trouble here.

As if to confirm, a huge refrigerator truck slowed down as it came through the traffic lights, and the driver rolled down the window and eased over to the curb, looked out, then suddenly gunned it when he saw the police car.

—No nig-knock today, shouted the cop to the passing truck.

The short one blanched a little when he looked back at me, and he gave a thin smile that creased his eyelids. He ran his hands over a tube of fat that bulged out at his waist.

—No trade today, he said, almost apologetically.

—So, what can we do for you, miss? said the other.

—I'm looking to return something.

—Oh, yeah?

—I have these things here. In my car.

—Where'd you get that? What is it? Like the 1850s?

—It's my husband's.

Two thin smiles, but they looked happy enough that I'd broken their tedium. They stepped over to my car and rumbled around, running their hands along the wooden dash, marveling at the hand brake. I had often wondered if Blaine and I had gone on our twenties kick simply so we could keep our car. We had bought it as a wedding present for ourselves. Every time I sat in it, it felt like a return to simpler times.

The second cop peered into the box of possessions. They were disgusting, but I was hardly in a position to say anything. I felt a sudden pang of guilt for the plastic bag of underwear that I had left behind at the hospital, as if it somehow might be needed now, to complete the person who was not around. The cop picked up the parking ticket and then the license from the bottom of the box. The younger one nodded.

—Hey, that's the Irish guy, the priest.

—Sure is.

—The one that was giving us shit. About the hookers. He drove that funky van.

—He's up there on the fifth floor. I mean, his brother. Cleaning out his stuff.

—A priest? I said.

—A monk or some such. One of these worker guys. Liberation theo-whateveritis.

—Theologian, said the other.

—One of those guys who thinks that Jesus was on welfare.

I felt a shudder of hatred, then told the cops that I was a hospital administrator and that the items needed to be returned—did they mind leaving them with the dead man's brother?

—Not our job, miss.

—See the path there? Around the side? Follow that to the fourth brown building. In to the left. Take the elevator.

—Or the stairs.

—Be careful, but.

I wondered how many assholes it took to make a police department. They had been made braver and louder by the war. They had a swagger to them. Ten thousand men at the water cannons. Shoot the niggers. Club the radicals. Love it or leave it. Believe nothing unless you hear it from us.

I walked toward the projects. A surge of dread. Hard to calm the heart when it leaps so high. As a child I saw horses trying to step into rivers to cool themselves off. You watch them move from the stand of buckeye trees, down the slope, through the mud, swishing off flies, getting deeper and deeper until they either swim for a moment, or turn back. I recognized it as a pattern of fear, that there was something shameful in it—these high-rises were not a country that existed in my youth or art, or anywhere else. I had been a sheltered girl. Even when drug-addled I would never have gone into a place like this. I tried to persuade myself onward. I counted the cracks in the pavement. Cigarette butts. Unopened letters with footprints on them. Shards of broken glass. Someone whistled but I didn't look his way. Some pot fumes drifted from an open window. For a moment, it wasn't like I was entering water at all: it was more like I was ferrying buckets of blood away from my own body, and I could feel them slap and spill as I moved.

The dry brown remnants of a floral wreath hung outside the main doors. In the hallway the mailboxes were dented and scorch-marked. There was a reek of roach spray. The overhead lights were spray-painted black for some reason.

A large middle-aged lady in a floral-patterned dress waited at the elevator. She kicked aside a used needle with a deep sigh. It settled into the corner, a small bubble of blood at its tip. I returned her nod and smile. Her white teeth. The bounce of imitation pearls at her neck.

—Nice weather, I said to her, though both of us knew exactly what sort of weather it was.

The elevator rose. Horses into rivers. Watch me drown.

I said good-bye to her on the fifth floor as she continued upward, the sound of the cables like the crack of old branches.

A few people were gathered outside the doorway, black women, mostly, in dark mourning clothes that looked as if they didn't belong to them, as if they'd hired the clothes for the day. Their makeup was the thing that betrayed them, loud and gaudy and one with silver sparkles around her eyes, which looked so tired and worn-down. The cops had said something about hookers: it struck me that maybe the young girl had just been a prostitute. I felt a momentary sigh of gratitude, and then the awareness stopped me cold, the walls pulsed in on me. How cheap was I?

What I was doing was unpardonable and I knew it. I could feel my chest thumping in my blouse, but the women parted for me, and I went through their curtain of grief.

The door was open. Inside, a young woman was sweeping the floor clean. She had a face that looked like it came from a Spanish mosaic. Her eyes were darkened with streaks of mascara. A simple silver chain around her neck. She was clearly no hooker. I felt immediately underdressed, like I was barging in on her silence. Beyond her, a replica of the man from the photo on the license, only heavier, jowlier, more sparsely stubbled. The sight of him knocked the oxygen out of me. He wore a white shirt and a dark tie and a jacket. His face was broad and slightly florid, his eyes puffy with grief. I stammered that I was from the hospital and that I was here to drop off the things that had belonged to a certain Mr. Corrigan.

—Ciaran Corrigan, he said, coming across and shaking my hand.

He seemed to me first the sort of man who would be quite happy doing crosswords in bed. He took the box and looked down, searched through it. He came to the keyring and gazed at it a moment, put it in his pocket.

—Thanks, he said. We forgot to pick these things up.

He had a touch of an accent to him, not very strong, but he carried his body like I had seen other Irishmen carry themselves, hunched into himself, yet still hyperaware. The Spanish woman took the shirt and brought it into the kitchen. She was standing by the sink and sniffing the cloth deeply. The black bloodstains were still visible. She looked across at me, lowered her gaze to the floor. Her small chest heaved. She suddenly ran the tap and plunged the cloth into the water and began wringing it, as if John A. Corrigan might suddenly appear and want to wear it again. It was quite obvious that I wasn't wanted or needed, but something held me there.

—We've got a funeral service in forty-five minutes, he said. If you'll excuse me.

A toilet flushed in the apartment above.

—There was a young girl too, I said.

—Yes, it's her funeral. Her mother's getting out of jail. That's what we heard. For an hour or two. My brother's service is tomorrow. Cremation. There've been some complications. Nothing to worry about.

—I see.

—If you'll excuse me.

—Of course.

A short heavyset priest made his way into the apartment, announcing himself as a Father Marek. The Irishman shook his hand. He glanced at me as if to ask why I was still there. I went to the door, stopped, and turned around. It looked like the door locks had been jimmied a number of times.

The Spanish woman was still in the kitchen, where she suspended the wet shirt from a hanger above the sink. She stood there with her head down, like she was trying to remember. She put her face in the shirt again.

I turned and stammered.

—Would you mind if I went to the girl's service?

He shrugged and looked at the priest, who scribbled a quick map on a scrap of paper, as if he was glad for something to do. He took me by the elbow and then down the corridor.

—Do you have any influence? the priest asked.

—Influence? I asked.

—Well, his brother has insisted on getting him cremated before he goes back to Ireland. Tomorrow. And I was wondering if you could talk him out of it.

—Why?

—It's against our faith, he said.

Down the corridor, one of the women had begun wailing. She stopped, though, when the Irishman stepped out the door. He had jammed his tie high on his neck and his jacket was pulled tight across his shoulders. He was followed by the Spanish woman, who had a stately pride about her. The corridor was hushed. He pressed the button for the elevator and looked at me.

—Sorry, I said to the priest. I don't have any influence.

I pulled away from him and hurried toward the elevator as it was closing. The Irishman put his hand in the gap and pulled the door open for me, and then we were gone. The Spanish woman gave me a guarded smile and said she was sorry she couldn't go to the girl's funeral, she had to go home and look after her own children, but she was glad that Ciaran had someone to go with.

I offered him a lift without thinking, but he said no, that he had been asked to travel in the funeral cortege, he didn't know why.

He wrung his hands nervously as he stepped out into the sunlight.

—I didn't even know the girl, he said.

—What was her name?

—I don't know. Her mother's Tillie.

He said it with a downward finality, but then he added: I think it's Jazzlyn, or something.

—

I PARKED THE CAR outside St. Raymond's cemetery in Throgs Neck, far enough away that nobody could see it. A hum came from the expressway, but the closer I got to the graveyard the more the smell of fresh-cut grass filled the air. A faint whiff of the Long Island Sound.

The trees were tall and the light fell in shafts among them. It was hard to believe that this was the Bronx, although I saw the graffiti scrawled on the side of a few mausoleums, and some of the headstones near the gate had been vandalized. There were a few funerals in progress, mostly in the new cemetery, but it was easy enough to tell which group was the girl's. They were carrying the coffin down the tree-lined road toward the old cemetery. The children were dressed in perfect white, but the women's clothes looked like they had been cobbled together, the skirts too short, the heels too high, their cleavage covered with wraparound scarves. It was like they had gone to a strange garage sale: the bright expensive clothes hidden with bits and pieces of dark. The Irishman looked so pale among them, so very white.

A man in a gaudy suit, wearing a hat with a purple feather, followed at the back of the procession. He looked drugged-up and malevolent. Under his suit jacket he wore a tight black turtleneck and a gold chain on his neck, a spoon hanging from it.

A boy who was no more than eight played a saxophone, beautifully, like some strange drummer boy from the Civil War. The music rang out in punctuated bursts over the graveyard.

I stayed in the background, near the road in a patch of overgrown grass, but as the service began, John A. Corrigan's brother caught my eye and beckoned me forward. There were no more than twenty people gathered around the graveside but a few young women wailed deeply.

—Ciaran, he said again, extending his hand, as if I might have forgotten. He gave me a thin, embarrassed smile. We were the only white people there. I wanted to reach up and adjust his tie, fix his scattered hair, primp him.

A woman—she could only have been the dead girl's mother—stood sobbing beside two men in suits. Another, younger woman stepped up to her. She took off a beautiful black shawl and draped it on the mother's shoulders.

—Thanks, Ange.

The preacher—a thin, elegant black man—coughed and the crowd fell silent. He talked about the spirit being triumphant in the body's fall, and how we must learn to recognize the absence of the body and praise

the presence of what is left behind. Jazzlyn had a hard life, he said. Death
could not justify or explain it. A grave does not equal what we have had in
our lifetime. It was maybe not the time or the place, he said, but he was
going to talk about justice anyway. Justice, he repeated. Only candor and
truth win out in the end. The house of justice had been vandalized, he
said. Young girls like Jazzlyn were forced to do horrific things. As they
grew older the world had demanded terrible things of them. This was a
vile world. It forced her into vile things. She had not asked for it. It had
become vile for her, he said. She was under the yoke of tyranny. Slavery
may be over and gone, he said, but it was still apparent. The only way to
fight it was with charity, justice, and goodness. It was not a simple plea,
he said, not at all. Goodness was more difficult than evil. Evil men knew
that more than good men. That's why they became evil. That's why it
stuck with them. Evil was for those who could never reach the truth. It
was a mask for stupidity and lack of love. Even if people laughed at the
notion of goodness, if they found it sentimental, or nostalgic, it didn't
matter—it was none of those things, he said, and it had to be fought for.

—Justice, said Jazzlyn's mother.

The preacher nodded, then looked up toward the high trees. Jazzlyn
had been a child who grew up in Cleveland and New York City, he said,
and she had seen those distant hills of goodness and she knew that one
day she was going to get there. It was always going to be a difficult journey. She had seen too much evil on the way, he said. She had some
friends and confidants, like John A. Corrigan, who had perished with her,
but mostly the world had tried her and sentenced her and taken advantage of her kindness. But life must pass through difficulty in order to
achieve any modicum of beauty, he said, and now she was on her way to
a place where there were no governments to chain her or enslave her, no
miscreants to demand the wrong thing, and none of her own people who
were going to turn her flesh to profit. He stood tall then and said: Let it be
said that she was not ashamed.

A wave of nods went around the crowd.

—Shame on those who wanted to shame her.

—Yes, came the reply.

—Let this be a lesson to us all, said the preacher. You will be walking
someday in the dark and the truth will come shining through, and behind you will be a life that you never want to see again.

—Yes.

—That bad life. That vile life. In front of you will stretch goodness. You will follow the path and it will be good. Not easy, but good. Full of terror and difficulty maybe, but the windows will open to the sky and your heart will be purified and you will take wing.

I had a sudden, terrible vision of Jazzlyn flying through the windshield. I felt dizzy. The preacher's lips moved, but for a moment I couldn't hear. He was looking at a single place in the crowd, his vision fixed on the man in the purple hat behind me. I glanced over my shoulder. The man was biting his upper lip in anger and his body seemed to curl into itself, coiling and getting ready to strike. The hat shadowed him but he looked to have a glass eye.

—The snakes will perish with the snakes, said the preacher.

—Yessir, came a woman's voice.

—They'll be gone.

—Yes they will.

—Be they out of here.

The man in the purple hat didn't move. Nobody moved.

—Go on! shouted Jazzlyn's mother, contorting herself. She looked like she was strapped down but she was wriggling and squirming out of it. One of the men in suits touched her arm. Her shoulders were going from side to side and her voice was raw with rage.

—Get the fuck out of here!

I wondered for a horrific moment if she was shouting at me, but she was staring beyond me, at the man in the feathered hat. The chorus of shouts rose higher. The preacher held his hands out and asked for calm. It was only then I realized that Jazzlyn's mother had kept her arms behind her back the whole time, shackled with handcuffs. The two black men in suits beside her were city cops.

—Get the fuck out, Birdhouse, she said.

The man in the hat waited a moment, stretched upward, gave a smile that showed all his teeth. He touched the brim, tilted it, turned, and walked away. A small cheer went up from the mourners. They watched the pimp disappear down the road. He raised his hat one time, without turning around, waved it in the air, like a man who was not really saying good-bye.

—The snakes are gone, said the preacher. Let them stay gone.

Ciaran steadied my arm. I was feeling cold and dirty: it was like putting on a fourth-hand blouse. I had no right to be there. I was treading on their territory. But something in the service was pure and true: *Behind you will be a life that you never want to see again.*

The wailing had stopped and Jazzlyn's mother said: Take these goddamn things off me.

Both cops stared straight ahead.

—I said take these goddamn things off me!

Finally, one of them stepped behind her and unlocked the handcuffs.

—Thank Jesus.

She shook her hands out and walked around the open grave, over toward Ciaran. Her scarf fell slightly and revealed the depth of her cleavage. Ciaran flushed red and embarrassed.

—I got a little story to tell, she said.

She cleared her throat and a swell went around the crowd.

—My Jazzlyn, she was ten. And she see'd a picture of a castle in a magazine somewheres. She went, clipped it out, and taped it on the wall above her bed. Like I say, nothing much to it, I never really thought that much about it. But when she met Corrigan . . .

She pointed over toward Ciaran, who looked to the ground.

— . . . and one day he was bringing around some coffee and she told him all about it, the castle—maybe she was bored, just wanted something to say, I don't know. But you know Corrigan—that cat would listen to just about anything. He had an ear. And, of course, Corrie got a kick out of that. He said he knew castles just like that where he growed up. And he said he'd bring her to a castle just like it one day. Promised her solid. Every day he'd come out and bring her coffee and he'd say to my little girl that he was getting that castle ready, just you wait. One day he'd tell her that he was getting the moat right. The next he said he was working on the chains that go to the gate bridge. Then he said he was working on the turrets. Then he'd say he was getting the banquet all squared away. They were gonna have mead—that's like wine—and lots of good food and there was gonna be harps playing and lots of dancing.

—Yes, said a woman in spangled makeup.

—Every day he had a new thing to say about that castle. That was their own little game, and Jazzlyn loved playing it, word.

She grabbed hold of Ciaran's arm.

—That's all, she said. That's all I have to say. That's it. That's fucking it, 'scuse me for saying it.

A chorus of amens went around the gathered crowd and then she turned to some of the other women and made a comment of some sorts, something strange and clipped about going to the bathroom in the castle. A ripple of laughter went around a portion of the crowd and an odd thing occurred—she began quoting some poet whose name I didn't catch, a line about open doors and a single beam of sunlight that struck right to the center of the floor. Her Bronx accent threw the poem around until it seemed to fall at her feet. She looked down sadly at it, its failure, but then she said that Corrigan was full of open doors, and he and Jazzlyn would have a heck of a time of it wherever they happened to be; every single door would be open, especially the one to that castle.

She leaned then against Ciaran's shoulder and started to weep: I've been a bad mother, she said, I've been a terrible goddamn mother.

—No, no, you're fine.

—There weren't ever no goddamn castle.

—There's a castle for sure, he said.

—I'm not an idiot, she said. You don't have to treat me like a child.

—It's okay.

—I let her shoot up.

—You don't have to be so hard on yourself . . .

—She shot up in my arms.

She turned her face to the sky and then grasped the nearest lapel.

—Where're my babies?

—She's in heaven now, don't you worry.

—My babies, she said. My baby's babies.

—They're just fine, Till, said a woman near the grave.

—They're being looked after.

—They'll come see you, T.

—You promise me? Who's got them? Where are they?

—I swear it, Till. They're okay.

—Promise me.

—God's honest, said a woman.

—You better fucking promise, Angie.

—I promise. All right already, T. I promise.

She leaned against Ciaran and then turned her face, looked him in the eye, and said: You remember what we done? You 'member me?

Ciaran looked like he was handling a stick of dynamite. He wasn't sure whether to hold it and smother it, or throw it as far away from himself as he could. He flicked a quick look at me, then the preacher, but then he turned to her and put his arms around her and held her very tight. He said: I miss Corrie too. The other women came around and they took their turns with him. They were hugging him, it seemed, as if he were the embodiment of his brother. He looked at me and raised his eyebrows, but there was something good and proper about it—one after the other they came.

He reached into his pocket and took out the keyring with the pictures of the babies, handed it to Jazzlyn's mother. She stared at it, smiled, then suddenly pulled away and slapped Ciaran's face. He looked like he was grateful for it. One of the cops half grinned. Ciaran nodded and pursed his lips, then stepped backward toward me.

I had no idea what sort of complications I had stepped myself into.

The preacher coughed and asked for silence and said he had a few final words. He went through the formalities of prayer and the old biblical *Ashes to ashes and dust to dust,* but then he said that it was his firm belief that ashes could someday return to wood, that was the miracle not just of heaven, but the miracle of the actual world, that things could be reconstituted and the dead could come alive, most especially in our hearts, and that's how he'd like to end things, and it was time to lay Jazzlyn to rest because that's what he wanted her to do, *rest.*

When the service was ended the cops put the handcuffs back on Tillie's wrists. She wailed just one single time. The cops walked her off. She broke down into soundless sobs.

I accompanied Ciaran out of the cemetery. He took off his jacket and hung it over his shoulder, not nonchalantly, but to beat the heat. We went down the pathway toward the gates on Lafayette Avenue. Ciaran walked a quarter of a step in front of me. People can look different from hour to hour depending on the angle of daylight. He was older than me, in his mid-thirties or so, but he looked younger a moment, and I felt protective of him, the soft walk, the little bit of jowliness to him, the roll of tubbiness at his waist. He stopped and watched a squirrel climb over a large tombstone. It was one of those moments when everything is out of balance, I suppose, and just watching an odd thing seems to make sense. The squirrel scampered up a tree trunk, the sound of its nails like water in a tub.

—Why was she in handcuffs?

—She got eight months or something. For a robbery charge on top of the prostitution.

—So they only let her out for the funeral?

—Yeah, from what I can gather.

There was nothing to say. The preacher had already said it. We walked out the gates and turned together in the same direction, toward the expressway, but he stopped and went to shake my hand.

—I'll give you a lift home, I said.

—Home? he said, with a half-laugh. Can your car swim?

—Sorry?

—Nothing, he said, shaking his head.

We went down along Quincy, where I had parked the car. I suppose he knew it the minute he saw the Pontiac. It was parked with its front facing us. One wheel was up on the curb. The smashed headlight was apparent and the fender dented. He stopped a moment in the middle of the road, half nodded, as if it all made sense to him now. His face fell in upon itself, like a sandcastle in time lapse. I found myself shaking as I got into the driver's side, leaned across to open up the passenger door.

—This is the car, isn't it?

I sat a long time, running my fingers over the dashboard, dusty with pollen.

—It was an accident, I said.

—This is the car, he repeated.

—I didn't mean to do it. We didn't mean for it to happen.

—We? he said.

I sounded exactly like Blaine, I knew. All I was doing was holding my hand up against the guilt. Avoiding the failure, the drugs, the recklessness. I felt so foolish and inadequate. It was as if I had burned the whole house down and was searching through the rubble for bits of how it used to be, but found only the match that had sparked it all. I was clawing around frantically, looking for any justification. And yet there was still another part of me that thought perhaps I was being honest, or as honest as I could get, having left the scene of the crime, having run away from the truth. Blaine had said that things just happen. It was a pathetic logic, but it was, at its core, true. Things happen. We had not wanted them to happen. They had arisen out of the ashes of chance.

I kept cleaning the dashboard, rubbing the dust and pollen on the leg of my jeans. The mind always seeks another, simpler place, less weighted. I wanted to rev the engine alive and drive into the nearest river. What could have been a simple touch of the brakes, or a minuscule swerve, had become unfathomable. I needed to be airborne. I wanted to be one of those animals that needed to fly in order to eat.

—You don't work for the hospital at all, then?

—No.

—Were you driving it? The car?

—Was I what?

—Were you driving it or not?

—I guess I was.

It was the only lie I've ever told that has made any sense to me. There was the faint crackle of something between us: cars as bodies, crashing.

Ciaran sat, staring straight ahead through the windshield. A little sound came from him that was closer to a laugh than anything else. He rolled the window up and down, ran his fingers along the ledge, then tapped the glass with his knuckles, like he was figuring a means of escape.

—I'm going to say one thing, he said.

I felt the glass was being tapped all around me: soon it would splinter and crumble.

—One thing, that's all.

—Please, I said.

—You should have stopped.

He thumped the dashboard with the heel of his hand. I wanted him to curse me, to damn me from a height, for trying to calm my own conscience, for lying, for letting me get away with it, for appearing at his brother's apartment. A further part of me wanted him to actually turn and hit me, really hit me, draw blood, hurt me, ruin me.

—Right, he said. I'm gone.

He had his hand on the handle. He pushed the door open with his shoulder and stepped partly out, then closed it again, leaned back in the seat, exhausted.

—You should've fucking stopped. Why didn't you?

Another car pulled into the gap in front of us to parallel-park, a big blue Oldsmobile with silver fins. We sat silently watching it trying to maneuver into the space between us and the car in front. It had just enough room. It angled in, then pulled out, then angled back in again. We watched it like it was the most important thing in the world. Not a movement between us. The driver leaned over his shoulder and cranked the wheel. Just before he put it in park he reversed once more and gently touched against the grille of my car. We heard a tinkle: the last of the glass left in the broken headlight. The driver jumped out, his arms held high in surrender, but I waved him away. He was an owl-faced creature, with spectacles, and the surprise of it made his face half comic. He hurried off down the road, looking over his shoulder as if to make sure.

—I don't know, I said. I just don't know. There's no explanation. I was scared. I'm sorry. I can't say it enough.

—Shit, he said.

He lit a cigarette, cracked the window slightly and blew smoke sideways out of his mouth, then looked away.

—Listen, he said finally. I need to get away from here. Just drop me off.

—Where?

—I don't know. You want to go for a coffee somewhere? A drink?

Both of us were flummoxed by what was traveling between us. I had witnessed the death of his brother. Smashed that life shut. I didn't say a word, just nodded and put the car in gear, squeezed it out of the gap, pulled out into the empty road. A quiet drink in a dark bar was not the worst of fates.

Later that night, when I got home—if home was what I could call it anymore—I went swimming. The water was murky and full of odd plants. Strange leaves and tendrils. The stars looked like nail heads in the sky—pull a few of them out and the darkness would fall. Blaine had completed a couple of paintings and had set them up around the lake in various parts of the forest and around the water edge. A doubt had kicked in, as if he knew it was a stupid idea, but still wanted to experiment with it.

There's nothing so absurd that you can't find at least one person to buy it. I stayed in the water, hoping that he'd leave and go to sleep, but he sat on the dock on a blanket and when I rose from the water, he shrouded me with it. Arm around my shoulder, he walked me back to the cabin. The last thing I wanted was a kerosene lamp. I needed switches and electricity. Blaine tried to guide me to the bed but I simply said no, that I wasn't interested.

—Just go to bed, I said to him.

I sat at the kitchen table and sketched. It had been a while since I had done anything with charcoal. Things took shape on the page. I recalled that, when we got married, Blaine had raised a glass in front of our guests and said with a grin: *'Til life do us part*. It was his sort of joke. We were married, I thought then—we would watch each other's last breath.

But it struck me, as I sketched, that all I wanted to do was to walk out into a clean elsewhere.

—

NOTHING MUCH HAD happened, earlier, with Ciaran, or nothing much had seemed to happen anyway, at least not at first. It seemed ordinary enough, the rest of the day. We had simply driven away from the cemetery, through the Bronx, and over the Third Avenue bridge, avoiding the FDR.

The weather was warm and the sky bright blue. We kept the windows down. His hair wisped in the wind. In Harlem he asked me to slow down, amazed by the storefront churches.

—They look like shops, he said.

We sat outside and listened to a choir practice in the Baptist Church on 123rd Street. The voices were high and angelic, singing about being in the bright valleys of the Lord. Ciaran tapped his fingers absently on the dashboard. It looked like the music had entered him and was bouncing around. He said something about his brother and him not having a dancing bone in their bodies, but their mother had played the piano when they were young. There was one time when his brother had wheeled the piano out into the street along the seafront in Dublin, he couldn't now for the life of him remember why. That, he said, was the funny thing about memory. It came along at the oddest moments. He hadn't remembered it in a long time. They had wheeled the piano along the beach in the sunshine. It was the one time in his life that he remembered being mistaken for his brother. His mother had mixed up the names and called him John—*Here, John, come here, love*—and even though he was the older brother it was a moment when he saw himself as firmly rooted in childhood, and maybe he was still there, now, today, and forever, his dead brother nowhere to be found.

He cursed and kicked his foot against the lower panels of the car: Let's get that drink.

At a Park Avenue overpass a kid swung on a harness and ropes, spraypainting the bridge. I thought of Blaine's paintings. They were a sort of graffiti too, nothing more.

We drove down the Upper East Side, along Lexington Avenue, and found a dumpy little joint around about Sixty-fourth Street. A young bartender in a giant white apron hardly looked us over as we strolled in. We blinked against the beer light. No jukebox. Peanut shells all over the floor. A few men with fewer teeth sat at the counter, listening to a baseball game on the radio. The mirrors were brown and freckled with age. The smell of stale fryer oil. A sign on the wall read: BEAUTY IS IN THE WALLET OF THE BEHOLDER.

We slid into a booth, against the red leather seats, and ordered two Bloody Marys. The back of my blouse was damp against the seat. A candle wavered between us, a small lambent glow. Flecks of dirt swam in the liquid wax. Ciaran tore his paper napkin into tiny pieces and told me all about his brother. He was going to bring him home the next day, after cremation, and sprinkle him in the water around Dublin Bay. To him, it didn't seem nostalgic at all. It just seemed like the right thing to do. Bring him home. He'd walk along the waterfront and wait for the tide to come in, then scatter Corrigan in the wind. It wasn't against his faith at all. Corrigan had never mentioned a funeral of any sort and Ciaran felt certain that he'd rather be a part of many things.

What he liked about his brother, he said, is that he made people become what they didn't think they could become. He twisted something in their hearts. Gave them new places to go to. Even dead, he'd still do that. His brother believed that the space for God was one of the last great frontiers: men and women could do all sorts of things but the real mystery would always lie in a different beyond. He would just fling the ashes and let them settle where they wanted.

—What then?

—No idea. Maybe travel. Or stay in Dublin. Maybe come back here and make a go of it.

He didn't like it all that much when he first came—all the rubbish and the rush—but it was growing on him, it wasn't half bad. Coming to the city was like entering a tunnel, he said, and finding to your surprise that the light at the end didn't matter; sometimes in fact the tunnel made the light tolerable.

—You never know, in a place like this, he said. You just never know.

—You'll be back, then? Sometime?

—Maybe. Corrigan never thought he'd stay here. Then he met someone. I think he was going to stay here forever.

—He was in love?

—Yeah.

—Why d'you call him Corrigan?

—Just happened that way.

—Never John?

—John was too ordinary for him.

He let the pieces of the napkin flutter to the floor and said something strange about words being good for saying what things are, but sometimes they don't function for what things aren't. He looked away. The neon in the window brightened as the light went down outside.

His hand brushed against mine. That old human flaw of desire.

I stayed another hour. Silence most of the time. Ordinary language escaped me. I stood up, a hollowness to my legs, gooseflesh along my bare arms.

—I wasn't driving, I said.

Ciaran folded his body all the way across the table, kissed me.

—I figured that.

He pointed to the wedding ring on my finger.

—What's he like?

He smiled when I didn't reply, but it was a smile with all the world of sadness in it. He turned toward the bartender, waved at him, ordered two more Bloody Marys.

—I have to go.

—I'll just drink them both myself, he said.

One for his brother, I thought.

—You do that.

—I will, he said.

Outside, there were two tickets in the window of the Pontiac—a parking fine, and one for a smashed headlight. It was enough to almost knock me sideways. Before I drove home to the cabin, I went back to the window of the bar and shaded my eyes against the glass, looked in. Ciaran was at the counter, his arms folded and his chin on his wrist, talking to the bartender. He glanced up in my direction and I froze. Quickly I turned away. There are rocks deep enough in this earth that no matter what the rupture, they will never see the surface.

There is, I think, a fear of love.

There is a fear of love.

WHAT HE HAS SEEN OFTEN in the meadow: a nest of three red-tailed hawks, chicks, on the ledge of a tree branch, in a thick intertwine of twigs. The chicks could tell when the mother was returning, even from far away. They began to squawk, a happiness in advance. Their beaks scissored open, and a moment later she winged down toward them, a pigeon in one foot, held by the talons. She hovered and alighted, one wing still stretched out, shielding half the nest from view. She tore off red hunks of flesh and dropped them into the open mouths of the chicks. All of it done with the sort of ease that there was no vocabulary for. The balance of talon and wing. The perfect drop of red flesh into their mouths.

It was moments like this that kept his training on track. Six years in so many different places. The meadow just one of them. The grass stretched for the better part of a half mile, though the line ran only 250 feet along the middle of the meadow, where there was the most wind. The cable was guy-lined by a number of well-tightened cavallettis. Sometimes he loosened them so the cable would sway. It improved his balance. He went to the middle of the wire, where it was most difficult. He would try hopping from one foot to the other. He carried a balancing pole that was too heavy, just to instruct his body in change. If a friend was visiting he would get him to thump the high wire with a two-by-four so that the cable swung and he learned to sway side to side. He even got the friend to jump on the wire to see if he could knock him off.

His favorite moment was running along the wire without a balancing pole—it was the purest bodyflow he could get. What he understood, even when training, was this: he could not be at the top and bottom all at once. There was no such thing as an attempt. He could catch himself with his hands, or by wrapping his feet around the wire, but that was a failure. He hunted endlessly for new exercises: the full turn, the tiptoe, the pretend fall, the cartwheel, bouncing a soccer ball on his head, the bound walk, with his ankles tied together. But they were exercises, not moves he would contemplate on a walk.

Once, during a thunderstorm, he rode the wire as if it were a surfboard. He loosened the guy cables so the wire was more reckless than ever. The waves the sway created were three feet high, brutal, erratic, side to side, up and down. Wind and rain all around him. The balancing pole touched against the tip of the grass, but never the ground. He laughed into the teeth of the wind.

He thought only later, as he went back to the cabin, that the pole in his hand had been a lightning rod: he could have been lit up with the storm—a steel cable, a balancing pole, a wide-open meadow.

The wood cabin had been deserted for several years. A single room, three windows, and a door. He had to unscrew the shutters to get light. The wind came in wet. A rusted water pipe hung from the roof and once he forgot and knocked himself out on it. He watched the acrobatics of flies bouncing on cobwebs. He felt at ease, even with the rats scratching at the floorboards. He decided to climb out the windows instead of through the door: an odd habit—he didn't know where it came from. He put the pole on his shoulder and walked out into the long grass toward the wire.

Sometimes there were Rocky Mountain elk that came to graze at the meadow edge. They raised their heads and peered at him and disappeared back into the treeline. He had wondered what they saw, and how they saw it. The sway of his body. The bar held out in the air. He was ecstatic when the elk began to stay. Clumps of two or three of them, keeping close to the treeline, but venturing forward a little more each day. He wondered if they would come and rub against the giant wooden poles that he had inserted into the ground, or if they would chew them and gnaw them away, leave the line to sag.

He came back one winter, not to train, but to relax and to go over the plans. He stayed in the log cabin, on a ridge overlooking the meadow. He spread the plans and photographs of the towers out across the rough-hewn table at the small window that looked out and down at the emptiness.

One afternoon he was astounded by a coyote stepping through the snow and jumping playfully just under his wire. At its lowest point in summer the wire had been fifteen feet in the air, but the snow was so deep now that the coyote could have leaped over.

After a while he went to put some wood in the stove and then suddenly the coyote was gone, like an apparition. He was sure he had dreamed it, except when he looked through binoculars there were still some paw marks in the snow. He went out in the cold to the path he had dug in the snow, wearing only boots, jeans, a lumber shirt, a scarf. He climbed the pegs in the pole, walked the wire without a balancing pole, and traveled out to meet the tracks. The whiteness thrilled him. It seemed to him that it was like stepping along the spine of a horse toward a cool lake. The snow reinstructed the light, bent it, colored it, bounced it. He was exuberant, almost stoned. I should jump inside and swim. Dive into it. He put one foot out and then hopped, arms stretched, palms flat. But in midflight he realized what he'd done. He didn't even have time to curse. The snow was crisp and dense, and he had jumped feet-first off the wire, like a man into a pool. I should just have fallen backward, given myself a different form. He was chest-deep in it and could not get out. Trapped, he tried swishing back and forth. His legs felt wrong, neither heavy nor light. He was encased, a cell of snow. He broke free with his elbows and tried to grab the wire above him but he was too far down. The snow leaked along his ankle, down into his boots. His shirt had ridden up on his body. It was like landing in a cold wet skin. He could feel the crystals on his ribcage, his navel, his chest. It was his business to live, to fight for it—it would be, he thought, his whole life's work just to get himself out of there. He gritted his teeth and tried inching himself upward. A long, tugging pain in his body. He sank back into his original form. The threat of gray sunset coming down. The far line of trees like sentries, watching.

He was the sort of man who could do chin-ups on one finger, but there was nothing to reach for—the wire was out of his grasp. There was the momentary thought of remaining there, frozen, until a thaw came, and he'd descend with the thaw until he was fifteen feet under the wire again, rotting, the slowest sort of falling, until he reached the ground, perhaps even gnawed at by the same coyote he admired.

His hands were fully free and he warmed them by tightening and untightening. He removed the scarf from his neck, slowly, in measured motion—he knew his heart would be slowing in the cold—and he looped the wire with it and tugged. Little beads of snow shook from the scarf. He could feel the scarf threads stretch. He knew the wire, the soul of it: it would not betray him, but the scarf, he thought, was old and worn. It could stretch or rip. Kicking his feet out beneath him, through the snow, making room, looking for somewhere compact. Don't fall backward. Each time he rose, the scarf stretched. He clawed upward and pulled himself higher. It was possible now. The sun had dipped all the way behind the trees. He made circles with his feet to loosen them, pushed his body sideways through the snow, exploded upward, tore his right foot from the snow and swung his leg, touched the wire, found grace.

He pulled his body onto the cable, kneeled, then lay a moment, looked at the sky, felt the cable become his spinal cord.

Never again did he walk in the snow: he allowed that sort of beauty to remind him of what could happen. He hung the scarf on a hook on the door and the next night he saw the coyote again, sniffing aimlessly around where his imprint still lay.

He sometimes went into the local town, along the main street, to the bar where the ranchers gathered. Hard men, they looked at him as if he were small, ineffectual, effete. The truth was that he was stronger than any of them. Sometimes a ranch hand would challenge him to an arm wrestle or a fight but he had to keep his body in tune. A torn ligament would be disaster. A separated shoulder would set him back six months. He placated them, showed them card tricks, juggled coasters. On leaving the bar he slapped their backs, pickpocketed their keys, moved their pickup trucks half a block, left the keys in the ignitions, walked home in the starlight, laughing.

Tacked inside his cabin door was a sign: NOBODY FALLS HALFWAY.

He believed in walking beautifully, elegantly. It had to work as a kind of faith that he would get to the other side. He had fallen only once while training—once exactly, so he felt it couldn't happen again, it was beyond possibility. A single flaw was necessary anyway. In any work of beauty there had to be one small thread left hanging. But the fall had smashed several ribs and sometimes, when he took a deep breath, it was like a tiny reminder, a prod near his heart.

At times he practiced naked just to see how his body worked. He tuned himself to the wind. He listened not just for the gust, but for the anticipation of the gust. It was all down to whispers. Suggestion. He would use the very moisture in his eyes to test for it. *Here it comes.* After a while he learned to pluck every sound from the wind. Even the pace of insects instructed him. He loved those days when the wind rushed across the meadow with a fury and he would whistle into it. If the wind became too strong he would stop whistling and brace his whole self against it. The wind came from so many different angles, sometimes all at once, carrying treesmell, bogwaft, elkspray.

There were times when he was so at ease that he could watch the elk, or trace the wisps of smoke from the forest fires, or watch the red-tail perning above the nest, but at his best his mind remained free of sight. What he had to do was reimagine things, make an impression in his head, a tower at the far end of his vision, a cityline below him. He could freeze that image and then concentrate his body to the wire. He sometimes resented it, bringing the city to the meadow, but he had to meld the landscapes together in his imagination, the grass, the city, the sky. It was almost like he was walking upward through his mind on another wire.

There were other places where he practiced—a field in upstate New York, the empty lot of a waterfront warehouse, a patch of isolated sea marsh in eastern Long Island—but it was the meadow that was hardest to leave. He'd look over his shoulder and see that figure, neck-deep in snow, waving good-bye to himself.

He entered the noise of the city. The concrete and glass made a racket. The thrup of the traffic. The pedestrians moving like water around him. He felt like an ancient immigrant: he had stepped onto new shores. He would walk the perimeter of the city but seldom out of sight of the towers. It was the limit of what a man could do. Nobody else had even dreamed it. He could feel his body swelling with the audacity. Secretly, he scouted the towers. Past the guards. Up the stairwell. The south tower was still unfinished. Much of the building was still unoccupied, nursed in scaffold. He wondered who the others walking around were, what their purpose was. He walked out onto the unfinished roof, wearing a construction hat to avoid detection. He took a mold of the towers in his head. The vision of the double cavallettis on the roof. The y-shaped spread of the wires as they would eventually be. The reflections from the windows and how they would mirror him, at angles, from below. He put one foot out over the edge and dipped his shoe in the air, did a handstand at the very edge of the roof.

When he left the rooftop he felt he was waving to his old friend again: neck-deep, this time a quarter of a mile in the sky.

He was checking the perimeter of the south tower one dawn, marking out the schedules of delivery trucks, when he saw a woman in a green jumpsuit, bent down as if tying her shoelaces, over and over again, around the base of the towers. Little bursts of feathers came from the woman's hands. She was putting the dead birds in little ziploc bags. White-throated sparrows mostly, some songbirds too. They migrated late at night, when the air currents were calmest. Dazzled by the building lights, they crashed into the glass, or flew endlessly around the towers until exhaustion got them, their natural navigational abilities stunned. She handed him a feather from a black-throated warbler, and when he left the city again he brought it to the meadow and tacked that too just inside the cabin wall. Another reminder.

Everything had purpose, signal, meaning.

But in the end he knew that it all came down to the wire. Him and the cable. Two hundred and ten feet and the distance it bridged. The towers had been designed to sway a full three feet in a storm. A violent gust or even a sudden change in temperature would force the buildings to sway and the wire could tighten and bounce. It was one of the few things that came down to chance. If he was on it, he would have to ride out the bounce or else he'd go flying. A sway of the buildings could snap the wire in two. The frayed end of a cord could even chop a man's head clean off in midflight. He needed to be meticulous to get it all right: the winch, the come-along, the spanners, the straightening, the aligning, the mathematics, the measuring of resistance. He wanted the wire at a tension of three tons. But the tighter a cable, the more grease that might ooze out of it. Even a change in weather could make a touch of grease slip from the core.

He went over the plans with friends. They would have to sneak into the other tower, put the cavallettis in place, winch the wire tight, look out for security guards, keep him up to date on an intercom. The walk would be impossible otherwise. They spread out plans of the building and learned them by heart. The stairwells. The guard stations. They knew hiding places where they would never be found. It was like they were planning a bank raid. When he couldn't sleep, he'd wander alone down to the toneless streets near the World Trade Center: in the distance, lights on, the buildings seemed one. He'd stop at a street corner and bring himself up there, imagine himself into the sky, a figure darker than the darkness.

The night before the walk he stretched the cable out the full length of a city block. Drivers stared at him as he unfurled it. He needed to clean the wire. Meticulously he went along and scrubbed it with a rag soaked in gasoline, then rubbed it with emery. He had to make sure there were no stray strands that might poke his foot through the slippers. A single splinter—a meat hook—could be deadly. And there were spaces in each cable where the wires needed to be seated. There could be no surprises. The cable had its own moods. The worst of all was an internal torque, where the cable turned inside itself, like a snake moving through a skin.

The cable was six strands thick with nineteen wires in each. Seven eighths of an inch in diameter. Braided to perfection. The strands had been wound around the core in a lay configuration, which gave his feet the most grip. He and his friends walked along the cable and pretended that they were high in the air.

On the night of the walk it took them ten hours to string the furtive cable. He was exhausted. He hadn't brought enough water. He thought perhaps he mightn't even be able to walk, so dehydrated that his body would crack on movement. But the simple sight of the cable tightened between the towers thrilled him. The call came across the intercom from the far tower. They were ready. He felt a bolt of pure energy move through him: he was new again. The silence seemed made for him to sway about in. The morning light climbed over the dockyards, the river, the gray waterfront, over the low squalor of the East Side, where it spread and diffused—doorway, awning, cornice piece, window ledge, brickwork, railing, roofline—until it took a lengthy leap and hit the hard space of downtown. He whispered into the intercom and waved to the waiting figure on the south tower. Time to go.

One foot on the wire—his better foot, the balancing foot. First he slid his toes, then his sole, then his heel. The cable nested between his big and second toes for grip. His slippers were thin, the soles made of buffalo hide. He paused there a moment, pulled the line tighter by the strength of his eyes. He played out the aluminum pole along his hands. The coolness rolled across his palm. The pole was fifty-five pounds, half the weight of a woman. She moved on his skin like water. He had wrapped rubber tubing around its center to keep it from slipping. With a curve of his left fingers he was able to tighten his right-hand calf muscle. The little finger played out the shape of his shoulder. It was the thumb that held the bar in place. He tilted upward right and the body came slightly left. The roll in the hand was so tiny no naked eye could see it. His mind shifted space to receive his old practiced self. No tiredness in his body anymore. He held the bar in muscular memory and in one flow went forward.

What happened then was that, for an instant, almost nothing happened. He wasn't even there. Failure didn't even cross his mind. It felt like a sort of floating. He could have been in the meadow. His body loosened and took on the shape of the wind. The play of the shoulder could instruct the ankle. His throat could soothe his heel and moisten the ligaments at his ankle. A touch of the tongue against the teeth could relax the thigh. His elbow could brother his knee. If he tightened his neck he could feel it correcting in his hip. At his center he never moved. He thought of his stomach as a bowl of water. If he got it wrong, the bowl would right itself. He felt for the curve of the cable with the arch and then sole of his foot. A second step and a third. He went out beyond the first guy lines, all of him in synch.

Within seconds he was pureness moving, and he could do anything he liked. He was inside and outside his body at the same time, indulging in what it meant to belong to the air, no future, no past, and this gave him the offhand vaunt to his walk. He was carrying his life from one side to the other. On the lookout for the moment when he wasn't even aware of his breath.

The core reason for it all was beauty. Walking was a divine delight. Everything was rewritten when he was up in the air. New things were possible with the human form. It went beyond equilibrium.

He felt for a moment uncreated. Another kind of awake.

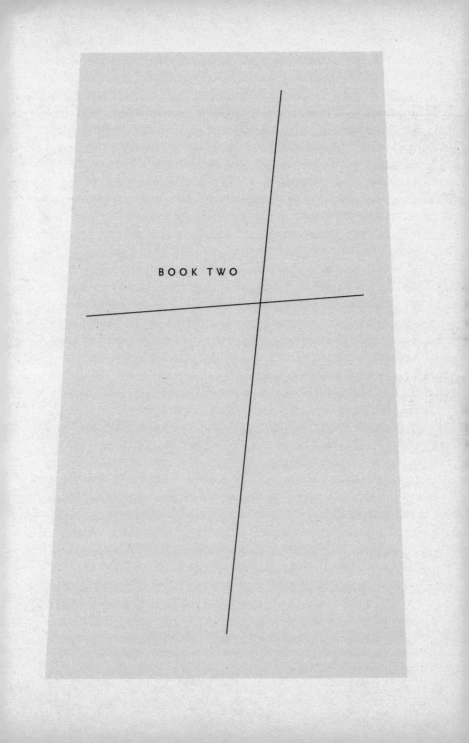

BOOK TWO

TAG

CATCH HIM HERE, IN THE CROOK of the carriages, with the morning already ovened up and muggy. Nine shots left on the roll. Nearly all the photos taken in darkness. Two of them, at least, the flash didn't work. Four of them were from moving trains. Another one, taken up in the Concourse, was a pure dud, he was sure of it.

He surfs the thin metal platform as the train jags south out of Grand Central. At times he gets dizzy just anticipating the next corner. That speed. That wild noise in his ears. The truth is, it frightens him. The steel thrumming through him. It's like he has the whole train in his sneakers. Control and oblivion. Sometimes it feels like he's the one driving. Too far left and the train might smash into the corner and there'll be a million mangled bodies along the rail. Too far right and the cars will skid sideways and it'll be good-bye, nice knowing you, see you in the headlines. He's been on the train since the Bronx, one hand on his camera, the other on the car door. Feet wide for balance. Eyes tight to the tunnel wall, looking for new tags.

He's on his way to work downtown, but to hell with those combs, those scissors, those shave bottles—he's hoping for the morning to open up with a tag. It's only thing that oils the hinges of his day. Everything else crawls, but the tags climb up into his eyeballs. PHASE 2. KIVU. SUPER

KOOL 223. He loves the way the letters curl, the arcs, the swerves, the flames, their clouds.

He rides the local just to see who's been there during the night, who came and signed, how deep they got into the dark. He doesn't have much time for the aboveground anymore, the railway bridges, the platforms, the warehouse walls, even the garbage trucks. Chumpwork that. Any chulo can do a throw-up on a wall: it's the underground tags he's grown to love the most. The ones you find in darkness. Way in the sides of the tunnels. The surprise of them. The deeper, the better. Lit up by the moving lights of the train and caught for just an instant so that he's never quite sure if he's seen them or not. JOE 182, COCO 144, TOPCAT 126. Some are quick scrawls. Others go from gravel to roof, maybe two or three cans' worth altogether, letters looping like they want to keep from ending, as if they've taken themselves a lungful of air. Others go five feet along the tunnel. The best of all is an eighteen-foot stretch under the Grand Concourse.

For a while they were tagging with just one color, mostly silver so it'd shine in the depths, but this summer they've gone up to two, three, four colors: red, blue, yellow, even black. That stumped him when he saw it first—putting a three-color tag where nobody would see it. Someone was high or brilliant or both. He walked around all day, just turning it over in his mind. The size of the flare. The depth. They were even using different-size nozzles on their cans: he could tell by the texture of the spray. He thought of the taggers scooting in and ignoring the third rail, the rats, the moles, the grime, the stink, the steel dust, the hatches, the steps, the signal lights, the wires, the pipes, the split tracks, the John 3:16's, the litter, the grates, the puddles.

The sheer cojones of it was that they were doing it underneath the city. Like the whole of upstairs had already been painted and the only territory left was here. Like they were hitting a new frontier. This is my house. Read it and weep.

Used to be, he dug the bombings, riding in a swallowed-up train, where he was just another color himself, a paint spot in a hundred other paint spots. Slamming downtown, through the rat alleys. No way out. He'd close his eyes and stand near the doors and roll his shoulders, think of the colors moving around him. Not just anyone could bomb a whole train. You had to be in the heart of things. Scale a yard fence, hop a track, hit a car, run off, send the steel out into the bright morning without a window to see through, the whole train tagged head to toe. He even tried a few times to hang out on the Concourse, where the 'Rican and Dominican taggers were, but they had no time for him, none of them, told him he didn't jive, called him names again, *Simplón, Cabronazo, Pendejo.* Thing was, he had been a straight-A student all year long. He didn't want to be, but that's how it turned out—he was the only one who hadn't cut classes. So they laughed him off. He slumped away. He even thought of going across to the blacks on the other side of the Concourse, but decided against it. He returned with his camera, the one he got from the barbershop, went to the 'Ricans, and said he'd be able to make them famous. They laughed again and he got bitch-slapped by a twelve-year-old Skull.

But then in the middle of summer, on his way to work, he stepped between the cars; the train had stopped just outside 138th Street, and he was tottering on the steel plate, just as the train started up again, when he caught the quick blur. He had no idea what it was, some enormous silver flying thing. It stayed on his retina, an afterburn, all the way through the barbershop day.

It was there, it was his, he owned it. It would not be scrubbed off. They couldn't put an underground wall in an acid bath. You can't buff that. A maximum tag. It was like discovering ice.

On the way home to the projects he rode the middle of the train again, just to check it out, and there it was once more, STEGS 33, fat and lonely in the middle of the tunnel with no other tags to brother it. It flat-fuck-out amazed him that the tagger had gone down into the tunnel and signed and then must just have walked straight back out, past the third rail, up the grimy steps, out the metal grating, into the light, the streets, the city, his name underneath his feet.

He walked across the Concourse then with a swagger, looked across at the taggers who'd been aboveground all day. Pendejos. He had the secret. He knew the places. He owned the key. He walked past them, shoulders rolling.

He began to ride the subway as often as he could, wondering if the taggers ever brought a flashlight down with them, or if they moved in teams of twos and threes, like the bombers in the train yards, one on the lookout, one with the flashlight, one to tag. He didn't even mind going downtown to his stepfather's barbershop anymore. At least the summer job gave him time to ride the rails. At first he pressed his face close to the windows, but then began surfing the cars, kept his gaze on the walls, looking for a sign. He preferred to think of the taggers working alone, blind to the light, except for a match here and there, just to see the outline, or to jazz up a color, or to fill in a blank spot, or to curve out a letter. Guerrilla work. Never more than half an hour between trains, even late at night. What he liked most were the big freestyle wraparounds. When the train went past he froze them tight in his head, and pulled them around in his mind all day long, followed the lines, the curves, the dots.

He has never once tagged a thing himself, but if he ever got a clear chance, no consequences, no stepfathersmack, no lockdown, he'd invent a whole new style, draw a little black in the blackness, a little white on deep white, or stir it up with some red, white, and blue, screw with the color scheme, put in some 'Rican, some black, go wild and stump them, that's what it was all about—make them scratch their heads, sit up and take notice. He could do that. Genius, they called it. But it was only genius if you thought of it first. A teacher told him that. Genius is lonely. He had an idea once. He wanted to get a slide machine, a projector, and put a photograph of his father inside. He wanted to project the image all around the house, so that at every turn his mother would see her gone husband, the one she kicked out, the one he has not seen in twelve years, the one she'd swapped for Irwin. He'd love to project his father there, like the tags, to make him ghostly and real in the darkness.

It's a mystery to him if the writers ever get to see their own tags, except for maybe one step back in the tunnel after it's finished and not even dry. Back over the third rail for a quick glance. Careful, or it's a couple of thousand volts. And even then there's the possibility a train will come. Or the cops make it down with a spray of flashlights and billy clubs. Or some long-haired puto will step out of the shadows, white eyes shining, knife blade ready, to empty out their pockets, crush and gut. Slam that shit on quick, and out you go before you get busted.

He braces against the shake of the carriage. Thirty-third Street. Twenty-eighth. Twenty-third. Union Square, where he crosses the platform and switches to the 5 train, slips in between the cars, waits for the shudder of movement. No new tags along the walls this morning. Sometimes he thinks he should just buy some cans, hop off the train, and begin spraying, but deep down he knows he doesn't have what it takes:

it's easier with the camera in his hands. He can photograph them, bring them out of the darkness, lift them up from the alleys. When the train picks up speed he keeps his camera under the flap of his shirt so it doesn't bounce around. Fifteen pictures already gone from a roll of twenty-four. He's not even sure any of them will come out. One of the customers in the barbershop gave him the camera last year, one of the downtown hotshots, showing off. Just handed it to him, case and all. Had no idea what to do with it. He threw it behind his bed at first, but then took it out one afternoon and examined it, started clicking what he saw.

Got to like it. Started carrying it everywhere. After a while his mother even paid for the photos to get developed. She'd never seen him so caught up before. A Minolta SR-T 102. He liked the way it fit in his hands. When he got embarrassed—by Irwin, say, or by his mother, or just coming out into the schoolyard—he could shade his face with the camera, hide behind it.

If only he could stay down here all day, in the dark, in the heat, riding back and forth between the cars, taking shots, getting famous. He heard of a girl, last year, who got the front page of *The Village Voice*. A picture of a bombed-out car heading into the tunnel at the Concourse. She caught it in the right light, half sun, half dark. The spray of headlights came straight at her and all the tags stretched behind. Right place, right time. He heard she made some serious money, fifteen dollars or more. He was sure at first it was a rumor, but he went to the library and found the back issue and there it was, with a double spread on the inside too, and her name in the bottom corner of the photos. And he heard there were two kids from Brooklyn out riding the rails, one of them with a Nikon, another with something called a Leica.

He tried it once himself. Brought a picture to *The New York Times* at the start of summer. A shot of a writer high on the Van Wyck overpass, spraying. A beautiful thing, all caught in shadow, the spray man hanging from ropes, and a couple of puffy clouds in the background. Front-page stuff, he was sure. He took a half-day from the barbershop, even wore a shirt and tie. He walked into the building on Forty-third and said he wanted to see the photo editor, he had a surefire photo, a master shot. He'd learned the lingo from a book. The security guard, a big tall moreno, made a phone call and leaned across the desk and said: "Just drop the envelope there, bro."

"But I want to see the photo editor."

"He's busy right now."

"Well, when's he unbusy? Come on, Pepe, please?"

The security guard laughed and turned away, once, then twice, then stared at him: "Pepe?"

"Sir."

"How old are you?"

"Eighteen."

"Come on, kid. How old?"

"Fourteen," he said, eyes downcast.

"Horatio José Alger!" said the security guard, his face open with laughter. He made a couple of phone calls but then looked up, eyes hooded, as if he already knew: "Sit right there, man. I'll tell you when he passes."

The lobby of the building was all glass and suits and nice smooth calf muscles. He sat for two straight hours until the guard gave him a wink. Up he went to the photo editor and thrust the envelope in his hand. The guy was eating half a Reuben sandwich. Had a piece of lettuce on his teeth. Would have been a photograph himself. Grunted a thanks and walked out of the building, off down Seventh Avenue, past the peep shows and the homeless vets, with the photo tucked under his arm. He followed him for five blocks, then lost him in the crush. And then he never heard a thing about it after that, not a thing at all. Waited for the phone call but it didn't come. He even went back to the lobby at the end of three shifts, but the security guard said he could do nothing more. "Sorry, my man." Maybe the editor lost it. Or was going to steal it. Or was going to call him any minute. Or had left a message at the barbershop and Irwin forgot. But nothing happened.

He tried a Bronx circular after that, a shitty little neighborhood rag, and even they flat-out said no: he heard someone chuckling on the other end of the telephone. Someday they'd come crawling up to him. Someday they'd lick his sneakers clean. Someday they'd be clambering over themselves to get at him. Fernando Yunqué Marcano. Imagist. A word he liked, even in Spanish. Made no sense but had a nice ring to it. If he had a card, that's what he would put on it. FERNANDO Y. MARCANO. IMAGIST. THE BRONX. U.S.A.

There was a guy he saw once on television who made his money knocking bricks out of buildings. It was funny, but he understood it in a way. The way the building looked different afterward. The way the light came through. Making people see differently. Making them think twice. You have to look on the world with a shine like no one else has. It's the sort of thing he thinks about while sweeping the floor, dunking the scissors, stacking the shave bottles. All the hotshot brokers coming in for a short back and sides. Irwin said there was art in a haircut. "Biggest gallery you're ever going to get. The whole of New York City at your fingertips." And he would think, Ah, just shut up, Irwin. You ain't my old man. Shut up and sweep. Clean the comb bottles yourself. But he was never quite able to say it. The disconnect between his mouth and his mind. That's where the camera came in. It was the unspoken thing between him and the others, the brush-off.

The train shudders and he presses nonchalantly with the palm of his hands on each car to keep himself steady, and the engine gets going, but then stops again with a quick halt, a screech of brakes, and he is shunted sideways, his shoulder taking the brunt of the whack and his leg presses hard against the chains. He quickly checks the camera. Perfect. No problem. His favorite moment, this. Stopped dead. In the tunnel, near the mouth. But still in the dark. He catches the metal lip of the door with his fingers. Rights himself and leans once more against the door.

Nonchalance. Ease. In the dark of tunnel now. Between Fulton and Wall Street. All the suits and haircuts getting ready to pile out.

There is no new rumble from the train and he likes these silences, gives him time to scope out the walls. He takes a quick look down the car to make sure there're no cops, places one foot on the chains and shunts himself up, grabs the lip of the car, one-arms himself high. If he stood on the roof he could touch the curve of the tunnel—good place for a tag— but he holds on to the lip of the car and peers out over the edge. Some red and white markings on the walls where they curve. A few yellow lights sulfurous in the distance.

He waits for his eyes to adjust, for the little retina stars to leave. Along the rear distance of the train, small bars of color bleed out from the edge of each car and spray outward. Nothing on the walls, though. A tagging Antarctica. What did he expect? Hardly going to be any writers downtown. But you never know. That would be the genius. That would be the point. Buff this, maricón.

He feels the chain jiggle beneath his feet, the first warning of movement, and he holds a little tighter to the rim of the car. None of the bombers ever get the ceiling. Virgin territory. He should start a movement himself, a brand-new space. He looks out along the length of the train, then goes a little higher on his toes. At the far end of the tunnel, he spies a patch of what could be paint on the east wall, a tag he hasn't seen before, something quick and oblong, with what looks like a tinge of red around silver, a *P* or an *R* or an *8*, maybe. Clouds and flames. He should make his way back through the cars—among the dead and dreaming—and get closer to the wall, decipher the tag, but just then the train jolts a second time and it's a warning signal—he knows it—he hops back down, braces himself. As the wheels grind, he trills the sighting through his mind, matches it up against all the old tags in other parts of the tunnel, and he figures it's brand new, it must be, yes, and he gives a quiet fist pump—someone's come and tagged downtown.

Within seconds the train is in the pale station light of Wall Street and the doors are hissing open, but his eyes are closed and he is mapping it out, the height, the color, the depth of the new tag, trying to put a geography on it for the way home, where he can take it back, own it, photograph it, make it his.

A radio sound. The static moving toward him. He leans out. Cops. Coming up from the end of the platform. They've seen him, for sure. Going to drag him out, give him a ticket. Four of them, belts jiggling. He slides open the door to the car, ducks inside. Waits for the slap of a hand on his shoulder. Nothing. He leans back against the cool metal of the door. Catches sight of them sprinting out past the turnstiles. Like there's some fire to get to. All of them clanging. Handcuffs and guns and night-sticks and notepads and flashlights and God knows what else. Someone's bought it, he thinks. Someone's gone and bought it.

He squeezes sideways through the closing doors, holding the camera sideways so it doesn't get scratched. Behind him, the door hisses shut. A jaunt in his step. Out the turnstile and up the stairs. To hell with the barbershop. Irwin can wait.

ETHERWEST

IT'S EARLY IN THE MORNING and the fluorescents are flickering. We're taking a break from the graphics hack. Dennis gets the blue-box program running through the PDP-10 to see if we can catch a good hook.

It's Dennis, Gareth, Compton, and me. Dennis is the oldest, almost thirty. We like to call him Grandpa—he did two tours in 'Nam. Compton graduated U.C. Davis. Gareth's been programming for must be ten years. Me, I'm eighteen. They call me the Kid. I've been hanging out at the institute since I was twelve.

—How many rings, guys? says Compton.

—Three, says Dennis, like he's already bored.

—Twenty, says Gareth.

—Eight, I say.

Compton flicks a look at me.

—The Kid speaks, he says.

True enough, most of the time I just let my hackwork do the talking. It's been like that since I sneaked in the basement door of the institute, back in '68. I was out skipping school, a kid in short pants and broken glasses. The computer was spitting out a line of ticker tape and the guys at the console let me watch it. The next morning they found me sleeping on the doorstep: Hey, look, it's the Kid.

Nowadays I'm here all day, every day, and the truth is I'm the best hacker they got, the one who did all the patches for the blue-box program.

The line gets picked up on the ninth ring and Compton slaps my shoulder, leans into the microphone, and says to the guy in his smooth clip so as not to freak him out: Hi, yeah, don't hang up, this is Compton here.

—Excuse me?

—Compton here, who's this?

—Pay phone.

—Don't hang up.

—This is a pay phone, sir.

—Who's speaking?

—What number're you looking for . . . ?

—I have New York, right?

—I'm busy, man.

—Are you near the World Trade Center?

—Yeah, man, but . . .

—Don't hang up.

—You must've got a wrong number, man.

The line goes dead. Compton hits the keyboard and the speed dial kicks in and there's a pickup on the thirteenth ring.

—Please don't hang up. I'm calling from California.

—Huh?

—Are you near the World Trade Center?

—Kiss my ass.

We can hear a half-chuckle as the phone gets slammed down. Compton pings six numbers all at once, waits.

—Hi, sir?

—Yes?

—Sir, are you in the vicinity of downtown New York?

—Who's this?

—We're just wondering if you could look up for us?

—Very funny, ha-ha.

The line goes dead again.

—Hello, ma'am?

—I'm afraid you must have the wrong number.

—Hello! Don't hang up.

—I'm sorry, sir, but I'm in a bit of a hurry.

—Excuse me . . .

—Try the operator, please.

—Bite me, says Compton to the dead line.

We're thinking that we should pack it all in and go back to the graphics hack. It's four or five in the morning, and the sun'll soon be coming up. I guess we could even go home if we wanted to, catch a few zees instead of sleeping under the desks like usual. Pizza boxes for pillows and sleeping bags among the wires.

But Compton hits the enter key again.

It's a thing we do all the time for kicks, blue-boxing through the computer, to Dial-A-Disc in London, say, or to the weather girl in Melbourne, or the time clock in Tokyo, or to a phone booth we found in the Shetland Islands, just for fun, to blow off steam from the programming. We loop and stack the calls, route and reroute so we can't be traced. We go in first through an 800 number just so we don't have to drop the dime: Hertz and Avis and Sony and even the army recruiting center in Virginia. That tickled the hell out of Gareth, who got out of 'Nam on a 4-F. Even Dennis, who's worn his OCCIDENTAL DEATH T-shirt ever since he came home from the war, got off on that one big-time too.

One night we were all lazing around and we hacked the code words to get through to the president, then called the White House. We layered the call through Moscow just to fool them. Dennis said: I have a very urgent message for the president. Then he rattled off the code words. Just a moment, sir, said the operator. We nearly pissed in our pants. We got past two other operators and were just about to get through to Nixon himself, but Dennis got the jitters and said to the guy: Just tell the president we've run out of toilet paper in Palo Alto. That cracked us up, but for weeks afterwards we kept waiting for the knock on the door. It became a joke after a while: we started calling the pizza boy Secret Agent Number One.

It was Compton who got the message on the ARPANET this morning—it came over the AP service on the twenty-four-hour message board. We didn't believe it at first, some guy walking the wires high above New York, but then Compton got on the line with an operator, pretended he was a switchman, testing out some verification trunks on the pay phones, said he needed some numbers down close to the World Trade buildings, part of an emergency line analysis, he said, and then we programmed the numbers in, skipped them through the system, and we each took bets on whether he'd fall or not. Simple as that.

The signals bounce through the computer, multifrequency bips, like something on a flute, and we catch the guy on the ninth ring.

—Uh. Hello.

—Are you near the World Trade Center, sir?

—Hello? 'Scuse me?

—This is not a joke. Are you near the World Trades?

—This phone was just ringing out here, man. I just . . . I just picked it up.

He's got one of those New York accents, young but grouchy, like he's smoked too many cigarettes.

—I know, says Compton, but can you see the buildings? From where you're standing? Is there someone up there?

—Who is this?

—Is there someone up there?

—I'm watching him right now.

—You what?

—I'm watching him.

—Far out! You can see him?

—I been watching him twenty minutes, more, man. Are you . . . ? This phone just rang and I—

—He can see him!

Compton slaps his hands against the desk, takes out his pocket protector, and flings it across the room. His long hair goes flying around his face. Gareth dances a little jig over by the printout table and Dennis walks by and takes me in a light headlock and knuckles my scalp, like he doesn't really care, but he likes to see us get our kicks, like he's still the army sergeant or something.

—I told you, shouts Compton.

—Who's this? says the voice.

—Far out!

—Who the hell is this?!

—Is he still on the tightrope?

—What's going on? Are you messing with me, man?

—Is he still there?

—He's been up there twenty, twenty-five minutes!

—All right! Is he walking?

—He's going to kill himself.

—Is he walking?

—No, he's stopped right now!

—Standing there?

—Yeah!

—He's just standing there? Midair?

—Yeah, he's got the bar going. Up and down in his hands.

—In the middle of the wire?

—Near the edge.

—How near?

—Not too near. Near enough.

—Like what? Five yards? Ten yards? Is he steady?

—Steady as shit! Who wants to know? What's your name?

—Compton. Yours?

—José.

—José? Cool. José. ¿Qué onda, amigo?

—Huh?

—¿Qué onda, carnal?

—I don't speak Spanish, man.

Compton hits the mute button and punches Gareth's shoulder.

—Can you believe this guy?

—Just don't lose him.

—I've seen SAT questions with more brains than this one.

—Just keep him on the line, man!

Compton leans into the console and takes the mike again.

—Can you tell us what's happening, José?

—Tell you what, man?

—Like, describe it.

—Oh. Well, he's up there . . .

—And?

—He's just standing.

—And . . . ?

—Where're you calling from, anyway?

—California.

—Seriously.

—I am serious.

—You're fucking with me, right?

—No.

—This a hoax, man?

—No hoax, José.

—Are we on TV? We're on TV, ain't we?

—We haven't got TV. We've got a computer.

—A what?

—It's complicated, José.

—You telling me I'm talking to a computer?

—Don't worry about it, man.

—What is this? Is this *Candid Camera*? Are you looking at me right now? Am I on?

—On what, José?

—I'm on the show? Ah, come on, you've got a camera here somewhere. Come clean, man. For real. I love that show, man! Love it!

—This is not a show.

—Are you Allen Funt, man?

—What?

—Where're your cameras? I don't see no cameras. Hey, man, are you in the Woolworth Building? Is that you up there? Hey!

—I'm telling you, José, we're in California.

—You're trying to tell me I'm talking to a computer?

—Sort of.

—You're in California . . . ? People! Hey, people!

He says it real loud, holding the receiver out, and we can hear voices chattering, and the wind, and I guess it's one of those pay phones in the middle of the street, covered in stickers with sexy girls and all, and we can hear some sirens going in the background, big high whoops, and a woman laughing, and a few muffled shouts, a car horn, a vendor roaring about peanuts, some guy saying he's got the wrong lens, he needs a better angle, and some other guy shouting: Don't fall!

—People! he says again. I got this nutjob here. Guy from California. Go figure. Hey. You there?

—I'm here, José. Is he up there still?

—You're a friend of his?

—No.

—How did you know, then? If you're calling in?

—It's complicated. We're phreaking. We hack the system . . . Man, is he still up there? That's all I want to know.

He pulls the phone away again and his voice sways.

—Where you from again? he shouts.

—Palo Alto.

—No kidding?

—Honestly, José.

—He says the guy's from Palo Alto! What's his name?

—Compton.

—The guy's name is Compton! Yeah, Comp-ton! Yeah. Yeah. Just a minute. Hey, man, there's a guy here wants to know, Compton what? What's his last name?

—No, no, my name is Compton.

—What's his name, man, *his* name?

—José, can you just tell me what's happening?

—Can I have some of what you're on? You're tripping, aren't you? You really a friend of his? Hey! Listen up! I got some whackjob on the phone from California. He says the guy's from Palo Alto. The tightrope walker's from Palo Alto.

—José, José. Listen to me a moment, please, okay?

—We got a bad line. What's his name?

—I don't know!

—I think we got a bad connection. We got some nutjob. I don't know, he's jabbering, man. Computers and shit. Oh, holy shit! Holy shit!

—What, what?

—Holy freakin' shit.

—What? Hello?

—No!

—José? You there?

—Jes-us.

—Hello, you there?

—Jesus H.

—Hello?

—I can't believe it.

—José!

—Yeah, I'm here! He just hopped. Did you see that?

—He what?

—He, like, hopped. Holy freakin' shit!

—He jumped?

—No!

—He fell?

—No, man.

—He's dead?

—No, man!

—What?

—He hopped from foot to foot! He's wearing black, man. You can see it. He's still up there! This guy's awesome! Holy shit! I thought he was a goner. He just went up on one foot and the other, oh, man!

—He hopped?

—'Zactly.

—Like a bunny hop?

—More like a scissors thing. He just . . . Man! Fuck me. Oh, man. Fuck me running backwards. He just like did a little scissors thing. On the wire, man!

—Far out.

—Can you freakin' believe that? He a gymnast or something? He looks like he's dancing. Is he a dancer? Hey, man, is your friend a dancer?

—He's not really my friend, José.

—I swear to Christ he must be tied to something, or something. Tied to the wire. I bet he's tied. He's up there and he just did the scissors thing! Far freakin' out.

—José. Listen up. We've got a bet going here. What's he look like?

—He's holding it, man, holding it.

—Can you see him well?

—Like a speck. Like a little thing! He's way the fuck up there. But he hopped. He's in black. You can see his legs.

—Is it windy?

—No. It's muggy as shit.

—It's not windy?

—Up there it's gotta be windy, man. Jesus! He's, like, all the way up there. I don't know how the fuck they're going to get him down. They got pigs up there. Lots of 'em.

—Huh?

—They got cops. Swarming 'round the top. On both sides.

—They trying to get him?

—No. He's way the fuck out there. He's standing now. Just holding the bar. Oh, no way! No!

—What? What is it? José?

—He's crouching. Check this shit out.

—Huh?

—You know, kneeling.

—He's what?

—He's sitting now, man.

—What d'you mean he's sitting?

—He's sitting on the wire. This guy is sick!

—José?

—Check it out!

—Hello?

There's another silence, his breath against the mouthpiece.

—José. Hey, amigo. José? My friend . . .

—No way.

Compton leans in closer to the computer, the microphone at his lips.

—José, buddy? Can you hear me? José? You there?

—Untrue.

—José.

—I ain't shittin' you . . .

—What?

—He's lying down.

—On the wire?

—Yes on the fucking wire.

—And?

—He's got his feet hooked in under him. He's looking up at the sky. He looks . . . weird.

—And the bar?

—The what?

—The pole?

—Across his stomach, man. This guy is unfuckingreal.

—He's just lying there?

—Yup.

—Like taking a nap?

—What?

—Like a siesta?

—Are you trying to mind-fuck me, man?

—Am I . . . what? 'Course not, José. No, no way. No.

There's a long silence on the phone, like José has just transported himself up there, alongside the tightrope walker.

—José? Hey. Hello. José. How's he going to get back up, José? José. I mean, if he's lying down, how's he going to get back up? Are you sure he's lying down? José? You there?

—Are you saying I'm a liar?

—No I'm just, like, speaking.

—Tell me this, man. You're in California?

—Yeah, man.

—Prove it.

—I can't really . . .

Compton mutes himself once again.

—Can someone pass me the hemlock?

—Get someone else, says Gareth. Tell him to give the phone to some-one.

—Some guy who can read, at least.

—His name's José and the dude can't even speak Spanish!

He leans right back in.

—Do me a favor there, José. Can you pass the phone along?

—Why?

—We're doing an experiment.

—You calling from California? No shit? You think I'm a retard? Is that what you think?

—Give me someone else there, will ya?

—Why? he says again, and we hear him pull the phone away from his mouth again and there's a crowd around him, jabbering away, oohs and ahhs, and then we hear the phone drop, and he says something about a freakball, and something else faint and whispery, and then he's shouting as the phone swings around, and the voices get caught in the wind.

—Anyone want to talk to this fruitcake? He thinks he's calling from California!

—José! Just pass the phone, man, will you?

The phone must be swinging in the air but it's getting slower, the voices steady, and behind them, some sirens, someone shouting now about hot dogs, and I can see it in my mind's eye, they're all down there, milling about, and the taxis are stopped and the necks are craned upwards and José is letting the phone swing at his knees.

—Oh, I don't know, man! he says. It's some dipshit from California. I don't know. I think he wants you to say something. Yeah. About it, like, what's happening. You wanna . . . ?

—Hey! José! José! Pass it along there, José.

After a second or two he picks up the phone and says: This guy's gonna talk to you.

—Oh, thank Christ.

—Hello, says a guy in a very low voice.

—Hi, this is Compton. We're out here in California . . .

—Hello, Compton.

—I'm just wondering if you could describe things for us there.

—Well, that's difficult right now.

—Why's that?

—Something terrible happened.

—Huh?

—He fell.

—He what?

—Smashed to the ground. Terrible commotion here. D'you hear that siren? You can't hear that? Listen.

—It's hard to hear.

—There's cops running through. They're crawling all over the place.

—José? José? Is that you? Did someone fall?

—He smashed here. Right here at my feet. It's all blood 'n' shit.

—Who's this? Is this José?

—Listen to the sirens, man.

—Get outta here.

—He splattered all over the place.

—Are you shittin' me?

—Man, it's horrible.

The phone slams, the line goes dead, and Compton looks around at us, eyes bugging.

—You think he bought it?

—Of course not.

—That was José! says Gareth.

—That was a different voice.

—No it wasn't. It was José. He was doggin' us! I can't believe he dogged us.

—Try the number again!

—You never know. Could be true. Could've fallen.

—Try it!

—I'm not paying any debt, Compton shouts, unless I hear it live!

—Oh, come on, says Gareth.

—Guys! says Dennis.

—We gotta hear it live. A bet's a bet.

—Guys!

—You're always welching on your bets, man.

—Try the number again.

—Guys, we've got work to do, says Dennis. I'm thinking that we could maybe even get that patch tonight.

He slaps me on the shoulder and says: Right, Kid?

—Tonight is already tomorrow, man, says Gareth.

—What if he did fall?

—He didn't fall. That was José, man.

—The line's busy!

—Get another one!

—Try the ARPANET, man.

—Get real.

—Get a pay phone!

—Bounce it.

—I can't believe it's busy.

—Well, unbusy it.

—I'm not God.

—Then find someone who is, man.

—Aww, brother. They're all just ringing out!

Dennis steps over the pizza boxes on the floor and passes the printout machine, slaps the side of the PDP-10, then thumps his chest, right by his OCCIDENTAL DEATH.

—Work, guys!

—Ah come on, Dennis.

—It's five in the morning!

—No, let's find out.

—Work, guys, work.

It's Dennis's company after all and he's the one who doles out the cash at the end of the week. Not that anyone buys anything except comics and copies of *Rolling Stone*. Dennis supplies everything else, even the toothbrushes in the basement bathroom. He learned everything he needed to know over there in 'Nam. He likes to say that he's in on the ground level, that he's making his own little xerox of Xerox. He makes his money on our hacks for the Pentagon, but the file-transferring programs are his real thing.

One of these centuries we're all going to have the ARPANET in our heads, he says. There'll be a little computer chip in our minds. They'll embed it at the base of our skulls and we'll be able to send each other messages on the electronic board, just by thinking. It's electricity, he says. It's Faraday. It's Einstein. It's Edison. It's the Wilt Chamberlain of the future.

I like that idea. That's cool. That's possible. That way we wouldn't even have to think of phone lines. People don't believe us, but it's true. Someday you'll just think something and it'll happen. *Turn off the light,* the light turns off. *Make the coffee,* the machine kicks on.

—Come on, man, just five minutes.

—All right, says Dennis, five. That's it.

—Hey, are all the frames linked? says Gareth.

—Yeah.

—Try it over there too.

—Have tone, will phone.

—Come on, Kid, get your ass over there. Call up the blue-box program.

—Let's go fishing!

I built my first crystal radio when I was seven. Some wire, a razor blade, a piece of pencil, an earphone, an empty roll of toilet paper. I made a variable capacitor from layers of aluminum foil and plastic, all pressed together using a screw. No batteries. I got the plans from a Superman comic. It only got one station, but that didn't matter. I listened late at night under the covers. In the room next door I could hear my folks fighting. They were both strung out. They went from laughter to crying and back again. When the station kicked off the air I put my hand over the earphone and took in the static.

I learned later, when I built another radio, that you could put the antenna in your mouth and the reception got better and you could drown out all the noise easily.

See, when you're programming too, the world grows small and still. You forget about everything else. You're in a zone. There are no backward glances. The sound and the lights keep pushing you onwards. You gather pace. You keep on going. The variations comply. The sound funnels inwards to a point, like an explosion seen in reverse. Everything comes down to a single point. It might be a voice recognition program, or a chess hack, or writing lines for a Boeing helicopter radar—it doesn't matter: the only thing you care about is the next line coming your way. On a good day it can be a thousand lines. On a bad one you can't find where it all falls apart.

I've never been that lucky in my life, I'm not complaining, it's just the way it is. But, this time, after just two minutes, I catch a hook.

—I'm on Cortlandt Street, she says.

I swivel on the chair and pump my first.

—Got one!

—The Kid's got one.

—Kid!

—Hang on, I tell her.

—Excuse me? she says.

There's bits of pizza lying around my feet and empty soda bottles. The guys run across and kick them aside and a roach scurries out from one of the boxes. I've rigged a double microphone into the computer, with foam ends from packing material, the stand from a wire hanger. These are highly sensitive, low distortion, I made them myself, just two small plates put close to each other, insulated. My speakers too, I made them from radio scrap.

—Look at these things, says Compton, flicking the big foam ends of the mike.

—Excuse me? says the lady.

—Sorry. Hi, I'm Compton, he says, pushing me out of my seat.

—Hi, Colin.

—Is he still up there?

—He's wearing a black jumpsuit thing.

—Told you he didn't fall.

—Well, not exactly a jumpsuit. A pantsuit thing. With a V-neck. Flared trousers. He's extremely poised.

—Excuse me?

—Getouttahere, says Gareth. Poised? Is she for real? *Poised?* Who says poised?

—Shut up, says Compton, and he turns to the mike. Ma'am? Hello? It's just the one man up there, right?

—Well, he must have some accomplices.

—What d'you mean?

—Well, surely it's impossible to get a wire from one side to the other. On your own, that is. He must have a team.

—Can you see anyone else?

—Just the police.

—How long has he been up there?

—Roughly forty-three minutes, she says.

—Roughly?

—I got out of the subway at seven-fifty.

—Oh, okay.

—And he'd just begun.

—Okay. Gotcha.

He tries to cover both mikes at once, but instead draws back and circles his finger at his temple like he's caught a crazy fish.

—Thanks for helping us.

—No problem, she says. Oh.

—You there? Hello.

—There he goes again. He's walking across again.

—How many times is that?

—That's his sixth or seventh time across. He's awfully fast this time. Awfully awfully fast.

—He's, like, running?

A big round of applause goes up in the background and Compton leans back from the mike, swivels the chair sideways a little.

—These things look like goddamn lollipops, he says.

He turns back to the microphone and pretends to lick it.

—Sounds crazy there, ma'am. Are there many people?

—This corner alone, well, there must be six, seven hundred people or more.

—How long d'you think he'll stay up there?

—My word.

—What's that?

—Well, I'm late.

—Just hang on there a minute more there, can you?

—I mean, I can't stand here talking all the time . . .

—And the cops?

—There are some policemen leaning out over the edge. I think they're trying to coax him back in. Mmm, she says.

—What? Hello!

No answer.

—What is it? says Compton.

—Excuse me, she says.

—What's going on?

—Well, there's a couple of helicopters. They're getting very close.

—How close?

—I hope they don't blow him off.

—How close are they?

—Seventy yards or so. A hundred yards, at most. Well, they're backing off right now. Oh, my.

—What is it?

—Well, the police helicopter backed off.

—Yes.

—Goodness.

—What is it?

—Right now, this very moment, he's actually waving. He's bending over with the pole resting on his knee. His thigh, actually. His right thigh.

—Seriously?

—And he's fluttering his arm.

—How do you know?

—I think it's called saluting.

—It's what?

—A sort of showboating. He bends down on the wire and he balances himself and he takes one hand off the pole and he, well, yes, he's saluting us.

—How do you know?

—Oops-a-daisy, she says.

—What? You okay? Lady?

—No, no, I'm fine.

—Are you still there? Hello!

—Excuse me?

—How can you see him so clearly?

—Glasses.

—Huh?

—I'm watching him through glasses. It's hard to balance glasses and the phone at once. One second, please.

—She's glassing him, says Dennis.

—You've got binoculars? asks Compton. Hello. Hello. You've got binocs?

—Well, yes, opera glasses.

—Getouttahere, says Gareth.

—I went to see Marakova last night. At the ABT. I forgot them. The glasses, I mean. She's wonderful by the way. With Baryshnikov.

—Hello? Hello?

—In my handbag, I left them there all night. Fortuitous, really.

—Fortuitous? says Gareth. This chick's a hoot.

—Shut the hell up, says Compton, covering my mike. Can you see his face, ma'am?

—One moment, please.

—Where's the helicopter?

—Oh, it's way away.

—Is he still saluting?

—Just a moment, please.

It sounds as if she's holding the phone away from herself for a moment, and we hear some high cheers and a few gasps of delight, and suddenly I want nothing more than for her to come back to us, forget about the tightrope man, I want our opera-glasses woman and the rich sound of her voice and the funny way she says *fortuitous*. I'd say she's old, but that doesn't matter, it's not like a sexy thing, I don't like her like that. It's not like I'm getting off on her or anything. I've never had a girlfriend, it's no big deal, I don't think that way, I just like her voice. Besides, it was me who found her.

I figure she's about thirty-five or more, even, with a long neck and a pencil skirt, but, who knows, she could be forty or forty-five, older, even, with her hair sprayed into place and a set of wooden dentures in her purse. Then again, she's probably beautiful.

Dennis is over in the corner, shaking his head and smiling. Compton's doing the finger-circling thing and Gareth is cracking up. All I want to do is push them out of my chair and stop them using my stuff—I got a right to my own stuff.

—Ask her why she's there, I whisper.

—The Kid speaks again!

—You okay, Kid?

—Just ask her.

—Don't be a drip, says Compton.

He leans backwards and laughs, covering my mike with both hands, starts bouncing back and forth in my chair. His legs are kicking up and down and the pizza boxes are scattering at his feet.

—Excuse me? says the lady. There's noise on the line.

—Ask her how old she is. Go on.

—Shut up, Kid.

—Shut up you, your goddamn self, Compton.

Compton smacks my forehead with the heel of his hand.

—Listen to the Kid!

—C'mon, just ask her.

—The beloved American right to the pursuit of horniness.

Gareth starts laughing his ass off and Compton leans into the mike again and says: Are you still there, ma'am?

—I'm here, she says.

—Is he still saluting?

—Well, he's standing now. The policemen are leaning out. Over the edge.

—The helicopter?

—Nowhere near.

—Any more bunny hops?

—Excuse me?

—Did he do any more bunny hops?

—I didn't see that. He didn't do any bunny hops. Who did bunny hops?

—From foot to foot, like?

—He's a real showman.

Gareth giggles.

—Are you taping me?

—No, no, no, honestly.

—I hear voices in the background.

—We're in California. We're cool. Don't worry. We're computer guys.

—As long as you're not taping me.

—Oh, no. You're cool.

—There are legal issues about that.

—Of course.

—Anyway, I really should . . .

—Just a moment, I say, leaning all the way across Compton's shoulder.

Compton pushes me back and asks if the tightrope walker's looking nervous and the woman takes a long time to answer, like she's chewing on the whole idea and wondering whether to swallow it.

—Well, he looks rather calm. His body, that is. He looks calm.

—You can't see his face?

—Not exactly, no.

She's beginning to fade, like she doesn't want to talk to us much anymore, evaporating down the line, but I want her just to hang on, I don't know why, it feels like she's my aunt or something, like I've known her a long time, which is impossible of course, but I don't care anymore, and I grab the microphone and bend it away from Compton and I say: You work there, ma'am?

Compton throws his head right back to laugh again and Gareth tries tickling my nuts and I mouth the word *asshole* at him.

—Well, yes, I'm a librarian.

—Really?

—Hawke Brown and Wood. In the research library.

—What's your name?

—Fifty-ninth floor.

—Your name?

—I really don't know if I should . . .

—I'm not trying to be rude.

—No, no.

—I'm Sam. I'm out here in a research lab. Sam Peters. We work on computers. I'm a programmer.

—I see.

—I'm eighteen.

—Congratulations, she laughs.

It's almost like she can hear me blush on the other end of the phone. Gareth is bent over double with laughter.

—Sable Senatore, she says finally in a voice like soft water.

—Sable?

—That's right.

—Can I ask . . . ?

—Yes?

—How old're you?

Silence again.

They're all cracking up, but there's a sweet point in her voice, and I don't want to hang up. I keep trying to imagine her there, under those big towers, looking upwards, opera glasses around her neck, getting ready to go to work in some law firm with wood paneling and pots of coffee.

—It's eight-thirty in the morning, she says.

—Excuse me?

—Hardly time for a date.

—I'm sorry.

—Well, I'm twenty-nine, Sam. A little old for you.

—Oh.

Sure enough, Gareth starts hobbling around like he's using a walking stick, and Compton is doing little caveman howls, even Dennis slides up against me and says: Loverboy.

Then Compton shoves me sideways from the table and says something about his bet, he's got to get the bet resolved.

—Where is he? Sable? Where's the guy now?

—Is this Colin again?

—Compton.

—Well, he's at the edge of the south tower.

—How long's the distance between the towers?

—Hard to judge. A couple of hundred . . . oh, there he goes!

A great big noise all around her and whooshing and cheering and it's like everything has become undone and is lapsing into babble, and I think of all the thousands off the buses and the trains, seeing it for the first time, and I wish I was there, with her, and I get a wobbly feeling in my knees.

—He lay down? asks Compton.

—No, no, of course not. He's done.

—He stopped?

—He just walked right in. He saluted again and waved and then walked right in. Very fast. Ran. Kind of.

—He's done?

—Shit.

—I win! says Gareth.

—Aww, he's done? You sure? That's it?

—The police at the edge are taking him in. They have the pole. Oh, listen.

There are huge hoots and a tremendous round of applause from near the phone. Compton looks annoyed and Gareth snaps his fingers like he's snapping money. I lean in and take the microphone.

—He's finished? Hello? Can you hear me?

—Sable, I say.

—Well, she says, I really must . . .

—Before you go.

—Is this Samuel?

—Can I ask you a personal question?

—Well, I guess you already have.

—Can I get your number? I ask.

She laughs, says nothing.

—Are you married?

Another laugh, a regret in it.

—Sorry, I say.

—No.

—Excuse me?

And I don't know whether she's said no to giving me her number, or no to being married, or maybe both at once, but then she lets out a little laugh that flutters away.

Compton is digging in his pocket for money. He slides a five-dollar bill across to Gareth.

—I was just wondering . . .

—Really, Sam, I must go.

—I'm not a weirdo.

—Toodle-pips.

And the line goes dead. I look up, and Gareth and Compton are staring at me.

—Toodle-pips, roars Gareth. Get a load of that! He's poised!

—Shut up, man.

—That's fortuitous!

—Shut up, asswipe.

—Touchy, touchy.

—Someone fell, says Compton with a grin.

—I was just messing with her. I was just fooling.

—Toodle-pips!

—Can I get your number, please?!

—Shut your mouth.

—Hey. The Kid gets angry.

I step over to the phone and hit the enter key on the keyboard again,
but it just rings and rings and rings. Compton's got this strange look on
his face, like he's never seen me before, like I'm some sort of brand-new
guy, but I don't care. I dial again: it just keeps ringing. I can see Sable, in
my mind's eye, walking away, down the street, up into the World Trade
Center towers, to the fifty-ninth floor, all woodwork and file cabinets, saying hello to the lawyers, settling down at her desk, putting a pencil behind her ear.

—What was the name of that law firm again?

—Toodle-pips, says Gareth.

—Forget about it, man, says Dennis.

He's standing there in his T-shirt, hair all askew.

—She ain't coming back, says Compton.

—What makes you so sure?

—Women's intuition, he says with a giggle.

—We got to work on that patch, says Dennis. Up and at it.

—Not me, says Compton. I'm going home. I haven't slept in years.

—Sam? How about you?

It's the Pentagon program he's talking about. We've signed a secrecy
agreement. It's an easy enough thing to do. Any kid could do it. That's
what I'm thinking. You just use the radar program, key in the gravita-

tional pull, maybe use some rotation differentials, and you can find out where any missile will land.

—Kid?

When there's a lot of computers going all at once, the place hums. It's more than white noise. It's the sort of hum that makes you feel that you're the actual ground lying under the sky, a blue hum that's all above and around you, but if you think about it too hard it will get too loud or big, and make you feel no more than just a speck. You're sealed in by it, the wires, the piping, the electrons moving, but nothing really moving, nothing at all.

I go to the window. It's a basement window that doesn't get any light. That's one thing I don't understand, windows in basements—why would anyone put a window in a basement? Once I tried to open it, but it doesn't move.

I bet the sun is coming up outside.

—Toodle-pips! says Gareth.

I want to go across the room and hit him, a punch, a real punch, something that'll really hurt him, but I don't.

I settle down at the console, hit Escape, then the N key, then the Y key, leave the blue-box hack. No more phreaking today. I open up the graphics program, use my password. SAMUS17. We've been working six months on it, but the Pentagon's been developing it for years. If there comes another war, they'll be using this hack, that's for sure.

I turn to Dennis. He's already hunched over his console.

The program boots. I can hear it clicking.

There's a high that you get when you're writing code. It's cool. It's easy to do. You forget your mom, your dad, everything. You've got the whole country onboard. This is America. You hit the frontier. You can go anywhere. It's about being connected, access, gateways, like a whispering game where if you get one thing wrong you've got to go all the way back to the beginning.

THIS IS THE HOUSE THAT HORSE BUILT

THEY DIDN'T LET ME GO to Corrigan's funeral. I woulda walked the bakery line to get there. They put me back in the pen instead. I weren't crying. I laid straight out on the bench with my hand over my eyes.

—

I saw my rap sheet, it's yellow with fifty-four entries. Typed up not so neat. You see your life with carbon copies. Kept in a file. Hunts Point, Lex and Forty-ninth, West Side Highway, all the way back to Cleveland. *Loitering. Prostitution offense. Class A misdemeanor. Criminal possesion controlled substance 7th degree. Criminel trespass 2nd degree. Criminal posession narcotic drug, Class E felony. Prostitution solicitation, Class A, Misdemeaner Degree o.*
The cops musta got a D in spelling.
The ones in the Bronx write worse than anyone. They get an F in everything except pulling us up on our prop'rties.

—

Tillie Henderson alias Miss Bliss alias Puzzle alias Rosa P. alias Sweet-Cakes.
Race, sex, height, weight, hair color, hair type, complexion, eye color, scars, marks, tattoos (none).

—

I got a taste for supermarket cakes. You won't find that on my yellow sheet.

—

The day they arrested us, Bob Marley was on the radio, singing, *Get up, stand up, stand up for your rights*. A funny-ass cop turned the volume higher and grinned over his shoulder. Jazzlyn shouted: "Who's gonna look after the babies?"

—

I left the spoon in the baby formula. Thirty-eight years old. There ain't no prizes.

—

Hooking was born in me. That's no exaggeration. I never wanted no square job. I lived right across from the stroll on Prospect Avenue and East Thirty-first. From my bedroom window I could see the girls work. I was eight. They wore red high heels and hair combed high.

The daddies went by on their way to the Turkish hotel. They caught dates for their girls. They wore hats big enough to dance in.

Every pimp movie you've ever seen has them pulling up in a Cadillac. It's true. Daddies drive Kitties. They like whitewall tires. The fuzzy dice don't happen so often, though.

I put on my first lipstick when I was nine. Shiny in the mirror. My mother's blue boots were too big for me at eleven. I could've hid down inside them and popped my head out.

When I was thirteen I already had my hands on the hip of a man in a raspberry suit. He had a waist like a lady's, but he hit me hard. His name was Fine. He loved me so much, he didn't put me on the stroll, he said he was grooming me.

—

My mother had religious readings. We were in the Church of the Spiritual Israel. You had to throw your head back and speak in tongues. She'd been on the stroll too. That was years ago. She left it when her teeth fell out. She said, "Don't you do what I done, Tillie."

So I done exactly that. My teeth haven't fallen out yet but.

—

I never tricked until I was fifteen. I walked into the lobby of the Turkish hotel. Someone gave a low whistle. Everyone's head turned, 'specially mine. Then I realized they were whistling at me. Right there I began walkin' with a bounce. I was turning out. My first daddy said: "Soon as you finish breakin' luck, honey, come on home to me."

Hose, hot pants, high heels. I hit the stroll with a vengeance.

One of the things you learn early on is you don't let your hair fall down in the open window. You do that, the crazy ones grab you by the locks and pull you in and then they beat you silly.

—

Your first daddy, you don't forget. You love him until he beats you with a tire iron. Two days later, you're changing wheels with him. He buys you a blouse that makes your body go out and around in all the right places.

—

I left baby Jazzlyn with my mother. She kicked her legs and looked up at me. She had the whitest skin when she was born. I thought first she wasn't mine. I never knew who her Daddy was. He coulda been any on a list long as Sunday. People said that he mighta been a Mexican, but I don't recall no Pablo sweating on me. I took her up in my arms and that's when I said to myself, *I'm gonna treat her good all her life.*

The first thing you do when you have a baby is you say, She's never gonna work the stroll. You swear it. Not my baby. She's never gonna be out there. So you work the stroll to keep her off the stroll.

I stayed that way nearly three years, on the stroll, running home to her, taking her in my arms, and then knew what I had to do. I said: "Look after her, Momma. I'll be right back."

—

The skinniest dog I ever seen is the one on the side of the Greyhound buses.

—

The first time I saw New York, I lay down on the ground outside Port Authority just so I could see the whole sky. Some guy stepped right over me without even looking down.

—

I started hooking my very first day. I went to the fleabag hotels over on Ninth. You can make a sky out of a ceiling, that's no problem. There were a lot of sailors in New York.

I used to like dancing with their hats on.

—

In New York you work for your man. Your man's your daddy, even if he's just a chili pimp. It's easy to find a daddy. I got lucky early on and I found TuKwik. He took me on and I worked the best stroll, Forty-ninth and Lexington. That's where Marilyn's skirt blew high. Up by the subway vent. The next best stroll was way over on the West Side, but TuKwik didn't like it, so I didn't go over there much. There wasn't as much scratch to be made on the West Side. And the cops were always throwing their badges, strictly on a prop'rty basis. They'd see how long it was since you was in jail by asking the date on your sheet. If you hadn't been inside in a while they'd curl their fingers and say, *Come with me.*

I liked the East Side, even if the cops were hard-asses.

They didn't get many colored girls on Forty-ninth and Lex. The girls were whiteys with good teeth. Nice clothes. Hair done fancy. They never wore no big rings because big rings get in the way. But they had beautiful manicures and their toenails sparkling. They looked at me and shouted: "What the fuck you doing here?" And I said, "I'm just doin' here, girls, that's all." After a while, we didn't fight no more. No more nails scraping flesh. No more trying to break each other's fingers.

—

I was the first nigger absolute regular on that stroll. They called me Rosa Parks. They used to say I was a chewing-gum spot. Black. And on the pavement.

That's how it is in the life, word. You joke a lot.

—

I said to myself, I said, I'm gonna make enough money to go home to Jazzlyn and buy her a big house with a fireplace and a deck out the back with lots of nice furniture. That's what I wanted.

I'm such a fuck-up. No one's a bigger fuck-up than me. No one's gonna know that, though. That's my secret. I walk through the world like I own it. Watch this spot. Watch it curve.

—

I got a cell mate here, she keeps a mouse in a shoe box. The mouse is the best friend she has. She talks to it and pets it. She even kisses it. Once she got bit on the lip. I laughed my ass off.

She's in for eight months on a stabbing. She won't talk to me. She'll be up-state soon. She says I ain't got no brains. Me, I'm not going upstate, no way, I made my deal with the devil—he was a little bald man with a black cape on.

—

When I was seventeen I had a body that Adam woulda dropped Eve for. Hot-potato time. It was prime, no lie. Nothing in the wrong place. I had legs a hundred miles long and a booty to die for. Adam woulda said to Eve, *Eve, I'm leaving you, honey,* and Jesus himself woulda been in the background saying, *Adam, you're one lucky motherfucker.*

—

There was a pizza place on Lexington. A picture on the wall of all these guys in tight shorts and good skin and a ball at their feet—they were fine. But the guys inside were fat and hairy and always making jokes about pepperonis. You had to dab their pizza with a napkin just to get the oil off. The syndicates used to come around too. You didn't want to mess with the syndicates. They had a crease in the trousers of their suits, and they smelled of brilliantine. They might bring you for a nice Guinea meal and then you end up taking a dirt nap.

—

TuKwik was flash. He had me on his arm like a piece of jewelry. He had five wives, but I was Wife Número Uno, top of the Christmas tree, freshest meat on the stack. You do what you can for your daddy, you light up fireworks for him, you love him to sunset, and then you go strolling. I made the most money of all, and he treated me nice. He had me ride in the front seat while the other wives watched from the street, steaming.

The only thing is, if he loves you more, he beats you more too. That's just the way it is.

One of the doctors in the emergency ward had a crush on me. He stitched together my eye after TuKwik beat me with a silver coffeepot. Then the doctor leaned down and kissed it. It tickled right on the part where the thread was coming through.

———

On a slow day, in the rain, we'd fight a lot, me and the other wives. I ran down the street carrying Susie's wig with a bit of flesh still lodged inside it. But most of the time we were a big family, word. No one believes it, but it's true.

———

On Lexington, they got hotels with wallpaper and room service and real gold paint on the rim of plates. They got rooms where they put chocolates on the pillows. They got businessmen come in for a day. Whiteys. In tighteys. They lift up their shirts, you can smell the husband panic off them, like their wife is gonna come out of the TV set.

The chambermaids put mints on pillows. I had a handbag full of green wrappers. I left the room with green wrappers and men already sweating out their marriage license.

I was strictly a lie-down girl, a flatbacker. Plain screwing was all I knew, but I made them feel like no one else. *Oh, baby, let me feel you. You make me so hot. Don't take that bone to another dog.*

I had a hundred little stupid sayings. It was like I was singing an old song. They lapped it up.

———

"Are you okay there, SweetCakes?" "Goddamn, but you make me feel fine!" (One minute thirty, ace, that's a record.)

"Gimme some sugar, sugar." "Aww, man, you're too kissable to kiss." (I'd rather lick the pipe in the sink.)

"Hey, girl, don't I do it good?" "Oh, you do it good, oh, yeah, you do, so good it's good, yeah, good." (Pity 'bout your little pork sword, though.)

—

On the way out of the Waldorf-Astoria I tipped the hotel detectives, the bellman, and the elevator boy. They knew all the girls on the stroll. The elevator boy had a thing for me. One night I blew him in the walk-in fridge. On the way out he stole a steak. Slipped it in under his shirt. Walked out, saying he always liked it medium-rare.

He was a cutie. Winked at me, even if the elevator was full.

—

I was a bug on keeping clean. I liked to shower before every time. When I got the trick to shower, I'd soap him all over and watch the dough rise. You'd say to him, "Honey, I want some'a that bread." Then I brought him to the oven, where he just about popped.

You try to get him finished after fifteen minutes, most. But you try to keep him going at least two minutes or so. Guys don't like it if they pop early. They don't get value. They feel dirty and cheap. I never had a guy who didn't come, never once. Well, not never, but if he wasn't coming I'd scratch his back and speak real nice to him, never dirty, and sometimes he'd cry and say, "I just wanna talk to you honey, that's all I wanna do, I just wanna talk." But then sometimes he'd turn over and get all vicious and scream, "Fuck you, I knew I could never get it on with you, you black bitch."

And I'd keep all pouty like he broke my heart, then I'd lean real close and whisper to him that my daddy was in the Panthers with lots of nigger dogs, and he wouldn't like to hear that sort of talk, dig? And then they'd pull up their trousers quick and get outta there lick lick lickety-split.

—

TuKwik got himself into fights. He carried a knuckle-duster in his sock. He had to be knocked down before he could get it. But he was smart. He oiled the cops and he oiled the syndicate and he kept all the rest for himself.

The smart daddy looks for the girl who walks alone. I walked alone for two weeks. Ohio. O-hi-o.

I became a modern woman. I took the Pill. I didn't want no new Jazz-lyn. I sent her postcards from the office on Forty-third. The guy behind the counter didn't recognize me at first. Everyone was hollering at me for skipping the line, but I just went right on up to him, swinging my ass. He blushed and slipped me some free stamps.

I always recognize my tricks.

—

I found a new daddy who was a famous player. His name was Jigsaw. He had a flash suit. He called it his vine. He kept a handkerchief in his pocket. His secret was that inside the handkerchief he had taped a row of razor blades. He could take it out and make a puzzle of your face. He had a little crimp in his walk. Everything perfect's got a flaw. The cops hated him. They arrested me more when they knew Jigsaw was mine.

They hated the idea of a nigger making money, especially if it's off a whitey, and it was nearly all whiteys on Forty-ninth Street. That was Chalktown.

Jigsaw had more scratch than God. He bought me a foxtail chain and a string of jade beads. He paid up, cash bonds. He even had a one-up on a Cadillac. He had a Rolls-Royce. Silver. That's no lie. It was old but it rolled. It had a wooden steering wheel. Sometimes we rode up and down Park Avenue. That's when being in the life was good. We rolled down the windows outside the Colony Club. We said, "Hi, ladies, anyone want a date?" They were terrified. We drove off, hollering, "Come on, let's go get ourselves some cucumber sandwiches."

We drove down to Times Square, howling. "Cut the crusts off 'em, baby!"

—

I got the most beautiful things from Jigsaw. He had an apartment on First and Fifty-eighth. Everything was boosted, even the carpets. Vases all over the place. And mirrors with golden edges. The tricks, they liked coming there. They walked right in and said, *Wow*. It was like they thought I was a businesswoman.

All the time they was looking for the bed. The thing is, the bed came down out of the wall. It was on electronic control.

That place was flash.

—

The guys who paid a hundred dollars, we called them Champagnes. Susie would say: "Here comes my Champagne," when a fancy car pulled up on the street.

One night I had one of them football guys from the New York Giants, a linebacker with a neck so big they called him Sequoia. He had a wallet too, like none I ever seen, fat with C-notes. I thought, Here comes ten Champagnes all at once. Here it comes, bubbly, the mighty G.

Turned out he just wanted a freebie, so I got down on the ground, bent down, looked between my legs, said, "HIKE!" and threw him a room-service menu.

Sometimes I just crack myself up.

—

I was calling myself Miss Bliss then, 'cause I was very happy. The men were just bodies moving on me. Bits of color. They didn't matter none. Sometimes I just felt like a needle in a jukebox. I just fell on that groove and rode in awhile. Then I'd pick the dust off and drop again.

—

The thing I noticed about the homicide cops is that they wore real nice suits. And their shoes were always polished. One of them, he had a three-legged shoeshine box right under his desk. Rags and black polish and all. He was cute. He wasn't looking for a freebie. He only wanted to know who iced Jigsaw. I knew, but I wasn't telling. When someone buys it, you keep your mouth shut. That's the law on the street, zip zip goes your mouth, zip zip not saying a word, zip zip zip zip zip.

—

Jigsaw walked into three neat bullets. I saw him lying there, on the wet ground. He had one in the center of his forehead, where it blew his brains open. And when the paramedics opened up his shirt it was like he had two extra red eyes in his chest.

There was blood spatter on the ground and on the lamp post and on the mailbox too. This guy from the pizza shop came out to clean the passenger-side mirror of his van. He was scrubbing it with his apron, shaking his head and muttering under his breath, like someone had just burned his calzones. As if Jigsaw *meant* to leave his brains on the guy's mirror! Like he did it deliberate!

He went back into the shop and the next time we went in the shop for a slice, he was like: "Hey, no hookers in here, get outta here, get your sellin' asses O-U-T, especially you, you N-I-G-G-E-R." We said, "Oh, he can spell," but I swear to God, I wanted to twist his Guinea balls up in his throat and squeeze them into one and call it his Adam's apple.

Susie said she hated racists, especially Guinea racists. We laughed our heads off and marched right on down to Second Avenue and got us a slice at Ray's Famous. It was so delicious we didn't even have to dab the oil off. After that we never went back to the place on Lex.

We weren't gonna give business to no racist pig.

—

Jigsaw had all that scratch, but he was buried in Potter's Field. I seen too many funerals. I guess I'm no different than nobody else. I don't know who got Jigsaw's money, but I'd say it was the syndicate.

There's only one thing moves at the speed of light and that's cold hard cash.

—

Couple of months after Jigsaw got scrambled, I saw Andy Warhol coming down the block. He had eyes that were big and blue and schizoid, like he just came from a day of token-sucking. I said, "Hey, Andy honey, you want a date?" He said, "I'm not Andy Warhol, I'm just a guy wearing an Andy Warhol mask, ha ha." I pinched his ass. He jumped back and went, "Ooohh." He was a bit square, but then he talked to me must've been ten minutes or more.

I thought he was going to put me in a movie. I was all jumping up and down in my stilettos. I woulda kissed him if he put me in a movie. But in the end he didn't want nothing except to find himself a boy. That's all he wanted, a young boy he could take home and do his thing with. I told him that I could use a big pink strap-on and he said: "Oh, stop, you're getting me hot."

I went around all night, saying: "I turned Andy Warhol on!"

—

I got another trick I thought I recognized. He was young but bald on top.
The bald spot was very white, like a little ice rink on his head. He got a
room in the Waldorf-Astoria. The first thing he did was he pulled the curtains tight and fell on the bed and said: "Let's get it on."

I was like, "Wow, do I know you, honey?"

He looked at me hard and said: "No."

"Are you sure?" I said, all cutesy and shit. "You look familiar."

"No," he said, real angry.

"Hey, take a chill pill, honey," I said. "I'm only axing."

I pulled off his belt and unzipped him and he moaned, *Ohyeah-
yeahyeah*, like they all do, and he closed his eyes and kept on moaning,
and then I don't know why, but I figured it out. It was the guy from the
weather report on CBS! Except he wasn't wearing his toupee! That was
his disguise. I finished him off and got myself dressed and waved good-
bye but turned at the door and said to him, "Hey man, it's cloudy in the
east with the wind at ten knots and a chance of snow."

There I was, cracking myself up again.

—

I used to love the joke where the last line was: *Your Honor, I was armed
with nothing more than a piece of fried chicken.*

—

The hippies were bad for business. They were into free love. I stayed
away from them. They stank.

The soldiers were my best clients. When they came back they just
wanted to pop—popping was the only thing on their minds. They'd had
their asses handed to them by a bunch of half-baked slanty-eyed mother-
fuckers and now they just needed to forget. And there ain't much better
to help you forget than popping with Miss Bliss.

I made up a little badge that said: THE MISS BLISS SOLUTION: MAKE WAR,
NOT LOVE. Nobody thought it was funny, not even the boys who were com-
ing home from 'Nam, so I threw it in the garbage can on the corner of
Second Avenue.

They smelled like small little graveyards walking around, those boys.

But they needed loving. I was like a social service, word. Doing my thing for America. Sometimes I'd hum that kiddie song while he scraped his fingers down my back. *Pop goes the weasel!* They got a kick outta that.

—

Bob was a pross cop with a hard-on for black girls. I musta seen his shield more'n I had hot breakfasts. He arrested me even when I wasn't working. I was in the coffee shop and he threw the badge and he said, "You're coming with me, Sambette."

He thought he was funny. I said, "Kiss my black ass, Bob." Still he took me down the pen. He had his quota. He got paid overtime. I wanted to slice him up with my nail file.

—

Once I had a man a whole week long at the Sherry-Netherlands. There was a chandelier surrounded with grapes 'n' vines in the ceiling and violins carved outta the plaster and all. He was small and fat and bald and brown. He put a record on the player. Sounded like snake music. He said, "Isn't this a divine comedy?" I said: "That's a weird thing to say." He just smiled. He had a nice accent.

We had crystal cocaine and caviar and champagne in a bucket. It was a blow date, but all he had me do was read to him. Persian poems. I thought maybe I was already in heaven and floating on a cloud. There was a lot of things being said about ancient Syria and Persia. I laid out on the bed buck naked and just read to the chandelier. He didn't even want to touch me. He sat in the chair and watched me reading. I left with eight hundred dollars and a copy of Rumi. I never read nothing like that before. Made me want to have a fig tree.

That's long before I went to Hunts Point. And that's long before I ended up under the Deegan. And that's long before Jazz and Corrie rode that van to doom.

But if I was given one week to live, just one week again, if that was my choice, that week at the Sherry-Netherlands is the one I'd repeat. I was just lying on the bed, naked and reading, and him being nice to me, and telling me I was fine, that I'd do well in Syria and Persia. I never seen Syria or Persia or Iran or whatever they call it. Someday I'm going to go, but I'll bring Jazzlyn's babies and I'll marry an oil sheik.

—

Except I been thinking about the noose.

—

Any excuse is a good excuse. When they ship you off to prison they give you a syphilis test. I came back clean. I was thinking maybe I wouldn't be clean this time. Maybe that'd be a good excuse.

—

I hate mops. I hate sweeping brushes. You can't trick your way outta prison. You have to wash windows, clean the floor, sponge the showers. I'm the only hooker in C-40. Everyone else is way upstate. One thing for sure, there ain't no pretty sunsets out the window.

All the butches are in C-50. All the femmes are where I am. The lesbians are called jaspers, I don't know why—sometimes words are weird. In the canteen, all the jaspers want to do is comb my hair. I'm not into that. Never have been. I won't wear no Oxfords. I like to keep my uniform short, but I won't wear a bow in my hair either. Even if you're going to die, you might as well die pretty.

—

I don't eat. At least I can keep my figure. I'm still proud of that.

I'm a fuck-up but I'm still proud of my body.

They wouldn't serve the food to dogs anyway. The dogs would strangle themselves after reading the menu. They'd start howling and puncture themselves dead with forks.

—

I got the keyring with the babies on it. I like to hang it on my finger and watch them twirl. I got this piece of aluminum foil too. It's not like a mirror, but you can look in it and you can guess that you're still pretty. It's better 'n talking to a mouse. My cell mate shaved the side of the bed in order to put the mouse in wood shavings. I read a book once about a guy with a mouse. His name was Steinbeck—the guy, not the mouse. I ain't stupid. I don't wear the dunce cap just 'cause I'm a hooker. They did an I.Q. test and I got 124. If you don't believe me, ask the prison shrink.

—

The library cart squeaks around once a week. They don't got no books I like. I asked them for Rumi and they said, "What the hell is that?"

In the gym I play Ping-Pong. The butches go, "Ooohh, look at her smash."

—

Most of the time, me and Jazz, we never robbed nobody. Wasn't worth it. But this asshole, he took us all the way from the Bronx to Hell's Kitchen and promised us all sorts of scratch. Turned out different, so all we done was we relieved him of the chore, that's the word, relieved him. Just lightened his pockets, really. I took the rap for Jazzlyn. She wanted back with the babies. She needed the horse too. I wanted her off it, but she couldn't go cold. Not like that. Me, I was clean. I could take it. I'd been clean six months. I was banging coke here and there, and sometimes I sold some horse that I got from Angie, but mostly I was clean.

In the station house Jazz was crying her eyes out. The detective leaned across his desk to me and said: "Look, Tillie, you wanna make things right for your daughter?" I'm like: "Yeah, babe." He said: "All right, gimme a confession and I'll let her go. You'll get six months, no more, I guarantee it." So, I sat down and sang. It was an old charge, robbery in the second degree. Jazz had jacked two hundred dollars from that guy and syringed that straight off.

That's how it goes.

Everything flies through the windshield.

—

They told me Corrigan smashed all the bones in his chest when he hit the steering wheel. I thought, Well at least in heaven his Spanish chick'll be able to reach in and grab his heart.

—

I'm a fuck-up. That's what I am. I took the rap and Jazzlyn paid the price. I am the mother and my daughter is no more. I only hope at the last minute that at least she was smiling.

I'm a fuck-up like none you've ever seen before.

—

Even the roaches don't like it here in Rikers. The roaches, they've got an aversion. The roaches, they're like judges and district attorneys and shit. They crawl out of the walls in their black coats and they say, Miss Henderson, I hereby sentence you to eight months.

Anyone who knows roaches know that they rattle. That's the word. They *rattle* across the floor.

—

The shower stall is the best place. You could hang an elephant from the pipes.

—

Sometimes I bang my head off the wall long enough that I just don't feel it anymore. I can bang it hard enough I finally sleep. I wake with a headache and I bang again. It only stings in the shower when all the butches are watching.

A white girl got sliced yesterday. With the filed-down side of a canteen tray. She had it coming. Whiter than her whiteness. Outside the pen it never used to bother me: white or black or brown or yellow or pink. But I guess the pen is the flip side of real life—too many niggers and not many whiteys, all the whiteys can buy their way out of it.

This the longest I ever spent inside. It gets you to thinking about things. Mostly about being such a fuck-up. And mostly about where to hang the noose.

—

When they first told me 'bout Jazzlyn I just stood there beating my head against the cage like a bird. They let me go to the funeral and then they locked me back up. The babies weren't there. I kept asking about the girls but everyone was saying: Don't worry about the babies, they're being looked after.

—

In my dreams I'm back in the Sherry-Netherlands. Why I liked him so much I don't really know. He wasn't a trick, he was a john—even with the bald head he was fine.

Men in the Middle Eastern life dig hookers. They like to spoil them and buy them things and walk around with the sheets wrapped around them. He asked me to stand by the window in silhouette. He positioned the light just so. I heard him gasp. All I was doing was standing. Nothing ever made me feel better than him just looking at me, appreciating what he saw. That's what good men do—they appreciate. He wasn't fooling with himself or nothing, he just sat in the chair watching me, hardly breathing. He said I made him delirious, that he'd give me anything just to stay there forever. I said something smart-ass, but really I was thinking the exact same thing. I hated myself for saying something disrespectful. I coulda had the floor swallow me up.

After a moment or two he relaxed, then sighed. He said something to me about the desert in Syria and how the lemon trees look like little explosions of color.

And all of a sudden—right there, looking out over Central Park—I got a longing for my daughter like nothing else before. Jazzlyn was eight or nine then. I wanted just to hold her in my arms. It's no less love if you're a hooker, it's no less love at all.

The park got dark. The lights came on. Only a few of them were working. They lit up the trees.

"Read the poem about the marketplace," he said.

It was a poem where a man buys a carpet in the marketplace, and it's a perfect carpet, without a flaw, so it brings him all sorts of woe 'n' shit. I had to switch on the light to read to him and it spoiled the atmosphere, I could tell straight off. Then he said, "Just tell me a story then."

I turned off the light and stood there. I didn't want to say nothing cheap.

I couldn't think of anything except a story I heard from a trick a few weeks before. So I stood there with the curtains in my hands and I said: "There was this old couple out walking by the Plaza. It was early evening. They were hand in hand. They were about to go into the park when a cop blew his whistle sharp and stopped them. The cop said, 'You can't go in there, it's gonna get dark, it's too dangerous to walk around the park, you'll get mugged.' The old couple said, 'But we want to go in there, it's our anniversary, we were here forty years ago exactly.' The cop said, 'You're crazy. Nobody walks in Central Park anymore.' But the old couple kept walking in anyway. They wanted to take the exact same walk they took all those years before, 'round the little pond. To remember. So they went hand in hand, right into the dark. And guess what? That cop, he walked behind at twenty paces, right around the lake, just to make sure them people weren't tossed, ain't that something?"

That was my story. I stayed still. The curtains were all damp in my hands. I could almost hear the Middle Eastern man smile.

"Tell it to me again," he said.

I stood a little closer to the window, where the light was coming in real nice. I told it to him again, with even more details, like the sound of their footsteps and all.

—

I never even told that story to Jazzlyn. I wanted to tell her but I never did. I was waiting for the right time. He gave me that Rumi book when I left. I shoved it in my handbag, didn't think much of it at first, but it crept up on me, like a street lamp.

I liked him, my little fat bald brown man. I went to the Sherry-Netherlands to see if he was there, but the manager kicked me out. He had a folder in his hand. He used it like a cattle prod. He said, "Out out out!"

I began to read Rumi all the time. I liked it because he had the details. He had nice lines. I began saying shit to my tricks. I told folks I liked the lines because of my father and how he studied Persian poetry. Sometimes I said it was my husband.

I never even had a father or a husband. Not one I knew of, anyways. I ain't whining. That's just a fact.

—

I'm a fuck-up and my daughter is no more.

—

Jazzlyn asked me once about her Daddy. Her real Daddy—not a daddy Daddy. She was eight. We were talking on the phone. Long-distance from

New York to Cleveland. It cost me nothing because all the girls knew how to get the dime back. We learned it from the vets who came back from 'Nam all messed up in the head.

I liked the bank of phones on Forty-fourth. I'd get bored and ring the phone right beside me. I picked it up and talked to myself. I got a big kick outta that. *Hi, Tillie, how you doin', baby? Not too bad, Tillie, how you? Swingin' it, Tillie, how's the weather there, girl? Raining, Tillie-o. No shit, it's raining here too, Tillie, ain't that a kicker?!*

———

I was on the drugstore phone on Fiftieth and Lex when Jazzlyn said: "Who's my real Daddy?" I told her that her Daddy was a nice guy but he went out once for a pack of cigarettes. That's what you tell a kid. Everyone says that, I don't know why—I guess all the assholes who don't want to hang around their kids are smokers.

She never even asked about him again. Not once. I used to think he was gone for cigarettes an awful long time, whoever the fuck he was. Maybe he's standing around still, Pablo, waiting for the change.

———

I went back to Cleveland to pick Jazzlyn up. That was '64 or '65, one of them years. She was eight or nine years old then. She was waiting for me on the doorstep. She wore a little hooded coat and she was sitting there all pouty and then she looked up and saw me. I swear it was like seeing a firework go off. "Tillie!" she shouted. She never really called me Mom. She jumped up from the step. No one ever gave me a bigger hug. No one. She like near smothered me. I sat right down beside her and cried my eyes out. I said, "Wait'll you see New York, Jazz, it's gonna blow you away."

My own mother was in the kitchen giving me snake eyes. I handed her an envelope with two thousand dollars. She said: "Oh, honey, I knew you'd come good, I just knew it!"

We wanted to drive across country, Jazzlyn and me, but instead we got a skinny dog all the way from Cleveland. The whole time there she slept on my shoulder and sucked her thumb, nine years old and still sucking her thumb. I heard later, in the Bronx, that was one of her things. She liked to suck her thumb when she was doing it with a trick. That makes me sick to the core. I'm a fuck-up and that's all. That's about all that matters.

Tillie Fuck-Up Henderson. That's me without ribbons on.

———

I ain't gonna kill myself until I see my baby's baby girls. I told the warden today that I'm a grandmother and she didn't say nothing. I said, "I want to see my grandbabies—why won't they bring my grandbabies?" She didn't bat an eyelid. Maybe I'm getting old. I'll have my thirty-ninth birthday inside. It'll take a whole week just to blow them candles out.

I begged her and begged her and begged her. She said the babies were fine, they were being looked after, social services had them.

———

It was a daddy who put me in the Bronx. He called himself L.A. Rex. He didn't like niggers, but he was a nigger himself. He said Lexington was for whiteys. He said I got old. He said I was useless. He said I was taking too much time with Jazzlyn. He said to me that I looked like a piece of cheese. He said, "Don't come down by Lex again or I'll break your arms, Tillie, y'hear me?"

So that's what he did—he broke my arms. He broke my fingers too. He caught me on the corner of Third and Forty-eighth and he snapped them like they was chicken bones. He said the Bronx was a good place for retirement. He grinned and said it was just like Florida without the beaches.

I had to go home to Jazzlyn with my arms in plaster. I was in convalescence for I don't know how long.

L.A. Rex had a diamond star in his tooth, that's no lie. He looked a bit like that Cosby guy on TV, except Cosby has some funky-ass sideburns. L.A. even paid my hospital bills. He didn't put me out on the stroll. I thought, *What the fuck is up with that?* Sometimes the world is a place you just can't understand.

So I got clean. I got myself housing. I gave up the game. Those were good years. All it took to make me happy was finding a nickel in the bottom of my handbag. Things were going so good. It felt like I was standing at a window. I put Jazzlyn in school. I got a job putting stickers on supermarket cans. I came home, went to work, came home again. I stayed away from the stroll. Nothing was going to put me back there. And then one day, out of the blue, I don't even remember why, I walked down to the Deegan, stuck out my thumb, and looked for a trick. I got a thump in the back of my head from a daddy called Birdhouse—he was wearing a surefire fuck-off hat that he never once took off 'cause he didn't like anyone to see his glass eye. He said, "Hey, babe, what's shakin'?"

—

Jazzlyn needed school books. I'm almost sure that's what it was.

—

I wasn't a parasol girl down on Forty-ninth and Lex. The parasol was a thing I started in the Bronx. To hide my face, really. That's a secret I won't tell nobody. I've always had a good body. Even for all those years I stuffed junk into it, it was good and curvy and extra delicious. I never had a disease I couldn't get rid of. It was when I got to the Bronx that I took up the parasol. They couldn't see my face but they could see my booty. I could shake it. I had enough electricity in my booty to jump-start the whole of New York City.

In the Bronx I got in the car quick and then they couldn't say no. Try kicking a girl out of your car unpaid: you might as well suck raindrops from a puddle.

It's always been the older girls that work the Bronx. All except Jazzlyn. I kept Jazz around for company. She only went downtown now and then. She was the most popular girl on the stroll. Everyone else was charging twenty, but Jazzlyn could go all the way to forty, even fifty. She got the young guys. And the older guys with the real bread, the fat ones who want to feel handsome. They came on all starry-eyed with her. She had straight hair and good lips and legs that went up to her neck. Some of the guys they called her Raf, 'cause that's what she looked like. If there'd've been trees under the Deegan she'd'd've been up there giraffing with her tongue.

That was one of the nicknames on her rap sheet. *Raf.* She was with this British guy once and he was making all these dive-bomber sounds. He was pumping away, saying shit like: "Here I am, rescue mission,

Flanders one-oh-one, Flanders one-oh-one! Coming down!" When he was finished he said, "See, I rescued you." And Jazzlyn's like: "You rescued me, is that right?" 'Cause men like to think they can rescue you. Like you got a disease and they got the special cure just waiting for you. *Come in here, honey, don't ya want someone to understand you? Me, I understand you. I'm the only guy knows a chick like you. I got a dick as long as a Third Avenue menu but I got a heart bigger'n the Bronx.* They fuck you like they're doing you a big favor. Every man wants a whore to rescue, that's the knockdown truth. It's a disease in itself, you ask me. Then, when they've shot their wad they just zip up and go and forget about you. That's something fucked up in the head.

Some of these assholes think you got a heart of gold. No one's got a heart of gold. I don't got no heart of gold, no way. Not even Corrie. Even Corrie went for that Spanish broad with the dumb little tattoo on her ankle.

—

When Jazzlyn was fourteen she came home with her first red mark on the inside of her arm. I as good as slapped the black off her, but she came back with the mark between her toes. She didn't even smoke a cigarette and there she was, on the horse. She was running with the Immortals then. They had a beef with the Ghetto Brothers.

I tried keeping her straight by keeping her on the streets. That's what I was thinking.

—

Big Bill Broonzy's got a song I like, but I don't like to listen to it: *I'm down so low, baby, I declare I'm lookin' up at down.*

—

By the time she was fifteen I was watching her shoot up. I'd sit down on the pavement and think, That's my girl. And then I'd say, Hold on a goddamn motherfucking second, is that my girl? Is that really *my* girl?

And then I'd think, Yeah that's my girl, that's my flesh 'n' blood, that's her, all right.

I made that.

—

There were times I'd strap the elastic around her arm to get the vein to pop. I was keeping her safe. That's all I was trying to do.

—

This is the house that Horse built. This is the house that Horse built.

—

Jazz came home one Friday and said: "Hey, Till, how'd you like to be a grandma?" I said, "Yeah, Grandma T., that's me." She started blubbering. And then she was crying on my shoulder—it woulda been nice if it weren't for real.

I went down to Foodland but all they had was a cheap-ass Entenmann's.

She was eating it and I looked at her and thought, That's my baby and she's having a baby. I didn't even take a slice until Jazz went to bed and then I wolfed that motherfucker down, got crumbs all over the floor.

—

Second time I came a grandmother, Angie organized a party for me. She talked Corrie into borrowing a wheelchair and she wheeled me along under the Deegan. We were high on coke then, laughing our asses off.

—

Oh, but what I shoulda done—I shoulda swallowed a pair of handcuffs when Jazzlyn was in my belly. That's what I shoulda done. Gave her a heads-up about what was coming her way. Say, Here you is, already arrested, you're your mother and her mother before her, a long line of mothers stretching way back to Eve, french and nigger and dutch and whatever else came before me.

Oh, God, I shoulda swallowed handcuffs. I shoulda swallowed them whole.

—

I spent the last seven years fucking in the inside of refrigerator cars. I spent the last seven years fucking in the inside of refrigerator cars.

Yeah. I spent the last seven years fucking in the inside of refrigerator cars.

—

Tillie Fuck-Up Henderson.

—

I get a call that I got a visitor. I'm, like, primed. I'm fixing my hair and putting on lipstick and making myself smell fine, jailhouse perfume and all. I'm flossing my teeth and plucking my eyebrows and even making sure my prison duds look good. I thought, There's only two people in the world ever going to come see me. I was bouncing down the prison steps. It was like coming down a fire escape. I could smell the sky. Watch out, babies, here comes your Momma's Momma.

I got to the Gatehouse. That's what they call the visiting room. I'm looking all 'round for them. There are lots of chairs and plastic windows and a big cloud of cigarette smoke. It's like moving through a delicious fog. I'm standing up on my toes and looking all around and everyone's settling down and meeting their honeys. There are big oohs and ahhs and laughing and shouting going on, all over the place, and kids scream-ing, and I keep standing up on my tiptoes to see my babies. Soon enough there's only one spot left at the chairs. Some white bitch is sitting oppo-site the glass. I'm thinking I half know her, but I don't know from where, maybe she's a parole officer, or a social worker or something. She's got blond hair and green eyes and pearly-white skin. And then she says: "Oh, hi, Tillie."

I'm thinking, Don't *Hi, Tillie* me, who the fuck're you? These whiteys, they come on all familiar. Like they understand you. Like they're your best friends.

But I just say, "Hi," and slide onto the chair. I feel like I got the air knocked out of me. She gives me her name and I shrug 'cause it don't mean nothing to me. "You got any cigarettes?" I say, and she says no, she quit. And I'm thinking, She's even less good to me than she was five min-utes ago, and five minutes ago she was useless.

And I say, "Are you the one who got my babies?"

She says, "No, someone else is looking after the babies."

Then she just sits there and starts asking me about prison life, and if

I'm eating good, and when am I going to get out? I look at her like she's ten pounds of shit wrapped in a five-pound bag. She's all nervous and stuff. And I finally out and say it so slow that she raises her eyebrows in surprise: "Who—the—fuck—are—you?" And she says, "I know Keyring, he's my friend." And I'm like, "Who the fuck is Keyring?" And then she spells it out: "C-i-a-r-a-n."

Then the cherry falls and I think, She's the one came to Jazzlyn's funeral with Corrigan's brother. Funny thing is, he's the one who gave me the keyring.

"Are you a holy roller?" I ask her.

"Am I what?"

"You on a Jesus kick?"

She shakes her head.

"Then why you here?"

"I just wanted to see how you were."

"For real?"

And she says: "For real, Tillie."

So I let up on her. I say, "All right, whatever."

And she's leaning forward, saying it's nice to see me again, the last time she saw me she just felt very badly for me, the way the pigs put me in handcuffs and all, at the graveside. She actually said "pigs," but I could tell she wasn't used to it, like she was trying to be tough but she wasn't. But I think, Okay, this is cool, I'll let it slide, I'll let fifteen minutes drift, what's fifteen, twenty minutes?

She's pretty. She's blond. She's cool. I'm telling her about the girl in C-40 with the mouse, and what it's like when you're a femme not a butch, and how the food tastes terrible, and how I miss my babies, and how there was a fight on TV night over the Chico show and Scatman Crothers and if he's a cardboard nigger. And she's nodding her head and going, Uh-huh, hmm, oh, I see, that's very interesting, Scatman Crothers, he's cute. Like she'd get it on with him. But she's hip to me. She's smiling and laughing. She's smart too—I can tell she's smart, a rich girl. She tells me she's an artist and she's dating Corrigan's brother, even though she's married, he went to Ireland to scatter Corrigan's ashes and came right back, they fell in love, she's getting her life together, she used to be an addict, and she still likes to drink. She says she'll put some money in my prison account and maybe I can get myself some cigarettes.

"What else can I get for you?" she says.

"My babies."

"I'll try," she says. "I'll see where they are. I'll see if I can get them to visit. Anything else, Tillie?"

"Jazz," I say.

"Jazz?" she goes.

"Bring Jazzlyn back too."

And she goes white at the gills.

"Jazzlyn's dead," she said, like I'm some fucking idiot.

She's got a look in her eyes like she just been kicked. She's staring at me and her lip is quivering. And then the goddamn bell goes off. It's visiting time over and we're saying good-bye to each other behind the glass, and I turn to her and say, "Why did ya come here?"

She looks down at the ground and then she smiles up at me, lip still quivering, but she shakes her head, and there are little teardrops in the corner of her eyes.

She slips a couple of books across the table and I'm like, Wow, Rumi, how the fuck did she know?

She says she'll come again, and I beg her again to bring the babies. She says she'll ask around, they're with social services or something. Then she waves bye-bye, scrubbing her eyes dry as she walks away. I'm thinking, What the fuck?

I was walking up the stairs again, still wondering how she knew about Rumi, and then I remembered. I started laughing to myself, but I was glad I didn't say anything to her about Ciaran and his little pork sword—what's the point? He was a good guy, Keyring. Anyone who's a brother of Corrie's is a brother of mine.

—

Nothing's righteous. Corrigan knew the deal. He never gave me no shit. His brother was a bit of an asshole. That's just a plain fact. But lots of people are assholes and he paid me well for the one time and I blinded him with Rumi. Corrigan's brother had some serious scratch in his pockets—he was a bartender or something. I looked down and I remember thinking, There's my dark tit in Corrigan's brother's hand.

—

I never saw Corrigan naked, but I imagine he was swell even if his brother was a Tweety Bird.

—

First time we saw Corrigan, we just flat-out knew he was undercover. They got Irishes undercover. Most of the cops're Irish—guys going a little to fat, with bad teeth but still a sense of making the world funny.

One day Corrigan's van was filthy and Angie wrote with her finger in the dirt: DON'T YOU WISH YOUR WIFE WAS THIS FILTHY? That had us crying we laughed so hard. Corrie didn't notice it. Then Angie wrote a smiley face and TURN ME OVER on the other side. He was scooting around the Bronx with that crazy shit written on his van and he never even saw it. He was in a world of his own, Corrie. Angie went up to him at the end of the week and showed him the words. He got all blushy like the Irish guys do and he began stammering.

"But I don't understand—I haven't got a wife," he said to Angie.

We never laughed so much since Christ left Cincinnati.

—

Every day we were hanging out with him, pleading with him to arrest us. And he was going: "Girls, girls, girls, please." The more we got to hugging on him the more he'd go, "Girls, girls, come on, now, girls."

Once, Angie's daddy broke us up and grabbed Corrie by the scruff of the neck and told him where he should go. He put a knife up under Corrie's neck. Corrie just stared at him. His eyes were big but it was like he didn't have no fear. We were like: "Yo, man, just leave." Angie's daddy flicked the knife and Corrie walked away with blood coming down his black shirt.

A couple of days later he was down again, bringing us coffees. He had a little bandage on his neck. We were like: "Yo, Corrie, you should get-the-fuck, you'll get tossed." He shrugged, said he'd be all right. Down came Angie's daddy and Jazzlyn's daddy and Suchie's daddy, all at once, like the Three Wise Men. I saw Corrie's face go white. I never seen him go that white before. He was worse'n chalk.

He held his hands up and said: "Hey, man, I'm just giving them coffee."

And Angie's daddy stepped forward. He said: "Yeah well, I'm just giving you the cream."

—

Corrie got the daylight kicked out of him seven ways to Sunday, I don't know how many times. That shit hurt. It hurt bad. Even Angie was hanging off her daddy's back, trying to scratch his eyes out, but we couldn't stop him. Still Corrie came back, day after day. Got to where the daddies actually respected him for it. Corrie never once called the cops, or the Guards, that's what he called them, that was his Irish word for the police. He said: "I'm not calling the Guards." Still the daddies knocked the shit out of him every now and then, just to keep him in line.

We found out later he was a priest. Not really a priest, but one of those guys who lived somewhere because he thought that he should, like he had a duty thing, morals, some sort of shit like that, a monk, with vows and shit, and that chastity stuff.

—

They say boys always want to be the first with girls, and girls always want to be the last with boys. But with Corrie all of us wanted to be the first. Jazz said, "I had Corrie last night, he was super-delicious, he was glad I was his first." And then Angie'd go: "Bullshit, I had that motherfucker for lunch, I ate him whole." And then Suchie'd go: "Shit, y'all, I spread him on my pancakes and sucked him down with coffee."

Anyone could hear us laughing, miles away.

—

He had a birthday once, I think he was thirty-one, he was just a kid, and I bought him a cake and all of us ate it together out under the Deegan. It was covered in cherries, musta been a million and six cherries on it, and Corrie didn't even get the joke, we were popping cherries in his mouth left and center and he's going, *Girls, girls please, I'll have to call the Guards.*

We almost wet ourselves laughing.

He cut up the cake and gave a piece out to everyone. He took the last piece for himself. I held a cherry over his mouth and got him to try to bite on it. I kept moving it away while he kept trying to snag it. He was stepping down the street after me. I had my swimsuit on. We musta looked a pair, Corrie and me, cherry juice all over his face.

Don't let no one tell you that it's all shit and grime and honkypox on the stroll. It's that, all right, sometimes, sure, but it's funny sometimes too. Sometimes you just hang a cherry out in front of a man. Sometimes you got to do it, sometimes, for putting a smile on your face.

When Corrie laughed he had a face that creased up deep.

—

"Say fuhgeddboudit, Corrie."

"Fergetaboutit."

"No no no, say fuhgeddboudit."

"Fergedboutit."

"Oh, man, fuhgeddboudit!"

"Okay, Tillie," he said, "I'll fuh-get-bout-it."

—

The only whitey I ever woulda slept with—genuine—was Corrigan. No bullshit. He used to tell me I was too good for him. He said I'd chuckle at his best and whistle for more. Said I was way too pretty for a guy like him. Corrigan was a stone-cold stud. I woulda married him. I woulda had him talk to me in his accent all the time. I woulda taken him upstate and cooked him a big meal with corn beef and cabbage and made him feel like he was the only whitey on earth. I woulda kissed his ear if he gave me a chance. I woulda spilled my love right down into him. Him and the Sherry-Netherlands guy. They were fine.

We filled his trash can seven, eight, nine times a day. That was nasty. Even Angie thought it was nasty and she was the nastiest of all of us—she left her tampons in there. I mean, nasty. I can't believe Corrie used to see that stuff and he never once gave us shit about it, just dumped it out and went on his way. A priest! A monk! The tinkling shop!

And those sandals! Man! We'd hear the slap of him coming.

—

He said to me once that most of the time people use the word *love* as just another way to show off they're hungry. The way he said it went something like: *Glorify their appetites.*

He said it just like that, but in his delicious accent. I could've eaten everything Corrie said, I coulda just gobbled it all down. He said, "Here's a coffee, Tillie," and I thought it was the nicest thing I ever heard. I went weak at the knees. He he was like a Motown whitey.

—

Jazzlyn used to say she loved him like chocolate.

—

It's been a long time since that Lara girl came to visit, maybe ten or thirteen days. She said she'd bring the babies. She promised. You get used to people, but. They always promise. Even Corrie made promises. The drawbridge shit and all.

—

A funny-ass thing happened with Corrie once. I'll never forget. It's the only time he ever brought us a trick to look after. Along he comes, real late one night, opens the back of the van and lifts out an old guy in a wheelchair. Corrie's all cagey and all. I mean, he's a priest or whatever and he's bringing us a trick! He's looking over his shoulder. He's worried. Feeling guilty, maybe. I said: "Hey, Daddy-o," and his face goes white, so I stayed quiet and didn't say nothing. Corrie's coughing into his fist and all. Turns out it's the old guy's birthday and he's been pleading and pleading and pleading with Corrie to take him out. Says he hasn't been with a woman since the Great Depression, which is like eight hundred million years ago. And the old guy's real abusive, calling Corrie all sorts of names 'n' all. But it just rolls off o' Corrie. He shrugs his shoulders and pulls the hand brake on the chair and leaves Methuselah there on the sidewalk.

"It's not my call, but Albee here wants servicing."

"I told ya not to tell 'em my name," shouts the old guy.

"Shut up," says Corrie, and he walks away.

Then he turns around once more and looks at Angie and says: "Just don't rob him, please."

"Me, dice him?" says Angie, with her eyes all starry and shit.

Corrie raises his eyes to heaven and shakes his head.

"Promise me," he says, and then he slams the door of his brown van and sits inside, waiting.

Corrie turns on the radio real loud.

We get down to work. It turns out Methuselah's got enough scratch to keep us all going awhile. He musta been saving for years. We decide to give him a party. So we lift him into the back of a fruit-and-vegetable truck and make sure his brake is on, and we take our clothes off and get to dancing. Shaking it in his face. Rubbing him up and down. Jazzlyn's jumping up and down on the fruit crates. And we're all naked, playing the Hike! game with bits of lettuce and tomatoes. It's hilarious.

The funny thing is, the old guy, he's about nineteen hundred years old at least, just closes his eyes and sits back against his wheelchair, like he's breathing us all in, a little smile on his face. We offer him whatever he wants, but he just keeps his eyes closed, like he's remembering something, and he's got that grin on his mug the whole time, he's in heaven. Eyes closed and nostrils flaring. He's like one of those guys who likes just to smell everything. He says to us something about being hungry and how he met his wife when he was hungry and then they crossed some border together into Austria and then she died.

He had a voice like Uri Geller. Most of the time when tricks say anything, we just say, "Ah-ha," like we understand them perfectly. He had tears rolling down his face, half of them were tears of joy, and half of them were something else, I don't know what. Angie shoved her titties in his face and shouted: "Bend this spoon, motherfucker."

Some girls like old guys because they don't want a lot. Angie don't mind them. But, me, I hate old guys, especially when they got their shirts off. They got these little droopy tits like icing off the side of a cake. But, hey, he was paying us and we kept telling him how good he looked. He was getting all red in the face.

Angie was shouting, "Don't give him a heart attack, girls—I hate the emergency ward!"

He let the brake on his wheelchair go and when we were done he paid us all twice as much as we asked. We lifted him out the truck and this old guy started looking for Corrie: "Where's that pussy asshole?"

Angie said: "Who you calling a pussy, you pussy-ass, shrivel-dick?"

Corrie switched off the radio and came out of his brown van, where he sat waiting, and said thank you to us all, and just pushed that old guy back to his van. Funny thing is, there was a piece of lettuce stuck to the old guy's wheelchair, inside the wheel. Corrie pushed him to the truck and the piece of lettuce went round and round and round.

Corrie was like: "Remind me never to eat salad, ever ever ever again."

That cracked us up. That was one of the best nights we ever had under the Deegan. I suppose Corrie was helping us out. That old guy was made of cash. He smelled a bit bad, but he was worth it.

———

Every time I get a piece of lettuce in the prison chow now, I just have to laugh.

———

The boss matron likes me. She had me in her office. She said: "Open your jumpsuit, Henderson." I opened it up and let my tits hang out. She just sat in her chair and didn't move, just closed her eyes and started breathing heavy. Then after a minute she said: "Dismissed."

———

The femmes have a different shower time than the butches. That don't make no difference. There's all sorts of crazy shit goes on in the showers. I thought I'd seen it all, but sometimes it looks like a massage salon. Someone brought in butter once from the kitchen. They had it already melted down. The matrons with their nightsticks love getting off on it. It's illegal but sometimes they bring the guards in from the male prison. I think I'd jerk them off just for a pack of cigarettes. You can hear the oohs and ahhs when they come around. But they don't fuck or rape us. They stop at that. They just stare and get off on it, like the boss matron.

I had a British trick once, and he called it *getting me jollies.* "Hey, luv, any chance of gettin' me jollies?" I like that. I'm gonna get my jollies. I'm gonna hang myself from the pipes in the shower room and then I'll get my jollies.

Watch me dance from the jolly pipe.

———

Once I wrote Corrie a letter and left it in his bathroom. I said: *I really dig you, John Andrew.* That was the only time I ever called him by his real name. He told it to me and said it was a secret. He said he didn't like the name—he was named after his father, who was an Irish asshole. "Read the note, Corrie," I said. He opened it up. He blushed. It was the cutest thing, him blushing. I wanted to pinch his cheeks.

He said, "Thanks," but it sounded like *Tanks,* and he said something about how he had to get himself good with God, but he liked me, he said, he really did, but really he had something going with God. He said it like he and God were having a boxing match. I said I'd stand ringside. He touched my wrist and said, "Tillie, you're a riot."

—

Where are my babies? One thing I know, I used to sugar them up way too much. Eighteen months old and they were already sucking on lollipops. That's a bad grandmother, you ask me. They're gonna have bad teeth. I'm gonna see them in heaven and they're gonna be wearing braces.

—

First time I ever turned a trick I went and bought myself a supermarket cake. Big white one with frosting. I stuck my finger into it and licked. I could smell the man on my finger.

When I first sent Jazzlyn out, I bought her a supermarket cake too. Foodland special. Just for her, to make her feel better. It was half eaten by the time she came back. She stood there in the middle of the room, tears in her eyes: "You ate my goddamn cake, Tillie."

And I was sitting there with icing all over my face, going, "No I didn't, Jazz, not me, no way."

—

Corrie was always talking that shit about getting her a castle and all. If I had a castle I'd let down the drawbridge and allow everyone to leave. I broke down at the funeral. I shoulda kept my 'posure, but I didn't. The babies weren't there. Why weren't the girls there? I woulda killed to see them. That's all I wanted to see. Someone said they were being looked after by social services, but someone else said that it'd be all right, they said the babies got a good babysitter.

That was always the hardest thing. Getting a babysitter so we could hit the stroll. Sometimes it was Jean and sometimes it was Mandy and sometimes Latisha, but the best of them all woulda been nobody, I know that.

I shoulda just stayed at home and ate all the supermarket cakes until I couldn't even get outta the chair.

—

I don't know who God is but if I meet Him anytime soon I'm going to get Him in the corner until He tells me the truth.

I'm going to slap Him stupid and push Him around until He can't run away. Until He's looking up at me and then I'll get Him to tell me why He done what He done to me and what He done to Corrie and why do all the good ones die and where is Jazzlyn now and why she ended up there and how He allowed me to do what I done to her.

He's going to come along on His pretty white cloud with all His pretty little angels flapping their pretty white wings and I'm gonna out and say it formal: Why the fuck did you let me do it, God?

And He's gonna drop His eyes and look to the ground and answer me. And if He says Jazz ain't in heaven, if He says she didn't make it through, He's gonna get himself an ass-kicking. That's what He's gonna get.

An ass-kicking like none He ever got before.

—

I ain't gonna whine either before or after I do it. Well, I guess there'd be no whining *after* anyway. If you think of the world without people it's about the most perfect thing there ever is. It's all balanced and shit. But then come the people, and they fuck it up. It's like you got Aretha Franklin in your bedroom and she's just giving it her all, she's singing just for you, she's on fire, this is a special request for Tillie H., and then all of a sudden out pops Barry Manilow from behind the curtains.

At the end of the world they're gonna have cockroaches and Barry Manilow records, that's what Jazzlyn said. She cracked me up too, my Jazz.

—

It weren't my fault. Peaches from C-49 came at me with a piece of lead pipe. She ended up in the infirmary with fifteen stitches across her back. People think I'm easy 'cause I'm cute.

If you don't want it to rain, don't fuck with the clouds over Tillie H. I just hit her one good whack. It weren't my fault. I didn't want to juice her up, that was all. I'm not into that. Simple fact is she needed an ass-kicking.

—

The boss matron was up in my face. She said I was gonna have to go upstate. She said: "We're shipping you upstate for the last few months of your sentence." I was like: "What the fuck?" She said: "You heard me, Henderson, no cursing in this office." I said: "I'll take it all off for you, boss, every stitch." She shouted: "How dare you! Don't insult me! That's disgusting." I said: "Please don't send me upstate. I want to see my babies." She said nothing and I got nervous and said something not too polite again. She said, "Get the hell out of here."

I went around the side of her desk. I was just going to open my jumpsuit to pleasure her, but she hit the panic button. In came the screws. I didn't mean to do what I done, I didn't mean to get her in the face, I just lashed out with my foot. I knocked her front tooth out. I guess it don't matter. I'm going upstate now for sure. I'm on the pony express.

The boss matron didn't even beat the shit out of me. She lay there on the floor a moment and I swear she almost smiled, and then she said: "I've got something real nice for you, Henderson." They put me in cuffs and they arraigned me, all formal and everything. They put me in the van and booked me and brought me to Queens court.

I pleaded guilty to assault and they gave me eighteen months more. That's near two years all together with time served. The defense lawyer told me it was a good deal, I coulda gotten three, four, five years, even seven. He said, "Honey, take it." I hate lawyers. He was the sort who walks around with a stick so far up his ass you could've waved a flag under his nose. Said he pleaded with the judge and all. He said to the judge: "It's just one tragedy after another, Your Honor."

I told him the only tragedy is that I don't see my babies nowhere. How come my babies weren't in the courtroom? That's what I wanted to know. I shouted it out. "How come they ain't here?"

I was hoping somebody would be there, that Lara girl or somebody, but there was nobody at all.

The judge, he was black this time, he must've gone to Harvard or something. I thought he woulda understood, but niggers can be worse on niggers sometimes. I said to him, "Your Honor, can you get me my babies? I just wanna see them once." He shrugged and said the babies were in a good place. He never once looked me in the face. He said: "Describe to me exactly what happened." And I said: "What happened is that I had a baby and then she had some babies of her own." And he said, "No, no, no—with the assault." And I said, "Oh, who the fuck cares a flying fuck about the fucking assault, god fucking damn it fuck me fuck you and fuck your wife." Then my lawyer shut me up. The judge looked down over his glasses at me and sighed. He said something about Booker T. Washington, but I wasn't listening too good. Finally, he said there was a specific request from a warden to put me in a penitentiary upstate. He said the word *penitentiary* like he was lording it over me. I said to him: "And fuck your parrot too, asshole."

He snapped his gavel on the bench and that was that.

—

I tried to scratch their eyes out. They had to put me in restraint and bring me to the hospital wing. Then on the bus upstate they had to restrain me again. Even worse, they didn't tell me they was going to move me from New York. I kept shouting out for the babies. Upstate woulda been okay, but Connecticut? I'm no country girl. They had a shrink meet me and then they gave me a yellow jumpsuit. You'd need a shrink for sure if you wanted to wear a yellow jumpsuit.

I was brought into an office and I told the shrink that I was real happy to be in suburban Connecticut. Real real happy. I said if she gave me a knife I'd show her just how happy. I'd trace it out on my wrist.

"Lock her up," she said.

—

They give me pills. Orange ones. They watch them go down. Sometimes I can fake it and tuck one of them in the hole in the back of my teeth. Someday I'm going to take them all together like one great big delicious orange, and then I'll reach up to the jolly pipe and say sayonara.

—

I don't even know my cell mate's name. She's fat and wears green socks. I told her I'm gonna hang myself and all about the jolly pipe and she said, "Oh." Then a few minutes later she said, "When?"

—

I guess that white woman, Lara, worked things out, or someone did, somehow, somewhere. I went down to the waiting room. The babies! The babies! The babies!

They were sitting there on the knee of a big black woman, long white gloves on her and a fancy red handbag, looking for all the world that she just woke up from the Lord's bed.

Down I ran straight to the glass wall and stuck my hands in the bottom opening.

"Babies!" I said. "Little Jazzlyn! Janice!"

They didn't know me. They were sitting on that woman's lap, sucking their thumbs and looking over her shoulder. Like to broke my heart. They kept snuggling into her bosom, smiling. I kept saying, "Come to Grandma, come to Grandma, let me touch your hands." That's all you can do through the bottom of the glass—they got a few inches and you can touch someone's hands. It's cruel. I just wanted to hug on them. Still they wouldn't budge—maybe it was the prison duds, I don't know. The woman had a southern accent, but I knew her face from the projects, I seen her before. I always thought she was a square, used to stand in the elevator and turn away. She said she was rightly conflicted whether she should bring the babies in or not, but she heard I really wanted to see them and they were living in Poughkeepsie now with a nice house and a nice fence, and it wasn't too far away. She'd been fostering them awhile now, she got them through the Bureau of Child Welfare, they had to spend a few days in a Seaman's home or something like that, but now they were being well looked after, she told me, don't you worry.

"Come to Grandma," I said again.

Little Jazzlyn turned her face into the woman's shoulder. Janice was sucking on her thumb. I noticed their necks were scrubbed clean. Their fingernails too were all perfect and round.

"Sorry," she said, "I guess they're just feeling shy."

"They look good," I said.

"They're eating healthy."

"Don't feed them too much shit," I said.

She looked at me a second from under her eyebrows, but she was cool, she was. She wasn't about to say nothing about me cursing. I liked her for that. She wasn't a stuck-up, she wasn't making judgments.

We were silent awhile and then she said that the girls have got a nice room in a little house on a quiet street, much quieter than the projects, she painted the baseboards for them, they got wallpaper with umbrellas on it.

"What color?"

"Red," she said.

"Good," I said, because I didn't want them having no pink parasols. "Come to Tillie and touch my hands," I said again, but the babies never once got off her lap. I begged and begged but the more I begged, the more they turned towards her. I guess maybe the prison frightened them, the guards and all.

The woman gave a smile that pinched her face some and said it was time for them to get going. I wasn't sure if I hated her or not. Sometimes my mind sways between good and bad. I wanted to lean across and smash the glass and grab her nappy hair, but then again, she was looking after my babies, they weren't in some horrible orphanage, starving, and I could've kissed her for not giving them too many lollipops and rotting their teeth.

When the bell rang she held the babies across to kiss me, against the glass. I don't think I'll ever forget the smell of them coming in through the little slot at the bottom of the glass, so delicious. I poked my little finger through and little Janice touched it. It was like magic. I put my face against the glass again. They smelled like real babies, like powder and milk and all.

When I was walking back out the courtyard to the pen I felt like someone came and carved my heart out, then put it walking in front of me. That's what I thought—there's my heart going right out in front of me, all on its own, slick with blood.

—

I cried all night. I ain't ashamed. I don't want them working no stroll. Why did I do what I done to Jazzlyn? That's the thing I'd like to know, Why did I do what I done?

—

What I hated the most: standing under the Deegan among all those splotches of pigeon shit on the ground. Just looking down and seeing them like they was my carpet. I flat-out hated that. I don't want the babies to see that.

—

Corrie said there are a thousand reasons to live this life, each one of them fine, but I guess it didn't do him no good now, did it?

—

My cell mate ratted me out. Said she was worried about me. But I don't need no prison-house shrink just to tell me that I ain't gonna be alive if I leave my feet dangling in the air. They pay her for that shit? I missed my calling. I coulda been a millionaire.

Here comes Tillie Henderson with the shrink hat on. You been a bad mother, Tillie, and you're a shitass grandmother. Your own mother was shitty too. Now give me a hundred bucks, thank you, very good, next in line please, no I don't take checks, cash only, please.

—

You're manic-depressive and you're manic-depressive too and you, you're definitely manic-depressive, girl. And you over there in the corner, you're just plain fucking depressive.

—

I'd like to have a parasol the day I go. I'll hang myself from the jolly pipes and look all pretty underneath.

I'll do it for the girls. They don't need no one like me. They don't need to be out on the stroll. They're better off this way.

Jolly pipe, here I come.

I'll look like Mary Poppins swinging underneath.

—

They got these religious meetings take place in the Gatehouse. I went this morning. I was talking to the chaplain about Rumi and shit, but he's like, "That's not spiritual, that's poetry." Fuck God. Fuck Him. Fuck Him sideways and backwards and any which way. He ain't coming for me. There ain't no burning bushes and there ain't no pillars of light. Don't talk to me about light. It ain't nothing more than a glow at the end of a street lamp.

Sorry, Corrie, but God is due His ass-kicking.

—

One of the last things I heard Jazz do, she screamed and dropped the
keyring out the door of the paddy wagon. Clink it went on the ground and
we saw Corrigan coming out to the street with a muscle in his step. He
was red in the face. Screaming at the cops. Life was pretty good then. I'd
have to say that's one of the good moments—ain't that strange? I remember it like yesterday, getting arrested.

—

There ain't no such thing as getting home. That's the law of living far as
I can see. I bet they don't have no Sherry-Netherlands in heaven. The
Sherry-Never-lands.

—

I gave Jazzlyn a bath once. She was just a few weeks old. Skin shining. I
looked at her and thought she gave birth to the word *beautiful*. I wrapped
her in a towel and promised her she'd never go on the stroll.
    Sometimes I want to stab my heart with a stiletto. I used to watch
men with her when she was all growed up. And I'd say to myself, Hey
that's my daughter you're fucking. That's my little girl you're pulling into
the front seat. That's my blood.
    I was a junkie then. I guess I always have been. That ain't no excuse.
    I don't know if the world'll ever forgive me for the bad I slung her way.
I ain't gonna sling it the way of the babies, not me.

—

This is the house that Horse built.

—

I'd say good-bye, except I don't know who to say it to. I ain't whining.
That's just the fuck-off truth. God is due His ass-kicking.
    Here I come, Jazzlyn, it's me.
    I got a knuckle-duster in my sock.

PHOTO: © FERNANDO YUNQUÉ MARCANO

THE RINGING GROOVES OF CHANGE

Before the walk, he would go to Washington Square Park to perform. It marked the beginning of the city's dangerous side. He wanted the noise, to build up some tension in his body, to be wholly in touch with the filth and the roar. He secured his wire from the ribbed edge of a light pole to another. He performed for the tourists, tiptoeing along in his black silk hat. Pure theater. The sway and fake fall. Defying gravity. He could lean over at an angle and still bring himself back to standing. He balanced an umbrella on his nose. Flipped a coin in the air from his toe: it landed perfectly on the crown of his head. Forward and backward somersaults. Handstands. He juggled pins and balls and flaming torches. He invented a game with a Slinky—it looked like the metal toy was unwrapping itself along his body. The tourists lapped it up. They threw money in a hat for him. Most of the time it was nickels and dimes, but sometimes he'd get a dollar, or even five. For ten dollars he would jump to the ground, doff his hat, bow, throw a backflip.

On the first day the dealers and junkies hovered near his show. They could see how much he was making. He stuffed it all in the pockets of his flares, but he knew they'd roll him for it. For his final trick he scooped up the last of his money, put the hat on his head, rode a unicycle along the rope, then simply pedaled off the ten-foot drop, onto the ground and away through the Square, down Washington Place. He waved over his shoulder. He came back the next day for his rope—but the dealers liked the trick enough that they let him stay, and the tourists he brought were easy hits.

He rented a cold-water apartment on St. Marks Place. One night he strung a simple rope across from his bedroom to the fire escape of a Japanese woman opposite: she had lit candles on the ironwork for him. He stayed eight hours, and when he emerged he found that some kids had tossed shoes up on the wire, a city custom, the laces tied together. He crawled out on the wire, which had grown loose and dangerous, but was still taut enough to hold him, and walked back in through his window. He saw immediately that the place had been ransacked. Everything. Even his clothes. All the money was gone from the pockets of his pants too. He never saw the Japanese woman again: when he looked across the candles were gone. Nobody had ever stolen from him before.

This was the city he had crawled into—he was surprised to find that there were edges beneath his own edge.

Sometimes he would get hired to go to parties. He needed the money. There were so many expenses and his savings had been plundered. The wire itself would cost a thousand dollars. And then there were the winches, the false I.D.'s, the balancing pole, the elaborate ploys to get it all up to the roof. He'd do anything to get the money together, but the parties were awful. He was hired as a magician, but he told the hosts that he couldn't guarantee that he'd do anything at all. They had to pay him, but still he might just sit there all night. The tension worked. He became a party regular. He bought a tuxedo and a bow tie and a cummerbund.

He'd introduce himself as a Belgian arms dealer, or an appraiser from Sotheby's, or a jockey who'd ridden in the Kentucky Derby. He felt comfortable in the roles. The only place he was entirely himself, anyway, was high on the wire. He could pull a long string of asparagus from his neighbor's napkin. He'd find a wine cork behind the ear of a host, or tug an endless unfolding scarf from a man's breast pocket. In the middle of dessert he might spin a fork in the air and have it land on his nose. Or he'd teeter backward on his chair until he was sitting on only one leg, pretending he was so drunk that he'd hit a nirvana of balance. The partygoers were thrilled. Whispers would go around the tables. Women would approach him in a cleavage lean. Men would slyly touch his knee. He would vanish from the parties out a window, or the back door, or disguised as a caterer, a tray of uneaten hors d'oeuvres above his head.

At a party at 1040 Fifth Avenue he announced, at the beginning of dinner, that he would, by the end of the evening, tell the exact birth dates of every single man in the room. The guests were enthralled. One lady who wore a sparkling tiara leaned right into him. *So, why not the women as well?* He pulled away from her. *Because it's impolite to tell the age of a lady.* He already had half the room charmed. He said nothing more the whole night: not a single word. *Come on,* the men said, *tell us our age.* He stared at the guests, switched seats, examined the men carefully, even running his fingers along their hairlines. He frowned and shook his head, as if baffled. When the sorbet came out, he climbed wearily into the middle of the table, pointed at each guest one by one and reeled off the birth dates of all but one in the room. January 29, 1947. November 16, 1898. July 7, 1903. March 15, 1937. September 5, 1940. July 2, 1935.

The women applauded and the men sat, stunned.

The one man who hadn't been pegged sat back smugly in his chair and said, *Yes, but what about me?* The tightrope walker whisked his hand through the air: *Nobody cares when you were born.*

The room erupted in laughter and the walker leaned over the women at the table and, one by one, he removed their husbands' driver's licenses, from their handbags, from their dinner napkins, from under their plates, even one from between her breasts. On each license, the exact birth date. The one man who hadn't been pegged leaned back in his chair and announced to the table that he'd never carried his wallet, never would: he'd never be caught. Silence. The tightrope walker got down from the table, pulled his scarf around his neck, and said to the man as he waved from the dining room door: *February 28, 1935.*

A flush went to the man's cheeks as the table applauded, and the man's wife gave a half-wink to the tightrope walker as he ghosted out the door.

———

THERE WAS AN ARROGANCE in it, he knew, but on the wire the arrogance became survival. It was the only time he could lose himself completely. He thought of himself sometimes as a man who wanted to hate himself. Get rid of this foot. This toe. This calf. Find the place of immobility. So much of it was about the old cure of forgetting. To become anonymous to himself, have his own body absorb him. And yet there were overlapping realities: he also wanted his mind to be in that place where his body was at ease.

It was so much like having sex with the wind. It complicated things and blew away and softly separated and slid back around him. The wire was about pain too: it would always be there, jutting into his feet, the weight of the bar, the dryness at his throat, the throb of his arms, but the joy was losing the pain so that it no longer mattered. So too with his breathing. He wanted his breath to enter the wire so that he was nothing. This sense of losing himself. Every nerve. Every cuticle. He hit it on the towers. The logic became unfixed. It was the point where there was no time. The wind was blowing and his body could have experienced it years in advance.

He was deep into his walk when the police helicopter came. Another small gnat in the air, but it didn't faze him. Together both helicopters sounded like ligaments clicking. He was quite sure they would not be so stupid as to try to approach. It amazed him how sirens could overtake all other sounds; they seemed to drain upward. And there were dozens of cops out on the roof now, screaming at him, running to and fro. One of them was leaning out from the side of the columns on the south tower, held by a blue harness, his hat off, his body leaning outward, calling him a motherfucker, that he better get off the motherfucking wire right motherfucking now before he sent the motherfucking helicopter in to pluck him from the motherfucking cable, you hear me, motherfucker, right motherfucking now!—and the walker thought, What strange language. He grinned and turned on the wire and there were cops on the opposite side too, these ones quieter, leaning into walkie-talkies, and he was sure he could hear the crackle of them, and he didn't want to taunt them but he wanted to remain: he might never walk like this again.

The shouting, the sirens, the dull sounds of the city. He let them become a white hum. He went for his last silence and he found it: just stood there, in the precise middle of the wire, one hundred feet from each tower, eyes closed, body still, wire gone. He took the air of the city into his lungs.

Someone on a megaphone was screaming at him now: "We'll send in the helicopter, we're sending the 'copter. Get off!"

The walker smiled.

"Get off now!"

He wondered if that was what the moment of death was about, the noise of the world and then the ease away from it.

He realized that he had thought only about the first step, never imagined the last. He needed a flourish. He turned toward the megaphone and waited a moment. He dropped his head as if in agreement. Yes, he was coming in. He lifted his leg. The dark form of his body showing to the people below. Leg held high for drama. Placed the side of his foot on the wire. The duck walk. And then the next foot and the next and then the next until it was pure machinery and then he ran—as quickly as he had ever run a highwire—using the center soles of his feet for grip, toes sideways, the balancing bar held far out in front of him, from the middle of the wire to the ledge.

The cop had to step back to grab him. The walker ran into his arms.

"Motherfucker," said the cop, but with a grin.

For years afterward he'd still be up there: slippered, dark-footed, agile. It would happen at odd moments, driving along the highway, or shuttering down the cabin window with boards before a storm, or walking in the fields of long grass around the shrinking meadow in Montana. In midair again, the cable taut through his toe. Cross-weaved by the wind. A sense of sudden height. The city beneath him. He could be in any mood or any place and, unbidden, it returned. He might simply be taking a nail from his carpenter's belt in order to hammer it into a piece of wood, or leaning across to open a car's glove compartment, or turning a glass under a stream of water, or performing a card trick at a party of friends, and all of a sudden his body would be drained of everything else but the bloodrush of a single stride. It was like some photograph his body had taken, and the album had been slid out again under his eyes, then yanked away. Sometimes it was the width of the city he saw, the alleyways of light, the harpsichord of the Brooklyn Bridge, the flat gray bowl of smoke over New Jersey, the quick interruption of a pigeon making flight look easy, the taxis below. He never saw himself in any danger or extremity, so he didn't return to the moment he lay down on the cable, or when he hopped, or half ran across from the south to the north tower. Rather it was the ordinary steps that revisited him, the ones done without flash. They were the ones that seemed entirely true, that didn't flinch in his memory.

Afterward, he was immediately thirsty. All he wanted was water and for them to unsnap the wire: it was dangerous to leave it there. He said: "You must take down the wire." They thought he was joking. They had no clue. It could tighten in the wind, snap, take off a man's head. They pushed him toward the center of the roof. "Please," he begged. He saw a man step toward the winch to loosen it, to take off the tension. He felt an enormous relief and tiredness sweep over him, sliding into his life again.

When he emerged from the towers, handcuffed, the onlookers cheered. He was flanked by cops, reporters, cameras, men in serious suits. The flashbulbs went off.

He had picked up a paper clip in the World Trade Center's station command and it was easy enough to open the cuffs: they clicked with a little lateral pressure. He shook out his hand as he walked, then raised it to a cheer. Before the cops even realized what he had done, he snapped the handcuffs shut again, behind his back.

"Smart-ass," said the cop, a sergeant, pocketing the paper clip. But there was admiration in the sergeant's voice: the paper clip would be a story forever.

The walker passed on through the gauntlet across the plaza. The squad car was waiting at the end of the steps. It was strange to revisit the world again: the slap of footsteps, the call of the hot-dog man, the sound of a pay phone ringing in the distance.

He stopped and turned to look at the towers. He could still make out the tightrope: it was being hauled in, slowly, carefully, attached to a chain, to a rope, to a fishing line. It was like watching a child's Etch A Sketch as the sky shook itself out: the line kept disappearing pixel by pixel. Eventually there would be nothing left there at all, just the breeze.

They were crowding him, shouting for his name, for his reasons, for his autograph. He stayed still, looking upward, wondering how the onlookers had seen it: what line of sky had been interrupted for them. A journalist in a flat white hat shouted, "Why?" But the word didn't come into it for him. He didn't like the idea of why. The towers were there. That was enough. He wanted to ask the reporter why he was asking him why. A children's rhyme slipped through his mind, a riffle of whys, good-bye, good-bye, good-bye.

He felt a gentle shove on his back and a pull on his arm. He looked away from the towers and was guided toward the car. The cop put his hand on the top of his head: "In you go, buddy." He was guided down onto the hard leather seats, handcuffs on.

The photographers put their lenses against the car window. An eruption of light against the glass. It briefly blinded him. He turned to face the other side of the car. More cameras. He stared ahead.

The sirens were turned on.

All was red and blue and wail.

BOOK THREE

PART OF THE PARTS

THE THEATER BEGAN SHORTLY AFTER LUNCH. His fellow judges and court officers and reporters and even the stenographers were already talking about it as if it were another of those things that just happened in the city. One of those out-of-the-ordinary days that made sense of the slew of ordinary days. New York had a way of doing that. Every now and then the city shook its soul out. It assailed you with an image, or a day, or a crime, or a terror, or a beauty so difficult to wrap your mind around that you had to shake your head in disbelief.

He had a theory about it. It happened, and re-happened, because it was a city uninterested in history. Strange things occurred precisely because there was no necessary regard for the past. The city lived in a sort of everyday present. It had no need to believe in itself as a London, or an Athens, or even a signifier of the New World, like a Sydney, or a Los Angeles. No, the city couldn't care less about where it stood. He had seen a T-shirt once that said: NEW YORK FUCKIN' CITY. As if it were the only place that ever existed and the only one that ever would.

New York kept going forward precisely because it didn't give a good goddamn about what it had left behind. It was like the city that Lot left, and it would dissolve if it ever began looking backward over its own shoulder. Two pillars of salt. Long Island and New Jersey.

He had said to his wife many times that the past disappeared in the city. It was why there weren't many monuments around. It wasn't like London, where every corner had a historical figure carved out of stone, a war memorial here, a leader's bust there. He could only really pinpoint a dozen true statues around New York City—most of them in Central Park, along the Literary Walk, and who in the world went to Central Park these days anyway? A man would need a phalanx of tanks just to pass Sir Walter Scott. On other famous street corners, Broadway or Wall Street or around Gracie Square, nobody felt a need to lay claim to history. Why bother? You couldn't eat a statue. You couldn't screw a monument. You couldn't wring a million dollars out of a piece of brass.

Even down here, on Centre Street, they didn't have many public backslaps to themselves. No Lady Justice in a blindfold. No Supreme Thinkers with their robes wrapped around themselves. No Hear No Evil, See No Evil, Speak No Evil carved into the upper granite columns of the criminal courts.

Which was one of the things that made Judge Soderberg think that the tightrope walker was such a stroke of genius. A monument in himself. He had made himself into a statue, but a perfect New York one, a temporary one, up in the air, high above the city. A statue that had no regard for the past. He had gone to the World Trade Center and had strung his rope across the biggest towers in the world. The Twin Towers. Of all places. So brash. So glassy. So forward-looking. Sure, the Rockefellers had knocked down a few Greek revival homes and a few classic brownstones to make way for the towers—which had annoyed Claire when she read about it—but mostly it had been electronics stores and cheap auction houses where men with quick tongues had sold everything useless under the sun, carrot peelers and radio flashlights and musical snow globes. In place of the shysters, the Port Authority had built two towering beacons high in the clouds. The glass reflected the sky, the night, the colors: progress, beauty, capitalism.

Soderberg wasn't one to sit around and decry what used to be. The city was bigger than its buildings, bigger than its inhabitants too. It had its own nuances. It accepted whatever came its way, the crime and the violence and the little shocks of good that crawled out from underneath the everyday.

He figured that the tightrope walker must have thought it over quite

a bit beforehand. It wasn't just an offhand walk. He was making a statement with his body, and if he fell, well, he fell—but if he survived he
would become a monument, not carved in stone or encased in brass, but
one of those New York monuments that made you say: *Can you believe it?*
With an expletive. There would always be an expletive in a New York sentence. Even from a judge. Soderberg was not fond of bad language, but he
knew its value at the right time. A man on a tightrope, a hundred and ten
stories in the air, can you possibly fucking believe it?

—

SODERBERG HIMSELF HAD just missed the walk. It upset him to think
so, but he had, just by minutes, seconds, even. He had taken a cab all the
way downtown. The driver was a sullen black man blaring music through
the speakers. A smell of marijuana in the cab. Sickening, really, the way
you couldn't get a clean, decent ride anymore. Rastafarian music from
the eight-track. The driver dropped him off at the rear of 100 Centre
Street. He walked past the D.A.'s office, stopped at the locked metal-
framed door on the side, an entrance only the judges used, their one concession, designed so they wouldn't have to mix with the visitors at the
front. It wasn't so much a furtive doorway, or even a privileged thing.
They needed their own entrance, just in case some idiot decided to take
matters into his own hands. Still, it brightened him: a secret passage into
the house of justice.

    At the door he took a quick look over his shoulder. In the upper
reaches of the next-door building he noticed a few people leaning out of
the windows, looking westward, pointing, but he ignored them, assumed
it was a car crash or another morning altercation. He unlocked the metal
door. If only he had turned around, paid attention, he might have been
able to go upstairs and see it all unfolding in the distance. But he keyed
himself in, pressed the button for the elevator, waited for the door to ac-
cordion open, and went up to the fourth floor.

    In the corridor he stepped along in his plain black everyday shoes.
The dark walls with a deep fungal smell. The squeak of his shoes
sounded out in the quiet. The place had the summer blues. His office
was a high-ceilinged room at the far end of the corridor. When he had
first become a judge he'd had to share chambers in a grimy little box not
fit for a shoeshine boy. He'd been astounded how he and his fellows were

treated. There were mouse droppings in the drawers of his desk. The walls desperately in need of paint. Cockroaches would perch and twitter on the edge of the windowsill, as if they too just wanted to get out. But five years had gone by and he'd been shunted around from office to office. His was a more stately chambers now, and he was treated with a modicum more respect. Mahogany desk. Cut-glass inkwell. Framed photos of Claire and Joshua by the sea in Florida. A magnetized bar that held his paper clips. The Stars and Stripes on a standing pole behind him, by the window, so that sometimes it fluttered in the breeze. It wasn't the world's fanciest office, but it sufficed. Besides, he wasn't a man to make frivolous complaints: he kept that powder dry in case he'd need it at other times.

Claire had bought him a brand-new swivel chair, a leather number with deep pouchy patterns, and he liked the moment, first thing every morning, when he sat and spun. On his shelves there were rows and rows of books. The Appellate Division Reports, the Court of Appeals Reports, the New York Supplements. All of Wallace Stevens, signed and arranged in a special row. The Yale yearbook. On the east wall, the duplicates of his degrees. And the *New Yorker* cartoon neatly framed by the doorway— Moses on the mountain with the Ten Commandments, with two lawyers peeping over the crowd: *We're in luck, Sam, not a word about retrospectivity.*

He switched on his coffeepot, spread *The New York Times* on the desk, shook out a few packets of creamer. Sirens outside. Always sirens: they were the shadow facts of his day.

He was halfway through the business section when the door creaked open and another shiny head peeped itself around. It was hardly fair, but justice was largely balding. It wasn't just a trend, but a fact. Together they were a team of shiny boys. It had been a phantom torment from the early days, all of them slowly receding: not many follicles among the oracles.

—G'morning, old boy.

Judge Pollack's wide face was flushed. His eyes were like small shining metal grommets. Something of the hammerhead about him. He was blabbering about a guy who had strung himself between the towers. Soderberg thought at first it was a suicide, a jump off a rope suspended to a crane or some such thing. All he did was nod, turn the paper, all Watergate, and where's the little Dutch boy when you need him? He made an off-color crack about G. Gordon Liddy putting his finger in the wrong hole this time, but it whizzed past Pollack, who had a small piece of cream cheese on the front of his black robe and some white spittle coming from his mouth. Aerial assault. Soderberg sat back in his chair. He was about to mention the stray breakfast when he heard Pollack mention a balancing bar and a tightrope, and the penny dropped.

—Say again?

The man Pollack was talking about had actually *walked* between the towers. Not only that, but he had lain down on the wire. He had hopped. He had danced. He had virtually run across from one side to the other.

Soderberg spun in the chair, a decisive quarter-turn, and yanked open the blinds and tried looking across the expanse. He caught the edge of the north tower, but the rest of the view was obstructed.

—You missed him, said Pollack. He just finished.

—Official, was it?

—Excuse me?

—Sanctioned? Advertised?

—'Course not. The fellow broke in during the night. Strung his wire across and walked. We watched him from the top floor. The security guards told us.

—He broke into the World Trade Center?

—A looney, I'd say. Wouldn't you? Take him off to Bellevue.

—How did he get the wire across?

—No idea.

—Arrested? Was he arrested?

—Sure, said Pollack with a chuckle.

—What precinct?

—First, old boy. Wonder who'll get him?

—I'm on arraignment today.

—Lucky you, said Pollack. Criminal trespass.

—Reckless endangerment.

—Self-aggrandization, said Pollack with a wink.

—That'll brighten the day.

—Get the flashbulbs going.

—Takes some gumption.

Soderberg wasn't quite sure if the word *gumption* was another phrase for balls or for stupidity. Pollack gave him a wink and a senatorial wave, closed the door with a sharp snap.

—Balls, said Soderberg to the closed door.

But it would indeed brighten the day, he thought. The summer had been so hot and serious and full of death and betrayal and stabbings, and he needed a little entertainment.

There were only two arraignment courts and so Soderberg had a fifty percent chance of landing the case. It would have to come through on time. It was possible that they could shove the tightrope walker swiftly through the system—if they found it newsworthy enough, they could do anything they wanted. They could have him squared away in a matter of hours. Fingerprinted, interviewed, Albany-ed, and away. Brought in on a misdemeanor charge. Perhaps him and some accomplices. Which made him think: How the hell had the walker gotten the cable from one side to the other? Surely the tightrope was a piece of steel? How did he toss it across? Couldn't be made of rope, surely? Rope would never hold a man that distance. How then did he get it from one side to the other? Helicopter? Crane? Through the windows somehow? Did he drop the tightrope down and then drag it up the other side? It gave Soderberg a shiver of pleasure. Every now and then there was a good case that would come along and add a jolt to the day. A little spice. Something that could be talked about in the backrooms of the city. But what if he didn't get the case? What if it went across the hall? Perhaps he could even have a word with the D.A. and the court clerks, strictly on the sly, of course. There was a system of favors in place in the courts. *Pass me the tightrope walker and I'll owe you one.*

He propped his feet on the desk and drank his coffee and pondered the pulse of the day with the prospect of an arraignment that wasn't, for once, dealing with pure drudge.

Most days, he had to admit, were dire. In came the tide, out they went again. They left their detritus behind. He didn't mind using the word *scum* anymore. There was a time when he wouldn't have dared. But that's what they mostly were and it pained him to admit it. *Scum.* A dirty tide coming in on the shores and leaving behind its syringes and plastic wrappers and bloody shirts and condoms and snotty-nosed children. He dealt with the worst of the worst. Most people thought that he lived in some sort of mahogany heaven, that it was a highfalutin job, a powerful career, but the true fact of the matter was that, beyond reputation, it didn't amount to much at all. It landed the odd good table in a fancy restaurant, and it pleased Claire's family no end. At parties people perked up. They straightened their shoulders around him. Talked differently. It wasn't much of a perk, but it was better than nothing. Every now and then there was a chance for promotion, to go upstairs to the Supreme Court, but it hadn't come his way yet. In the end so much of it was just mundanity. A bureaucratic babysitting.

At Yale, when he was young and headstrong, he'd been sure that one day he'd be the very axis of the world, that his life would be one of deep impact. But every young man thought that. A condition of youth, your own importance. The mark you'd make upon the world. But a man learns sooner or later. You take your little niche and you make it your own. You ride out the time as best you can. You go home to your good wife and you calm her nerves. You sit down and compliment the cutlery. You thank your lucky stars for her inheritance. You smoke a fine cigar and you hope for an occasional roll in the silk sheets. You buy her a nice piece of jewelry at DeNatale's and you kiss her in the elevator because she still looks beautiful, and well preserved, despite the years rolling by, she really does. You kiss her good-bye and you go downtown every day and you soon figure out that your grief isn't half the grief that everyone else has. You mourn your dead son and you wake up in the middle of the night with your wife weeping beside you and you go to the kitchen, where you make yourself a cheese sandwich and you think, Well, at least it's a cheese sandwich on Park Avenue, it could be worse, you could have ended up far worse: your reward, a sigh of relief.

The lawyers knew the truth. The court clerks too. And the other judges, of course. Centre Street was a shithouse. They actually called it that: *the shithouse*. If they met one another at official functions. *How was the shithouse today, Earl? I left my briefcase in the shithouse.* They had even made it into a verb: *Are you shithousing it tomorrow, Thomas?* He hated admitting it even to himself, but it was the truth. He thought of himself as being on a ladder, a well-dressed man on a ladder, a man of privilege and style and learning, in a dark robe, in the house of justice, using his bare hands to pull the rotting leaves and the twigs from the shithouse gutters.

It didn't bother him half as much as it used to. The fact was that he was part of a system. He knew that now. A small piece of skin on a large elaborate creature. A cog that turned a set of wheels. Perhaps it just was a process of growing older. You leave the change to the generations that come behind you. But then the generation that comes behind you gets blown asunder in Vietnamese cafés, and you go on, you must go on, because even if they're gone they still can be remembered.

He was not the maverick Jew that he had once set out to be; still Soderberg refused to surrender. It was a point of honor, of truth, of survival.

When he first got called, back in the summer of '67, he thought that he'd take the job and be a paragon of virtue. He wouldn't just survive, but flourish. He packed up his job and took a fifty-five percent pay cut. He didn't need the money. He and Claire had already set a good deal aside, their accounts were healthy, the inheritance strong, and Joshua was squared away at PARC. Even if the idea of being a judge came as a complete surprise, he loved it. He had spent some early years in the U.S. Attorney's office, sure, and he had put his time in, had served on a tax commission, built himself a track record, buttered up the right people. He had taken a few difficult cases in his time, had argued well, had struck a balance. He'd written an editorial for *The New York Times* questioning the legal parameters of the draft dodgers and the psychological effects conscription had on the country. He had weighed the moral and constitutional aspects and came out firmly on the side of the war. At parties on Park Avenue he had met Mayor Lindsay, but only glancingly, and so when the appointment was suggested, he thought it was a ruse. He put the phone down. Laughed it off. It rang again. *You want me to do what?* There was talk of eventual promotion, first as acting judge of the Supreme Court of New York, and then, who knows—from there anything was still possible. A lot of the promotions had stalled when the city started to go bankrupt, but he didn't mind, he would surf it out. He was a man who believed in the absolute of the law. He would be able to weigh and dissect and ponder and make a change, give something back to the city where he'd been born. He always felt that he had skirted the city's edges and now he would take a pay cut and be at its core. The law was fundamental to how it was imparted and to what degree it could contain the excesses of human folly. He believed in the notion that even when laws were written down they ought not to remain unaltered. The law was work. It was there to be sifted. He was interested not just in the meaning of what could be, but also what ought to be. He would be at the coal face. One of the important miners of the morality of the city. The Honorable Solomon Soderberg.

Even the name rang right. Perhaps he had been used as judicial fodder, a balancing of the books, but he didn't mind too much; the good would outweigh the bad. He'd be rabbinical, wise, caring. Besides, every lawyer had a judge inside him.

He had walked in, his very first day, with his heart on fire. Through the front entrance. He wanted to savor it. He'd bought a brand-new suit from a swanky tailor on Madison Avenue. A Gucci tie. Tassels on his shoes. He approached the building in a great swell of anticipation. Etched outside the wide gold-colored doors were the words THE PEOPLE ARE THE FOUNDATION OF POWER. He stood a moment and breathed it all in. Inside, in the lobby, there was a blur of movement. Pimps and reporters and ambulance chasers. Men in purple platform shoes. Women dragging their children behind them. Bums sleeping in the window alcoves. He could feel his heart sink with each step. It seemed for just a moment that the building could still have the aura—the high ceilings, the old wooden balustrades, the marble floor—but the more he walked around the more his spirit sank. The courtrooms were even worse than he remembered. He shuffled around, dazed and disheartened. The corridor walls were graffitied. Men sat smoking in the back of the courtrooms. Deals were going down in the bathrooms. Prosecutors had holes in their suits. Crooked cops roamed about, looking for kickbacks. Kids were doing complicated handshakes. Fathers sat with smacked-out daughters. Mothers wept over their long-haired sons. On the courtroom doors, the fancy red leather pouching was slit. Attorneys went by with battered attaché cases. He ghosted past them all, took the elevator upstairs, then pulled up a chair at his new desk. There was a piece of dried chewing gum underneath the desk drawer.

Still and all, he said to himself, still and all, he would soon have it all sorted out. He could handle it. He could turn things around.

He announced his intentions in chambers one afternoon, at a retirement party for Kemmerer. A snicker went around the room. *So sayeth Solomon,* said one sad sack. *Slice the baby, boys.* Great hilarity and the tinkling of glasses. The other judges told him he'd get used to it eventually, that he'd see the light and it'd still be in a tunnel. The greatest part of the law was the wisdom of toleration. One had to accept the fools. It came with the territory. Every now and then the blinkers had to be lowered. He had to learn to lose. That was the price of success. *Try it,* they said. *Buck the system, Soderberg, and you'll be eating pizza in the Bronx. Be careful. Play the game. Stick with us.* And if he thought Manhattan was bad, he should go up to where the real fires were raging, to American Hanoi itself, at the end of the 4 train, where the very worst of the city played itself out every day.

He refused to believe them for many months, but slowly it dawned on him that they were correct—he was caught, he was just a part of the system, and the word was appropriate, a part of the Parts.

So many of the charges were just whisked away. The kids pleaded out, or he gave them time served, just so he could clear the backlog. He had his quota sheet to fill. He had to answer to the supervisors upstairs. The felonies got knocked down to misdemeanors. It was another form of demolition. You had to swing the wrecking ball. He was being judged on how he judged: the less work he gave to his colleagues upstairs, the happier they were. Ninety percent of the cases—even serious misbehavior—had to be disposed of. He wanted the promised promotion, yes, but even that couldn't stifle the feeling that he had taken whatever idealism he once had and stuffed it inside a cheap black robe, and now, when he went searching, he couldn't even find it inside the darkest slits.

He arrived at 100 Centre Street five days a week, put on his robe, wore his shiniest shoes, pulled his socks up around his ankles, and prevailed when he could. It was, he knew, about choosing his fights. He could have easily had a dozen pitched battles a day, more if he wanted. He could've taken on the whole system. He could have given the graffiti writers fines of a thousand dollars so that they'd never be able to pay it. Or he could've sentenced the firework kids on Mott Street to six months. He could've sent the drug addicts down for a full year. Chained them with a heavy bail. But it would all rebound, he knew. They would refuse to plead. And he would get the book slung at him for clogging up the courts. The shoplifters, the shoeshine boys, the hotel sneaks, the three-card-monte kids, they were all entitled eventually to say, Not guilty, Your Honor. And then the city would choke. The gutters would fill up. The slime would spill over. The sidewalks would fill. And he'd be blamed.

At the worst of times he thought, I'm a maintenance guy, I'm a gatekeeper, I'm a two-bit security man. He watched the parade come in and out of his courtroom, whichever Part he was in that day, and he wondered how the city had become such a disgusting thing on his watch. How it lifted babies by the hair, and how it raped seventy-year-old women, and how it set fires to couches where lovers slept, and how it pocketed candy bars, and how it shattered ribcages, and how it allowed its war protesters to spit in the faces of cops, and how the union men ran roughshod over their bosses, and how the Mafia took a hold of the boardwalks, and how fathers used daughters as ashtrays, and how bar fights spun out of control, and how perfectly good businessmen ended up urinating in front of the Woolworth Building, and how guns were drawn in the pizza joints, and how whole families got blown away, and how paramedics ended up with crushed skulls, and how addicts shot heroin into their tongues, and how shysters ran scams and old ladies lost their savings, and how shopkeepers gave back the wrong change, and how the mayor wheezed and wheedled and lied while the city burned down to the ground, got itself ready for its own little funeral of ashes, crime, crime, crime.

There wasn't a bad thing in the city that didn't pass through Soderberg's gutter watch. It was like surveying the evolution of slime. You stand there long enough and the gutter gets slick, no matter how hard you battle against it.

All these idiots kept coming from their grind houses, strip joints, freak shows, novelty stores, peep shows, fleabag hotels, and they looked even worse for having spent some time in the Tombs. Once, when he was in court, he saw a cockroach literally climb from a defendant's pocket and crawl along his shoulder and up along the side of his neck before the man even noticed. When he realized it, the defendant just whisked it away, and continued his guilty plea. Guilty, guilty, guilty. They nearly all pleaded guilty and in exchange got a sentence they could live with, or they went for time served, or they coughed up a small fine, and went along their merry way, a swagger in their walk, out into the world, just so they could turn around and do the same foolish thing and be back in his courtroom a week or two later. It put him in a state of constant agitation. He bought a hand exerciser that fit in the pocket. He slid his hand underneath the slit in his robe and took it from his suit pocket. It was a spring-loaded thing with two wooden handles that he squeezed surreptitiously under his garments. He only hoped he wasn't seen. It could of course be misinterpreted, a judge fumbling beneath his gown. But it calmed him as his cases came and went, and his quota filled. The heroes of the system were the judges who disposed of the most cases in the quickest amount of time. Open the sluice gates, let them go.

Anyone who swung by, anyone who participated in the system in any way, got sideswiped. The crimes got to the prosecutors—the rapes, the manslaughters, the stabbings, the robberies. The young assistant D.A.'s stood horrified by the enormity of the lists in front of them. The sentences got to the court officers: they were like disappointed cops, and would sometimes hiss when the judges were soft on crime. The slurring got to the court reporter. The blatant sideswipes got to the Legal Aid lawyers. The terms got to the probation officers. The vulgar simplicities got to the court psychologists. The paperwork got to the cops. The fines—light as they were—got to the criminals. The low bail figures got to the bondsmen. Everyone was in a jam and it was his job to sit at the center of it, to dole out the justice and balance it between right and wrong.

Right and wrong. Left and right. Up and down. He thought himself up there, standing at the edge of the precipice, sick and dizzy, unaccountably looking upward.

Soderberg downed his coffee in one smooth swallow. It tasted cheap with creamer.

He would get the tightrope man today—he was sure of it.

He picked up his phone and dialed down to the D.A.'s office, but the phone rang on and on and when he looked up at his little desktop clock it was time for the morning's clear-out.

Wearily, Soderberg rose, then smiled to himself as he followed a straight line along the floor.

—

HE LIKED THE BLACK gossamer robe in summertime. It was a little worn at the elbows, but no matter, it was breezy and light. He picked up his ledgers, tucked them under his arm, caught a quick glance of himself thick-bodied in the mirror, the tracery of blood vessels in his face, the deepening eye sockets. He pasted the last few hairs on his pate down, walked out solemnly through the corridor and past the elevator bank. He took the stairs down, a little skip in his step. Past the correction officers and probation people, into the rear hallway of Arraignment Part 1A. The worst part of the journey. At the back of the court, the prisoners were kept in the pens. The abattoir, they called it. The upper holding cells ran the length of half a block. The bars were painted a creamy yellow. The air was rank with body odor. The court officers went through four bottles of air freshener every day.

There were plenty of police and court officers lined up along the gauntlet and the criminals were smart enough to keep quiet as he went along the chute. He walked quickly, head down, among the officers.

—Good morning, Judge.

—Like the shoes, Your Honor.

—Nice to see you again, sir.

A quick simple nod to whoever acknowledged him. It was important to maintain a democratic aloofness. There were certain judges who bantered and mocked and joked and buddied up, but not Soderberg. He walked quickly out along the chute, in through the wooden door, into civility, or remnants of it, the dark wood bench, the microphone, the fluorescent lights, up the steps, to his elevated seat.

In God We Trust.

The morning slipped away quickly. A full calendar of cases. The usual roll call. Driving on an expired license. Threatening a police officer. Assault in the second degree. Lewd public act. A woman had stabbed her aunt in the arm over food stamps. A deal was cut with a tow-headed boy on grand theft auto. Community service was handed out to a man who'd put a peephole into the apartment below him—what the Peeping Tom didn't know was that the woman was a Peeping Tom too, and she peeped him, peeping her. A bartender had been in a brawl with a customer. A murder in Chinatown got sent upstairs immediately, bail set and the matter passed along.

All morning long he wheeled and bartered and crimped and cringed.

—Is there an outstanding warrant or not?

—Tell me, are you moving to dismiss or not?

—The request to withdraw is granted. Be nice to each other from here on in.

—Time served!

—Where's the motion, for crying out loud?

—Officer, would you please tell me what happened here? He was what? Cooking a chicken on the sidewalk?! Are you kidding me?

—Bail set at two thousand dollars' bond. Cash one thousand two hundred fifty.

—Not you again, Mr. Ferrario! Whose pocket was picked this time?

—This is an arraignment court, counselor, not Shangri-La.

—Release her on her own recognizance.

—This complaint does not state a crime. Dismissed!

—Has anybody here ever heard of privilege?

—I've no objection to a nonjail disposition.

—In exchange for his plea, we'll reduce the felony to a misdemeanor.

—Time served!

—I think your client was overserved in the narcissism department this morning, counselor.

—Give me something more than elevator music, please!

—Will you be finished by Friday?

—Time served!

—Time served!

—Time served!

There were so many special tricks to learn. Seldom look the defendant in the eye. Seldom smile. Try to appear as if you have a mild case of hemorrhoids: it will give you a concerned, inviolable expression. Sit at a slightly uncomfortable bend, or at least one that appears uncomfortable. Always be scribbling. Appear like a rabbi, bent over your writing pad. Stroke the silver at the side of your hair. Rub the pate when things get out of hand. Use the rap sheet as a guide to character. Make sure there are no reporters in the room. If there are, all rules are underlined twice. Listen carefully. The guilt or the innocence is all in the voice. Don't play favorites with the lawyers. Don't let them play the Jew card. Never respond to Yiddish. Dismiss flattery out of hand. Be careful with your hand exerciser. Watch out for masturbation jokes. Never stare at the stenographer's rear end. Be careful what you have for lunch. Have a roll of mints with you. Always think of your doodles as masterpieces. Make sure the carafe water has been changed. Be outraged at water spots on the glass. Buy shirts at least one size too big in the neck so you can breathe.

The cases came and went.

Late in the morning he had already called twenty-nine cases and he asked the bridge—his court officer, in her crisp white shirt—if there was any news on the case of the tightrope walker. The bridge told him that it was all the buzz, that the walker was in the system, it seemed, and he would likely come up in the late afternoon. She wasn't sure what the charges were, possibly criminal trespass and reckless endangerment. The D.A. was already deep in discussion with the tightrope walker, she said. It was likely that the walker would plead to everything if given a good enough deal. The D.A. was keen on some good publicity, it seemed. He wanted this one to go smoothly. The only hitch might be if the walker was held over until night court.

—So we have a chance?

—Pretty good, I'd say. If they push him through quick enough.

—Excellent. Lunch, then?

—Yes, Your Honor.

—We'll reconvene at two-fifteen.

—

THERE WAS ALWAYS Forlini's, or Sal's, or Carmine's, or Sweet's, or Sloppy Louie's, or Oscar's Delmonico, but he had always liked Harry's. It was the farthest away from Centre Street, but it didn't matter—the quick cab ride relaxed him. He got out on Water Street and walked to Hanover Square, stood outside and thought, This is my place. It wasn't because of the brokers. Or the bankers. Or the traders. It was Harry himself, all Greek, good manners, arms stretched wide. Harry had worked his way through the American Dream and come to the conclusion that it was composed of a good lunch and a deep red wine that could soar. But Harry could also make a steak sing, pull a trumpet line out of a string of spaghetti. He was often down in the kitchen, slinging fire. Then he would step out of his apron, put on his suit jacket, slick back his hair, and walk up into the restaurant with composure and style. He had a special inclination toward Soderberg, though neither man knew why. Harry would linger a moment longer with him at the bar, or slide up a great bottle and they'd sit underneath the monk murals, passing the time together. Perhaps because they were the only two in the place who weren't deep in the stock business. Outsiders to the clanging bells of finance. They could tell how the day was going in the markets by the decibel level around them.

On the wall of Harry's, the brokerage houses had private lines connected to a battery of telephones on the wall. Guys from Kidder, Peabody over there, Dillon, Read there, First Boston over there, Bear Stearns at the end of the bar, L. F. Rothschild by the murals. It was big money, all the time. It was elegant too. And well mannered. A club of privilege. Yet it didn't cost a fortune. A man could escape with his soul intact.

He sidled up to the bar and called Harry across, told him about the walker, how he'd just missed him early in the morning, how the kid had been arrested and was coming through the system soon.

—He broke into the towers, Har.

—So . . . he's ingenious.

—But what if he had fallen?

—The ground'd hardly cushion the fall, Sol.

Soderberg sipped his wine: the deep red heft of it rose to his nose.

—My point is, Har, he could've killed someone. Not just himself. Could've made hamburger of someone . . .

—Hey, I need a good line man. Maybe he could work for me.

—There's probably twelve, thirteen counts against him.

—All the more reason. He could be my sous chef. He could prepare the steamers. Strip the lentils. Dive into the soup from high above.

Harry pulled deeply on a cigar and blew the smoke to the ceiling.

—I don't even know if I'm going to get him, said Soderberg. He may be held over until night court.

—Well, if you do get him, give him my business card. Tell him there's a steak on the house. And a bottle of Château Clos de Sarpe. Grand Cru, 1964.

—He'll hardly tightrope after that.

Harry's face creased into a suggested map of what it would become years later: full, sprightly, generous.

—What is it about wine, Harry?

—What d'ya mean?

—What is it that cures us?

—Made to glorify the gods. And dull the idiots. Here, have a little more.

They clinked glasses in the slant of light that came through the upper windows. It was as if, looking out, they might've seen the walk re-enacted up there, on high. It was America, after all. The sort of place where you should be allowed to walk as high as you wanted. But what if you were the one walking underneath? What if the tightrope walker really had fallen? It was quite possible that he could have killed not just himself, but a dozen people below. Recklessness and freedom—how did they become a cocktail? It was always his dilemma. The law was a place to protect the powerless, and also to circumscribe the most powerful. But what if the powerless didn't deserve to be walking underneath? It sometimes put him in mind of Joshua. Not something he liked thinking about, not the loss at least, the terrible loss. It brought too much heartache. Pierced him. He had to learn that his son was gone. That was the extent of it. In the end Joshua had been a steward, a custodian of the truth. He had joined up to represent his country and came home to lay Claire flat with grief. And to lay him flat also. But he didn't show it. He never could. He would weep in the bath of all places, but only when the water was running. Solomon, wise Solomon, man of silence. There were some nights he kept the drain open and just let the water run.

He was the son of his son—he was here, he was left behind.

Little things got to him. The mitzvah of *maakeh*. Build a fence around your roof lest someone should fall from it. He questioned why he had bought the toy soldiers all those years ago. He fretted over the fact that he'd made Joshua learn "The Star-Spangled Banner" on the piano. He wondered if, when he taught the boy to play chess, he had somehow instilled a battle mentality? Attack along the diagonals, son. Never allow a back-rank mate. There must have been somewhere that he'd hard-wired the boy. Still, the war had been just, proper, right. Solomon understood it in all its utility. It protected the very cornerstones of freedom. It was fought for the very ideals that were under assault in his court every day. It was quite simply the way in which America protected itself. A time to kill and a time to heal. And yet sometimes he wanted to agree with Claire that war was just an endless factory of death; it made other men rich, and their son had been dispatched to open the gates, a rich boy himself. Still, it was not something he could afford to think of. He had to be solid, firm, a pillar. He seldom talked about Joshua, even to Claire. If there was anyone to talk to, it would be Harry, who knew a thing or two about longing and belonging, but it wasn't something to talk about right now. He was careful, Soderberg, always careful. Maybe too careful, he thought. He sometimes wished he could let it all out: *I'm the son of my son, Harry, and my son's dead.*

He lifted the glass to his face, sniffed the wine, the deep, earthy aroma. A moment of levity—that's what he wanted. A good, quiet moment. Something gentle and without noise. While away a few hours with his good pal. Or perhaps even call in sick for the rest of the day, go home, spend an afternoon with Claire, one of those afternoons when they could just sit together and read, one of those pure moments he and his wife shared increasingly as their marriage went along. He was happy, give or take. He was lucky, give or take. He didn't have everything he wanted, but he had enough. Yes, that's what he wanted: just a quiet afternoon of nothingness. Thirty-odd years of marriage hadn't made a stone out of him, no.

A little bit of silence. A gesture toward home. A hand on Harry's wrist and a word or two in his ear: *My son.* It was all he needed to say, but why complicate it now?

He lifted the glass and clinked with Harry.

—Cheers.

—To not falling, said Harry.

—To being able to get back up.

Soderberg was beginning to swing away from wanting the tightrope walker in his courtroom now: it would be too much of a headache, surely. He would have preferred to just fritter the day away at the long bar, with his dear friend, toasting the gods and letting the light fall.

—

—CRIMINAL COURT ARRAIGNMENT Part One-A, now in session. All rise.

The court officer had a voice that reminded him of seagulls. A peculiar caw to her, the tail end of her words swerving away. But the words demanded an immediate silence and the buzz in the rear of the court died.

—Quiet, please. The Honorable Judge Soderberg presiding.

He knew immediately he had the case. He could see the reporters in the pews of the spectator section. They had that jowly, destroyed look to them. They wore open-neck shirts and oversize slacks. Unshaven, whiskied. The more obvious giveaways were the notebooks with yellow covers jutting out of their jacket pockets. They were craning their necks to see who might emerge from the door behind him. A few extra detectives sat on the front bench for the show. Some off-duty clerks. Some businessmen, possibly even Port Authority honchos. A few others, maybe a security man or two. He could even see a tall, red-headed sketch artist. And that meant only one thing: the television cameras would be outside.

He could feel the wine at his toes. He wasn't drunk—nowhere near it—but he could still feel it swishing at the edges of his body.

—Order in the court. Silence. The court is now in session.

The doors creaked open behind him and in slouched a line of nine defendants toward the benches along the side wall. The usual riffraff, a couple of con men, a man with his eyebrow sliced open, two clapped-out hookers, and, walking at the rear of them all, a grin stretched from ear to ear, a slight bounce in his step, was a young white man, strangely clad: it could only be the tightrope walker.

In the gallery there was a stir. The reporters reached for their pencils. A slap of noise, as if a liquid had suddenly splashed through them.

The funambulist was even smaller than Soderberg had imagined. Impish. Dark shirt and tights. Strange, thin ballet slippers on his feet. There was something even washed-out about him. He was blond, in his mid-twenties, the sort of man you might see as a waiter in the theater district. And yet there was a confidence that rolled off him, a swagger that Soderberg liked. He looked like a small, squashed-down version of Joshua, as if some brilliance had been deposited in his body, programmed in like one of Joshua's hacks, and the only way out for him was through performance.

It was obvious that the tightrope walker had never been arraigned before. The first-timers were always dazed. They came in, huge-eyed, stunned by it all.

The walker stopped and looked from one side of the courtroom to the other. Momentarily frightened and bemused. As if there was way too much language in this place. He was thin, lithe, a quality of the leonine to him. He had quick eyes: the glance ended up on the bench.

Soderberg made a split second of eye contact. Broke his own rule, but so what? The walker understood and half nodded. There was something gleeful and playful there in the walker's eyes. What could Soderberg do with him? How could he manipulate it? After all, it was reckless endangerment, at the very least, and that could end upstairs, a felony, with the possibility of seven years. What about disorderly conduct? Soderberg knew deep down that it'd never go in that direction. It'd be kept a minor misdemeanor and he'd have to work it out with the D.A. He'd play it smart. Pull something unusual from the hat. Besides, the reporters were there, watching. The sketch artist. The TV cameras, outside the courtroom.

He called his bridge over and whispered in her ear: Who's on first? It was their little joke, their judicial Abbott and Costello. She showed him the calendar and he skimmed down quickly over the cases, flicked a quick look at the sin bin, sighed. He didn't have to do them in order, he could juggle things around, but he tapped his pencil against the first pending case.

The bridge stepped away and cleared her throat.

—Docket ending six-eight-seven, she said. The People versus Tillie Henderson and Jazzlyn Henderson. Step up, please.

The assistant D.A., Paul Concrombie, shook out the creases in his jacket. Opposite him, the Legal Aid attorney brushed back his long hair and came forward, spreading the file out on the shelf. In the back of the court, one of the reporters let out an audible groan as the women stood up from the bench. The younger hooker was milky-skinned and tall, wearing yellow stilettos, a neon swimsuit under a loose black shirt, a baubled necklace. The older one wore a one-piece swimsuit and high sil- ver heels, her face a playground of mascara. Absurd, he thought. Sun- bathing in the Tombs. She looked as if she had been around awhile, that she'd done her share of circling the track.

—Aggravated robbery in the second degree. Produced on an out- standing warrant from November 19, 1973.

The older hooker blew a kiss over her shoulder. A white man in the gallery blushed and lowered his head.

—This isn't a nightclub, young lady.

—Sorry, Your Honor—I'd blow you one too 'cept I'm all blowed out.

A quick snap of laughter circled the room.

—I'll have decorum in my court, Miss Henderson.

He was quite sure he heard the word *asshole* creeping out from under her tongue. He always wondered why they dug such pits for themselves, these hookers. He peered down at the rap sheets in front of him. Two il- lustrious careers. The older hooker had at least sixty charges against her over the years. The younger one had begun the quick portion of the slide: the charges had started to come with regularity and she would only accel- erate from here on in. He'd seen it all too often. It was like opening up a tap.

Soderberg adjusted his reading glasses, sat back a moment in the swivel chair, addressed the assistant D.A. with a withering look.

—So. Why the wait, Mr. Concrombie? This happened almost a year ago.

—We've had some recent developments here, Your Honor. The defendants were arrested in the Bronx and . . .

—Is this still in the complaint form?

—Yes, Your Honor.

—And is the assistant D.A. interested in disposing of this on a criminal-court level?

—Yes, Your Honor.

—So, the warrant is vacated?

—Yes, Your Honor.

He was hitting his stride, getting it done with speed. All a bit of a magic trick. Sweep out the black cape. Wave the white wand. Watch the rabbit disappear. He could see the row of nodding heads in the spectators' area, caught on the current, rolling along with him. He hoped the reporters were getting it, seeing the control he had in his courtroom, even with the wine at the corners of his mind.

—And what're we doing now, Mr. Concrombie?

—Your Honor, I've discussed this with the Legal Aid lawyer, Mr. Feathers here, and we've agreed that in the interests of justice, taking everything into consideration, the People are moving to dismiss the case against the daughter. We're not going to go further with it, Your Honor.

—The daughter?

—Jazzlyn Henderson. Yes, sorry, Your Honor, it's a mother-daughter team.

He flicked a quick look at the rap sheets. He was surprised to see that the mother was just thirty-eight years old.

—So, you two are related.

—Keeping it in the family, Y'r Honor!

—Miss, I'll ask you not to speak again.

—But you axed me a question.

—Mr. Feathers, instruct your client, please.

—But you axed me.

—Well, I will *axe* you, yes, young lady.

—Oh, she said.

—Okay. Miss . . . Henderson. Zip it. Do you understand that? Zip it. Now. Mr. Concrombie. Go on.

—Well, Your Honor, after studying the file, we don't believe that the People will be able to sustain our burden of proof. Beyond reasonable doubt.

—For what reason?

—Well, the identification is problematic.

—Yes? I'm waiting.

—The investigation revealed that there was a matter of mistaken identity.

—Whose identification?

—Well, we have a confession, Your Honor.

—Okay. Don't bowl me over with your certainty about this, Mr. Concrombie. So you're dropping the case against Miss, uh, Miss Jazzlyn Henderson?

—Yes, sir.

—And all parties are agreed?

A little nodding field of heads around the room.

—Okay, case dismissed.

—Case dismissed?

—You serious? said the young girl. That's it?

—That's it.

—Done and dusted? He's cutting me loose?

Under her breath he was sure he could hear her say: Getdefuckouttahere!

—What did you say, young lady?

—Nothing.

The Legal Aid lawyer leaned across and whispered something vicious in her ear.

—Nothing, Your Honor. Sorry. I said nothing. Thanks.

—Get her out of here.

—Lift the rope! One coming out!

The younger hooker turned to her mother, kissed her square on the eyebrow. Strange place. The mother, beaten down and tired, accepted the kiss, stroked the side of her daughter's face, pulled her close. Soderberg watched as they embraced. What sort of deep cruelty, he wondered, allows a family like that?

Still, it always surprised him, the love these people could display for each other. It was one of the few things that still thrilled him about the courtroom—the raw edge it gave to life, the sight of lovers embracing after beating each other up, or families glad to welcome back their son the petty thief, the surprise of forgiveness when it shone in the core of his court. It was rare, but it happened, and like everything, the rarity was necessary.

The young hooker whispered in the mother's ear and the mother laughed, waved over her shoulder again at the white man in the spectators' section.

The court officer didn't lift the rope. The young hooker did it herself. She swayed as she walked, as if she was already selling herself. She brazened her way down the center of the aisle toward the white man with graying flecks at the side of his hair. She took off the black shirt as she went, so that only her swimsuit could be seen.

Soderberg could feel his toes curl at the sheer audacity of it.

—Put that shirt back on, right now!

—It's a free world, ain't it? You dismissed me. It's his shirt.

—Put it on, said Soderberg, leaning close into his microphone.

—He wanted to dress me up nice for court. Didn't you, Corrie? He got it sent down to me in the Tombs.

The white man was trying to drag her across by the elbow, whispering something urgently in her ear.

—Put on the shirt or I'll pull you up on contempt. . . . Sir, are you related to that young woman?

—Not exactly, said the man.

—And what does *not exactly* mean?

—I'm her friend.

He had an Irish accent, this gray-haired pimp. He raised his chin like an old-fashioned boxer. His face was thin and his cheeks were sunken.

—Well, friend, I want to make sure that she keeps the shirt on at all times.

—Yes, Y'r Honor. And, Y'r Honor . . . ?

—Just do what I say.

—But, Y'r Honor . . .

Soderberg slammed the gavel down: Enough, he said.

He watched the younger hooker as she kissed the Irishman on the cheek. The man turned away, but then took her face gently in his hands. A strange-looking pimp. Not the usual type. No matter. They came in all sizes and packages. Truth was, the women were victims of the men, always were, always would be. At the essential core, it was idiots like the pimp who should've been jailed. Soderberg let out a sigh and then turned toward the assistant D.A.

An eyebrow raise was language enough between the two of them. There was still the matter of the mother to take care of, and then he'd get to the centerpiece.

He flicked a quick look across at the tightrope walker sitting at the benches. A befuddled gaze on the walker's face. His own crime so unique that he surely had no idea what he was even doing here.

Soderberg tapped the microphone and those in the courtroom perked up.

—As I understand it, the remaining defendant, the mother here . . .

—Tillie, Y'r Honor.

—I'm not talking to you, Miss Henderson. As I understand it, counselors, this is still a complaint with a felony. Is it going to be acceptable to dispose of it as a misdemeanor?

—Your Honor, we already have a disposition here. I have discussed it with Mr. Feathers.

—That's right, Your Honor.

—And . . . ?

—The People are moving to reduce the charge from robbery to petty larceny in exchange for the defendant's plea of guilty.

—Is this what you want, Miss Henderson?

—Huh?

—You are willing to plead guilty to this crime?

—He said it'd be no more'n six months.

—Twelve is your maximum, Miss Henderson.

—Long as I can see my babies . . .

—Excuse me?

—I'll take anything, she said.

—Very well, for the purpose of this plea, the outstanding charges are reduced to petty larceny. Do you understand that if I accept your plea pursuant to this decision you've made, that I have the power, that I could sentence you to up to one year in jail?

She leaned over quickly to her Legal Aid lawyer, who shook his head and put his hand on her wrist and half smiled at her.

—Yeah, I understand.

—And you understand you're pleading to petty larceny?

—Yeah, babe.

—Excuse me?

Soderberg felt a stab of pain, somewhere between the eyes and the back of the throat. A stunned flick. Had she really called him *babe*? It couldn't be. She was standing, staring at him, half smiling. Could he pretend that he didn't hear? Dismiss it? Call her up in contempt? If he made a fuss, what would happen?

In the silence the room seemed to shrink a moment. The lawyer beside her looked as if he might bite her ear off. She shrugged and smiled and waved back over her shoulder again.

—I'm sure you didn't mean that, Miss Henderson.

—Mean what, Y'r Honor?

—We will move on.

—Whatever you say, Y'r Honor.

—Keep your language in check.

—Cool, she said.

—Or else.

—You got it.

—You understand that you are giving up your right to trial?

—Yeah.

The Legal Aid lawyer's lips recoiled as they touched, accidentally, against the woman's ear.

—I mean, yessir.

—You have discussed pleading guilty with your lawyer and you are satisfied with his services? You are pleading guilty of your own free will?

—Yessir.

—You understand that you're giving up your right to trial?

—Yessir, you bet.

—Okay, Miss Henderson, how do you plead to petty larceny?

Again, the Legal Aid lawyer leaned across to school her.

—Guilty.

—Okay, so very well, tell me what happened here.

—Huh?

—Tell me what occurred, Miss Henderson.

Soderberg watched as the court officers moved to reduce the yellow-back form to a blue-back for the misdemeanor crime. In the spectators' section the reporters were fidgeting with the spirals on their books. The buzz in the room had died slightly. Soderberg knew that he would have to move quickly if he was going to pull out a good performance for the tightrope walker.

The hooker raised her head. The way she stood, he knew for certain she was guilty. Just by the lean of the body, he knew. He always knew.

—It's a long time ago. So, I was, like, I didn't want to go to Hell's Kitchen, but Jazzlyn and me, well me, I got this date in Hell's Kitchen, and he was saying shit about me.

—All right, Miss Henderson.

—Shit like I was old and stuff.

—Language, Miss Henderson.

—And his wallet just jumped out in front of me.

—Thank you.

—I weren't finished.

—That'll do.

—I ain't all bad. I know you think I'm all bad.

—That'll do, young lady.

—Yeah, Pops.

He saw one of the court officers smirk. His cheeks flushed. He lifted his glasses high on his head, pinned her with a stare. Her eyes, suddenly, seemed wide and pleading, and he understood for a moment how she could attract a man, even in the worst of times: some layered beauty and fierceness, some history of love.

—And you understand that by pleading guilty you are not being co-erced?

She tottered close to her lawyer and then she turned, heavy-eyed, to the bench.

—Oh, no, she said, I ain't being coerced.

—Mr. Feathers, do you consent to immediate sentence and waive your right to presentence report?

—Yes, we do.

—And, Miss Henderson, do you wish to make a statement before I give sentence?

—I want to be in Rikers.

—You understand, Miss Henderson, that this court cannot determine which prison you will be in.

—But they said I'd be in Rikers. That's what they said.

—And why, pray tell, would you like to be in Rikers? Why would anyone like . . .

—Cuz'a the babies.

—You've got babies?

—Jazzlyn's got.

She was pointing over her shoulder at her daughter, slumped in the spectators' section.

—Very well, there is no guarantee, but I'll make a note to the court officers to be so disposed. In the case of the People versus Tillie Henderson, the plea is guilty and I sentence you to no more than eight months in prison.

—Eight months?

—Correct. I can make it twelve, if you like.

She opened her mouth in an unsounded whimper.

—I thought it were gonna be six.

—Eight months, young lady. Do you wish to adjust your plea?

—Shit, she said and she shrugged her shoulders.

He saw the Irishman in the spectators' section grab the arm of the young hooker. He was trying to make his way forward in the court to say something to Tillie Henderson, but the court officer prodded him in the chest with a billy club.

—Order in the court.

—Can I say a word, Your Honor?

—No. Now. Sit. Down.

Soderberg could feel his teeth grind.

—Tillie, I'll be back later, okay?

—Sit. Or else.

The pimp stopped in the aisle and looked up at Soderberg. The pupils small, the eyes very blue. Soderberg felt exposed, open, unlayered. A blanket of quiet fell over the court.

—Sit! Or else.

The pimp lowered his head and retreated. Soderberg let out a quick breath of relief, then turned slightly in his chair. He picked up the calendar of cases, put his hand over the microphone, nodded across to the court officer.

—All right, he whispered. Get the tightrope walker up.

Soderberg glanced at Tillie Henderson as she was escorted out the door to his right. She walked with her head low and yet there was a learned bounce in her gait. As if she were already out and doing the track. She was held on each side by a court officer. The jacket she wore was crumpled and dirty. The sleeves were way too long. It looked as if two women could have fit inside it. Her face looked odd and vulnerable, and yet still held a touch of the sensual. Her eyes were dark. Her eyebrows were plucked thin. There was a shine to her, a glisten. It was as if he were seeing her for the first time: upside down, the way the eye first sees, and then must correct. Something tender and carved about the face. The long nose that looked as if it might have been broken a few times. The flare of her nostrils.

She turned at the door and tried to look over her shoulder, but the court officers blocked her.

She mouthed something toward her daughter and the pimp, but it was lost, and she gave a little winded sigh as if she were on the beginning of a long journey. Her face seemed for a second almost beautiful, and then the hooker turned and shuffled and the door was closed behind her, and she vanished into her own namelessness.

—Get the tightrope walker up, he said again to his bridge. Now.

CENTAVOS

THERE IS, AT LEAST, ALWAYS THIS: It is a Thursday morning. My first-floor apartment. In a clapboard house. In a street of clapboard houses. Through the window, a quick flit of dark against the blue sky. It is a surprise to me that there are birds of any sort in the Bronx. It is summertime so there is no school for Eliana or Jacobo. But they are already awake. I can hear the sound of the television turned high. Our ancient set is stuck on one channel and the only program playing is *Sesame Street*. I turn in the sheets towards Corrigan. It is the first time that he has ever slept over. We have not planned it: it has just happened this way. He stirs in his sleep. His lips are dry. The white sheets move with his body. A man's beard is a weather line: an intersperse of light and dark, a flurry of gray at the chin, a dark hollow beneath his lip. It amazes me how it darkens him, this morning beard, how it has grown in such a short time, even the little flecks of gray where there was none the night before.

The thing about love is that we come alive in bodies not our own.

One arm of Corrigan's shirt is on, one arm off. In our haste we have not even undressed properly. Everything is forgiven. I lift the weight of his arm and unbutton the shirt. Wooden buttons that slip through a cloth loop. I pull the shirt along the length of his arm and off. His skin is very white, the color of newly sliced apple, beneath his brown neck. I kiss his shoulder. The religious chain around his throat has left a tan mark, but not the cross, since it sits underneath his shirt, and it looks like he wears a necklace of white skin that finishes in midair. Some bruises on his skin still: his blood disorder.

He opens his eyes and blinks a moment, makes a sound that is somewhere between pain and awe. He pushes his feet out from under the sheets, looks around the room.

"Oh," he says, "it's morning."

"It is."

"How did my trousers get over there?"

"You drank too much vino."

"¿De veras?" he says. "And I became what—an acrobat?"

From upstairs, the sound of footsteps, our neighbors awakening. He waits out the sounds, the eventual thump of their feet into shoes.

"The children?"

"They're watching *Sesame Street*."

"We drank a lot."

"We did."

"I'm not used to it anymore." He runs his hands over the sheets, comes to the curve of my hip, draws away.

More sounds from above, a shower, the fall of something heavy, the click of a woman's high heels across the floor. Mine is the apartment that receives all noises, even from the basement below. For one hundred and ten dollars a month, I feel as if I live inside a radio.

"Are they always this loud?"

"Just wait until their teenagers wake."

He groans and looks up at the ceiling. I wonder what it is Corrigan is thinking: up there, his God, but first my neighbors.

"Doctor, help me," he says. "Tell me something magnificent."

He knows that I have always wanted to be a doctor, that I have come all the way from Guatemala with this intention, that I was not able to finish medical school at home, and he knows too that I have failed here, I never even got to the steps of a university, that there was probably never a chance in the first place, and yet still he calls me "Doctor."

"Well, I woke up this morning and diagnosed a very early case of happiness."

"Never heard of it," he says.

LET THE GREAT WORLD SPIN

"It's a rare disease. I caught it just before the neighbors woke."

"Is it contagious?"

"Don't you have it yet?"

He kisses my lips, but then turns away from me. The unbearable weight of the complications he carries, his guilt, his joy. He lies on his left shoulder, his legs tuck into a bend, and he puts his back to me—he looks as if he wants to crouch and protect himself.

The first time I saw Corrigan, I was looking out the window of the nursing home. He was there, through the dirty panes, loading up Sheila and Paolo and Albee and the others. He had been in a fight. There were cuts and bruises on his face and he looked at first glance like exactly the sort of man I should stay away from. And yet there was something about him that was loyal—that's the only word I knew, *fidelidad*—he seemed to be loyal to them because maybe he knew what their lives were. He used wooden planks to roll the wheelchairs up into the van and he strapped them in. He had pasted his van with peace and justice stickers: I thought maybe he had a sense of humor to go along with his violence. I found out later that the cuts and the bruises were from the pimps—he took their worst punches and never hit back. He was loyal to the girls too, and to his God, but even he knew that the loyalty had to break somewhere.

After a moment he turns to me, runs his finger along my lips, then out of the blue he says: "Sorry."

We were hasty last night. He fell asleep before I did. A woman might think it thrilling to make love to a man who had never in his life made love before, and it was, the thought of it, the movement towards it, but it was as if I was making love to a number of lost years, and the truth is that he cried, he put his head on my shoulder, and he could not keep hold of my gaze, couldn't bear it.

A man who holds a vow that long is entitled to anything he wants.

I told him that I loved him and that I'd always love him and I felt like a child who throws a centavo into a fountain and then she has to tell someone her most extraordinary wish even though she knows that the wish should be kept secret and that, in telling it, she is quite probably losing it. He replied that I was not to worry, that the penny could come out of the fountain again and again and again.

He wanted to repeat the attempt at lovemaking. Each time another surprise and doubt, as if he did not trust himself, what was happening.

But there is a moment when he wakes now—on this day that I will remember over and over again—when he turns to me and there's still a hint of wine on his breath.

"So," he says, "you took my shirt off too."

"It's a trick."

"A good one," he says.

My hand travels across the sheet to meet him.

"We have to cover the mirilla," I say.

"The what?"

"The mirilla, the peephole, the spy thing, whatever it is called."

There is a spyhole in every door of my apartment. The landlord, it seems, once got a good deal on these doors, and hung them all around. You can look from one room to the other and the curved glass makes it either narrow or wide, depending on what side you happen to be on. If you look into my kitchen, the world is tiny. If you look out, it stretches. The bedroom spyhole faces inwards, where Jacobo and Eliana can look in upon me while I am sleeping. They call it the carnival door. It seems to them, through the distortion, as if I lie in the biggest bed in the world. I puff myself up on the world's largest pillows. The walls curve around me. The first day we moved in I stuck my toes out from under the covers. *Mama, your feet are bigger than your head!* M'ijo said that the world inside my bedroom seemed stretchy. M'ija said it was made of chewing gum.

Corrigan shifts sideways out of bed. His thin, bare back, his long legs. He steps to the closet. He puts his black shirt on a hanger, wedges the metal end of the hanger in the gap between door and frame. The dangling black shirt covers the spyhole in the door. From outside, the sound of the television.

"We should lock it too," I say.

"¿Estás segura?"

These small Spanish phrases he uses sound like stones in his mouth, his accent so terrible it makes me laugh.

"Won't they worry?"

"Not if we don't."

He returns to the bed, naked, embarrassed, covering himself. He slips beneath the covers, nudges against my shoulder. Singing. Off-key. "Can you tell me how-to-get, how-to-get to Sesame Street?"

I know already that I will return to this day whenever I want to. I can bid it alive. Preserve it. There is a still point where the present, the now, winds around itself, and nothing is tangled. The river is not where it begins or ends, but right in the middle point, anchored by what has happened and what is to arrive. You can close your eyes and there will be a light snow falling in New York, and seconds later you are sunning upon a rock in Zacapa, and seconds later still you are surfing through the Bronx on the strength of your own desire. There is no way to find a word to fit around this feeling. Words resist it. Words give it a pattern it does not own. Words put it in time. They freeze what cannot be stopped. Try to describe the taste of a peach. Try to describe it. Feel the rush of sweetness: we make love.

I do not even hear the pounding at the door, but Corrigan stops and grins and kisses me, a rim of sweat at the top of his brow.

"That'll be Snuffleupagus."

"I think it's Oscar the Grouch."

I step out of bed and remove the shirt from the hanger in front of the spyhole, look down. I see the tops of their heads: their eyes look tiny and confused. I pull Corrigan's shirt on and open the door. Bend down to eye level. Jacobo holds an old blanket in his hands. Eliana an empty plastic glass. They are hungry they say, first in English and then in Spanish.

"Just a minute," I tell them. I am a terrible mother. I should not do this. I close the door again, but open it just as quickly, rush out into the kitchen, fill two bowls with cereal, two glasses of water.

"Quiet now, niños. Promise me."

I step back to the bedroom, glance at my children through the spyhole, in front of the television, spilling cereal on the carpet. I cross the room and jump on the bed. I throw the sheet to the floor, and then I fall beside Corrigan, pull him close. He is laughing, his body at ease.

We rush, him and I. We make love again. Afterwards, he showers in my bathroom.

"Tell me something magnificent, Corrigan."

"Like what?"

"Come on, it's your turn."

"Well, I just learned to play the piano."

"There's no piano."

"Exactly. I just sat down at it and could immediately play every note."

"Ha!"

It's true. That is how it feels. I go into the bathroom where he is show-ering, pull back the curtain, kiss his wet lips, then pull on my robe and go out to look after the children. My bare feet on the curling linoleum floor. My painted toes. I'm vaguely aware that every fiber in me is still making love to Corrigan. Everything feels new, the tips of my fingers alive to every touch, a stove top.

He comes out of the room with his hair so wet that at first I think the gray at the side temples has disappeared. He is wearing his dark trousers and his black shirt since he has nothing else to change into. He has shaved. I want to tell him off for using my razor. His skin looks shiny and raw.

A week later—after the accident—I will come home and tap out his hairs at the side of my sink, arrange them in patterns, obsessively, over and over. I will count them out to reconstitute them. I will gather them against the side of the sink and try to create his portrait there.

I saw the X-rays in the hospital. The swollen heart-shadow from the blunt chest trauma. His heart muscle getting squeezed by the blood and fluid. The jugular veins, massively enlarged. His heart went in and out of gallop. The doctor stuck a needle into his chest. I knew the routine from my years as a nurse: drain the pericardium. The blood and fluid were taken out, but Corrigan's heart kept on swelling. His brother was saying prayers, over and over. They took another X-ray. The jugular veins were massive, they were squeezing him shut. His whole body had gone cold.

But, for now, the children just look up and say: "Hi, Corrie," as if it is the most natural thing in the world. Behind them, the television plays. *Count to seven. Sing along with me. When the pie was opened the birds began to sing.*

"Niños, apaguen la tele."

"Later, Mom."

Corrigan sits at the small wooden table at the rear of the television set. He has his back to me. My heart shudders every time he sits near the por-trait of my dead husband. He has never asked me to move the photo. He never will. He knows the reason it is there. No matter that my husband was a brute who died in the war in the mountains near Quezaltenango— it makes no difference—all children need a father. Besides, it is just a photo. It takes no precedence. It does not threaten Corrigan. He knows my story. It is contained within this moment.

And I suddenly think, as I look across the table at him, that these are the days as they will be. This is the future as we see it. The swerve and the static. The confidence and the doubt. Corrigan glances back at me, smiles. He fingers one of my medical textbooks. He even opens it to a random page and scans it, but I know he isn't reading at all. Sketches of bodies, of bones, of cartilage.

He skips through the pages as if looking for more space.

"Really," he says, "that'd be a good idea."

"What?"

"To get a piano and learn how to play it."

"Yes, and put it where?"

"On top of the television set. Right, Jacobo? Hey, Bo, that would work, wouldn't it?"

"Nah," says Jacobo.

Corrigan leans across the sofa and knuckles my son's dark hair.

"Maybe we'll get a piano with a television set inside it."

"Nah."

"Maybe we'll get a piano and TV and a chocolate machine all in one."

"Nah."

"Television," says Corrigan, smiling, "the perfect drug."

For the first time in years I wish for a garden. We could go outside in the cool fresh air and sit away from the children, find our own space, shorten the nearby buildings into blades of grass, have the stonemasons carve flowers at our feet. I have often dreamed of bringing him back to Guatemala. There was a place my childhood friends and I used to go, a butterfly grove, down the dirt road towards Zacapa. The path dipped through the bushes. The trees opened into the grove, where the bushes grew low. The flowers were in the shape of a bell, red and plentiful. The girls sucked on the sweet flowers while the boys tore the butterflies apart to see how they were made. Some of the wings were so colorful they could only be poisonous. When I left my home and arrived in New York, I rented a small apartment in Queens, and, one day, distraught, I got a tattoo on my ankle, the wings spread wide. It is one of the stupidest things I have ever done. I hated myself for the cheapness I had become.

"You're daydreaming," Corrigan says to me.

"Am I?"

My head against his shoulder, he laughs as if the laughter wants to travel a good distance, down through my body also.

"Corrie?"

"Uh-huh?"

"You like my tattoo?"

He prods me playfully. "I can live with it," he says.

"Tell me the truth."

"No, I like it, I do."

"Mentiroso," I say. He creases his forehead. "Fibber."

"I'm not fibbing. Kids! Kids, do you think I'm fibbing?"

Neither of them says a word.

"See?" says Corrigan. "I told you."

My desire for him now is raw and sharp. I lean forward and kiss his lips. It is the first time we have kissed in front of the children, but they do not seem to notice. A sliver of cold at my neck.

There are times—though not often—when I wish that I didn't have children at all. Just make them disappear, God, for an hour or so, no more, just an hour, that's all. Just do it quickly and out of my sight, have them go up in a puff of smoke and be gone, then bring them back fully intact, as if they didn't leave at all. But just let me be alone, with him, this man, Corrigan, for a tiny while, just me and him, together.

I leave my head on his shoulder. He touches the side of my face absently. What can be on his mind? There are so many things to pull him away from me. Sometimes, I feel he is made of a magnet. He bounces and spins in midair around me. I go to the kitchen and make him café. He likes it very strong and hot with three spoonfuls of sugar. He lifts the spoon out and licks it triumphantly, as if the spoon has gotten him through an ordeal. He breathes on the spoon and then hangs it off the end of his nose, so it dangles there, absurdly.

He turns to me. "What do you think, Adie?"

"Que payaso."

"Gracias," he says in his awful accent.

He walks over in front of the television set with the spoon still hanging off the end of his nose. It falls and he catches it and then he breathes on it once more, does his trick. The children explode in laughter. "Let me, let me, let me."

These are the little things I am learning. He is ridiculous enough to hang spoons off the end of his nose. This, and he likes to blow his café cool, three short blows, one long blow. This, and he has no taste for cereal. This, and that he's good at fixing toasters.

The children return to the television show. He sits back and finishes his café. He stares at the far wall. I know he is thinking again of his God and his church and his loss if he decides to leave the Order. It is like his own shadow has leaped up to get him. I know all this because he smiles at me and it is a smile that contains everything, including a shrug, and then he suddenly gets up from the table, stretches, goes to the couch and falls over the back of it, sits between the children, as if they can protect him. He drapes his arms around them, over their shoulders. I like him and dislike him for this, both at once. I feel a desire for him again, in my mouth now, sharp like salt.

"You know," he says, "I've work to do."

"Don't go, Corrie. Just hang around awhile. Work can wait."

"Yeah," he says, as if he might believe it.

He pulls the children closer to him and they allow it. I want him to make up his mind. I want to hear him say that he can have both God and me, also my children and my little clapboard house. I want him to remain here—exactly here—on the couch, without moving.

I will always wonder what it was, what that moment of beauty was, when he whispered it to me, when we found him smashed up in the hospital, what it was he was saying when he whispered into the dark that he had seen something he could not forget, a jumble of words, a man, a building, I could not quite make it out. I can only hope that in the last minute he was at peace. It might have been an ordinary thought, or it might have been that he had made up his mind that he would leave the Order, and that nothing would stop him now, and he would come home to me, or maybe it was nothing at all, just a simple moment of beauty, a little thing hardly worth talking about, a random meeting, or a word he had with Jazzlyn or Tillie, a joke, or maybe he had decided that, yes, he could lose me now, that he could stay with his church and do his work, or maybe there was nothing on his mind at all, perhaps he was just happy, or in agony, and the morphine had scattered him—there are all these things and there are more—it is impossible to know. I hold in confusion the last moments of his language.

There was a man walked the air, I heard about that. And Corrigan had spent the night sleeping in his van down near the courthouse. He got a ticket for it. On John Street. Perhaps he woke up, stumbled out of his van in the early morning, and saw the man high up there, challenging God, a man above the cross rather than below—who knows, I cannot tell. Or maybe it was the court case, that the walker got off free, while Tillie was sent away for eight months, maybe that annoyed him—these things are tangled, there are no answers, maybe he thought she deserved another chance, he was angry, she shouldn't have gone to jail. Or maybe something else got to him.

He told me once that there was no better faith than a wounded faith and sometimes I wonder if that is what he was doing all along—trying to wound his faith in order to test it—and I was just another stone in the way of his God.

In my worst moments I am convinced that he was rushing home to say good-bye, that he was driving too fast because he made up his mind, and it was finished, but in my best, my very best, he comes up on the doorstep, smiling, with his arms spread wide, in order to stay.

And so this is how I will leave him as much, and as often, as I can. It was—it is—a Thursday morning a week before the crash, and it fits in the space of every other morning I wake into. He sits between Eliana and Jacobo, on the couch, his arms spread wide, the buttons of his black shirt open, his gaze fixed forward. Nothing will ever really take him from the couch. It is just a simple brown thing, with mismatching cushions, and a hole in the armrest where it has been worn through, a few coins from his pocket fallen down into the gaps, and I will take it with me now wherever I go, to Zacapa, or the nursing home, or any other place I happen to find.

ALL HAIL AND HALLELUJAH

I KNEW ALMOST RIGHT OFF. Them two babies needed looking after. It was a deep-down feeling that must've come from long ago. Sometimes thinking back on things is a mistake arising out of pride, but I guess you live inside a moment for years, move with it and feel it grow, and it sends out roots until it touches everything in sight.

I grew up in southern Missouri. The only girl with five brothers. It was the years of the Great Depression. Things were falling apart, but we held together as best we could. The house we lived in was a small A-frame, like most houses on the colored side of town. The unpainted timbers sagged around the porch. On one side of the house was the long parlor, furnished with cane chairs, a purple divan, and a long table, rough-hewn from the bed of a broken cart. Two large oak trees shaded the other side of the house, where the bedrooms were built to face east into sunrise. I hung buttons and nails from the branches, a wind chime. Inside, the floors of the house were unevenly spaced. At night, raindrops fell on the metal roof.

My father used to say he liked to sit back and listen to the whole place make noise.

The days I recall finest were about as ordinary as they come—playing hopscotch on the slab of broken concrete, following my brothers through the cornfields, trailing my schoolbag through the dust. My older brothers and I read a lot of books back then—a bookmobile came around our street once every few months, staying fifteen minutes. When the sun bubbled yellow on the broken fence we ran out from the house, down towards the back of Chaucer's grocery store, to play in a stream that strikes me now as paltry, but back then was a waterway to contend with. We'd sail steamships down that mighty creek, and we'd have Nigger Jim whopping on Tom Sawyer for all he was worth. Huck Finn was not one we knew quite what to do with, and we mostly left him out of our adventures. The paper boats went around the corner and away.

My father was a house painter most of the time, but the thing he loved to do was hand-paint signs on the doorways of businesses in town. The names of important men on frosted glass. Gold-leaf lettering and careful silver curlicues. He got occasional work with the trading companies, the mills, and the small-town detective agencies. Every now and then a museum or an evangelical church wanted its welcome signs touched up. His business was nearly all in the white part of town, but when he worked on our side of the river we would go along with him and hold his ladder, hand him brushes and cloths. He painted wooden signs that swung in the wind for real estate and riverbed clams and sandwiches that cost a nickel. He was a short man who dressed impeccably for every job, no matter where it was. He wore a creased shirt with a starched collar and a silver tie pin. His trousers were cuffed at the bottom and he was happy to say that if he looked hard enough he could see the reflection of his work in his shoes. He never mentioned a single thing to us about money, or the lack of it, and when the Depression really kicked in, he simply went around to all of his old jobs and touched up the paint in the hope that the business would stay alive, and they might slip him a dollar or two when times were good.

The lack of money didn't bother my mother too much—she was a woman who had known the worst of times and best of times: she was old enough to have heard all the slave stories firsthand, and wise enough to see the value of getting out from under its yoke, or at least as far as anyone could get out from it in southern Missouri in those days.

She had been given, as a memento, the exchange slip from when my grandmother had been sold, and it was something she carried to remind her of where she came from, but when she finally got a chance to sell it, she did—to a museum curator who came from New York. She used the money to buy herself a secondhand sewing machine. She had other jobs too, but mostly she worked as a cleaner in the newspaper office in the center of town. She came home with papers from all over the country and at night read us the stories she considered the good ones, stories that opened up the windows of our house, simple tales about climbing a tree for cats, or boy scouts helping the fire brigade, or colored men fighting for what was good and right, what our mother called *justful*.

She wasn't from the Marcus Garvey choir: she held no rancor nor any desire to go back, but she wasn't averse to thinking that a colored woman could get herself a better place in the world.

My mother had the most beautiful face I knew, perhaps the most beautiful one I've ever known: dark as darkness, full, perfectly oval, with eyes that looked like my father had painted them, and a mouth that had a slight downturn of sadness, and the brightest teeth, so that when she smiled, it threw her whole face into another relief. She read in a high African singsong that I guess came down along the line from Ghana long ago, something that she made American, but tied us to a home we'd never seen.

Up until the age of eight I was allowed to sleep alongside my brothers, and, even after that, our mother would still put me in the bed beside them and read us all to sleep. Then she slipped her wide arms under me and carried me to my own mattress, which, because of the layout of the house, was in the narrow hallway outside her bedroom. I can still to this day hear my folks whispering and laughing before they went off to sleep: perhaps it is all I want to recall, perhaps our stories should stop on a dime, maybe things could begin and end right there, at the moment of laughter, but things don't begin and end really, I suppose; they just keep on going.

On an August evening when I was eleven, my father walked through the door with a splatter of paint on his shoes. My mother, who was baking bread, just stared at him. He had never before, not once, ruined his clothes while out painting. She dropped a teaspoon to the ground. A little patch of melted butter spread on the floor. "What in the name of Luther happened t'you?" she whispered. He stood pale and drawn, and gripped the edge of the red-and-white-checked tablecloth. He seemed like he was swallowing to steady his voice. He faltered a little and his knees buckled. She said: "Oh, Lord, it's a stroke." She put her arms around him.

My father's narrow face in her big hands. His eyes skipping past hers. She looked up and shouted at me: "Gloria, go get the doctor."

I slid out the door in my bare feet.

It was a dirt road in those days and I can recall the texture of each step—it sometimes feels that I'm running that road still. The doctor was sleeping off a league of hangovers. His wife said he couldn't be disturbed, and she slapped me twice on either side of the face when I tried to break past her up the stairs. But I was a girl with a good set of lungs. I screamed good and loud. He surprised me when he came to the head of the stairs, peered down, and then got his little black bag. I rode for my very first time in a motorcar, back to our house, where my father was still sitting at the kitchen table, clutching his arm. It was, it turned out, a mild enough heart attack, not a stroke, and it didn't change my father much, but it took the wind from my mother's heart. She wouldn't let him out of her sight: she was afraid he'd collapse at any moment. She lost her job at the newspaper when she insisted that he had to come sit with her as she cleaned: the editors couldn't abide the thought of a colored man sifting through their papers, though they saw nothing wrong with a woman doing it.

One of the most beautiful things I ever saw—still, to this day—was the sight of my father getting ready to go fishing one afternoon with some friends he'd made at the local corner store. He bumbled his way around the house, packing. My mother didn't want him to carry any of it, not even the rod and tackle, for fear it might strain him. He slammed more tackle into the picnic basket and shouted that he'd carry any damn thing he wanted. He even loaded the basket with extra beer and tuna-fish sandwiches for his friends. When a whistle came from outside, he turned and kissed her at the door, tapped her rear end, and whispered something in her ear. Mama snapped her head back and laughed, and I figured years later that it must've been something good and rude. She watched him go until he was almost out of sight beyond the corner, then she came back inside and got on her knees—she wasn't a godly woman, mind; she used to say that the heart's future was in a spadeful of dirt—but she began praying for rain, an all-out serious prayer that might bring my father back quickly so she could be with him.

That was the sort of everyday love I had to learn to contend with: if you grow up with it, it's hard to think you'll ever match it. I used to think it was difficult for children of folks who really loved each other, hard to get out from under that skin because sometimes it's just so comfortable you don't want to have to develop your own.

I will not for the life of me forget the sign they painted for me a few years later, after I'd lost two of my brothers in the Second World War over Anzio, and after the bombs had been dropped on Japan, after the speeches and the glad-handing. I was on my way up north to attend college in Syracuse, New York, and they had written on a little sign with my father's favorite paint, the precious gold that he kept for high-class jobs, and they held it up at the bus station, the placard built strong like a kite with a diamond-shaped back so it wouldn't flap in the wind: COME HOME SOON, GLORIA.

I didn't come home soon. I didn't come home at all. Not then, at least. I stayed up north, not so much running wild as having my head in books, and then my heart in a quick marriage, and then my soul in a sling, and then my head and heart in my own three little boys, and letting the years slip by, like folk do, watching my ankles puff up, and the next time I truly came home, to Missouri, years later, I was freedom-riding on the buses, and hearing stories about the police dragging out the water cannons, and I could hear my mother's voice in my ears: Gloria, you've done nothing all this time, nothing at all, where have you been, what have you done, why didn't you come back, didn't you know I was praying for rain?

—

I'VE GOT A BODY NOW, near thirty years later, that people think is church-going. I've got dresses that pull tight in the rear and keep my bosom from swaying. I thread the left shoulder of my blackest dress with a gold-colored brooch. I carry a white handbag with a looping handle. I wear hose stockings right up to my knees and sometimes I pull on a set of white gloves that go high to my elbows.

I've got a voice, too, with an undertow, so people look at me and think that I'm about to break into some old cane-field spiritual, but the truth is I haven't seen God since those early days when I left Missouri and I'd rather go home to my room in the Bronx and pull the bedsheets high and listen to Vivaldi slide through the stereo speakers than listen to any preacher ranting on about how to save the world.

In any case, I can hardly fit in pews anymore: it's never been comfortable to slide my body through.

I lost two marriages and three boys. They left in different ways, all of which broke my heart, but God isn't about to patch any of it back together. I know I made a fool of myself at times, and I know God made a fool of me just as often. I gave up on Him without too much guilt. I tried doing the right thing most of my life, but it wasn't in the Lord's house. Still and all, I know that *churchy* is the impression I've come around to giving. They look at me and listen and think I'm leading them towards the gospel. Everyone has their own curse, and I suppose—for a while at least—Claire saw me fitting in that peculiar box.

She wasn't a woman with whom I had any dispute. She seemed perfectly fine to me, as gentle-wayed as they come. It wasn't as if she tried to beat me upside the head with her tears. They came natural, like anyone else. She was embarrassed too, I could tell, with her curtains, her china, her husband painted on the wall, the teacup rattling on her saucer. She looked like she could fly out the window to Park Avenue at any time, with the streak of gray in her hair, her thin, bare arms, her long neck with blue veins. There were university diplomas on the wall in the corridor, and anyone could see that she was born on the right side of the river. She kept her house neat and scrubbed and she had a tiny southern lilt to her voice, so if there was any one of the ladies I felt a kinship with, it was her.

That morning glided by, like most good mornings do.

We had our flipflap with the tightrope man and then we wandered down from the roof and ate the doughnuts and sipped the tea and rattled on some. The living room was flooded with light. The furniture had a deep sheen to it. The ceilings were high and trimmed with a fancy molding. On the shelf, a small four-legged clock in a glass bell. My flowers were sitting in the center of the table. They had already begun to open a little in the heat.

The others were giddy with Park Avenue, I could tell. When Claire disappeared to the kitchen, they kept picking up their cups and glancing at the bottom to see what sort of stamp was there. Janet even lifted a glass ashtray. There were two cigarette butts squeezed into it. She held it up in the air to see if she could find some mark there, like it might have come from Queen Elizabeth herself. I could hardly contain my smile. "Well, you never know," said Janet, in a fierce whisper. She had a way of flipping her hair sideways without hardly moving her head. She placed the ash-tray back down on the table and gave a little sniff as if to say, *How dare you*. She rearranged her hair with another flick and looked across at Jacqueline. They had the white-woman language going between them, I've seen it enough times to know, it's all in the eyes, they dip a little to the side, they hold the gaze a moment, and then they look away. They got centuries of practice at it—I'm surprised some people aren't frozen in it.

I glanced towards the kitchen, but Claire was still beyond the louvered door—I could see her thin outline, bustling away, getting more ice. The snap of an ice tray. A running tap.

"Be with you in a jiffy," she called from the kitchen.

Janet stood and tiptoed over to the portrait on the wall. He was painted very fine, the husband, like a photograph, sitting in an antique chair with his jacket and blue tie on. It was one of those paintings where you'd hardly notice a brushstroke. He was looking out at us very seriously. Bald, with a sharp nose, and a little hint of wattle at his neck. Janet slid up next to the portrait and made a face. "Looks like he's got a stick up his rear end," she whispered. It was funny, and true, I suppose, but I couldn't help but feel a tightening in my chest, thinking that Claire was going to come out of the kitchen at any moment. I said to myself, *Say nothing, say nothing, say nothing*. Janet reached across and put her hand on the frame of the painting. Marcia had a wicked smile on her face. Jacqueline was biting her lip. All three of them were on the point of bursting out in laughter.

Janet's hand moved up along the frame and hovered over his thigh. Marcia threw herself back on the couch and clasped her mouth as if it was the funniest thing ever to happen. Jacqueline said: "Don't excite the poor man."

A hush and a few more giggles. I wondered what might happen if I were the one to get up and touch his knee, run my hand along the inside of his leg—imagine that—but I stayed rooted, of course, to the chair.

We heard the push of the louvered door and Claire was out and about, a big jug of ice water in her hands.

Janet stood away from the painting, Marcia turned into the couch and pretended to cough, and Jacqueline lit herself another cigarette. Claire held the plate out to me. Two bagels and three doughnuts. One with glazing, one with sprinkles, one plain.

"If I have another doughnut, Claire," I said, "I'll spill out into the street."

That was like letting the air out of a balloon and allowing it to fly around the room. I didn't mean for it to be that funny, but by all accounts it was, and the room let out a big breath. We soon fell to talking again with our serious faces on—truth, it was good talk, honest talk, remembering our boys, how and what they were, and what they went and fought for. The clock ticked on the shelf near the bookcase and then Claire walked us down the corridor, past the paintings and the university diplomas, to her boy's room.

She pushed open the door like it was the first time she'd done it in years. It creaked and swung on its hinges.

The room looked as if it had hardly been touched. Pencils, sharpeners, papers, baseball charts. Rows of books on the shelves. An oak dresser on tall legs. A Mickey Mantle poster above the bed. A water stain on the ceiling. A creak in the floorboards. It surprised me some, the smallness of the room—it just about fit all five of us. "Let me crack the window," said Claire. I was careful to take the end of the bed where there was most support—I didn't want it creaking. I put my hands down on the mattress so it wouldn't bounce and I leaned against the wall where I could feel the cool of the plaster against my back. Janet sat on the beanbag chair—she hardly made a dent in it—and the others took the far end of the bed, while Claire herself took a small white chair by the window where the breeze came in.

"Here we are," she said.

The sound in her voice like we'd come to the end of a very long journey.

"Well, it's lovely," said Jacqueline.

"It really is," said Marcia.

The ceiling fan spun and the dust settled like little mosquitoes around us. Along the shelves there were lots of radio parts and flat boards with electronic gizmos, wires hanging down. Big batteries. Three screens, their backs open and tubes showing.

"He liked his televisions?" I said.

"Oh, they're bits of computers," said Claire.

She reached across and picked up a photo of him in a silver frame on

his table, passed it around. The frame was heavy and it had a MADE IN EN-
GLAND sticker on the back velvet. In the photo Joshua was a thin little
white boy with pimples on his chin. Dark glasses and short hair. Eyes that
weren't comfortable looking in the camera. He wasn't in uniform either.
She said it was taken just before his graduation from high school, when
he was valedictorian. Jacqueline rolled her eyes again but Claire didn't
notice—every word she said about her son seemed to spread the smile on
her face. She picked up a snow globe from his desk, shook it up and
down. The globe was from Miami, and I thought, There's someone with
a touch of funny—snow falling over Florida. But when she turned it upside down it was like there was some other gravity in the world: she
waited until every little flake had settled and then she turned it again and
she told us all about him, Joshua, where he went to school, the notes he
liked on the piano, what he was doing for his country, how he read all the
books on the shelves, how he even built himself his own adding machine, went to college, then out to some park somewhere—he was the
sort of boy who was once liable to put another man on the Moon.

I had asked her once if she thought Joshua and my boys were friends,
and she said yes, but I knew nothing was probably further from the truth.

No shame in saying that I felt a loneliness drifting through me. Funny
how it was, everyone perched in their own little world with the deep need
to talk, each person with their own tale, beginning in some strange middle point, then trying so hard to tell it all, to have it all make sense, logical and final.

No shame in saying either that I let her rattle on, even encouraged her
to get it all out. Years ago, when I was at university in Syracuse, I developed a manner of saying things that made people happy, kept them talking so I didn't have to say much myself, I guess now I'd say that I was
building a wall to keep myself safe. In the rooms of wealthy folk, I had
perfected my hard southern habit of *Mercy* and *Lord* and *Landsakes*. They
were the words I fell back on for another form of silence, the words I've
always fallen back on, my reliables, they've been my last resort for I don't
know how long. And sure enough, I fell into the same ditch in Claire's
house. She spun off into her own little world of wires and computers and
electric gadgets, and I spun right back.

Not that she noticed, or seemed to notice anyway; she just peeked up at me from under her gray streak, and smiled, like she was surprised to be talking and nothing could stop her now. She was a picture of pure happiness, collecting one thought after the other, circling around, going back, explaining another thing about the electronics, detailing another about Joshua's time in school, rattling on about a piano in Florida, doing her own peculiar hopscotch through that boy's life.

It grew hot in the room, all five of us stuffed together. The hand of the clock by the bedside table didn't move anymore, maybe the batteries were expired, but it got to ticking in my mind. I could feel myself drifting. I didn't want to fall asleep. I had to bite the inside of my lip to keep myself from nodding off. Sure enough, it wasn't just me, we were all getting a little itchy, I could feel it, the shifting of bodies, and the way Jacqueline was breathing and the little cough that came every now and then from Janet, and Marcia wiping her brow with her little handkerchief.

I could feel a case of pins and needles coming on. I kept trying to move my toes and tighten my calf muscles—I guess I was grimacing a little, moving my body, making too much noise.

Claire smiled at me but it was one of those smiles that has a little zipper in it, a little too tight at the edges. I gave her a smile back, and tried hard not to make it seem like I was fidgety and awkward both. It wasn't as if she was boring me, it had nothing at all to do with what she was telling me, just my body giving me a hard time. I tightened my toes again, but that didn't work, and as quiet as possible I started knocking my knee off the edge of the bed, trying to get that half-gone feeling out of my leg. Claire gave me a look like she was disappointed, but it wasn't me who stood up at all; it was Marcia who finally stretched herself up in the air and flat-out yawned—yawned, like a child pulling a piece of chewing gum from her mouth, a thing that said, Look at me, I'm bored, I'm going to yawn and nobody's going to stop me.

"Excuse me," she said with a half-apology.

There was a lockdown for a moment. It was like seeing the air fall apart so that you could recognize all the separate things that go together to make it.

Janet leaned across and tapped Claire on the knee and said: "Go on with your story."

"I forget what I was saying," she said. "What was I saying?"

Nobody stirred.

"I know I was saying something important," she said.

"It was about Joshua," said Jacqueline.

Marcia glared across the room.

"I can't for the life of me recall what it was," said Claire.

She smiled another one of her quick zipper smiles, like her brain was refusing to accept the bold-faced evidence, and took a deep breath and jumped right in. Soon she was traveling on that highballing Joshua train again—he was at the cusp of something so entirely new, she said, that the world would never quite know what it missed, he was bringing machines to a place where they would do good things for man and mankind, and someday these machines would talk to each other just like people, even our wars would be fought through machines, it might be impossible to understand, but believe me, she said, it was the direction the world was going.

Marcia stood up again and stretched near the doorway. Her second yawn was not as bad as the first, but then she said: "Has anyone got the timetable for the ferry?"

Claire stopped cold.

"I didn't mean to interrupt you. Sorry. I just don't want to get caught up in any rush hour," said Marcia.

"It's lunchtime."

"I know, but it gets very busy sometimes."

"Oh, it does, yes," piped Janet.

"Sometimes you have to wait in line for hours."

"Hours."

"Even on Wednesdays."

"We could order something in," said Claire. "There's a new Chinese place on Lexington."

"Really, no. Thank you."

I could see the red rising to Claire's cheeks. She tried to smile again, a neutral smile, and I thought of that old yea-saying line *A little bit of poison helped her along,* from an old song my mother had taught me as a child.

Claire was pulling at her dress, straightening it, making sure it wasn't puckered. Then she picked the photo of her Joshua off the window ledge, and got to her feet.

"Well, I can't thank you enough for coming," she said. "It's been I don't know how long since someone has been in this room."

Her smile could've broken glass.

Marcia smiled a hammer blow right back. Jacqueline wiped her brow like she'd just been through the longest ordeal. The room filled with hems and haws and pauses and coughs, but Claire still clutched the photo frame right into her dress. Everyone began saying what a wonderful morning it was, and thank you so much for the hospitality, and wasn't Joshua such a brave guy, and yes we'll meet as soon as we can, and wasn't it a wonder that he was so smart, and Lord give me the address of the bakery that made the doughnuts, and whatever other specimen of word-fill we could find to plug the silence around us.

"Don't forget your umbrella, Janet."

"I was born with my umbrella in hand."

"It won't rain, will it?"

"Impossible to get a cab when it rains."

In the corridor Marcia adjusted her lipstick in the mirror and hung her handbag on her wrist.

"Next time I'm here, remind me to bring a tent."

"A what?"

"I'll camp right here."

"Me too," said Janet. "It's really a glorious apartment, Claire."

"A penthouse," said Marcia.

All sorts of lies were flying through the air, going back and forth, colliding with each other, and even Marcia was afraid to be the first to turn the handle of the door. She stood by the hat stand with the ball-and-claw feet. Her shoulder touched against it. The feet tottered and the handles swayed.

"I'll call you first thing next week."

"That would be wonderful," said Claire.

"We'll begin again in my house."

"Great idea—I can't wait."

"We'll put out yellow balloons," said Janet. "Remember those?"

"Did we have yellow balloons?"

"In the trees."

"I can't recall," said Marcia. "My mind's shot." Then she leaned across and whispered something in Janet's ear and they both giggled.

We could hear the clack outside from the elevator going up and down.

"Delicate question?" said Marcia. She had a guilty look on her face. She touched Claire's forearm.

"Please, please."

"Should we tip the elevator boy?"

"Oh, no, of course not."

I took a quick last look in the hallway mirror, and checked the clasp of my handbag, when all of a sudden Claire tugged my elbow and brought me down the corridor a little ways.

"Would you like some extra bagels, Gloria?" she said for all to hear.

"Oh, I've got enough bagels," I said.

"Just stay here a little while," she said under her breath.

There was a little rim of moist at her eye.

"Really, Claire, I got enough bagels."

"Stay awhile," she whispered.

"Claire," I said, trying to move away, but she had a hold of my elbow like she was clutching a last piece of twine.

"After everyone leaves?"

I could see the little tremble going in her nostrils. She had the type of face when you look closely at it, you think it's gone all a sudden old. There was a pleading in her voice. Janet and Jacqueline and Marcia were down the far end of the corridor, tickling their ribs now at one of the paintings on the wall.

Sure, I didn't want to leave Claire there with all those leftover crumbs on the carpet, and the crushed-out cigarettes in the ashtrays and I suppose I could've easily stayed, rolled up my sleeves, and started washing the dishes and cleaning the floor and tucking the lemons away in the Tupperware, but the thing is, I had the thought that we didn't go freedom-riding years ago to clean apartments on Park Avenue, no matter how nice she was, no matter how much she smiled. I had nothing against her. Her eyes were big and wide and generous. I was pretty sure I could've just sat down on the sofa and she would've served me hand and foot, but we didn't go marching for that either.

"Mercy," I said.

I couldn't help it.

"Ah-hem," went Jacqueline from the front door, like she was clearing her throat for speech.

"Coca-Cola one two three," said Marcia.

I could hear the tip-tap of Janet's shoes against the wooden floors. Jacqueline gave another little cough. Marcia was adjusting her hair in the mirror and muttering something under her breath.

There it was, I might never have believed it at any other time in my life—three white women wanting me to leave with them, and one of them trying to get me to hold back with her. I was flat-out dilemma'd, tied to a galloping horse. My heart began going hammer and tongs. There was moistness gathering in Claire's eyes and she was looking at me like I had to decide quickly. One choice was, I went with the others, down the elevator and out into the street, where we could stand and say our good-byes. The next choice was I stayed with Claire. I didn't want to lose our run of mornings by playing favorites, no matter how good-hearted she was, or how fancy her apartment, and so I stepped back and flat-out lied to her.

"Well, I got to make my way home to the Bronx, Claire, I got a church appointment in the afternoon, the choir."

I felt plain-out awkward for the way I was lying. She said of course, yes, she understood, how silly of her, and then she kissed me gentle on the cheek. Her lips brushed against the side of my hair clip and she said: "Don't worry."

I don't know the words for how she looked at me—there are few words—it was a welling up, a rising, a lifting up on the surface from the water, it was the sort of thing that could not be told. It felt for a moment that something had unthreaded down my spine, and my skin got tight, but what could I say? She grabbed hold of my wrist and tweaked it, saying a second time that she understood and she didn't mean to take me away from the choir. I stood away from her. It was over then, I was sure, happily solved, and the corridor brightened up for me and a few more smiles went around among us, and we declared we'd see each other at Marcia's next time—though it felt to me that there'd probably never be another time, that was the heartbreaker, I had a good idea that we'd let it slip away now, we had all had our chance, we'd brought our boys back to life for a little while—and we stepped out into the hallway, where Claire pressed the button for the elevator.

The iron gate was opened by the elevator boy. I was last to step in, and

Claire pulled me back by the elbow and brought me close again, a sadness settling over her face.

She whispered: "You know, I'd be happy to pay you, Gloria."

———

MY GRANDMOTHER WAS a slave. Her mother too. My great-grandfather was a slave who ended up buying himself out from under Missouri. He carried a mind-whip with him just in case he forgot. I know a thing or two about what people want to buy, and how they think they can buy it. I know the marks that got left on women's ankles. I know the kneeling-down scars you get in the field. I heard the stories about the gavel coming down on children. I read the books where the coffin ships groaned. I heard about the shackles they put on your wrists. I was told about what happened the first night a girl came to bloom. I heard the way they like their sheets tight on the bed so you can bounce a coin off them. I've listened to the southern men in their crisp white shirts and ties. I've seen the fists pumping in the air. I joined in the songs. I was on the buses where they lifted their little children to snarl in the window. I know the smell of CS gas and it's not as sweet as some folks say.

If you start forgetting you're already lost.

Claire panicked the moment she said it. It was like all of her face whirlpooled down to her eyes. She got sucked up into her own unexpected words. The bottom of her eyelids trembled a second. She opened a limp, resigned palm, and stared at it as if to say that she had disappeared from herself and all she had left was this strange hand she was holding out in the air.

I stepped quickly into the elevator.

The elevator boy said: "Have a nice afternoon, Mrs. Soderberg."

I could see her eyes as the door was pulled across: the tender resignation.

The door slid shut. Marcia sighed with relief. A giggle came from Jacqueline. Janet made a shushing sound and stared ahead at the elevator boy's neck, but I could tell she was holding back a grin. I just thought to myself that I wasn't going to fall into their game. They wanted to go off and whisper about it. *You know, I'd be happy to pay you, Gloria.* I was sure they had heard it, that they'd dissect it to death, maybe in some coffee shop, or some luncheonette, but I couldn't stand the thought of any more talking, any more doors closing, any more rattle of cups. I would just leave them behind, go for a walk, a little way uptown, clear my head, glide a little, put one foot in front of the other, and just mash this over in my mind.

Downstairs, the light was pouring clear across the tiles. The doorman stopped us and said: "Excuse me, ladies, but Mrs. Soderberg called down on the intercom and she'd like to see you again a moment."

Marcia gave one of her long sighs, and Jacqueline said how maybe she was bringing us some leftover bagels, like it was the funniest thing in the world, and I felt the heat pulse up in my cheeks.

"I have to go," I said.

"Ooh, somebody's hot under the collar," said Marcia. She had sidled up beside me and laid her hand on my forearm.

"I've got choir practice to go to."

"Lordy," she said, her eyes reduced to a slit.

I stared right back at her, then stepped out the door, up the avenue, the burn of their eyes on my back.

"Gloria," they called. "Glor-ia."

All around me, people were walking surefooted and shiny down the street. Businessmen and doctors and well-dressed ladies on the way to lunch. The taxis were driving by with their lights off all of a sudden for a colored woman, since they didn't want to pick me up, even in my best dress, in the bright afternoon, in the summer heat. Maybe I'd take them the wrong way, out of the city, where the money and the paintings were, to the Bronx, where the money and the paintings weren't. Everyone knows the taxi drivers hate a colored woman anyway—she won't tip him, or at the very best she'll nickel-and-dime him, that's the thinking, and there's no way to change it, no amount of freedom-riding is ever going to shift that. So I just kept placing one foot in front of the other. They were my best shoes, my going-to-opera leathers, and they were comfortable at first, they weren't too bad, and I thought the walking would shuck the loneliness.

"Gloria," I heard again, as if my own name were drifting away from me.

I didn't look back. I was sure that Claire would run after me, and I kept wondering if I'd done the right thing, leaving her behind, with the radio parts spread around her son's room, the books, the pencils, the baseball cards, the snow globes, the sharpeners, all neatly arranged on the shelves. Her face came back to me, the slide of sadness along her eyes.

Walk, don't walk.

I flat-out wanted to go home and curl up, to be buried in my apartment, away from traffic signals. I didn't want the shame, or anger, or jealousy, even—I just wanted to be home, the doors locked, the stereo on, some libretto sounding out around me, to sit on the broken-backed sofa, drowning everything else until it was all invisible.

Walk, don't walk.

Then again, I was thinking that I shouldn't be acting this way, maybe I was getting it all wrong, maybe the truth is that she was just a lonely white woman living up on Park Avenue, lost her boy the exact same way as I lost three of mine, treated me well, didn't ask for nothing, brought me in her house, kissed me on the cheek, made sure my teacup was full, and she just flat-out made a mistake by running her mouth off, one silly little statement I was allowing to ruin everything. I had liked her when she was fussing all over us, and she didn't mean harm, maybe she was just nervous. People are good or half good or a quarter good, and it changes all the time—but even on the best day nobody's perfect.

I could imagine her there, staring at the elevator, watching the numbers go down, chewing on her fingers, watching it all descend. Kicking herself for trying too hard. Running back to the intercom and begging us to stay just a minute more.

After almost ten blocks I got a little stab in my stomach, a stitch. I leaned up against the doorway of a doctor's office on Eighty-fifth Street, under the awning, breathing heavily, and weighing it all up in my mind, but then I thought, No, I'm not going to turn back, not now, I'm going to keep right on going, that's my duty and nobody's going to stop me.

Sometimes you get a bug in your mind. I'm going to make it all the way home even if it takes me a week, I thought, I'm going to step every inch of the way, gospel, that's what I had to do, no matter what, back to the Bronx.

Marcia, Janet, Jacqueline weren't calling after me anymore. Part of me was relieved that they let me go, that I didn't give in to them, didn't turn around. I wasn't sure what sort of response I would've let loose if they came trundling up alongside me. But another part of me thought that

Claire at least should have kept after me, I deserved that much, I wanted her to come tap me on the shoulder and beg a second time so that I knew it mattered, like our boys mattered. And I didn't want that to be the end of things for my boys.

I looked up the avenue. Park was gray and wide and there was a small rise of hill up ahead, a stepping-stone of traffic lights. I tightened the buckles on my shoes and stepped out into the crosswalk.

—

WHEN I LEFT MISSOURI, I was seventeen years old, and I made my way to Syracuse, where I survived on an academic scholarship. I fared pretty well, even if I say so myself. I had gifts for putting together some fine written sentences, and I could juggle a good slice of American history, and so—like a few young colored women my age—we were invited to elegant rooms, places with wooden panels and flickering candles and fine crystal glasses, and we were asked to give opinions on what had happened to our boys over Anzio, and who W.E.B. Du Bois was, and what it really meant to be emancipated, and how the Tuskegee Airmen came about, and what Lincoln would think of our achievements. People listened to our answers with that glazed-over look in their eyes. It was like they really wanted to believe what was being said in their presence, but they couldn't believe they were present for it.

Late in the evenings I played the piano stiffly, but it was as if they wanted jazz to leap from my fingers. This was not the Negro they expected. Sometimes they would look up, jolted, as if they'd just brought themselves, cold, out from a dream.

We were ushered to the door by the dean of one school or another. I could tell the parties only really began after the door closed and we were gone.

After visiting those splendid houses, I didn't want to go back to my little dorm room anymore. I walked around the city, down by Thornden Park and out to White Chapel gardens, sometimes until the blue dawn rose, wearing holes in my shoes.

Most of the rest of my college days were spent clutching my school satchel close to my chest and pretending not to hear the suggestions of the fraternity boys who wouldn't have minded a colored woman for a trophy: they had a safari intent to them.

Sure, I ached for the backroads of my hometown in Missouri, but leaving behind a scholarship would've been a defeat for my folks, who had no idea what it was like for me—they who thought their little girl was up north learning the truth of America in the sort of place where a young woman could cross the thresholds of the rich. They told me that my southern charm would get me by. My father wrote letters that began: *My Little Glorious*. I wrote back on airmail paper. I told them how much I loved my history classes, which was true. I told them I loved walking the woods, true too. I told them that I always had clean linen in my dorm room, true as well.

I gave them all the truth and none of the honesty.

Still, I graduated with honors. I was one of the first colored women at Syracuse to do so. I went up the steps, looked down on the crowd of gowns and hats, emerged into a stunned applause. A light rain fell across the college courtyard. I stepped past my college mates, terrified. My mother and father, up from Missouri, hugged me. They were old and ruined and held each other's hands as if they were just one piece. We went to a Denny's to celebrate. My mother said that we'd come a long way, us and our people. I shrank back down in the seat. They had packed the car so there was space for me in the back. No, I told them. I'd rather stay a little while as long as they didn't mind, I wasn't ready to return just yet. "Oh," they said, in unison, grinning just a little, "you're a Yankee now?" It was a grin that held pain—I guess you'd call it a grimace.

My mother, in the passenger seat, adjusted the rearview mirror as they drove off: she watched me go and waved out the window and shouted at me to hurry home.

I went into my first marriage, blank to the schemes of love. My husband-to-be was from a family in Des Moines. He was an engineering student and a well-known debater on the all-Negro debating circuit: he could hold any subject in the palm of his hand. He had bad skin and a beautiful bent nose. His hair was cut into a conservative Afro, tinged cinnamon at the edges. He was the sort of man who adjusted his glasses, precisely, with a middle finger. I met him on the night when he said that what America didn't realize was that it was forever censored, forever would be, unless common rights were changed. They were the words he used instead of civil rights: *common rights*. It brought a silence to the hall. My desire for him gripped my throat. He glanced across the room at me.

He had a lean boyishness, a full mouth. We dated for six weeks, then took the plunge. My parents and two remaining brothers drove north to join us for the wedding. The party had been arranged in a run-down hall on the outskirts of town. We danced until midnight and then the band left, dragging their trombones behind them. We searched around for our coats. My father had been silent most of the time. He kissed my cheek. He told me that not many people were ordering hand-painted signs any-more, that they were all going neon, but if he had one sign he could put on the world he would say that he was Gloria's father.

My mother gave advice—I still can't remember a single thing she said—and then my new husband whisked me away.

I looked across at him and smiled and he smiled back, and we both knew instantly that we'd made a mistake.

Some people think love is the end of the road, and if you're lucky enough to find it, you stay there. Other people say it just becomes a cliff you drive off, but most people who've been around awhile know it's just a thing that changes day by day, and depending on how much you fight for it, you get it, or you hold on to it, or you lose it, but sometimes it's never even there in the first place.

Our honeymoon was a disaster. The cold sunlight slanted through the windows of a rooming house in a small upstate New York town. I'd heard there were lots of wives who spent their wedding nights apart from their husbands. It didn't alarm me at first. I saw him curled, sleeplessly, on the couch, trembling as if in a fever. I could give him time. He insisted he was tired and spoke gravely of the strain of the day—I found out years later that he had spent absolutely all of his family savings on the marriage ceremony. I still felt a strong residue of desire for him when I heard him speak, or when he called me on the phone to tell me he wouldn't be home—it seemed that words had an affection for him, the way he spoke was magical, but after a while even his voice began to grate and he began to remind me of the colors of the walls in the hotel rooms in which he stayed: the colors leached into him and took him over.

After a while he didn't seem to have a name.

And then he said—in 1947, after eleven months of marriage—that he had been looking for another empty box to fit inside. This was the boy who had been the star of the Negro debating team. *Another empty box*. It felt as if my skull was being lifted from my flesh. I left him.

I avoided going home. I made up excuses, elaborate lies. My parents were still clinging on—what use was it to hurt them? The thought of them knowing that I had failed was coiled up inside me. I couldn't stand it. I didn't even tell them that I was divorced. I would phone my mother and tell her that my husband was in the bath, or down at the basketball courts, or out on a big job interview for a Boston engineering firm. I'd stretch the phone all the way to the front door and press the bell and say: "Oh, gotta go, Mom—Thomas has a friend here."

Now that he was gone he had a name again. Thomas. I wrote it in blue eyeliner on my bathroom mirror. I looked through it, beyond, at myself.

I should have gone back to Missouri, found myself a good job, settled back with my folks, maybe even uncovered a husband who wasn't scared of the world, but I didn't go back; I kept pretending I would, and soon enough my parents passed. My mother first, my father a broken man just one week later. I remember thinking that they went like lovers. They could not survive without each other. It was like they had spent their lives breathing each other's breath.

There was a loss lit in me now, and a rage, and I wanted to see New York. I heard it was a city that danced. I arrived at the bus station with two very fancy suitcases, high heels, and a hat. Men wanted to carry my cases but I walked on, head held high, down Eighth Avenue. I found a rooming house and applied to a scholarship foundation but heard nothing, and took the first job I could find: as a clerk for a betting outfit at the Belmont racetrack. I was a window girl. Sometimes we just walk into something that is not for us at all. We pretend it is. We think we can shrug it off like a coat, but it's not a coat at all, it's more like another skin. I was more than overqualified, but I took it anyway. Out I went to the racetrack every day. I thought I'd get out of the job in a matter of weeks, that it was just a moment, a blip of pleasure for a girl who knew what pleasure was but hadn't fully tasted it. I was twenty-two years old. All I wanted was to make my life thrilling for a while: to take the ordinary objects of my days and make a different argument out of them, no obligations to my past. Besides, I loved the sound of the gallop. On mornings, before the races, I would walk down among the stalls and breathe in all the scents of the hay and the soap and the saddle leather.

There's a part of me that thinks perhaps we go on existing in a place even after we've left it. In New York, at the racetrack, I loved to see the horses up close. Their flanks looked as blue as insect wings. They swished their manes back in the air. They were like Missouri to me. They smelled of home, of fields, of creek sides.

A man came around the corner with a horse brush in his hand. He was tall, dark, elegant. He wore overalls. His smile was so very wide and white.

My second and last marriage was the one that left me eleven floors up in the Bronx projects with my three boys—and I suppose, in a way, with those two baby girls.

Sometimes you've got to go up to a very high floor to see what the past has done to the present.

—

I WENT STRAIGHT on up Park and made it to 116th Street, at the crosswalk, and had begun to ponder just how exactly I was going to make my way across the river. There were always the bridges, but my feet had begun to swell and my shoes were cutting the back of my heels. The shoes were a half-size too big. I had bought them that way on purpose, for the opera on Sundays, when I liked to lean back and quietly flip the shoe off, let the cool take me. But now they rode up with each step and cut a little trench in my heels. I tried adjusting my stride, but the flaps of skin were beginning to come away. Each step dug a little deeper. I had a dime for the bus and a token for the subway but I had insisted to myself that I'd walk, that I'd make it back home under my own steam, one foot after the other. So, I kept on north.

The streets of Harlem felt like they were under siege—fences and ramps and barbed wire, radios in the windows, kids out on the sidewalks. Up in the high windows women leaned out on their elbows like they were looking back into a better decade. Below, wheelchair beggars with scraggly beards raced each other to cars stopped at the lights: they took their chariot duel seriously, and the winner dipped to pick a dime off the ground.

I caught glimpses of people's rooms: a white enamel jar against a window frame, a round wooden table with a newspaper spread out, a pleated shade over a green chair. What, I wondered, were the sounds filling those rooms? It had never occurred to me before but everything in New York is built upon another thing, nothing is entirely by itself, each thing as strange as the last, and connected.

A small blade of pain shot through me each time I stepped, but I could handle it—there were worse things than a torn-up pair of heels. A pop song traveled across my memory, Nancy Sinatra singing about her boots being made for walking. I had it in my thoughts that the more I hummed the less my feet would hurt. *One of these days these boots are gonna walk all over you.* One corner to another. One more crack in the pavement. That's the way we all walk: the more we have to occupy our minds the better. I started humming louder, not caring a bit who saw or heard me. Another corner, another note. As a little girl I had walked home through the fields, my socks disappearing into my shoes.

The sun was still high. I'd been walking slow, two hours or more.

Water ran down a drain: up ahead some kids had opened a fire hydrant and were dancing through the spray in their underwear. Their shiny little bodies were beautiful and dark. The older kids hung out on stoops, watching their brothers and sisters in their wet underclothes, maybe wishing they too could be that young again.

I crossed to the bright side of the street.

Over the years, in New York, I've been mugged seven times. There is an inevitability to it. You can feel it coming, even if from behind. A ripple in the air. A pulse in the light. An intent. In the distance, waiting for you, at a street garbage can. Under a hat, or a sweatshirt. The eye flick away. The glance back again. For a split second, when it happens, you're not even in the world. You're in your handbag and it's moving away. That's how it feels. There goes my life down the street, being carried by a pair of scattering shoes.

This time, the young girl, a Puerto Rican, stepped out of a vestibule on 127th. Alone. A swagger to her. Shadows from a fire escape crisscrossing her. She held a knife in under her own chin. A drugged-out shine to her eyes. I had seen that look before: if she didn't slice me she'd slice herself. Her eyelids were painted bright silver.

"The world's bad enough," I said to her, using my church tone, but she just pointed the blade of the knife at me.

"Give me your fucking bag."

"It's a sin to make it worse than it is."

She looped the handbag on the blade of the knife. "Pockets," she said.

"You don't have to do this."

"Oh, shut the fuck up," she said, and pulled the handbag high on her

elbow. It was as if she already knew from the weight that there was nothing inside but a handkerchief and some photographs. Then, swiftly, she
leaned forward with the knife and sliced open the side pocket of my
dress. The knife blade ran against my hip. My purse, my license, and two
more photos of my boys were kept inside the pocket. She sliced open the
second side.

"Fat bitch," she said as she walked around the corner.

The street throbbed around me. Nobody's fault but my own. The bark
of a dog flew by. I pondered the notion that I had nothing to lose anymore, that I should follow her, rip the empty handbag from her, rescue
my old self. It was the photographs that bothered me the most. I went to
the corner. She was already far down the street. The photos were scattered in a line down the pavement. I stooped and picked up what remained of my boys. I caught the eye of a woman, older than me, peeping
out the window. She was framed by the rotting wood. The sill was lined
with plaster saints and a few artificial flowers. I would have swapped my
life for hers at that moment, but she closed the window and turned away.
I propped the empty white handbag against the stoop and walked on
without it. She could have it. Take it all, except the photos.

I stuck out my hand and a gypsy cab stopped immediately. I slid into
the backseat. He adjusted his rearview mirror.

"Yeah?" he said, drumming away on the steering wheel.

Try measuring certain days on a weighing scale.

"Hey, lady," he shouted. "Where you going?"

Try measuring them.

"Seventy-sixth and Park," I said.

I had no idea why. Certain things we just can't explain. I could just as
easily have gone home: I had enough money tucked away under my mattress to pay for the cab fare ten times over. And the Bronx was closer than
Claire's house, that I knew. But we wove into the traffic. I didn't ask the
driver to turn around. The dread rose in me as the streets clicked by.

The doorman buzzed her and she ran down the stairs, came right out
and paid the cab driver. She glanced down at my feet—a little barrier of
blood had bubbled up over the edge of my heel, and the pocket of my dress
was torn—and something turned in her, some key, her face grew soft. She
said my name and discomforted me a moment. Her arm went around me
and she took me straight up in the elevator, down the corridor towards her

bedroom. The curtains were drawn. A deep scent of cigarettes came from her, mixed with fresh perfume. "Here," she said as if it was the only place in the world. I sat on the clean unrumpled linen as she ran the bath. The splash of water. "You poor thing," she called. There was a smell of perfumed salts in the air.

I could see my reflection in the bedroom mirror. My face looked puffed and worn. She was saying something, but her voice got caught up in the noise of the water.

The other side of the bed was dented. So, she had been lying down, maybe crying. I felt like flopping down into her imprint, making it three times the size. The door opened slowly. Claire stood there smiling. "We'll get you right," she said. She came to the edge of the bed, took my elbow, led me into the bathroom, sat me on a wooden stool by the bath. She leaned over and tested the warmth of the water with her knuckle. I unrolled the hose from my legs. Bits of skin came off my feet. I sat at the edge of the bath and swung my legs across. The water stung. The blood slid from my feet. Some vanishing sunset, the red glow dispersing in the water.

Claire laid a white towel out in the middle of the bathroom floor, at my feet. She handed me some sticky bandages, the back paper already peeled off. I couldn't help the thought that she wanted to dry my feet with her hair.

"I'm okay, Claire," I told her.

"What did they steal?"

"Only my handbag."

I felt charged with dread: she might think that all I wanted was the money she had offered me earlier to stay, to get my reward, my slave purse.

"There was no money in it."

"We'll call the police anyway."

"The police?"

"Why not?"

"Claire . . ."

She looked at me blankly and then an understanding traveled across her eyes. People think they know the mystery of living in your skin. They don't. There's no one knows except the person who carts it around her own self.

I bent down and put the bandages on the backs of my heels. They weren't quite wide enough for the cut. I could already feel the sharp sting of having to take them off later.

"You know the worst of it?" I said.

"What?"

"She called me fat."

"Oh, Gloria. I'm sorry."

"It's your fault, Claire."

"Excuse me?"

"It's your fault."

"Oh," she said, a tremble of nerves in her voice.

"I told you I shouldn't've had those extra doughnuts."

"Oh!"

She threw her head back until her neck was taut, and reached out to touch my hand.

"Gloria," she said. "Next time it's bread and water."

"Maybe a little pastry."

I leaned down to towel my toes. Her hand drifted to my shoulder, but then she rose and said: "You need slippers."

She rummaged in the closet for a pair of felt slippers for me and a dressing gown that must've belonged to her husband since her own wouldn't have fit me. I shook my head, and hung the gown on a hook on the door. "No offense," I said. I could live in my torn dress. She guided me into the living room. None of the plates or cups had been cleared from earlier. A bottle of gin sat in the center of the table. More emptiness than gin in the bottle. Ice was melting in a bowl. Claire was using the lemons we had cut instead of limes. She held the bottle high in the air and shrugged. Without asking she took out a second glass. "Excuse my fingers," she said as she dropped ice into the glass.

It had been years since I'd had a drink. It felt cool at the back of my throat. Nothing mattered but that momentary taste.

"God, that's good."

"Sometimes it's a cure," she said.

Sunlight shone through Claire's glass. It caught the color of lemon and the glass turned in her hands. She looked like she was weighing the world. She leaned back against the white of the couch and said: "Gloria?"

"Uh-huh?"

She looked away, over my head, to a painting in the corner of the room.

"The truth?"

"The truth."

"I don't normally drink, you know. It's just today, with, you know, all that talking. I think I made a bit of a fool of myself."

"You were fine."

"I wasn't silly?"

"You were fine, Claire."

"I hate making a fool of myself."

"You didn't."

"Are you sure?"

"Sure I'm sure."

"The truth's not foolish," she said.

She was swiveling her glass and watching the gin swirl in circles, a cyclone she wanted to drown herself in.

"I mean, about Joshua. Not the other stuff. I mean, I felt very silly when I said I'd pay you to stay. I just wanted someone to hang around. With, you know, with me. Selfish, really, and I feel awful."

"It happens."

"I didn't mean it." She looked away. "And then when you left, I called your name. I wanted to run after you."

"I needed to walk, Claire. That's all."

"The others were laughing at me."

"I'm sure they weren't."

"I don't think I'll ever see them again."

"Of course we will."

She let out a long sigh and threw back the drink, poured herself another, but mostly tonic this time, not gin.

"Why did you come back, Gloria?"

"To get paid, of course."

"Excuse me?"

"A joke, Claire, joke."

I could feel the gin working under my tongue.

"Oh," she said. "I'm a little slow this afternoon."

"I've no idea, really," I said.

"I'm glad you did."

"Nothing better to do."

"You're funny."

"That's not funny."

"It's not?"

"It's the truth."

"Oh!" she said. "Your choir. I forgot."

"My what?"

"Your choir. You said you had choir."

"I don't have choir, Claire. Never did. Never will. Sorry. No such thing."

She seemed to chew on the thought for a moment and then broke out in a grin.

"You'll stay awhile, though? Rest your feet. Stay for dinner. My husband should be home around six or so. You'll stay?"

"Oh, I don't think I should."

"Twenty dollars an hour?" she said with a grin.

"You've got me," I laughed.

We sat in happy quiet and she ran her fingers over the rim of her glass, but then she perked up and said suddenly: "Tell me about your boys again."

Her question rankled. I didn't want to think about my boys anymore. In a strange way, all I wanted was to be surrounded by another, to be a part of somebody else's room. I took a piece of lemon and slid it between my teeth and gums. The acid jarred me. I guess I wanted another sort of question altogether.

"Can I ask you something, Claire?"

"Of course."

"Could we put on some music?"

"What?"

"I mean, I suppose I'm just still in a little bit of shock."

"What sort of music?"

"Whatever you have. It makes me feel, I don't know, it calms me down. I like having an orchestra around. Do you have opera?"

"Afraid not. You like opera?"

"All my savings. I go to the Met every chance I get. Way up in the gods. Slip off my shoes and away I go."

She rose and went to the record player. I couldn't see the sleeve of the record she took out. She cleaned the vinyl with a soft yellow cloth and then she lifted the needle. She did everything small as if it was extraordinary and necessary. The music filled the room. A deep, hard piano: the hammers rippling across the strings.

"He's Russian," she said. "He can stretch his fingers to thirteen keys."

—

I WAS HAPPY ENOUGH the day my second husband found himself a younger version of the train he was riding towards oblivion. His hat had always been a helping too large on his head anyway. He upped and left me with three boys and a view of the Deegan. I didn't mind. My last thought of him was that nobody ought to be as lonely as him, walking away. But it didn't break my heart to close the door on him, or even to suck up the pride of a monthly check.

The Bronx was too hot in the summer, too cold in the winter. My boys wore brown hunting caps with earflaps. Later they threw the caps away and grew up into Afros. They hid pencils in their hair. We had our good days. I recall one summer afternoon when all four of us went to Foodland and raced up and down the frozen-food aisles with our shopping cart, keeping ourselves cool.

It was Vietnam that brought me to my knees. In she came and took all three of my boys from right under my nose. She picked them up out of their beds, shook the sheets, and said, These ones are mine.

I asked Clarence one day why he was going and he said one or two things about liberty, but mostly he was doing it because he was bored. Brandon and Jason said about the same thing too when their draft cards were dropped in our mailbox. It was the only mail that didn't get stolen in the houses. The mailman carried around huge bags of gloom. There was heroin all over the projects in those years and I thought maybe my boys were right, they were getting themselves free. I'd seen far too many children slouched down in the corners with needles in their arms, little spoons sticking out of their shirt pockets.

I as much as opened the windows and told them to be on their merry way. They flew off. Not one of them came back.

Every time a branch of mine got to being a decent size, that wind just came along and broke it.

I sat in my chair in my living room, watching afternoon soap operas.

I guess I ate. I suppose that's what I did. I ate whatever I could. Alone. Surrounded by packets of Velveeta and saltines, trying hard not to remember, switching channels and crackers and cheeses so the memories didn't get me. I watched my ankles swell. Every woman with her own curse, and I suppose mine was not much worse than a whole lot of them.

Everything falls into the hands of music eventually. The only thing that ever rescued me was listening to a big voice. There are years accumulated in a sound. I took to listening on the radio every Sunday and spent whatever extra grief money the government gave me on tickets to the Metropolitan. I felt like I had a room full of voices. The music pouring out over the Bronx. I sometimes turned the stereo so loud the neighbors complained. I bought earphones. Huge ones that covered half my head. I wouldn't even look at myself in the mirror. But there was a medicine in it.

That afternoon, too, I sat in Claire's living room and let the music float over me: it wasn't opera, it was piano, but it was a new pleasure—it thrilled me.

We went through three or four records. In the late afternoon or early evening, I wasn't quite sure, but I opened my eyes and she was putting a light blanket on my knees. She sat back against the white of the couch, the glass held at her lips.

"You know what I'd like to do?" said Claire.

"What's that?"

"I'd love to have a cigarette, right here, right now, in this room."

She fumbled around on the table for a package.

"My husband hates it when I smoke indoors."

She fished out a single cigarette. It was turned the wrong way around in her mouth and for a moment I thought she was going to light it that way, but she laughed and flipped it. The matches were wet and they dissolved at the touch.

I sat up and picked another book of matches off the table. She touched my hand.

"I think I'm a little tipsy," she said, but her voice was elegant.

I had the horrific feeling then—right then—that she might lean across and try to kiss me, or make some strange approach, like you read about in magazines. We lose ourselves sometimes. I felt hollow inside and there seemed to be a cool wind moving along my body like a breeze down a street, but it was nothing of the sort—all she did was sit back and blow the smoke to the ceiling and allow the music to wash over us.

A short while later she set the table for three and heated up a chicken pot pie. The phone rang a few times but she didn't answer. "I guess he's going to be late," she said.

On the fifth ring she picked it up. I could hear his voice but couldn't make out what he was saying. She held the mouthpiece close and I could hear her whispering the words *Dear* and *Solly* and *I love you*, but the conversation was quick and sharp, as if she were the only one talking, and I got the strangest feeling that the response at his end of the line was silence.

"He's in his favorite restaurant," she told me, "celebrating with the D.A."

It didn't make much difference—it's hardly like I wanted him to step down off the wall and get all friendly with me, but Claire had a far-off look in her eyes, like she wanted to be asked about him, and so I did. She launched into a long story about a promenade, a walk she was taking, a man who came towards her in long white flannel trousers, how he was the friend of some famous poet, how they used to go to Mystic every weekend, to a little restaurant there where he sampled their martinis; she went on and on and on, her eyes towards the front door, waiting for him to come home.

What drifted across my mind was how unusual it must have been, if anyone could have watched us from the outside, sitting with the light dimming outside, letting simple talk drift over us.

—

I CAN'T RECALL what it was led me to the small ad that was in the back of *The Village Voice*. It was not a paper I had any particular fondness for, but it was there one day, like sometimes happens, Marcia's ad, by the strangest chance, her, of all people. I sat down to compose a letter that maybe I wrote fifty or sixty times over, at the small counter in my kitchen. I explained everything about my boys, over and over again, the Lord knows how many times, saying how I was a colored woman, how I was living in a bad place but I kept it real nice and clean, how I had three boys and how I'd been through two husbands, how I'd really wanted to get back to Missouri but I never had the chance or the courage, how I'd be fine and happy to meet up with other people like me, how I'd be privileged. Each time I tore the letter up. It just didn't seem right. In the end all I wrote was: *Hello, my name is Gloria and I'd like to meet up too.*

—

IT MUST HAVE BEEN ten in the evening when her husband stumbled through the door. From the corridor he actually called: "Honey, I'm home."

In the living room, he stopped and stared, as if he were in the wrong place. He slapped his pockets like he might find a different set of keys there.

"Is something wrong?" he said to Claire.

He looked as if he could have aged some and then stepped right out of the portrait on the wall. His tie was a little askew but his shirt was buttoned up to the neck. The bald dome shone. He carried a leather briefcase with a silver snap. Claire introduced me. He pulled himself together and walked across to shake my hand. A faint scent of wine rolled from him. "Pleasure to meet you," he said, in the sort of way that meant he had no idea whatsoever why it might be a pleasure, but he had to say it anyway; he was bound to it by pure politeness. His hand was chubby and warm. He placed his briefcase at the foot of the table and frowned at the ashtray.

"Girls' night out?" he said.

Claire kissed him high, on the cheek, near his eyelid, and loosened his tie for him.

"I had some friends over."

He held the empty gin bottle to the light.

"Come sit with us," she said.

"I'm going to run and have a shower, hon."

"Come join us, come on."

"I'm pooped," he said, "but, boy, do I have a story for you."

"Oh, yeah?"

"Boy oh boy."

He was undoing the buttons on his shirt and for a moment I thought he might take the shirt off in front of me, stand in the middle of the room like some round white fish.

"Guy walked a tightrope," he said. "World Trade."

"We heard."

"You heard?"

"Well, yes, everyone's heard. The whole world's talking about it."

"I got to charge him."

"You did?"

"Came up with the perfect sentence too."

"He got arrested?"

"Quick shower first. Yes, of course. Then tell you all."

"Sol," she said, pulling his sleeve.

"I'll be right out, tell you everything."

"Solomon!"

He glanced at me. "Let me freshen up," he said.

"No, tell us, tell us now." She stood. "Please."

He flicked a look in my direction. I could tell he resented me, just being there, that he thought I was some housekeeper, or some Jehovah's Witness who had somehow come into his house, disturbed the rhythm, the celebration he wanted to give himself. He opened another button on his shirt. It was like he was opening a door at his chest and trying to push me out.

"The D.A. wanted some good publicity," he said. "Everyone in the city's talking about this guy. So we're not going to lock him up or anything. Besides the Port Authority wants to fill the towers. They're half empty. Any publicity is good publicity. But we have to charge him, you know? Come up with something creative."

"Yes," said Claire.

"So he pleaded guilty and I charged him a penny per floor."

"I see."

"Penny per floor, Claire. I charged him a dollar ten. One hundred and ten stories! Get it? The D.A. was ecstatic. Wait 'til you see. *New York Times* tomorrow."

He went to the liquor cabinet, his shirt a full three-quarters open. I could see the protrusion of his flabby chest. He poured himself a deep glass of amber liquid, sniffed it deeply, and exhaled.

"I also sentenced him to another performance."

"Another walk?" said Claire.

"Yes, yes. We'll get front-row tickets. In Central Park. For kids. Wait until you see this character, Claire. He's something else."

"He'll go again?"

"Yes, yes, but somewhere safe this time."

Claire's eyes skittered around the room, as if she was looking at different paintings and trying to hold them together.

"Not bad, huh? Penny per floor."

Solomon clapped his hands together: he was enjoying himself now. Claire looked at the ground, like she could see all the way through to the molten iron, the core of everything.

"And guess how he got the wire across?" said Solomon. He put his hand to his mouth and coughed.

"Oh, I don't know, Sol."

"Go on, guess."

"I don't really care."

"Guess."

"He threw it?"

"Thing weighs two hundred pounds, Claire. He was telling me all about it. In court. It'll be in all the papers tomorrow. Come on!"

"Used a crane or something?"

"He did it illegally, Claire. Stealth of night."

"I don't really know, Solomon. We had a meeting today. There were four of us, and me, and . . ."

"He used a bow and arrow!"

" . . . we sat around talking," she said.

"This guy should've been a Green Beret," he said. "He was telling me all this! His buddy shot a fishing line across first. Bow and arrow. Into the wind. Judged the angle just right. Hit the edge of the building. And then they fed the lines across until it could take the weight. Amazing, isn't it?"

"Yes," said Claire.

He put his bell-shaped glass on the coffee table with a sharp snap, then sniffed at his shirtsleeve. "I really must have a shower."

He walked over towards me. He became aware of his shirt and pulled it across without buttoning it. A waft of whiskey rolled from him.

"Well," he said. "Gosh, I'm sorry. I didn't really catch your name."

"Gloria."

"Good night, Gloria."

I swallowed hard. What he really meant was "good-bye." I had no idea what sort of reply he expected. I simply shook his hand. He turned his back and walked out along the corridor.

"Pleasure to meet you," he called over his shoulder.

He was humming a tune to himself. Sooner or later they all turn their backs. They all leave. That's gospel. I've been there. I've seen it. They all do.

Claire smiled and shrugged her shoulders. I could tell she wanted him to be someone better than what he was, that she must have married him for some good reason, and she wanted that reason to be on display, but it wasn't, and he had dismissed me, and it was the last thing she wanted from him. Her cheeks were red.

"Give me a moment," she said.

She went down the corridor. A mumble of voices from her bedroom. The faint sound of a bath running. Their voices raised and dipped. I was surprised when he emerged with her, just moments later. His face had softened: as if just being a moment with her had relaxed him, allowed him to be someone different. I guess this is what marriage is, or was, or could be. You drop the mask. You allow the fatigue in. You lean across and kiss the years because they're the things that matter.

"I'm sorry to hear about your sons," he said.

"Thank you."

"I didn't mean to be so brusque."

"Thank you."

"You'll excuse me?" he said.

He turned and then he said, with his gaze to the floor: "I miss my boy too sometimes." And then he was gone.

I suppose I've always known that it's hard to be just one person. The key is in the door and it can always be opened.

Claire stood there, beaming ear to ear.

"I'll drop you home," she said.

The thought of it flushed me with warmth but I said: "No, Claire, that's all right. I'll just get a taxi. Don't you worry."

"I'm going to drop you home," she said, with a sudden clarity.

"Please, just take the slippers. I'll get you a bag for your shoes. We've had a long day. We'll take a car service."

She rummaged in a drawer and pulled out a small phone book. I could hear the sound of the bath still running. The water pipes kicked in and there was a groan from the walls.

—

DARK HAD FALLEN OUTSIDE. The driver was waiting, propped, smoking a cigarette, against the hood of the car. He was one of those old-time drivers, with a peaked hat and a dark suit and a tie. He suddenly stubbed the cigarette out and ran to open the rear door for us. Claire slid in first. She was agile across the rear seat and she swung her legs across the well in the middle of the seats. The driver took my elbow and guided me inside. "There we go," he said in a big false voice. I felt a little old-black-ladyish, but that was all right—he was just doing his best, wasn't trying to make me feel bad.

I told him the address and he hesitated a moment, nodded, went around to the front of the car.

"Ladies," he said.

We sat in silence. On the bridge she flicked a quick look back at the city. All was light—offices that looked as if they were hovering on the void, the random pools from street lamps, headlights flashing across our faces. Pale concrete pillars flashed by. Girders in strange shapes. Naked columns capped with steel beams. The sweep of the river below.

We crossed over into the Bronx, past shuttered bodegas and dogs in doorways. Fields of rubble. Twisted steel pipes. Slabs of broken masonry. We drove beyond railroad tracks and the flashing shadows of the underpass, through the fire-blown night.

Some figures lumbered along among the garbage cans and the piles of refuse.

Claire sat back.

"New York," she sighed. "All these people. Did you ever wonder what keeps us going?"

A big smile went between us. Something that we knew about each other, that we'd be friends now, there wasn't much could take it from us, we were on that road. I could lower her down into my life and she could probably survive it. And she could lower me into hers and I could rummage around. I reached across and held her hand. I had no fear now. I could taste a tincture of iron in my throat, like I had bitten my tongue and it had bled, but it was pleasing. The lights skittered by. I was reminded how, as a child, I used to drop flowers into large bottles of ink. The flowers would float on the surface for a moment and then the stem would get swamped, and then the petals, and they would bloom with dark.

There was a commotion outside the projects when we pulled up. Nobody even noticed our car. We glided up by the fence, shadowed by the overpass. The black steel beams were shimmying with streetlight. None of the women of the night were out, but a couple of girls in short skirts were huddled under the light in the entrance. One was leaning across the shoulder of another and sobbing.

I had no time for them, the hookers, never had. I didn't hold any rancor for them nor any bleeding heart. They had their pimps and their white men who felt sorry for them. That was their life. They'd chosen it.

"Ma'am," said the driver.

I still had my hand in Claire's.

"Good night," I said.

I opened the door, and just then I saw them come out, two darling little girls coming through the globes of lamplight.

I knew them. I had seen them before. They were the daughters of a hooker who lived two floors above me. I had kept myself away from all that. Years and years. I hadn't let them near my life. I'd see their mother in the elevator, a child herself, pretty and vicious, and I'd stared straight ahead at the buttons.

The girls were being guided down the path by a man and a woman. Social workers, their pale skin shining, a scared look on their faces.

The girls were dressed in little pink dresses, with bows high on their chests. Their hair was done in beads. They wore plastic flip-flops on their feet. They were no more than two or three years old, like twins, but not twins. They were both smiling, which is strange now when I think back on it: they had had no idea what was happening and they looked a picture of health.

"Adorable," said Claire, but I could hear the terror in her voice.

The social workers wore the straitjacket stare. They were pushing the kids along, trying to guide them through the remaining hookers. A cop car idled farther up the block. The onlookers were trying to wave to the little girls, to lean down and say something, maybe even gather them up in their arms, but the social workers kept pushing the women away.

Some things in life just become very clear and we don't need a reason for them at all: I knew at that moment what I'd have to do.

"They're taking them away?" said Claire.

"I suppose."

"Where'll they go?"

"Some institution somewhere."

"But they're so young."

The kids were being bundled towards the back of the car. One of them had started crying. She was holding on to the antenna of the car and wouldn't let go. The social worker tugged her, but the child hung on. The woman came around the side of the car and pried the child's fingers off.

I stepped out. It didn't seem to me that I was in the same body anymore. I had a quickness. I stepped off the pavement and onto the road. I was still in Claire's slippers.

"Hold on," I shouted.

I used to think it had all ended sometime long ago, that everything was wrapped up and gone. But nothing ends. If I live to be a hundred I'll still be on that street.

"Hold on."

Janice—she was the older of the two—let her fingers uncurl and reached out to me. Nothing felt better than that, not in a long time. The other one, Jazzlyn, was crying her eyes out. I looked over my shoulder to Claire, who was still in the backseat, her face shining under the dome light. She looked frightened and happy both.

"You know these kids?" said the cop.

I guess I said yes.

That's what I finally said, as good a lie as any: "Yes."

BOOK FOUR

ROARING SEAWARD, AND I GO

October 2006

S HE OFTEN WONDERS WHAT IT is that holds the man so high
in the air. What sort of ontological glue? Up there in his haunted silhouette, a dark thing against the sky, a small stick figure in the vast expanse.
The plane on the horizon. The tiny thread of rope between the edges of
the buildings. The bar in his hands. The great spread of space.

The photo was taken on the same day her mother died—it was one of
the reasons she was attracted to it in the first place: the sheer fact that
such beauty had occurred at the same time. She had found it, yellowing
and torn, in a garage sale in San Francisco four years ago. At the bottom
of a box of photographs. The world delivers its surprises. She bought it,
got it framed, kept it with her as she went from hotel to hotel.

A man high in the air while a plane disappears, it seems, into the edge
of the building. One small scrap of history meeting a larger one. As if the
walking man were somehow anticipating what would come later. The in-
trusion of time and history. The collision point of stories. We wait for the
explosion but it never occurs. The plane passes, the tightrope walker gets
to the end of the wire. Things don't fall apart.

It strikes her as an enduring moment, the man alone against scale, still capable of myth in the face of all other evidence. It has become one of her favorite possessions—her suitcase would feel wrong without it, as if it were missing a latch. When she travels she always tucks the photo in tissue paper along with the other mementoes: a set of pearls, a lock of her sister's hair.

—

At the security line in Little Rock she stands behind a tall man in jeans and a battered leather jacket. Handsome in an offhand way. In his late thirties or early forties, maybe—five or six years older than she is. A bounce in his step as he moves up the line. She edges a little closer to him. The tag on his bag reads: DOCTORS WITHOUT BORDERS.

The security guard bristles and examines his passport.

—Are you carrying any liquids, sir?

—Just eight pints.

—Excuse me, sir?

—Eight pints of blood. I don't think they'll spill.

He taps his chest and she chuckles. She can tell that he's Italian: the words stretched with a lyrical curl. He turns to her and smiles, but the security guard stands back, stares at the man, as if at a painting, and then says: Sir, I need you to step out of line, please.

—Excuse me?

—Step out of line, please. Now.

Two other guards swing across.

—Listen, I'm only joking, says the Italian.

—Sir, follow us, please.

—Just a joke, he says.

He's pushed in the back, toward an office.

—I'm a doctor, I was just making a joke. Just carrying eight pints of blood, that's all. A joke. A bad one. That's all.

He flings out his hands to plead, but his arm is twisted high behind his back, and the door is closed behind him with a thump.

The rancor passes down the line to her and the other passengers in the security area. She feels a thread of cold along her neck as the security guard stares her down. She has a bottle of perfume sealed in a little ziploc bag, and she places it carefully in the tray.

—Why are you bringing this in carry-on, miss?

—It's less than three ounces.

—And the purpose of your travel?

—Personal. To see a friend.

—And what's your final destination, miss?

—New York.

—Business or pleasure?

—Pleasure, she says, the word catching at the back of her throat.

She answers calmly, practiced, controlled, and when she goes through the metal detector she automatically stretches her arms out to be searched, even though she doesn't set off the alarm.

—

The plane is near empty. The Italian finally slouches on, quiet, embarrassed, contrite. He has a hunch to his shoulders as if he can't quite deal with his height. His light-brown hair in a havoc. A small shadow of gray-tinged beard on his chin. He catches her eye as he takes the seat behind her. A smile travels between them. She can hear him, behind her, as he takes off his leather jacket and sighs down into his place.

Halfway through the flight she orders a gin and tonic and he extends a twenty-dollar bill across the seat to pay for her drink.

—They used to give things out free, he says.

—You're used to traveling in style?

She is annoyed at herself—she didn't mean to be so curt, but sometimes it happens, the words come out at the wrong angle, like she's on the defensive from the very beginning.

—No, not me, he says. Style and I never got along.

She can tell it's true, the wide collar on his shirt, an ink spot on the breast pocket. He looks like the sort of man who might give himself his own haircut. Not your normal Italian, but what's a normal Italian anyway? She has grown tired of the people who tell her that she's not a normal African-American, as if there were only one great big normal box that everyone had to pop out of, the Swedish, the Poles, the Mexicans, and what did they mean anyway that she wasn't normal, that she didn't wear gold hoop earrings, that she moved tightly, dressed tightly, kept everything in line?

—So, she says, what did they tell you in the airport?

—Not to make jokes anymore.

—God bless America.

—The bad-joke police. Did you hear the one . . .

—No, no!

— . . . about the man who went to the doctor's office with the carrot up his nose?

Already she is laughing. He gestures to the aisle seat.

—Please, yes.

She is surprised by the immediate comfort she feels, inviting him to sit, even turning toward him, bridging the distance over the middle seat. She is often nervous around men and women her own age, their attention, their desires. A tall, willowy beauty, she has cinnamon skin, white teeth, serious lips, no makeup, but her dark eyes always seem to want to escape her good looks. It adds up to a strange force around her: she strikes people as intelligent and dangerous, an otherland stranger. Sometimes she tries to claw her way through the awkwardness, but falls back down, suffocating. It's as if she feels it all bubbling up inside, all that wild ancestry, but she can't get it to boil.

At work she is known as one of the bosses with ice in her veins. If there's a joke e-mail sent around the offices, she is seldom copied on it: she would love to be, but seldom is, even among her closest colleagues. In the foundation the volunteers talk about her behind her back. When she steps into jeans and a T-shirt to join them in the field there is always something stiff about it, her shoulders in a controlled line, her demeanor mannered.

— . . . and the doctor says, I know exactly what's wrong with you.

—Yes?

—You're not eating properly.

—Ba dah boom, she says, bringing her head alarmingly close to his shoulder.

—

Four small plastic bottles of gin rattle on his airplane tray. He is, she thinks, already too complicated. He is from Genoa and divorced, with two children. He has worked in Africa, Russia, and Haiti, and spent two years in New Orleans working as a doctor in the Ninth Ward. He has just moved to Little Rock, he says, where he runs a small mobile clinic for veterans home from the wars.

—Pino, he says, extending his hand.

—Jaslyn.

—And you? he asks.

—Me?

A charm in his eyes.

—What about you?

What can she tell him? That she comes from a long line of hookers, that her grandmother died in a prison cell, that she and her sister were adopted, grew up in Poughkeepsie, their mother Gloria went around the house singing bad opera? That she got sent to Yale, while her sister chose to join the army? That she was in the theater department and that she failed to make it? That she changed her name from Jazzlyn to Jaslyn? That it wasn't from shame, not from shame at all? That Gloria said there was no such thing as shame, that life was about a refusal to be shamed?

—Well, I'm sort of an accountant, she says.

—A sort of accountant?

—Well, I'm at a small foundation. We help with tax preparation. It's not what I thought I'd do, I mean, when I was younger, but I like it. It's good. We go around the trailer parks and hotels and all. After Rita and Katrina and all. We help people fill out their tax forms and take care of things. 'Cause often they don't even have their driver's licenses anymore.

—Great country.

She eyes him suspiciously, but wonders if perhaps he means it. He could—it's possible, she thinks—why not, even in these times.

The more he talks the more she notices that his accent has a couple of continents in it, like it has landed in each place and picked up a few sounds in each. He tells her the story of how, as a child in Genoa, he used to go to the soccer games and help bandage the wounded who were involved in stadium fights.

—Serious injuries, he says. Especially when Sampdoria played Lazio.

—Sorry?

—You have no idea what I'm talking about, do you?

—No, she laughs.

He cracks the small seal on another bottle of gin, pours half in her glass, half in his own. She feels herself loosening further around him.

—Well, she says, I once worked at McDonald's.

—You're kidding.

C O L U M   M c C A N N

—Kind of. I tried to be an actor. Same thing, really. Learn your lines—
you want fries with that? Hit your mark—you want fries with that?

—Film?

—Theater.

She reaches across for her glass, lifts it, drinks. It is the first time in
years that she's opened herself to a stranger. It's as if she has bitten into
the skin of an apricot.

—Cheers.

—Salute, he says in Italian.

The plane banks out over the city. Storm clouds and a driving rain
against the windows. The lights of New York like shadows of light, under
the clouds, ghostly, rain-dampened, dim.

—So? he says, gesturing out the window, the darkness webbed over
Kennedy.

—Excuse me?

—New York. You staying long?

—Oh, I'm going to see an old friend, she says.

—I see. How old?

—Very old.

———

When she was young and not so shy, she used to love going out on the
street in Poughkeepsie, outside their small house, where she would run
along with one foot on the pavement and the other on the road. It took
some gymnastics: she had to extend one leg and keep the other slightly
bent, running at close to full pace.

Claire came to visit in a chauffeured town car. Once she sat and
watched the trick for a long time, with delight, and said that Jaslyn was
running an extended entrechat, half on, half off, half on, half off, half on.

Later, Claire sat with Gloria on wooden chairs in the back garden, by the
plastic pool, near the red fence. They looked so different, Claire in her neat
skirt, Gloria in her flowered dress, as if they too were running on different
levels of pavement, but in the same body, the two of them combined.

———

At the luggage carousel, Pino waits beside her. He has no suitcase to pick
up. She rubs her hands together, nervously. Why, still, this small feeling

of tightness at her core? Not even her own two gin and tonics have done their work. But he too is edgy, she notices, as he moves from foot to foot and adjusts his shoulder bag. She likes his nervousness—it brings him down to earth, makes him solid. He has already suggested that he can share a taxi with her into Manhattan, if she'd like. He is on his way to the Village, wants to hear some jazz.

She wants to tell him that he doesn't look like a jazz man, that there's something folk-rock about him, that he might fit well into a Bob Dylan song, or he might be found with the liner notes for Springsteen in his pocket, but jazz doesn't fit. Yet she likes complications. She wishes she could turn and say: I like people who unbalance me.

So much of her time spent like this: dreaming up things to say and never quite saying them. If only she could turn to Pino and say that she'll come with him tonight, to a jazz club, sit at a table with a tasseled lamp, feel the saxophone trill through her, stand and move to the tiny dance floor and align her long body against his, maybe even allow him to rub his lips along her neck.

She watches the line of suitcases tumble from the conveyor belt onto the carousel below: none of them hers. A group of kids on the far side jump on and off the carousel, to the amusement of their parents. She waves across and mugs a face at the youngest, who is perched atop a giant red suitcase.

—Your children, she says as she turns to Pino. Do you have photographs?

A silly, awkward question. She has spoken without thinking, leaned too close to him, asked too much. But he pulls out a cell phone and scrolls through the pictures, shows her a young teenage girl, dark, serious, attractive. He starts to scroll again for a picture of his boy, when a security guard comes right up beside him.

—No cell phone use in the terminal, sir.

—Excuse me?

—No cell phones, no cameras.

—Not your day, she says, smiling, as she leans down to pick up her small traveling bag.

—Maybe, maybe not, he says.

Across the way, a high yelp. The kids riding suitcases on the moving carousel have fallen afoul of the security guard too. She and Pino turn to each other. She feels much younger all of a sudden: the thrill of flirtation, her whole body shot through with lightness.

As they step from the terminal he says that they'll take the Queensboro Bridge, if that's okay with her. He will drop her off first and then go downtown.

So he knows the city, she thinks. He's been here before. This place belongs to him too. Another surprise. She's always thought that one of the beauties of New York is that you can be from anywhere and within moments of landing it is yours.

Sabine Pass and Johnson's Bayou, Beauregard and Vermilion, Acadia and New Iberia, Merryville and DeRidder, Thibodaux and Port Bolivar, Napoleonville and Slaughter, Point Cadet and Casino Row, Moss Point and Pass Christian, Escambia and Walton, Diamondhead and Jones Mill, Americus, America.

Names in her mind, flooding.

Rain outside the terminal. He stands under a small ledge, pulls a packet of cigarettes from his inside pocket. He tamps the pack with the heel of his hand, shifts a cigarette upward, offers it. She shakes her head no. She used to smoke, not anymore, an old habit from her days at Yale; almost everyone in the theater smoked.

But she likes the fact that he lights up and lets the smoke blow in her direction, that it will get in her hair, that she will own the scent of it later.

The taxi slides through the rain. The last of the storm has blown over the city, a final exhausted bow, an endfall. He hands her a card before the taxi pulls in by the awning on Park Avenue. He scribbles his name and the number of his cell on the back.

—Fancy, he says, surveying the street.

He picks her small bag out of the back of the cab, leans across and kisses her on each cheek. She notices with a smile that he has one foot on, one foot off the curb.

He fumbles in his pocket. She looks away and she hears a sudden click. He has taken her photograph with his cell phone. She is not quite sure how to respond. Erase it, file it, make it his screen saver? She thinks of herself, there, pixelated, alongside his children, carried around in his pocket, to his jazz club, to his clinic, to his home.

She has never done this with a man before, but she takes her own card out and tucks it into his shirt pocket, taps it closed with the palm of her hand. She feels her face tighten again. Too forward. Too flirtatious. Too easy.

It used to bother her terribly, as a teenager, that her mother and grandmother had worked the streets. She thought it might rebound on her someday, that she would find herself too much in love with love. Or that it might be dirty. Or that her friends would find out. Or, worse, that she might ask a boy to pay for it. She was the last of her high school friends to even kiss a boy: a kid in school once called her the Reluctant African Queen. Her first kiss ever was just after science class before social studies. He had a broad face and dark eyes. He held her in the doorway and kept his foot on the frame. Only the constant knocking on the door from a teacher separated them. She walked home with him that day, hand in hand, through the streets of Poughkeepsie. Gloria saw her from the porch of their small house and smiled deeply. She and the boy lasted all the way through college. She had even contemplated marrying him, but he went to Chicago to take a trading job. She went home to Gloria then, wept for a day.

Afterward, Gloria said to her that it was necessary to love silence, but before you could love silence you had to have noise.

—So you'll call me, then? she asks him.

—I'll call you, yes.

—Really? she asks with arched brow.

—Of course, he replies.

He extends his shoulder playfully. She rocks backward as if in a cartoon, her arms spread wide, flailing. She is not sure why she does it, but for a moment she doesn't really care—there is an electricity to it, it makes her laugh.

He kisses her again, this time on the lips, quickly, smartly. She almost wishes her co-workers were here, that they could see her, bidding good-bye to an Italian man, a doctor, on Park Avenue, in the dark, in the cold, in the rain, in the wind, in the night. Like there might some secret camera that beams it all back to the offices in Little Rock, everyone looking up from the tax forms to watch her wave good-bye, to see him turn his body in the back of the cab, his arm raised, a shadow on his face, a smile.

She hears the hiss of the taxi tires as the car pulls away. Then she cups her hands out beyond the awning and runs some rainwater through her hair.

—

The doorman smiles, although it has been years since she's seen him. A Welshman. He used to sing on Sundays when she, Gloria, and her sister came to visit. She can't quite recall his name. His mustache has gone gray.

—Miss Jaslyn! Where've you been?

And then she remembers: Melvyn. He reaches for the small bag and for a moment she thinks he's going to say how much she's grown. But all he says is, in a grateful way: They put me on the night shift.

She is not quite sure if she should kiss his cheek or not—this evening of kissing—but he solves the dilemma by turning away.

—Melvyn, she says, you haven't changed a bit.

He pats his stomach, smiles. She is wary of elevators, she would like to take the stairs, but a teenage boy is there with his hat and white gloves on.

—Madame, says the elevator boy.

—You staying long, Miss Jaslyn? asks Melvyn, but already the gate is closing.

She smiles at him from the back of the elevator.

—I'll call up to Mrs. Soderberg's, he says through the grille, and let them know you're here.

The elevator boy stares straight ahead. He takes great care with the Otis. He doesn't engage her in conversation, his head tilted slightly to the ceiling and his body as if it's counting out rhythm. She gets the sense that he will be here ten years from now, twenty, thirty. She would like to step up behind him and whisper, Boo! in his ear, but she watches the panel and the small circular white lights as they rise.

He pulls the lever, aligns the elevator and the floor perfectly. He slides his foot out to test his workmanship. A young man of precision.

—Madame, he says. First door on your right.

—

The door is opened by a tall Jamaican nurse, a man. They are momentarily confused, as if they should know each other somehow. The exchange is rapid-fire. I'm Mrs. Soderberg's niece. Oh, I see, come in. Not her niece, really, but she calls me her niece. Please come in. I called earlier. Yes, yes, she's sleeping now. Step inside. How is she? Well . . . he says.

And the *well* is drawn out, a pause, not an affirmative—Claire is not well at all; she is at the bottom of a dark well.

Jaslyn hears the sound of other voices: a radio, perhaps?

The apartment seems as if it has been sunk in aspic. It used to terrify her and her sister as children, on those occasions when they came into the city with Gloria, the dark hallway, the artwork, the smell of old wood. She and her sister held hands as they walked down the corridor. The worst thing was the portrait of the dead man on the wall. The painting had been done in such a way that his eyes seemed to follow them. Claire would talk about him all the time, that Solomon had loved this and Solomon loved that. She had sold some of the other paintings—even her Miró, to help pay the expenses—but the Solomon portrait remained.

The nurse takes her bag and settles it in the corner against the hat stand.

—Please, he says, and he motions her toward the living room.

She is stunned to see six people, most of them her own age, around the table and on the sofa. They are casually dressed but sipping cocktails. Her heart thumps against the wall of her chest. They too freeze at the sight of her. Well, well. The true nieces, nephews, cousins, perhaps? Song of Solomon. He is dead fourteen years but she can see him in their faces. One, almost certainly, is Claire's niece, with a streak of gray in her hair.

They stare at her. The air like ice around her. She wishes that she had taken Pino upstairs alongside her, so he could help take control, calmly, smoothly, or at least draw attention. She can still feel the kiss on her lips. She touches them with her fingers, as if she can hold the memory of it there.

—Hi, I'm Jaslyn, she says with a wave.

An idiotic wave. Presidential, almost.

—Hi, says a tall brunette.

She feels as if she has been nailed to the floor, but one of the nephews strides across the room. He has something of the petulant college boy about him, chubby face, a white shirt, a blue blazer, a red handkerchief in the breast pocket.

—Tom, he says. Lovely to meet you, Jaslyn, finally.

He says her name like something he wants to flick off his shoe, and the word *finally* stretches into rebuke. So he knows about her. He has heard. He probably thinks she's here to dig. So be it. Gold digger. The truth is, she couldn't care less about the will; if she got anything she would probably give it away.

—A drink?

—I'm fine, thanks.

—We figured that Auntie would've wanted us to enjoy ourselves even in the worst of times. He lowers his voice: We're making Manhattans.

—How is she?

—She's sleeping.

—It's late—I'm terribly sorry.

—We have soda too, if you want.

—Is she . . . ?

She cannot finish the sentence. The words hang in the air between her and Tom.

—She's not well, he says.

That word again. A hollow echo all the way down to the ground. No splash. A constant free fall. Well well.

She dislikes them for drinking, but then she knows she should join them, that she should not be apart. Bring Pino back, let him slide some charm among them, let him take her off into the evening upon his arm, nestled up against his leather jacket.

—Maybe I'll take a drink, she says.

—And so, says Tom, what exactly brings you here?

—Excuse me?

—I mean, what exactly do you do now? Weren't you working for the Democrats or something?

She hears a slight giggle from across the room. They are facing her, all of them, watching, as if she has, at last, made it to the stage.

—

She likes the people with the endurance to tolerate the drudge, the ones who know that pain is a requirement, not a curse. They arrange their lives in front of her, a few sheets of paper, a pay stub, a welfare check, all they have left. She adds up the figures. She knows the tax credits, the loopholes, the exits and entrances, the phone calls that must be made. She tries to nullify mortgage payments on a house that has floated down to the sea. She gets around insurance demands on cars that are at the bottom of the bayou. She tries to stop bills for very small white coffins.

She has seen others from the Little Rock foundation cleave people open immediately, but she has never been able to get to them so quickly. At first they are stilted with her, but she has learned how to listen all the same. After a half hour or so she gets to them.

It's as if they're talking to themselves, as if she is a mirror in front of them, giving them another history of themselves.

She is attracted to their darkness, but she likes the moment when they turn again and find some meaning that sideswipes them: *I really loved her. I loosened his shirt before he drifted through the floodgates. My husband put the stove on a layaway plan.*

And before they know it, their taxes are done, the insurance claim is laid out, the mortgage companies have been noted, the paper is slid across the table for them to sign. Sometimes it takes them an age just to sign, since they have something else to say—they are off and chatting about the cars they bought, the loves they loved. They have a deep need just to talk, just to tell a story, however small or reckless.

Listening to these people is like listening to trees—sooner or later the tree is sliced open and the watermarks reveal their age.

—

There was an old woman about nine months ago—she sat in a Little Rock hotel room, her dress spread out. Jaslyn was trying to figure out payments that the woman wasn't getting from her pension fund.

—My boy was the mailman, the woman said. Right there in the Ninth. He was a good boy. Twenty-two years old. Used to work late if he had to. And he worked, I ain't lying. People loved getting his letters. They waited for him. They liked him coming knocking on the door. You listenin'?

—Yes, ma'am.

—And then the storm blowed in. And he didn't come back. I was waiting. I had his dinner ready. I was living on the third floor then. Waiting. Except nothing happened. So I waited and waited. I went out after two days looking for him, went downstairs. All those helicopters were flying over, ignoring us. I waded out into the street, I was up to my neck, near drowning. I couldn't find no sign, nothing, 'til I was down there by the check-cashing store and I found the sack of mail floating and I pulled it in. And I thought, Holy.

The woman's fingers clamped down, gripping Jasyln's hand.

—I was sure he'd come floating around the next corner, alive. I looked and looked. But I never did see my boy. I wish I woulda drowned right there and then. I found out two weeks later that he was caught up high in a treetop just rotting in the heat. In his mailman uniform. Imagine that, caught in the tree.

The woman got to her feet, and went across the hotel room, went to a cheap dresser, yanked a drawer open.

—I still got his mail here, see? You can take it if you want it.

Jaslyn held the sack in her hands. None of the envelopes had been touched.

—Take it, please, the woman said. I can't stand it no more.

—

She took the sack of letters out to the lake near Natural Steps at the outskirts of Little Rock. The last light of day, she walked on the bank, her shoes sinking in the loam. Birds rose by pairs, bursting upward and wheeling overhead with the sun red on their cupped underwings. She wasn't sure what she should do with the mail. She sat down on the grass and sorted them out, magazines, flyers, personal letters to be returned with a note: *This got lost some time ago. I hope it's okay to send it on again now.*

She burned the bills, all of them. Verizon. Con Ed. The Internal Revenue Service. That grief wouldn't be needed now, no, not anymore.

—

She stands by the window, the dark down. A chatter in the room. She is reminded of white birds, flapping. The cocktail glass she holds feels fragile. If she holds it too tight, she thinks, it might shatter.

She has come to stay, to be with Claire for a day or two. To sleep in the spare room. To accompany her dying, the same way she accompanied Gloria's dying six years ago. The slow car journey back to Missouri. The smile on Gloria's face. Her sister, Janice, in the front seat, driving. Playing games with the rearview mirror. Both of them pushing Gloria in a wheelchair along the banks of the river. *Up a lazy river where the robin's song wakes a brand-new morning as we roll along.* It was a celebration, that day. They had dug their feet down into happiness and weren't prepared to let go. They threw sticks into an eddy and watched them circle. Put a blanket down, ate Wonder Bread sandwiches. Later in the afternoon, her sister began crying, like a change in the weather, for no reason except the popping of a wine cork. Jaslyn handed her a wadded tissue. Gloria laughed at them and said that she'd overtaken grief a long time ago, that she was tired of everyone wanting to go to heaven, nobody wanting to die. The only thing worth grieving over, she said, was that sometimes there was more beauty in this life than the world could bear.

Gloria left with a smile on her face. They closed her eyes with the glare of the sun still on them, rolled the wheelchair up the hill, stayed a little while looking out over the land until the insects of evening gathered.

They buried her two days later in a plot near the back of her old house. She had told Jaslyn once that everyone knows where they are from when they know where it is they want to be buried. A quiet ceremony, just the girls and a preacher. They put Gloria in the ground with one of her father's old hand-painted signs and a sewing tin she'd kept from her own mother. If there was any good way to go, it was a good way to go.

Yes, she thinks, she would like to stay and be with Claire also, spend a few moments, find some silence, let the moments crawl. She has even brought her pajamas, her toothbrush, her comb. But it is clear to her now that she is not welcome.

She had forgotten that there might be others too, that a life is lived in many ways—so many unopened envelopes.

—May I see her?

—I don't think she should be disturbed.

—I'll just pop my head around the door.

—It's a little late. She's sleeping. Would you like another drink . . . ?

His voice rises high on the question, unfinished, as if searching for her name. But he knows her name. Idiot. A crass, lumbering fool. He wants to own the grief and throw a party for it.

—Jaslyn, she says and smiles thinly.

—Another drink, Jaslyn?

—Thank you, no, she says, I have a room at the Regis.

—The Regis, awesome.

It's the fanciest hotel she can think of, the most expensive place. She has no idea even where it is, just somewhere nearby, but the name changes Tom's face—he smiles and shows his very white teeth.

She wraps a napkin around the bottom of her drink, places it down on the glass coffee table.

—Well, I should say good night. It's been a pleasure.

—Please, I'll show you down.

—It's okay, really.

—No, no, I insist.

He touches her elbow and she cringes. She resists the urge to ask him if he has ever been president of a frat house.

—Really, she says at the elevator, I can let myself out.

He leans forward to kiss her cheek. She allows him her shoulder and she gives a slight nudge against his chin.

—Good-bye, she says with a singsong finality.

Downstairs, Melvyn hails her a cab and soon she is alone again, as if none of the evening has happened at all. She checks in her pocket for the card from Pino. Turns it over in her fingers. It's as if she can feel the phone already ringing itself out in his pocket.

—

The only room at the St. Regis costs four hundred and twenty-five dollars for the night. She thinks about trying to find another hotel, even thinks about a phone call to Pino, but then slides her credit card across the counter. Her hands shake: it is almost a month and a half's rent in Little Rock. The girl behind the desk asks for I.D. Not a moment worth arguing over, though the couple in front of her were not asked for theirs.

The room is tiny. The television sits high on the wall. She clicks on the remote. The end of the storm. No hurricanes this year. Baseball scores, football scores, another six dead in Iraq.

She flops down on the bed, arms behind her head.

—

She went to Ireland shortly after the attacks on Afghanistan. It was supposed to be a vacation. Her sister was part of the team coordinating the
U.S. flights into Shannon Airport. They were spat on in the streets of Galway when they were leaving a restaurant. *Fucken Yanks go home.* It wasn't
as bad as being called a nigger, which happened when they rented a car
and ended up on the wrong side of the road.

Ireland surprised her. She had expected backroads of green and high
hedges, men with locks of dark hair, isolated white cottages on the hills.
Instead she got flyovers and ramps and lectures from heavy-faced drunks
on just exactly what world policy meant. She found herself pulling into a
shell, unable to listen. She'd heard bits and pieces about the man, Corrigan, who had died alongside her mother. She wanted to know more. Her
sister was the opposite—Janice wanted nothing to do with the past. The
past embarrassed her. The past was a jet that was coming in with dead
bodies from the Middle East.

So she drove to Dublin without her sister. She did not know why but
slow tears caught in her eyelashes: she had to squeeze them out to restore
her vision of the road. She drew in deep, silent breaths as the roads grew
bigger.

It was easy enough to find Corrigan's brother. He was the CEO of an
Internet company in the high glass towers along the Liffey.

—Come and see me, he said on the phone.

Dublin was a boomtown. Neon along the river. The seagulls embroi-
dered it. Ciaran was in his early sixties with a small peninsula of hair on
his forehead. Half an American accent—his other office, he said, was in
Silicon Valley. He was impeccably dressed in a suit and expensive open-
necked shirt. Gray chest hair peeking out. They sat in his office and he
talked her through a life of his late brother, Corrigan, a life that seemed
rare and radical to her.

Outside the window, cranes swung on the skyline. The Irish light
seemed lengthy. He took her across the river, to a pub, tucked down an al-
leyway, a genuine pub, all hardwood and beerscent. A row of silver kegs
outside. She ordered a pint of Guinness.

—Was my mother in love with him?

He laughed. Oh, I don't think so, no.

—Are you sure?

—That day, he was just giving her a lift home, that's all.

—I see.

—He was in love with another woman. From South America—I can't remember where, Colombia, I think, or Nicaragua.

—Oh.

She recognized the need for her mother to have been in love at least once.

—That's a pity, she said, her eyes moistening.

She scoured her sleeve across her eyes. She hated the sight of tears, anytime. Showy and sentimental, the last thing she wanted.

Ciaran had no idea what to do with her. He went outside and called his wife on his cell phone. Jaslyn stayed at the bar and drank another beer, felt warm but light-headed. Maybe Corrigan had secretly loved her mother, maybe they were on their way to a rendezvous, perhaps a deep love had struck them both at the last instant. It occurred to her that her mother would only be forty-five or forty-six years old if she were still alive. They might have been friends. They could have talked about these things, could have sat in a bar together, spent some time, shared a beer. But it was ridiculous, really. How could her mother have crawled away from that life and started anew? How could she have walked away intact? With what, sweeping brooms, dust pans? Here we go, honey, grab my high-heeled boots, put them in the wagon, westward we go. Stupid, she knew. Still. Just one evening. To sit with her mother and watch the way she painted her nails, maybe, or see the way she put coffee in a cup, or watch her kick her shoes off, a single moment of the ordinary. Running the bath. Humming out of tune. Cutting the toast. Anything at all. *Up a lazy river, how happy we could be.*

Ciaran breezed back into the pub and said to her in a distinctly American accent: Guess who's coming to dinner?

He drove a brand-new silver Audi. The house was just off the seafront, whitewashed, with roses out front and a dark ironwork fence. It was the same place the brothers had grown up. He had sold it once and had to buy it back for over a million dollars.

—Can you believe it? he said. A million plus.

His wife, Lara, was working in the garden, snipping roses with pruning shears. She was kind, slim, gentle, her gray hair pulled back into a bun. She had the bluest eyes, they looked like small drops of September sky. She pulled her gardening gloves off. There were spatters of color on her hands. She drew Jaslyn close, held her for a moment longer than expected: she smelled of paint.

Inside, there was a lot of artwork on the walls. They wandered around, a glass of crisp white wine for each of them.

She liked the paintings: radical Dublin landscapes, translated as line, shadow, color. Lara had published an art book and managed to sell some in the outdoor art shows in Merrion Square, but she had lost, she said, her American touch.

There was something of the beautiful failure about her.

They ended up in the back garden again, sitting at the patio, a bone of white light in the sky. Ciaran talked of the Dublin real estate market: but really, Jaslyn felt, they were talking about hidden losses, not profits, all the things they had passed by over the years.

After dinner, all three walked along the seafront together, past the Martello Tower and back around. The stars over Dublin sat like paint marks in the sky. The tide was long gone. An enormous stretch of sand disappeared into black.

—That way's England, said Ciaran, for no reason she could discern.

He put his jacket around her and Lara took her elbow, walked along, wedged between them. She broke free as delicately as she could, drove back to Limerick first thing the next morning. Her sister's face was glowing. Janice had just met a man. He was on his third tour, she said— imagine that. He wore size-fourteen boots, she added with a wink.

—

Her sister got shipped to the embassy in Baghdad two years ago. Every now and then she still gets a postcard from her. One of them is a picture of a woman in a burka: *Fun in the sun.*

—

The day dawns winter bright. She finds out in the morning that breakfast is not included in her hotel bill. She can only smile. Four hundred and twenty-five dollars, breakfast not included.

Upstairs, she takes all the soaps from the bathroom, the lotion, the shoeshine cloth, but still leaves a tip for the housekeepers.

She walks in the neighborhood for coffee, up north from Fifty-fifth Street.

The whole world a Starbucks, and she can't find a single one.

She settles on a small deli. Cream in her coffee. A bagel with butter. She circles back around to Claire's apartment, stands outside, looks up. It is a beautiful building, brickworked and corniced. But it's too early to stop by yet, she decides. She turns and walks east toward the subway, her small bag slung over her shoulder.

—

She loves the immediate energy of the Village. It is as if all the guitars have suddenly taken to the fire escapes. Sunlight on the brickwork. Flowerpots in high windows.

She is wearing an open blouse and tight jeans. She feels at ease, as if the streets are releasing her.

A man passes her with a dog inside his shirt. She smiles and watches them go. The dog crawls to the top of the man's shoulder and looks back at her, its eyes large and tender. She waves, sees the dog disappear down the man's shirt again.

She finds Pino in a coffee shop on Mercer Street. It is just as easy as she has imagined: she has no idea why, but she was convinced that it would be simple to find him. She could have called him on his cell phone but decided against it. Better to seek him out, find him, in this city of millions. He is alone and hunched over a coffee, reading a copy of *La Repubblica*. She has the sudden fear that there is a woman somewhere nearby, perhaps even one who is due to join him at any moment, but she doesn't care.

She buys a coffee, and slides back the chair, joins him at the table. He lifts his reading glasses to the top of his forehead and leans back in the chair, laughs.

—How did you find me?

—My internal GPS. How was your jazz?

—Oh, it was jazz. Your old friend, how is she?

—Not sure. Yet.

—Yet?

—I'll see her later today. Tell me. Can I ask? Just, well, y'know. What brings you here? The city?

—You really want to know? he says.

—I think so, yeah.

—Are you ready?

—As I'll ever be.

—I'm buying a chess set.

—You what?

—It's a handmade thing. There's a craftsman on Thompson Street. I'm picking it up. It's a bit of an obsession of mine. It's for my son, actually. It's a special Canadian wood. And the guy is a master . . .

—You came all the way from Little Rock to pick up a chess set?

—I suppose I needed to get out for a while.

—No kidding.

—And, well, I'll bring it to him in Frankfurt. Spend a few days with him, have some fun. Go back to Little Rock, return to work.

—How's your carbon footprint?

He smiles, drains his coffee. She can already tell that they will spend the morning here, that they will while the time away in the Village, they will have an early lunch, he will lean forward and touch her neck, she will cradle his hand there, they will go to his hotel, they will make love, they will open the curtains, they will tell stories, they will laugh, she will fall asleep again with her hand on his chest, she will kiss him good-bye, and later, back in Arkansas, he will call on her message machine, and she will leave his number on her night desk, to decide.

—Another question?

—Yeah?

—How many pictures of women are on your cell phone?

—Not many, he says with a grin. And you? How many guys?

—Millions, she says.

—Really?

—Billions, in fact.

—

There was only one time she ever went back to the Deegan. It was ten years ago, when she had just finished college. She wanted to know where it was her mother and grandmother had strolled. She drove a rental from JFK airport, got stopped in traffic, bumper to bumper. At least a half-mile of cars up ahead. In the rearview mirror the traffic pinned her into place. A Bronx sandwich.

So, she was home again, but it didn't feel like a homecoming.

She hadn't been in the neighborhood since she was five. She remembered the pale gray corridors and a mailbox stuffed with flyers: that was all.

She put the car in park and was fidgeting with her stereo when she caught a glimpse of movement far up the road. A man was rising out from the top of a limousine, strange and centaurian. She saw his head first, then his torso coming up through the open sunroof. Then the sharp swivel of his head as if he had been shot. She fully expected a spray of blood along his roof. Instead the man extended his arm and pointed as if directing traffic. He swiveled again. Each turn was quicker and quicker. He was like an odd conductor, wearing a suit and tie. The outstretched tie looked like a dial on the roof of the car as he turned. His hands rose on either side of him and he pulled his whole body up through the sunroof and then he was out and standing on top of the limousine, legs splayed wide and his fingers outstretched. Roaring at nearby drivers.

She noticed then that others were out and about, with their arms draped over their open doors, a little row of heads turning in the same direction, like sunflowers. Some secret between them. A nearby woman started beeping her car horn, she heard screaming, and it was then that she noticed the coyote trotting through the traffic.

It looked entirely calm, loping along in the hot sun, stopping and twisting its body, as if it were in some weird wonderland to be marveled at.

The thing was that the coyote was going toward the city, not back out. She remained seated and watched it come toward her. It crossed lanes two cars in front of her, passed alongside her window. It didn't look up, but she could see the yellow of the eyes.

In the rearview mirror she watched it go. She wanted to scream at it to turn, that it was going the wrong way, it needed to double back, just swivel and sprint free. Far behind her she noticed siren lights turning. Animal control. Three men with nets were circling through the traffic.

When she heard the crack of the rifle shot she thought at first it was just a car backfiring.

—

She likes the word *mother* and all the complications it brings. She isn't interested in *true* or *birth* or *adoptive* or whatever other series of mothers there are in the world. Gloria was her mother. Jazzlyn was too. They were like strangers on a porch, Gloria and Jazzlyn, with the evening sun going down: they just sat there together and neither could say what the other one knew, so they just kept quiet, and watched the day descend. One of them said good night, while the other waited.

—

They find each other slowly, tentatively, shyly, drawing apart, merging again, and it strikes her that she has never really known the body of another. Afterward they lie together without speaking, their bodies touching lightly, until she rises and dresses quietly.

—

The flowers are cheap, she thinks, the moment she buys them. Waxy flower paper, thin blooms, a strange scent to them, like someone in the deli has sprayed them with a false fragrance. Still, she can find no other open florist. And the light is dimming, the evening disappearing. She heads west, toward Park, her body still tingling, his phantom hand at her hip.

In the elevator the cheap scent of the flowers rises. She should have looked around and found a better shop, but it's too late now. No matter. She gets out on the top floor, her shoes sinking into the soft carpet. There is a newspaper on the ground, by Claire's door, the slick hysteria of war. Eighteen dead today.

A shiver along her arms.

She rings the doorbell, props the flowers against the frame as she hears the latches click.

—

It is the Jamaican nurse who opens the door for her again. His face is broad and relaxed. He wears short dreadlocks.

—Oh, hi.

—Is there anyone else here?

—Excuse me? he says.

—Just wondering if there's anybody else home.

—Her nephew's in the other room. He's napping.

—How long has he been here?

—Tom? He spent the night. He's been here a few days. He's been having people over.

There is a momentary standoff as if the nurse is trying to figure out just exactly why she has returned, what she wants, how long she'll stay. He keeps his hand around the doorframe, but then he leans forward and whispers conspiratorially: He brought a couple of real estate people to his parties, y'know.

Jaslyn smiles, shakes her head: it doesn't matter, she will not allow it to matter.

—Do you think I can see her?

—Be my guest. You know she had a stroke, right?

—Yes.

She stops in the hallway.

—Did she get my card? I sent a big goofy card.

—Oh, that's yours? says the nurse. That one's funny. I like that one.

He sweeps his hand along the corridor, points her down toward the room. She moves through the half-dark, as if pushing back a veil. She stops, turns the glass handle on the bedroom door. It clicks. The door swings. She feels as if she is stepping off a ledge. The room looks dark and heavy, a thick tenor to it. A tiny triangle of light where the curtains don't quite meet.

She stands a moment to let her eyes adjust. Jaslyn wants to part the dark, open the curtains, crack the window, but Claire is asleep, eyelids closed. She pulls up a chair by the bed, beside a saline drip. The drip is not attached. There is a glass on the bedside table. And a straw. And a pencil. And a newspaper. And her card among many other cards. She peers in the dark. *Get well soon, you funny old bird.* She is not sure now whether it is humorous at all; perhaps she should have bought something cute and demure. You never know. You cannot know.

The rise and fall of Claire's chest. The body a thin failure now. The shrunken breasts, the deep lids, the striated neck, the intricate articulation. Her life painted on her, receding on her. A brief flutter of her eyelids. Jaslyn leans close. A waft of stale air. An eyelid flutter once more. The eyes open and stare. In the dark, their whites. Claire opens her eyes, wider still, does not smile or say a word.

A pull on the sheets. Jaslyn looks down as Claire moves her left hand. The fingers go up and down as if playing a piano. The yellow rufflework of age. The person we know at first, she thinks, is not the one we know at last.

A clock sounds.

Little else to distract attention from the evening, just a clock, in a time not too distant from the present time, yet a time not too distant from the past, the unaccountable unfolding of consequence into tomorrow's time, the simple things, the grain of bedwood alive in light, the slight argument of dark still left in the old woman's hair, the ray of moisture on the plastic lifebag, the curl of the braided flower petal, the chipped edge of a photo frame, the rim of a mug, the mark of a stray tea line along its edge, a crossword puzzle sitting unfinished, the yellow of a pencil dangling over the edge of the table, one end sharpened, the eraser in midair. Fragments of a human order. Jaslyn turns the pencil around to safety, then rises, rounds the far end of the bed, toward the window. Her hands on the windowsill. She parts the curtains a little more, opens the triangle, lifts the window frame minutely, feels the curl of breeze on her skin: the ash, the dust, the light now pressing the dark out of things. We stumble on, now, we drain the light from the dark, to make it last. She lifts the window higher. Sounds outside, growing clearer in the silence, traffic at first, machine hum, cranework, playgrounds, children, the tree branches down on the avenue slapping each other around.

The curtain falls back but still a corridor of brightness has opened up on the carpet. Jaslyn steps to the bed again, takes off her shoes, drops them. Claire parts her lips ever so slightly. Not a word, but a difference in her breathing, a measured grace.

We stumble on, thinks Jaslyn, bring a little noise into the silence, find in others the ongoing of ourselves. It is almost enough.

Quietly, Jaslyn perches on the edge of the bed and then extends her feet, moves her legs across slowly so as not to disturb the mattress. She fixes a pillow, leans, picks a hair out of Claire's mouth.

Jaslyn thinks again of an apricot—she does not know why, but that's what she thinks, the skin of it, the savor, the sweetness.

The world spins. We stumble on. It is enough.

She lies on the bed beside Claire, above the sheets. The faint tang of the old woman's breath on the air. The clock. The fan. The breeze.

The world spinning.

AUTHOR'S NOTE

Philippe Petit walked a tightrope wire between the World Trade Center towers on August 7, 1974. I have used his walk in this novel, but all the other events and characters in this work are fictional. I have taken liberties with Petit's walk, while trying to remain true to the texture of the moment and its surroundings. Readers interested in Petit's walk should go to his book *To Reach the Clouds* (Faber and Faber, 2002) for an intimate account. The photograph used on page 237 is by Vic DeLuca, Rex Images, August 7, 1974, copyright Rex USA. To both of these artists I'm deeply indebted.

The title of this book comes from the Alfred, Lord Tennyson poem "Locksley Hall." That in turn was heavily influenced by the "Mu'allaqat," or the "Suspended Poems," seven long Arabic poems written in the sixth century. Tennyson's poem mentions "pilots of the purple twilight dropping down with costly bales," and the "Mu'allaqat" asks, "Is there any hope that this desolation can bring me solace?" Literature can remind us that not all life is already written down: there are still so many stories to be told.

ACKNOWLEDGMENTS

THIS PARTICULAR STORY owes enormous thanks to many—the police officers who drove me around the city; the doctors who patiently answered my questions; the computer technicians who guided me through the labyrinth; and all of those who helped me during the writing and editing process. The fact of the matter is that there are many hands tapping the writer's keyboard. I fear I will forget some names but I'm deeply grateful to the following for all of their support and help: Jay Gold, Roger Hawke, Maria Venegas, John McCormack, Ed Conlon, Joseph Lennon, Justin Dolly, Mario Mola, Dr. James Marion, Terry Cooper, Cenelia Arroyave, Paul Auster, Kathy O'Donnell, Thomas Kelly, Elaina Ganim, Alexandra Pringle, Jennifer Hershey, Millicent Bennett, Giorgio Gonella, Andrew Wylie, Sarah Chalfant, and all at the Wylie Agency, Caroline Ast and everyone at Belfond in Paris. Thanks to Philip Gourevitch and all at *The Paris Review*. For my students and colleagues at Hunter College, especially Peter Carey and Nathan Englander. And in the end nobody deserves more thanks than Allison, Isabella, John Michael, and Christian.

THE BABY-SITTERS CLUB

Keep Out, Claudia!
Ann M. Martin

AN
APPLE
PAPERBACK

SCHOLASTIC INC.
New York Toronto London Auckland Sydney

ISBN 0-590-45657-1

12 11 10 9 8 7 6 5 4 3 2 1   2 3 4 5 6 7/9

Printed in the U.S.A.   40

First Scholastic printing, August 1992

For Olivia Ford
Thank you

Keep Out, Claudia!

CHAPTER 1

"Claudia? Do you think Shea is playing that song right?" Jackie Rodowsky wanted to know. He gazed at me from under a fringe of red bangs.

I listened carefully to the piano music drifting from the living room. "What's he supposed to be playing?" I asked.

Jackie shrugged. " 'A doggie-o.' "

" 'A doggie-o'?" I repeated. I had never heard of "a doggie-o." Then again, I don't know much about music, except that I like certain groups and singers. And that I have recently started to like Bach. No kidding. His music is awesome, if you really listen to it.

From the other room I heard plink, plinkety, plink, plink, *blam*. (Oops.) Shea started over. Plink, plinkety, plink, plink, *blam*.

"Bullfrogs!" Shea yelled.

"I guess he isn't playing it right," said Jackie.

"I guess not."

"Duh," added Archie, who is Jackie and Shea's little brother.

It was Monday afternoon and I was baby-sitting at the Rodowskys' for three freckle-faced redheads. Shea is nine, Jackie is seven, and Archie is four. Shea was practicing for his upcoming piano recital. I hoped he would be ready.

Blam. "Bullfrogs!"

Jackie and Archie giggled.

Then Jackie looked up from the enormous rocket ship he and Archie were building with Legos. The Rodowsky boys have a Lego supply bigger than what you could find in most toy stores. "I wish I could play the piano. Or some instrument," Jackie said. He reached for a handful of Legos — and knocked a fin off the spaceship. The fin fell to the floor and split into pieces just as Bo, the Rodowskys' dog, tore into the rec room. He skittered on the Legos and crashed into the table on which the spaceship was being built.

"Cowabunga!" shrieked Archie, as the table collapsed and the rocket ship slid to the floor and smashed.

Jackie looked at me balefully. "Was that my fault?" he asked.

I tried to smile. "Not really," I told him. "Bo helped. Maybe Bo needs some exercise. Why don't you take him outside? Archie and I will try to put the spaceship back together."

Jackie sighed. "Okay," he replied. "But don't be surprised if I ram into the toolshed or wreck up the lawn or something."

Jackie is the teeniest bit accident-prone. Sometimes this bothers him — but mostly he is pretty happy-go-lucky.

Plink, plinkety, plink, plink, *blam*. "Bull-frogs!"

"You know what *I* wish, Claudia?" Archie said when Jackie and Bo were safely out the door. "I wish I could be in a play. Or in a show. I want to stand on a stage in front of a lot of people. I want the people to clap for me, and laugh at my jokes."

"You want to be an entertainer?" I said. "Hmm. And Jackie wants to play an instrument, and Shea is getting ready for his recital. You guys must like show business."

"Yup," replied Shea. "Don't you?"

To be truthful, I hadn't given it much thought. I have other interests. Like art and baby-sitting. And junk food.

My name is Claudia Kishi. Claudia Lynn Kishi, to be exact. I'm thirteen years old. I live here in the small town of Stoneybrook, Connecticut. I have a mom and a dad and an older sister. I don't have any pets, but I do have lots of friends. My best friends are the members of a business called the Baby-sitters Club. I happen to be the vice-president of that club (which us members call the BSC).

I've been the vice-president of the BSC ever since the club started, which was back at the beginning of seventh grade. Now I'm in eighth grade at Stoneybrook Middle School. I'll tell you a secret about school and me. I am not a very good student. I am especially not a good speller. It isn't that I'm dumb, although sometimes I *feel* dumb. It's just that I don't think school is very interesting. Except for art class. And when I'm at home I can usually find about a dozen things to do that are more exciting than homework. My parents say I have to learn discipline and responsibility. I say I am disciplined and responsible . . . but who needs to know about hypotenuses (hypotenusi?) or what letter "psychiatrist" begins with? (Anyone with half a brain would spell that word "sikiatrist." It would make much more sense. Furthermore, if you really think about it, in general, you hardly need the letter "c" at all. You could spell most "c" things with an "s" or a "k." You only need that "c" for spelling "chocolate" or "cheesecake," which by the way, *could* be spelled "choklit" and "chezkak." Just a thought. But is it any wonder I'm a bad speller?)

I'll tell you something. I bet I wouldn't feel

dumb sometimes if my sister Janine wasn't so smart. Janine is a genius. She is sixteen and basically a junior at Stoneybrook High, but already she takes courses at the local college. She did that last year, too. Can you imagine? She was fifteen and going to school with students who were, like, six years older than she was. Well, some of them were. And Janine's grades were as good as theirs. Or better. I think I'm just dumb by com*pari*son. What I mean is I'm *not* dumb. But next to Janine I *look* dumb.

Maybe if I got glasses and dressed in frumpy, dowdy clothes like Janine — no. I could never do that. I hope this doesn't sound conceited or shallow, but clothes and fashion are very important to me. Well, they are. They're almost as important as art and children and baby-sitting. I like to look good, and I'm good at looking good. All my friends say so. Sometimes they even copy my style. I wear pretty trendy clothes, and I like to be imaginative and try new things. I have to admit that the money I earn baby-sitting goes for art supplies (first) and then for jewelry and accessories and stuff. I have not saved much at all. (Unlike my friends Kristy and Jessi who hoard their money like squirrels hoard acorns.)

As Archie and I knelt on the floor and picked up pieces of the rocket ship, I thought about

5

the upcoming meeting of the BSC. My friends and I hold our meetings in my bedroom, and we were due for one later that afternoon. Mrs. Rodowsky had said she would be home before five, and the meeting would begin at five-thirty. Perfect. That would give me just enough time to fly home and straighten up my room. Ordinarily I don't bother. (My friends are used to my messes.) But that day my room was extra messy because I'd been experimenting with making ceramic mobiles, and little figures and pieces of wire were *every*-where. (Along with Snickers bars and M&M's and Neccos and Fritos and ranch-style potato chips and crackers and popcorn . . .)

The back door opened and Bo bounded into the room, followed by Jackie. "The toolshed is still standing," Jackie announced. "If I broke anything out there, I don't know about it."

I smiled. "Don't worry. You didn't mean to bump into the rocket ship. It was just an accident."

"An*oth*er accident," Jackie corrected me.

"Well, anyway, Shea and I have already put most of the spaceship back together. See? It broke into big pieces."

Jackie the walking disaster grinned. "Good," he said.

Plink, plinkety, plink, plink, *blam*. "Bullfrogs!" yelled Shea. (This time even *he* giggled.)

"Hey, Shea! You can stop practicing now!" I called. "Time's up."

"Okay!" he called back. But he didn't stop. I think he was getting worried about the recital.

"Lucky-duck Shea," said Archie as we lifted the spaceship back onto the table. "I could put on a show, too, you know. I can play 'Mary Had a Little Lamb' on the piano."

"With one finger," murmured Jackie. Then he hurried on. "I bet I could play the . . . the, um, the . . . well, I could play something."

"And I could dance," added Archie, "and sing. I could be a star."

Mrs. Rodowsky came back promptly at 4:45 that afternoon. As soon as she had paid me, I climbed onto my bicycle and pedaled home. As I rode along, I thought about Jackie, who wished he could play an instrument, and about Archie's words: "I could be a star." It was time for my friends and me to cook up a musical project for the kids we sit for. Obviously the Rodowsky boys would want to be involved in something like that. And I was sure other kids would, too.

I was so lost in thought when I reached

home that I nearly tripped over Janine who was sitting on our front stoop reading one of her sociology texts. Her bookbag was perched beside her.

"Oof! Sorry," I said. "What are you doing here?" The weather that day was gorgeous — warm and sunny — but Janine prefers to study in her room. She is not an outdoor person.

"I'm locked out," she said. "I can't find my key."

"Well, I'm here to save the day," I replied.

Our parents both work, so at my house forgetting or losing your key could mean trouble. Dad is a broker with a company in Stamford, Connecticut, which is the nearest city, and Mom is the head librarian at the Stoneybrook Public Library.

I unlocked the front door and let Janine inside.

She checked her watch. "You have a meeting soon, don't you?"

"Yup," I said. "I'm going to clean up my room. Want to keep me company?" Janine may be dowdy, and she may be a genius who makes me look dumb next to her, but she is still my sister, and I love her.

"All right." Janine followed me upstairs and along the hall to my room. "Goodness. What are you working on?" she asked. She cleared

8

a space on my bed so she could sit down.

"Mobiles," I answered. "Want to see?" I held up a half-finished one with ceramic cowboy boots, a cactus, and a coyote hanging from delicate curving wires. Then I showed her a still life I was painting, a charcoal sketch I was finishing up, and an idea for making jewelry with beads, sequins, and lace. And then I began to tidy up.

Janine watched with a half smile as I dug a package of Ring-Dings out from under a pile of papers and drawings on my desk, and tried to make order out of chaos. "Are you going to be ready in time?" she asked.

"Barely," I answered.

And at that moment I heard our front door open and close, and then feet running up the stairs. "I'm here!" yelled Stacey McGill.

CHAPTER 2

By five-thirty, Janine had left my room and settled herself in front of her computer. In her place were the six other members of the Baby-sitters Club: Kristy Thomas, Mary Anne Spier, Stacey McGill, Dawn Schafer, Jessi Ramsey, and Mallory Pike.

"This meeting of the BSC will now come to order," announced Kristy. She was sitting in my director's chair, one leg crossed over the other, a visor perched on her head, a pencil stuck over her ear, and a notebook open in her lap. Kristy is the president. She gets to call meetings to order. (She has a mouth which is suited to that purpose.)

It seems like forever that my friends and I have met in my room every Monday, Wednesday, and Friday afternoon from five-thirty until six but, as I mentioned, the BSC has only been around since the beginning of seventh grade. The club was Kristy's idea, and when it first began, there were just four members — Kristy, Stacey, Mary Anne, and me. As business grew, so did the club. Soon Dawn joined, and later Mal and Jessi joined, too.

How does our business work? It's simple, really. When parents in Stoneybrook (especially in our neighborhood) need a sitter for their children, they call us during one of our club meetings. Since they reach seven capable sitters at once, they're bound to line up someone with just one call (instead of making a million phone calls, trying to find a sitter who's free). My friends and I get tons of jobs this way, which is great, since we *adore* children. (We like the money we earn, too.)

As president, Kristy runs things smoothly and professionally. Every club member has her own duties and responsibilities. Kristy's duties are to be in charge, and to keep coming up with her good ideas. Kristy is famous for her ideas. She thought up the club, and she thought up a lot of other things. Like Kid-Kits. A Kid-Kit is a cardboard box (we each have one now) that we've decorated and filled with our old books, toys, and games, plus art supplies, activity books, and so on. We often take them along when we go on a sitting job. Kids love to explore them, which is one reason we're popular sitters.

Kristy also decided that keeping a notebook

and a record book would help our club to be efficient and organized. The notebook is more like a diary. In it, each of us writes up every single job we go on. Then we're responsible for reading the notebook once a week to find out how our friends solved sitting problems, and to stay in touch with the lives of our clients. The record book is where we keep track of all kinds of information: our clients' names, addresses, and phone numbers; the rates they pay; and notes about the children we sit for regularly, such as whether they have food allergies or special fears, or have to take any kind of medication. These things are extremely helpful to us.

Sometimes when I think about all the great ideas Kristy has had for the BSC, I'm amazed. At other times I think that's just part of who Kristy is. She's always had great ideas. I should know since she and Mary Anne and I grew up together. Before our lives began to change, our families lived on Bradford Court. Kristy lived across the street from me, and Mary Anne lived next door to her. (Now I'm the only one who still lives on Bradford Court.) Anyway, even when we were little kids Kristy had one great idea after another. Who knows why?

Kristy's family is a pretty interesting one, as far as I'm concerned. She has two older brothers, Sam and Charlie (they're in high school with my sister), and a little brother David Michael (he's seven). Her dad walked out on the family when David Michael was just a baby. For a long time, Kristy's mother struggled to support her four kids by herself — and she did a terrific job. She's some kind of big executive with a company in Stamford. When Kristy was in seventh grade her mom met and fell in love with a man named Watson Brewer. Guess what. Watson is an actual millionaire. And during the summer between seventh and eighth grade, Watson and Kristy's mom got married, and Watson moved the Thomases into his mansion (yes, mansion) across town. So Kristy acquired a stepfather. At the same time she acquired a little stepsister and stepbrother, Karen and Andrew, who are seven and four. Later, she acquired an adopted sister! Not long ago, Watson and Kristy's mom adopted Emily Michelle, a two-and-a-half-year-old girl who had been born in Vietnam.

As you can imagine, the Thomas/Brewer household is pretty wild sometimes. Even though Karen and Andrew live there only part time (mostly, they live with their mother and stepfather, who are also in Stoneybrook), the house is zooey, what with all those kids, Kristy's grandmother Nannie (who moved in to help care for Emily), and various pets.

What sort of person is Kristy? Well, she's energetic and outgoing and she talks a lot. Even *she* admits she has a big mouth. She loves sports and kids, which is why she decided to organize and coach a softball team for little kids, called Kristy's Krushers. Kristy has a fun sense of humor, and she's a good student. She's brown-eyed and brown-haired and the shortest kid in her class. (By the way, Kristy is thirteen, like me. So are the other members of the Baby-sitters Club, except for Mal and Jessi who are eleven and in sixth grade.) One thing that does *not* interest Kristy is clothes. She's happiest wearing jeans and a sweat shirt, maybe a turtleneck, baggy socks, old running shoes, and sometimes a baseball cap. If forced, she will put on a little makeup or jewelry, but she rarely thinks of that herself.

Would you be surprised to find out that Kristy has a boyfriend? Well, she does, although I think she'd kill me if she heard me say that. But she and Bart Taylor, who lives in her new neighborhood, have been spending a lot of time together, and not just on the softball field (Bart coaches a rival team, Bart's Bashers). They've even gone to a few school dances together.

Let's see. On to the vice-president of the BSC, and that's me. You already know a lot about me and my family, but let me tell you

14

why I was elected V.P. It is mainly because I have a phone in my room. Not only that, I have my very own phone *number*. This is important, considering how many calls we usually receive during a club meeting. Using a parent's phone would be pretty inconvenient (we'd tie it up three times a week and get calls during meetings that were for other people). So we're lucky to have my phone. As vice-president, I also offer around my supply of junk food when my friends and I meet. More importantly, I deal with calls that come in when we're not meeting.

One last thing about me. I'm Japanese-American. This is what I look like: extra-long black hair, almond-shaped eyes, and a good complexion, especially considering the amount of junk food I eat.

Mary Anne Spier is the secretary of the club. Her duties are complicated — to schedule each and every job that is phoned in. To do that, she has to know when I have art lessons, when Mal has orthodontist appointments, when Jessi will be at her ballet classes, and so forth. She keeps track of our jobs on the appointment pages in the record book. As far as anyone knows, she has never made a mistake. Mary Anne is also in charge of keeping the entire record book up-to-date and in order.

When I tell you about the kind of person

Mary Anne is, I think you'll be surprised to find out that she's Kristy's best friend. I'm still surprised — and I've known Mary Anne and Kristy all my life. Okay, remember that Kristy has a big mouth? Well, Mary Anne is quiet and softspoken, shy and sentimental. She cries easily. She is *so* sensitive. Not that Kristy is *in*sensitive; but she's tough-skinned, and Mary Anne is not. Still, Mary Anne is a survivor. Her life hasn't been exactly easy. Her mom died when Mary Anne was little and, after that, Mary Anne was raised by her *very* strict father. Mr. Spier loves his daughter, that's for sure, but he overprotected her and treated her like a baby. Only recently was Mary Anne allowed to wear her hair long (instead of in braids) and to choose her own clothes (which are slowly becoming trendier and less little-girl-like). It's practically a miracle that she has a steady boyfriend, Logan Bruno. But she does. They've been going out for quite awhile now (except for the time when they were going through The Big Separation). Logan is a really great guy. He's sweet, and he's very understanding of Mary Anne. He's also an associate member of the BSC. Honest. He's a terrific baby-sitter, so we call on him at those times when a job comes in that the rest of us can't take. (Or we call on Shannon Kilbourne.

16

She's our other associate member; she lives across the street from Kristy.)

You will never guess what happened to Mary Anne Spier earlier this year. Her dad finally remarried, so Mary Anne wound up with a stepmother, a stepbrother, and a stepsister. Here's the unbelievable part. Her stepsister is Dawn Schafer, Mary Anne's other best friend. Can you imagine having a best friend who becomes your stepsister?

This is the story. In the middle of seventh grade, Dawn moved to Stoneybrook with her mother and her brother Jeff after her parents got divorced. They moved clear across the country from California, where Dawn and Jeff had been born, since their *mother* had been born here in Stoneybrook. Dawn and Mary Anne became friends right away, and soon Dawn joined the Baby-sitters Club. Around the same time Mr. Spier began going out with Mrs. Schafer and poof! They got married. The next thing we knew, Mary Anne, her dad, and her kitten Tigger had moved into Dawn's house (it's bigger than the one Mary Anne had lived in), and Mary Anne and Dawn had become stepsisters. Whew. You never know what's around the corner.

Here's a theory of mine: Life is just one big surprise.

I guess I should tell you about Dawn next since I've sort of introduced you to her already. Our California girl is the alternate officer of the BSC. If anyone can't make a club meeting, Dawn steps in and takes over her duties. This means she has to know how to do everyone's jobs, which isn't easy. But Dawn is dependable. We can always count on her.

Dawn is also an individual. She tends to go her own way, and not worry much about what other people think. I don't mean she's uncaring. I just mean that she believes what she wants to believe, does the things she wants to do, dresses the way she wants to dress, and so on without being swayed by other people's opinions. If kids don't agree with Dawn, she doesn't care (much). She's a very strong person. I really admire her.

Dawn has lo-o-o-o-ong blonde hair. It's about the color of corn silk. Her eyes are blue. When she lived in California she sported a nice tan, but that has faded, thanks to our Connecticut winters. Remember I said that I'm a junk-food addict? Well, Dawn is a health-food addict. She lives on fruits, vegetables, and stuff like tofu and rice. No red meat or sugar for her. I could live without meat, I think, but it's the sugar thing I don't understand. How

18

does Dawn live without Twinkies and Three Musketeers bars?

Okay, it's time for me to tell you about *my* best friend. She's Stacey McGill, the treasurer of the BSC. Stacey (who's an only child) lives in Stoneybrook (duh), but she's a New York City girl at heart. That's where she grew up. And her dad still lives there. Like Dawn, Stacey and her mom settled here after the McGills got a divorce. But Stace is much more like me than like Dawn. We're sophisticated and boy-crazy, although we don't have steady boy-friends. And we love fashion. Stacey is allowed to wear pretty much whatever she wants, and to have her blonde hair permed. *Un*like me, Stacey is excellent at math, which is how she became the club treasurer. Stacey's in charge of keeping track of the money we earn, and of collecting our dues every Monday. Then she doles out the dues money as it's needed — to help pay my phone bills, to buy new items for the Kid-Kits, and so forth.

Also, unlike me, Stacey can't eat sweets. This is because she has a disease called diabetes. Her body doesn't process sugar the way it should, so Stacey has to help things along by sticking to a strict diet, and giving herself injections (yes, in*jec*tions) of something called insulin. None of this is easy, but Stacey copes well. I guess she's a survivor, too. (Actually, in our own way, we're all survivors.)

The two youngest officers of the Baby-sitters Club are our junior members, Jessi and Mal. "Junior member" means that they are too young to be allowed to sit at night, unless they're sitting for their own brothers and sisters and, believe me, they have plenty of brothers and sisters between them. Jessi has one younger sister and a baby brother, and Mal has *seven* brothers and sisters. She's the oldest of eight kids.

Jessi and Mal are another pair of best friends. And Jessi is another newcomer to Stoneybrook. Her family moved here at the beginning of the school year when her father's job changed. (Mal grew up in Stoneybrook.) Jessi is an extremely talented ballet dancer, and Mal likes to write and draw, and plans to create picture books when she's older.

Jessi and Mal don't look a thing alike. Jessi is African-American. Her skin is the color of cocoa, and (because of her dance classes) she often wears her hair up, or pulled back. Her legs are the long legs of a dancer and her eyelashes are so long she looks as if she's wearing mascara, even though she isn't allowed to use makeup.

Mal is white. Her hair is red and curly, and her face is covered with freckles. Plus, she wears glasses and braces. Her braces are the clear kind that don't show up much. Even so, Mallory doesn't feel particularly attractive. At least she and Jessi were allowed to have their ears pierced. Now if Mal could just get contact lenses, but her parents say no; not until she's older.

I have a feeling that both Jessi and Mal spend quite a bit of time wishing they were older. They think eleven is the pits. They feel grown-up and want to be treated as adults, but their parents still see them as kids, even when they baby-sit. Oh, well. Everyone is eleven at one time. We all live through it.

"Thank you . . . thank you . . . thank you . . ." The Monday afternoon meeting of the BSC was underway, and Stacey was collecting our dues. She was being very polite, considering none of us particularly likes to part with our money.

When she had finished, and had added our dues to the treasury (a manila envelope), the room grew quiet. We were waiting for the phone to ring. When it didn't, I decided to tell my friends about my afternoon with the Rodowsky boys.

"And so," I said finally, "what I've been thinking is that maybe we should come up with some kind of project — planning a musical performance — with the kids we sit for. Whoever's interested."

"That's a terrific idea!" exclaimed Jessi.

"But what, exactly, should we do?" I asked. "I mean, we've helped the kids put on some plays and skits already."

"And none of *us* is terribly musical," Kristy pointed out.

"I don't think that matters too much," said Mal. "We can help the kids organize and plan a show or something. They'll learn a lot just by experimenting. And don't forget. Some of *them* are pretty musical."

"Like the Perkins girls," I said.

"And Shea Rodowsky," added Mary Anne. "Remember his piano lessons. Other kids take lessons, too, like Marilyn Arnold. Plus, we can help them play simple homemade instruments such as drums — you know, oatmeal cartons? — and bells and tambourines."

Ring, ring.

"And telephones," said Stacey, giggling. Then she composed herself and reached for the receiver. "Hello, Baby-sitters Club," she said. A pause followed. Then, "Yes? . . . Yes. . . . Oh, mm-hmm." She was not talking to one of our regular clients. It was somebody she didn't know well. Stacey jotted down a few notes and told the caller she'd phone back in a few minutes. When she hung up, she was

22

smiling. "New clients," she announced. "They saw one of our fliers."

"Cool," said Dawn. "Who are they?"

"Their name is Lowell. That was Mrs. Lowell. She and her husband have three children. They're eight, six, and three. Two girls and a boy, I think she said. She doesn't know much about us. Just what she read in the flier. Also, she heard from somewhere that we're very reliable."

"Our reputation is spreading," said Kristy proudly.

"She needs a sitter for Friday afternoon," Stacey continued. She glanced at Mary Anne who was already checking the record book.

"Let's see. Mal, you're free." Mary Anne frowned. "And Claud, so are you, unless you're going to that art thing you mentioned last week. Oh, and I'm free. Who wants the job?"

"I told Vanessa I'd take her to the bookstore on Friday," said Mal. (Vanessa is Mallory's nine-year-old sister. She's a bookworm, like Mal.)

"And I did decide to go to the 'art thing,' " I said. "It's an art *show*. At a gallery."

"That leaves me." Mary Anne penciled herself in for the job. Then Stacey telephoned Mrs. Lowell to tell her who to expect on Friday.

The numbers on my digital clock flipped from 5:59 to 6:00.

"Well, I guess that's that," said Kristy. "Good meeting, you guys."

My friends and I stood up. Kristy removed the pencil from over her ear and stuck it in the back pocket of her jeans.

"See you in school tomorrow!" Jessi called to Mal as they ran down the hallway to the staircase.

"I'll call you tonight!" Mary Anne said to Kristy.

"Kristy, your brother's here to pick you up!" Dawn yelled.

And Stacey, my best friend, said, " 'Bye, Claud. Phone me tonight and we'll *tawk*." I laughed. I watched my friends leave the house.

CHAPTER 3

Friday

Today I met the Lowell kids. They are Caitlin (eight), MacKenzie (six), and Celeste (three). MacKenzie is called Mackie. I love those names! Caitlin, Mackie, and Celeste. And I love the kids. They're really pretty, all three of them. They look kind of like china dolls. Uh-oh. I'm off the subject.

When I arrived at the Lowells' house, Mrs. Lowell was waiting to show me around. She's very organized. And the kids seemed obedient and helpful.

Mary Anne's afternoon with the Lowell kids was easy, especially considering it was a new job. Sometimes an unfamiliar baby-sitter can be upsetting to kids, but the Lowells were as good as gold, according to Mary Anne.

Promptly at three-thirty, Mary Anne rang the Lowells' bell. Mrs. Lowell answered the door. Before she said hello, she glanced up and down at Mary Anne. She did it very quickly, but Mary Anne said it made her feel kind of strange, like she was being inspected. Anyway, Mrs. Lowell must have approved of what she saw because she stretched her mouth into a smile. Then she said, "I guess you're Mary Anne Spier." She seemed like any other mom.

"Yes," Mary Anne replied. And then she added formally, "From the Baby-sitters Club." She held up her Kid-Kit as if it were proof of this.

"Come inside. I'm Denise Lowell. I'm glad you were available. Do you mind if I ask you some questions?"

Mary Anne shook her head. "Nope."

"Terrific." Mrs. Lowell and Mary Anne sat in the kitchen. "So you are . . . how old?" asked Mrs. Lowell.

"Thirteen."

26

"And how long have you been baby-sitting?"

"About two years. Before that, some moms let me be mother's helpers, though. I've taken care of all ages of kids, even babies."

Mrs. Lowell nodded with satisfaction. Then she told Mary Anne where to find emergency numbers. And *then* she called, "Children! Caitlin, Mackie, Celeste!"

In less than a minute, the Lowell kids had run into the kitchen and were standing in a line. At first, Mary Anne just gazed at them. This was when she decided they looked like dolls. The children stood silently in their line. They didn't smile, but they gazed back at Mary Anne with clear blue eyes. The children were blond, their hair as light as Dawn's, and their complexions were pale. Caitlin and Mackie were dressed in what Mary Anne guessed were private school uniforms. Caitlin wore a blue plaid skirt, a blazer, a white blouse and white tights, and red shoes. Mackie wore neatly pressed pants, a blazer, and brown oxfords. And Celeste, a large bow in her hair, was wearing a white blouse and a pink pinafore.

"Thank you, children," said their mother after a moment, and the kids left the kitchen quietly. Mrs. Lowell turned to Mary Anne.

27

"I'll only be gone for about an hour and a half today," she said, and gave Mary Anne a short list of instructions. A few moments later, she left. Celeste cried briefly, then calmed down.

"So what do you guys want to do this afternoon?" asked Mary Anne. She was in the family room, holding the sniffling Celeste in her lap.

Caitlin looked thoughtful. "Tell us about your family," she said.

Mary Anne was startled. "My family?"

"Yeah. Do you have any pets?"

"Oh." Mary Anne smiled. She likes curious kids. "I have a kitten," she replied. "His name is Tigger."

"What color is he?" asked Mackie.

"And is he a he or a she?" asked Caitlin.

"He's a he. And he's gray striped."

"Does he talk?" Celeste tipped her head back to see Mary Anne's face. Her tears were drying on her cheeks.

"Does he talk? Well, he mews," said Mary Anne.

"Do you pretend he talks?" Celeste pressed.

"Sometimes."

"Do you have brothers and sisters?" asked Caitlin. Then she added, "I'm lucky. I have one of each."

"Me, too," said Mary Anne. "Well, really they are my stepbrother and stepsister. Guess

28

what. My stepsister is also my best friend. And she's the same age as me."

"Ooh," said Mackie. "What's a stepsister?"

Mary Anne tried to explain. When she had finished, she said, "Dawn is also a baby-sitter, like me. We both belong to the Baby-sitters Club."

Well, of course then Caitlin wanted to know about the other members of the BSC. Mary Anne began with Mallory. "She has *seven* brothers and sisters!" she exclaimed.

Caitlin raised her eyebrows. "She must be Catholic," she said.

Mary Anne raised her own eyebrows. "I — " she began to say.

But Mackie interrupted her. "What religion are you?" he asked.

"Well . . . my family doesn't go to church very often," Mary Anne replied, "but when we do, we go to the Presbyterian Church."

"Tell us more about your kitty," said Celeste. By that time she had turned herself around so that she was sitting face to face with Mary Anne. "Do you dress him up?"

So many questions! Mary Anne had never encountered kids like the Lowells. Even Karen Brewer (Kristy's little sister) who is an incredible talker, doesn't ask question after question. (Maybe that's because she'd rather talk than listen.)

Mary Anne told Celeste that Tigger doesn't like to wear clothes (he prefers his fur), and then she managed to engage the kids in some outdoor games, after they had changed their clothes of course. They played mother, may I? and red light, green light, statues, and hide-and-seek.

Finally, Celeste plopped herself down on the lawn and said, "I'm tired. My legs won't hold me up anymore."

"Let's go inside then," said Mary Anne. "Caitlin? Do you have homework?"

"Not on Friday!"

"How about you, Mackie?"

"Not in first grade!"

"Can we watch TV?" asked Caitlin. "*Leave It to Beaver* is on. Mommy always lets us watch that."

"Sure," replied Mary Anne, and she led the kids inside. They settled themselves in the family room — but no one could find *Leave It to Beaver*, no matter how often Caitlin switched the channels.

Soon Celeste grew bored, so Mary Anne found crayons and paper. Celeste announced that she was going to draw a picture of Tigger.

"Great," replied Mary Anne. "I'll watch."

It was while Celeste was adding huge purple eyes to Tigger's wobbly, wavy head that Mary Anne heard giggling from Caitlin and Mackie.

"Did you find *Leave It to Beaver*?" she asked. She glanced at the TV, but saw only an Asian girl and boy riding their bicycles along a neighborhood street.

The show was in color, so Mary Anne knew it wasn't *Leave It to Beaver*. Also, she guessed she had missed the funny part. Then she heard Mackie cry, "Look at their eyes!" and giggle harder.

Mary Anne glanced at the TV again. The scene hadn't changed. She shrugged, not seeing the humor. Oh, well.

"Hello!" called a voice as the back door opened and closed.

"Mommy!" shrieked Celeste, and abandoned her drawing. She raced to her mother and wrapped her arms around Mrs. Lowell's knees.

Five minutes later, Mary Anne was dashing across the Lowells' yard on her way to my house for Friday's meeting of the BSC. She arrived breathless. And early.

So did Kristy. The three of us piled onto my bed for a chat, just like we used to do years ago when we were little.

"Hey, guess what," I exclaimed. "I had a great idea!"

"That's *my* job," teased Kristy.

"No, really. I was thinking about Jackie and his brothers and a musical performance or something, and well, how about helping the kids form a band? The kids who take music lessons can play their own instruments and the other kids can *make* instruments, like you suggested Mary Anne."

"Way cool!" said Kristy. And she wasn't the only one who felt that way. After the meeting started, Kristy asked me to tell the others about the band. Everyone liked the idea.

"Excellent," said Kristy. "There's nothing like a new project."

CHAPTER 4

"Round and round and round she goes," I said, circling my finger in the air, "where she'll stop, nobody . . . knows!" When I said *knows* I touched the nose of Lucy Newton, who squealed with laughter.

Lucy is just a baby, and she loves that game. But Jamie, her brother, is four and wants to do more grown-up things.

"Let's play Popeye!" he cried, jumping up and down. "Let's play Teeny Mutant Stinky Turtles!" (He never gets that right.) "Let's go outside! Let's play on the swings!"

"Whew, hold it, Jamie," I said. "You're wearing me out, and I'm still sitting down. How about inviting a friend over?"

"I have a friend," said Jamie. "His name is Boris and he lives under the stairs. Want to meet him?"

"I meant a real friend."

"Boris is real!"

"Okay, a friend you can see, not an invisible one."

"We-ell . . ."

"Dawn is baby-sitting for the Perkins girls. Do you want to invite Myriah over? And maybe Gabbie?"

"Okay," replied Jamie, "but not Laura. She's another baby."

Laura did come over, though. That was because Dawn came over, so of course she brought all the girls with her. The Perkins family had moved into Kristy's old house, across the street from me. There are three Perkins girls. Myriah is five and a half, Gabbie is two and a half, and Laura is the baby. Jamie has become good friends with Myriah and Gabbie, and I can see why. They're lots of fun. They love to sing and dance and put on shows. And Myriah takes all kinds of lessons and classes — tap dancing, acting, singing. She and Gabbie know the words to lots of long songs. When Laura is older, she'll probably join her sisters in their acts. Right now she just watches them, cooing and smiling. (Sometimes I look at Lucy and Laura, who are practically the same age, and wonder if they'll grow up together and become best friends, like Mary Anne and Kristy did.)

When the Newtons' doorbell rang, Jamie

greeted our visitors with his call of, "Hi-hi! Hi-hi!"

"Hi-hi!" replied Dawn, Myriah, and Gabbie obediently.

"Hi-hi," I said to Dawn, and giggled.

We were about to take the five children into the Newtons' backyard when the phone rang. I dashed for it. "Hello, Newtons' residence," I said.

"Hi, Claud, it's me."

"Hi, Stace! What's going on?"

"The weather's so beautiful that even Charlotte wants to be out in it."

"No kidding." Stacey was baby-sitting at another house in the neighborhood, for eight-year-old Charlotte Johanssen. Charlotte is a wonderful kid — we all love her. She's quiet and sensitive (a little like Mary Anne), and extremely bright. She's already skipped a grade in school. Charlotte's main interests are reading and studying. (She has friends, though. Her very best friend is Becca Ramsey, Jessi's younger sister.) Anyway, Charlotte's request to play outside was a little unusual. "Come on over here," I said. "Dawn just came by with Myriah and Gabbie and Laura. Maybe Charlotte would like to play with the kids."

"Okay. Thanks. We'll walk Carrot over." Carrot is the Johanssens' schnauzer. He's getting a little fat. I mean, for a schnauzer.

No sooner had I hung up the phone than it rang again. "Sheesh," I mumbled. I picked up the receiver. "Hello, Newtons' residence."

"Hi, Claud."

"Mary Anne?"

"Yeah. I'm at the Hobarts'. I'm sitting for Mathew and Johnny."

The Hobarts have four boys. And they live in Mary Anne's old house! Mary Anne was watching the two younger Hobarts. (Mathew is six and Johnny is four. The oldest Hobart, Ben, is Mallory's very first boyfriend.) "So what are you doing?" Mary Anne asked.

"Dawn's here with the Perkins girls, and Stacey's on her way over with Charlotte. And Carrot."

"Oh. Darn. Johnny wanted Jamie to come over here."

"Why don't you bring the boys *here*? We'll have a play group."

"Awesome! We'll be right over."

Before I knew it, the Newtons' backyard was crawling with kids. (And one dog.) Jamie, Lucy, Myriah, Gabbie, Laura, Charlotte, Mathew, and Johnny. (And Carrot.)

My friends and I watched them for a few moments.

"Hey, you know what?" I cried suddenly. "You know what we have here?"

36

"A zoo?" suggested Stacey.

"No, a band. Or the beginnings of one. Lucy and Laura are too little, of course, and I don't know if Charlotte would want to be part of something like that, but here are five other kids."

"Yeah!" said Dawn. "Well, let's see what they think. Hey, you guys!" she called to the children swarming over Jamie's swingset.

"What?" Jamie called back.

"Come here!"

"Me?"

"All of you. We have an idea."

When the kids had gathered around us, my friends looked expectantly at me. "Um." I cleared my throat. "Would you guys like to be in a band?"

"Whose band?" asked Myriah.

"Yours. I mean, ours. We'll start our own band."

"What's a band?" Gabbie wanted to know.

Hmm. Good question. "Well, it's a group of people playing songs together on musical instruments," I replied.

"Are you going to teach us to play the instruments?" asked Jamie.

"Some of you," answered Stacey. "Some of you already play instruments."

"I play the violin," spoke up Mathew, proudly.

"I play the guitar," added Charlotte, sounding shy.

"You do? I didn't know that," said Stacey.

"I just started taking lessons. I was going to wait until I got good before I told anybody about it."

"You mean you'd want to be in the band?" said Mary Anne incredulously.

"I think so." Char's voice was a whisper, but she was smiling.

"Maybe the band should have some singers," suggested Myriah. "Gabbie and I are very good singers."

"I want to play the drums," said Johnny Hobart, "only I don't have any. We rented a violin for Mathew, but I don't have drums."

"Then we'll make some," said Mary Anne. "It's easy."

The kids were becoming excited.

"What could I play?" asked Jamie.

"We'll need more instruments," said Charlotte.

"How about some other band members?" I asked.

"Becca!" exclaimed Charlotte. "If I'm in the band, she's in the band."

"Maybe the Pike kids," suggested Stacey.

"Cool. We'll invite them over."

"Right now?" asked Mary Anne.

"Why not?"

Twenty minutes later the yard was even more jam-packed. The twelve of us had been joined by Jessi with Becca, and Mal with Nicky, Margo, and Claire, the three youngest Pikes. Nicky is eight, Margo is seven, and Claire is five.

I explained the band to its four newest members, and now all I could hear were cries of, "I want to play the tambourine!" "I want to play a harmonica!" "I want to make lots of noise!" (That was Nicky.) "Does anyone have a tuba?" (That was Claire, who has never played the tuba. "You don't even know what a tuba *looks* like," Margo said witheringly to her sister.)

Mary Anne, our dutiful club secretary, found a pencil and a memo pad in the Newtons' kitchen. She brought them into the backyard and began making notes: who wanted to sing, who wanted to play instruments, who *needed* instruments, and so forth.

"Someone should call Kristy and tell her what's going on," said Dawn.

"We should call the Rodowskys, too. After all, they gave me the idea for the band," I pointed out.

"We should probably call a lot of other kids," added Stacey. "We don't want to leave anyone out."

Mary Anne flipped to another page on the

memo pad and carefully wrote: KIDS TO
CALL. We listed Kristy's younger brothers
and sister, the Barretts, the Arnold twins,
Jenny Prezzioso, Nina Marshall, and the
Braddocks.

"Anyone else?" I asked during a lull in the
activity.

"Maybe the Papadakis kids," said Dawn.

"How about the Lowells?" added Mary
Anne. "Since they're new clients of the BSC,
it might be nice to ask them to join. Anyway,
I like the kids. For one thing, they're obedient.
They'll be able to follow directions."

I grinned. "Good idea. I'm sitting at the
Lowells' tomorrow, so I'll ask them then."

Mary Anne scribbled furiously on her pad.

CHAPTER 5

Mrs. Lowell had asked me to arrive at three-thirty the next afternoon. I didn't want to be late for my new job, so I raced directly to the Lowells' as soon as school let out. I didn't bother to go home first. As a result I was standing on the Lowells' front doorstep at exactly 3:19. Good, I thought. It can't hurt to show up early for new clients.

I pressed the doorbell and heard chimes ring in the house. When the door opened, I put on a bright smile. "Hi!" I said.

The woman standing in the entryway did not smile. And she hesitated before saying, "Hello. I'm Mrs. Lowell. Claudia?"

I nearly replied, "Yes, ma'am." Mrs. Lowell made me feel . . . formal. But my mouth had gone dry, so I just nodded.

Mrs. Lowell nodded back. "Well, come on inside." She walked away, leaving me to open the screen door and let myself inside. I followed her into the kitchen, trying to think of something to say.

The best I could come up with was, "Mary Anne really liked Caitlin and Mackie and Celeste. Um, are they here?"

"Caitlin and Mackie aren't home from school yet. Celeste is napping," was the reply. Mrs. Lowell looked everywhere but at me.

Suddenly I knew what was wrong. I'd eaten a bag of cashews on the way to the Lowells' house. I bet bits of nuts were stuck between my teeth. And Mrs. Lowell was so embarrassed for me she didn't know what to say. But I ran my tongue over my teeth and felt nothing. Hmm. Maybe my mascara had smeared. Or my hair was parted strangely. Or I had arrived *too* early after all.

"Claudia? Are you paying attention to me?" snapped Mrs. Lowell.

"Yes, ma'am." (Actually, I wasn't.)

"Our next-door neighbor is Mr. Selznick," she went on. "He's usually home during the day. You can call him in an emergency."

"Does he work at home?" I asked. (Maybe he was an artist.)

"What does it matter?"

I know I blushed then. I just know it. My face grew hot. It must have turned the color of a fire engine.

I shrugged and looked down. As I did, I caught sight of my black leggings and high-topped sneakers, my fringed blue-jean vest and beaded Indian belt, my six silver rings and . . .

Uh-oh. That was it. Mrs. Lowell didn't approve of my outfit. She thought it was too wild. It wasn't appropriate for her kids. That must be it. Mary Anne had written about the Lowell kids' clothes in the club notebook, how neatly and properly they were dressed, especially Caitlin and Mackie in their school uniforms. Of course, Mary Anne would have been neatly and properly dressed, too. She always is, thanks to her father. No wonder Mrs. Lowell didn't like me. And no wonder she had liked Mary Anne.

As Mrs. Lowell was finishing up her list of instructions, the front door burst open and then a girl and boy rushed into the kitchen.

"Hi, Mom!" cried the girl.

"Hi, Mommy!" cried the boy.

Mrs. Lowell's face softened into a warm smile. "Hi, kids. How was school? Come have a snack."

"But, Mom, who's *that*?" The girl was pointing at me.

"Caitlin, Mackie, this is your baby-sitter, Claudia Kishi," said Mrs. Lowell. She paused, then added, "Please be nice to her."

I forced a smile. "Hi, Caitlin. Hi, Mackie," I said.

Mackie said nothing, but Caitlin covered her mouth and giggled. I hoped that was a good sign.

"Well," said Mrs. Lowell presently, "I suppose I should go now." But she didn't. She couldn't seem to leave the room.

"Don't worry about Celeste," I said. "I mean, if you're afraid she'll be scared when she wakes up and finds a sitter here."

"No, it isn't that," said Mrs. Lowell vaguely.

So what *was* it?

I didn't find out. Mrs. Lowell finally managed to leave. Whew. Oh, well. I would only have to face her for a few more minutes at the end of the afternoon. In between I would have fun with the obedient, curious, and well-behaved children Mary Anne had liked so much.

Wrong.

The afternoon started off badly.

Caitlin and Mackie ate four Oreos each and reached for more. "Wait!" I cried. "That's enough!"

"We're hungry," said Caitlin, and grabbed a handful of cookies before I could put the package away.

She and her brother ate greedily, then

jumped up and ran out of the kitchen, leaving a crumb-covered table behind. I began to clean the kitchen while they shrieked through the house.

"Quiet!" I hissed.

They shrieked around until I could hear someone crying.

"Who's hurt?" I called.

"Nobody!" Mackie replied. "Celeste's awake!"

Well, no wonder. I dashed upstairs. "Caitlin, Mackie," I said, "please wipe the kitchen table while I get Celeste up."

The kids disappeared downstairs, then returned quickly.

"We have to talk to Celeste," Caitlin announced. "We have to tell her about her new baby-sitter."

Maybe that was a good idea. Celeste was still crying. She was probably confused. Her sister and brother would be able to calm her down. I stepped into the hallway, leaving the three kids in Celeste's room. Several minutes passed and the sound of crying faded away. I could hear only the low murmur of voices.

"Everything all right in there?" I called.

"Yup!" replied someone, probably Caitlin.

"Okay, then I'm coming in." When I returned to Celeste's room, she gazed at me from where she was sitting on her bed sandwiched between her brother and sister. And she didn't stop staring until Mackie nudged her in her side.

"Celeste, do you want a snack?" I asked.

She nodded. And Mackie cried, "Me, too!"

"You just had one," I reminded him.

"Well, I want another."

"So do I," added Caitlin.

"No way."

"I'll tell Mom you were a mean sitter," said Caitlin, eyes narrowed.

I stood before the Lowell children, trying to decide how to handle the situation. I remembered the time Stacey had tried something she called "reverse psychology" on the two bratty Delaney kids who used to live across the street from Kristy's new house. How had that worked? Had she told them to do the opposite of what she really wanted them to do? That sounded right.

"Okay," I said, "I guess you guys didn't have enough to eat before. You better try to finish off that package of cookies."

"The whole package?!" exclaimed Caitlin.

"Really? You mean it?" cried Mackie.

Uh-oh. Now what? This wasn't how Stacey's reverse psychology was supposed to work. I could picture what would happen that afternoon. The kids would gorge themselves with Oreos and be sick to their stomachs by

46

the time their mother came home. That would be great, just great.

"Um," I began.

Ring, ring.

"Telephone! I'll get it!" shrieked Caitlin. She dashed out of Celeste's room. Several moments later I heard her call, "Claudia! For you!"

Caitlin handed me the extension in the hallway. It's probably Mrs. Lowell, I thought miserably. She's phoning to check up on me.

But the caller was Mary Anne.

"I'm at the Hobarts'," she said. "A whole bunch of us are here. We're planning the band. Do the Lowells want to join?"

"Oh, my gosh! I forgot to ask them. I think we'll just walk on over there so the kids can see what's going on. We need to get out of the house. We'll be there in a few minutes."

The Lowells forgot about the cookies when I told them we were going to take a walk and meet some new kids, and that they would get to see Mary Anne again. Soon we were milling around the Hobarts' backyard along with Myriah and Gabbie, who had run over from next door; Jamie Newton; Mallory with Nicky, Margo, and Claire; Kristy with David Michael, Karen, and Andrew; Stacey with Charlotte; Dawn with the Rodowsky boys; and Mary Anne with Jenny Prezzioso. A few other

47

neighborhood kids had arrived, too.

The yard was full of noise and fun.

"I brought my kazoo," announced Jackie.

"I found a pair of tom-toms in our basement," said Haley Braddock. "Matt can play those because he can feel the beat." (Haley's brother Matt is profoundly deaf.)

Celeste spotted Mary Anne, ran to her, and clung to her hands (what was wrong with *me*?), but Mackie and Caitlin joyfully joined the other kids in planning the band and deciding what songs to learn. They had so much fun that when it was time to leave I hated to call them away. And believe me, they did not want to be called away.

"I don't *want* to leave!" cried Mackie.

"Maybe," said Caitlin, eyeing me, "Claudia will let us eat Oreos when we get home. We never got to eat our extras."

"No Oreos," I said. "It's too close to dinner now."

"But we're hungry!" said Mackie.

"Good, then you'll have plenty of room for your supper."

I walked the Lowell kids home (after I pried Celeste away from Mary Anne), and they whined and complained the entire way.

"You *prom*ised us Oreos," said Caitlin.

"I promised you Oreos when it was four o'clock. Now it's too late."

"Hmphh."

Back at the Lowells' house, I settled the kids into a game of Memory. They kept slipping out of the family room, though. One at a time. Soon I discovered what they were doing. Sneaking grapes.

"I said no snacking!" I cried.

"No, you didn't!" replied Mackie. "You said no Oreos."

I sighed.

I prayed for Mrs. Lowell's safe and quick return.

I couldn't get out of there fast enough.

CHAPTER 6

"Junk food, anyone?" I asked. I pulled a sack of Payday bars from the depths of one of my bureau drawers.

"Got any chips or Fritos?" asked Stacey.

"Or wheat germ biscuits?" asked Dawn.

"Oh, yeah. Right. Wheat germ biscuits. I have them hidden here under the bed along with my endless supply of tofu." (Dawn laughed.) "Will you settle for unsalted stone-ground wheat crackers?" I asked.

Dawn raised her eyebrows. "Sure!" she exclaimed.

"Me, too!" added Stacey. Then she frowned. "Oh, you're kidding. I get it. Silly me. For a moment, I thought — "

"No, I really do have them," I interrupted her. "I bought them just for you guys." I found the box of crackers on the floor under a pile of clean laundry. "Here we go," I said. "I aim to please."

It was 5:25 and another meeting of the BSC was about to begin. We were sitting comfortably in our usual places. Kristy was ensconced in the director's chair; Mary Anne and Stacey and I were lined up on my bed; Dawn was seated backward at the desk chair, her arms dangling over the top rung; and Jessi and Mal were curled up on the floor.

"Okay, please come to order," said Kristy when the food had been handed around and we were munching away.

We settled down. And right away the phone rang.

"I got it!" said Mal. "Hello, Baby-sitters Club. Mallory Pike speaking. . . . Hi, Mrs. Lowell. . . . Kristy? Okay, just a sec." Mallory put her hand over the receiver and said, "Kristy, Mrs. Lowell wants to talk to you."

"Okay," Kristy answered, frowning. She reached for the phone.

Requesting a particular sitter is not club policy.

"Maybe she isn't calling about a job," whispered Jessi.

"That must be it," I agreed.

But Kristy's end of the conversation certainly sounded work-related. "Two hours?" she said. Then she went on, "But — Well, okay. I mean, that isn't . . . um, did something happen? Why don't you want . . ."

I looked at Kristy. Her eyes were downcast. She seemed to be studying her sneakers. So I looked at the rest of my friends. They were exchanging puzzled glances.

Finally Kristy said, "I'll call you right back, okay?"

"What was that all about?" I asked as soon as she'd hung up.

"I'll explain in a few minutes," Kristy replied. "Who's free on Wednesday afternoon, Mary Anne?"

"This Wednesday? Let me see. . . . Just Jessi."

"Want to sit for the Lowells, Jessi?" asked Kristy.

"Sure. Why not?"

Kristy called Mrs. Lowell back, then faced the rest of us BSC members, looking serious. "I have to tell you this," she said, "and I might as well tell you straight out. When Mrs. Lowell called, she said she needed a sitter, but she asked for someone besides Claudia."

I gasped. "What?" I whispered.

Kristy shook her head. "I don't understand it, but that's what she said. Did anything happen when you were there, Claud? If it did, you should have told me about it."

"There's nothing to tell. It wasn't my best sitting job ever, but nothing horrible happened. Nobody got hurt, nothing was broken."

"Is one of the Lowells a walking disaster like Jackie Rodowsky?" asked Jessi. She looked worried. I knew she was beginning to wonder about the job she'd just accepted.

"No! Not at all. Think of the horrible things that have happened when we've sat for Jackie. Broken vases, grape juice on the carpet, skinned knees, banged heads. The Lowells were angels compared to Jackie." I felt numb. And I was angry that I had to defend myself when nothing had happened.

"The Lowells *are* sort of angelic, aren't they?" said Mary Anne.

I paused. "Actually, I didn't have quite the experience with them that you did," I said after a moment.

"Wait. I'm confused, Claudia," said Kristy. "Were the Lowells okay or not? What did go on when you sat for them?"

"Well, nothing. But something." Kristy looked very frustrated, so I rushed on. "Okay. The kids and I didn't really get along. Remember the Delaneys? Well, Caitlin and Mackie reminded me of Amanda and Max Delaney."

"You know, they *do* sort of look like them," spoke up Mary Anne.

"I mean they acted like them. They wouldn't

obey me. They tried to get away with things. They snuck food before dinner. When I set limits, they said they were going to tell on me, tell their mom I was mean to them or something."

"You should have let me know," Kristy said again.

"Well, I wrote about it in the notebook," I pointed out. "And anyway, like I said, none of the things that happened seemed that bad. No broken lamps, no grape juice stains, not even a skinned knee."

Now Mary Anne was frowning. "The kids were perfect when I sat for them. They did everything I suggested. And when Mrs. Lowell came home she kept smiling and telling me what a wonderful job I'd done and commenting on how happy the kids looked."

"What did I do wrong? Maybe the kids *really* spoiled their appetites when they snuck that food."

"What did they eat?" asked Stacey.

"Some grapes."

"That's *it*? Some grapes? You mean a couple of bunches?"

"No. Just a few grapes each. I checked the fruit bowl."

"That wouldn't spoil their appetites," said Dawn. "I thought you meant they raided the cookie jar."

54

"Nope. But maybe they have small stomachs. Or maybe the problem is something totally different. Maybe the kids told their mother they didn't have fun at the Hobarts'."

"Oh, they had a great time," said Mary Anne. "I was watching them."

"Then maybe Mrs. Lowell didn't like my taking them somewhere else to play. But she didn't say not to leave the yard."

"And the Hobarts are so close by," added Jessi.

"Maybe she doesn't like the Hobarts?" I wondered.

"I don't think the Lowell kids had ever *met* the Hobarts before," said Mallory. "I don't think they knew any of the kids there."

"I know! Mrs. Lowell didn't like my outfit!" I exclaimed. "I forgot about that. I'm positive she was looking at it and she thought it was too wild, especially considering what Caitlin and Mackie and Celeste were wearing."

"But why didn't she just say so?" asked Dawn.

I shrugged. So did Kristy.

"Well, I *did* get there a little early," I said after a moment.

"That's no reason to ask you not to sit again," Kristy pointed out.

Mr. Ohdner phoned then, needing a sitter. And then several more clients called. Our meeting became very busy. We couldn't talk about the Lowells again until nearly six o'clock.

"I hope," I said, "that you all noticed no one else asked me not to sit for them. Did you notice that?"

Kristy smiled. "I'm sorry if I sounded like I was accusing you before, but Mrs. Lowell was so clear about not wanting you to sit. The only logical explanation was that something had happened. Maybe I should phone Mrs. Lowell and talk to her tonight. I feel funny about that, though. And anyway, she does want to keep using the BSC," said Kristy.

"Maybe I'll find out something when I sit," said Jessi.

"Dress nicely," I advised her. "And keep the kids at home."

"Okay," agreed Jessi solemnly. Then she grinned. "I'll keep them out of the grapes, too."

CHAPTER 7

Wednesday—

I don't really see the point in writing up my "job" at the Lowells' yesterday, since there was no job after all. But a rule is a rule, so I'll write it up anyway. Here is what happened: nothing. I didn't get past the front door. Okay. Is everybody satisfied with my entry?

Later:

Sorry, you guys. I didn't mean to sound angry at you. Because I'm not. I'm angry at Mrs. Lowell, I guess, but I don't even know why.

57

After that weird club meeting, the one during which Mrs. Lowell phoned and requested any baby-sitter *except* me, Jessi decided she ought to be better prepared than usual when she met her new sitting charges. She wanted the afternoon to go perfectly so that Mrs. Lowell wouldn't be able to find a single fault with Jessi's work.

Jessi planned carefully. When the meeting was over she ran home, and after dinner she opened her Kid-Kit and examined the contents.

"Hmm. Low on crayons," she murmured. "And not enough books for little kids. I better find some that Celeste will like." Jessi removed a couple of items from the kit (to make room for more books), and wandered into her family's rec room. From a shelf, she pulled *Blueberries For Sal*, *The Snowy Day*, *A Chair For My Mother*, and *Good Dog, Carl*. She placed them by the kit.

Now, she thought, do I have enough toys for six-year-old boys? The kit was stocked with plenty of art materials (good for boys and girls of all ages), some easy jigsaw puzzles, and a bunch of Matchbox cars and trucks.

"Now for eight-year-old girls," muttered Jessi, and she marched upstairs to her sister's room.

58

"Becca?"

"Yeah?" Jessi's sister was sitting at her desk, writing something on a sheet of paper with wide lines on it.

"What are you doing?" asked Jessi.

"My homework. We're supposed to write a story called 'The Ghost in My Room.' It has to be two pages long." Becca looked pained.

"That sounds like fun!" exclaimed Jessi. "Listen, Becca, I have to put some stuff in my Kid-Kit that eight-year-old girls will especially like. Do you have any ideas?"

"Barbies," said Becca, without looking up from her paper. "And stickers. Oh, and Charlotte and I like to play office."

"Great, Becca. Thanks," said Jessi.

What a terrific idea! Jessi decided to put together an office package for Caitlin. Before she did that, though, she phoned Mary Anne. "I'm getting ready for my job at the Lowells'," she told her. "I want to make sure I have special stuff in my Kid-Kit for each of the children. And guess what Becca suggested. She said Caitlin might like to play office. What do you think?"

"I think that sounds great. I mean, we didn't play office when I baby-sat, but I'm sure Caitlin would like that game."

"Okay. I'm going to make up an office set for her."

It took Jessi half an hour (when she should have been working on an assignment for her French class), but finally she had filled a plastic box with colored pencils, Magic Markers, pens, erasers, paper clips (red, white, and blue), blunt scissors, tape, memo pads, rubber bands, stickers, animal stamps, writing paper, and envelopes.

"There," she said. "Boy. I should win the Best Baby-sitter Award.

On the day of her job at the Lowells', Jessi made sure to arrive exactly five minutes early — early enough to make a good impression, but not so early as to annoy Mrs. Lowell (in case that's what I had done). Jessi was determined to please her new clients.

Jessi paused on the Lowells' front stoop, clutching her Kid-Kit. She pictured the office set tucked inside. She was pretty sure Caitlin would like it. Jessi had shown it to Becca the night before, and Becca not only had fallen in love with it, but had begged her sister to put together one just for her — which Jessi had done.

Jessi drew in a breath and pressed the bell.

A few moments later the door swung open.

Jessi smiled at the woman standing before her. "Hi," she said. "I'm Jessi Ramsey. I'm the baby-sitter."

Mrs. Lowell looked shocked. When Jessi told us her story that afternoon, that was the only word she used to describe the expression on Mrs. Lowell's face. "Shocked," Jessi repeated to us. "I don't know how else to put it."

Mrs. Lowell stared at Jessi for a full six seconds and, during that time, Jessi did just what I had done when Mrs. Lowell and I faced each other. She tried to figure out what could possibly be wrong with what Mrs. Lowell saw. Had she buttoned her shirt crookedly? Were her jeans unzipped? Wait! Maybe Mrs. Lowell expected girls to wear dresses. . . . No. Jessi knew that Caitlin and Celeste owned blue jeans. Nervously, Jessi glanced down at herself, then back at Mrs. Lowell.

"Did — did I come at the wrong time?" Jessi stammered, checking her watch.

"No, um . . . No." Mrs. Lowell took a step backward. "I don't need a sitter after all," she finally managed to say. "I forgot to tell you."

Mrs. Lowell closed the front door.

Jessi remained motionless on the stoop. She felt like crying, although she wasn't quite sure why. She hadn't been yelled at or scolded or injured. Yet she was hurt. And a familiar thought nagged at her but wouldn't make itself known.

Jessi turned around slowly and walked

down the Lowells' driveway. When she reached the sidewalk she turned around and looked at the house. She couldn't see anyone; not Mrs. Lowell, not the children. Just a curtain moving near a window by the front door.

The Wednesday afternoon meeting of the BSC wouldn't begin for almost two hours. Jessi, carrying the Kid-Kit, walked toward Mallory's house. For some reason she didn't feel like going home and telling anyone what had just happened at the Lowells'. Jessi scuffed down the street thinking of the office set she'd made for Caitlin, of the half hour she *should* have spent doing her homework.

By the time she reached the Pikes' house she was crying.

But by the time she and Mal arrived in BSC headquarters, she had stopped. She simply looked puzzled — as puzzled as I still felt.

"Maybe Mrs. Lowell expected someone older," suggested Jessi when the meeting was underway. "Maybe she thought I would be thirteen, like Mary Anne and Claudia."

"But why wouldn't she just have said so?" asked Kristy, who was scowling under her visor. Clearly, she thought Mrs. Lowell was Trouble. I could tell she was trying to figure out what to do about her. Clients must be handled delicately.

"I don't know. She looked embarrassed,"

replied Jessi. "Well, no, that's not true. Like I said, she mostly looked shocked. And you know what? She practically slammed the door in my face!"

I gave Jessi a sympathetic glance. Then, to make her feel better, I asked her to show us the office kit she had put together. We all exclaimed over it, and about half of us decided to put together kits of our own.

But we could not forget about Mrs. Lowell.

"Maybe she'll call during the meeting," said Kristy.

She didn't. Each time the phone rang we looked at it expectantly. Once Dawn even said, staring at the receiver, "I *will* you to be Mrs. Lowell." The caller was Mr. Hobart.

"I guess I could phone Mrs. Lowell," said Kristy uncertainly. "In fact, I probably ought to. As club president, it's my job to find out if we have a dissatisfied client."

"Hey!" exclaimed Jessi, brightening. "Wait a sec! We're making too much of this. Maybe Mrs. Lowell really *did* forget she didn't need a sitter. Her plans changed and she forgot to call us to cancel. So she was embarrassed."

"I don't know," I said, not wanting to deflate Jessi, but wanting to be honest with her. "That doesn't explain why she never wants *me* to sit for her kids again."

Jessi sagged. "True."

For several minutes the seven of us sat in silence. At last Mary Anne sighed, then said, "Well, I'm supposed to sit for the Lowells again next week. Should we wait and see how that goes?"

"Sure," Kristy answered. "Why not? I don't know what else to do."

The clock turned to six and Kristy adjourned the meeting. My friends wandered quietly out of my room, through the hall, down the stairs, out the front door.

At dinner, I tried to be cheerful.

CHAPTER 8

"You know what we need?" asked Jackie Rodowsky. "We need a name. That's what. And it should be, like, catchy."

Jackie was talking about the band. My friends and I had managed to get the kids together several times and, by now, everyone had chosen whether to be a singer or a player, the players had decided on instruments, and the instruments had been either found or made. The band was heavy on kazoos and percussion (a lot of the littler kids had insisted on playing drums, tambourines, sticks, and cymbals), but we also featured a couple of piano players, a flute player, a trumpet player, a violin player, and Charlotte, our guitar player. Myriah, Gabbie, Buddy Barrett, and Margo Pike were our singers.

At our first band practice, the kids had unanimously voted to learn the song "Tomorrow" from the musical *Annie*.

Now, sitting for the Rodowskys one Saturday, the boys were rehearsing — and Jackie had decided the band needed a name.

"You know you're right," I replied. "Any suggestions, Jackie?"

Jackie bit his lip and stared into space. He fiddled with his kazoo. "How about the Beatles?"

"I think that's been taken."

"The Little Beatles? The Baby Beatles?"

"Your name should say more about *you*."

"Jackie Rodowsky's All-Star Orchestra!"

"It isn't *your* band, Jackie," said Archie indignantly.

And Shea added, "*I* think the name should be funny."

"String Beans!" said Archie.

"Turtle Toes!" said Shea.

I giggled. "Come on, you guys."

The Rodowsky boys grew quiet, thinking. After a moment Jackie said seriously, "You know what? I think we should call ourselves All the Children, like short for All the Children of the World. Because we *are* all kids, and we're all different kinds of kids; different ages, different colors — "

"Yeah!" said Shea, catching on. "And our families come from all different countries. We're Polish," he said proudly.

"And I'm Japanese," I added. "And Hannie

and Linny Papadakis are Greek, and the Hobarts are Australian."

"Did you know," spoke up Archie, "that Jamie Newton's great-great-great-grandfather was an Indian? So Jamie is a real, true American, because the Indians lived in America before anyone else did. And they're called Native Americans now. My teacher said so."

"Well I like All the Children," I said. "It's a great name for the band."

"I like it, too," said Shea and Archie at the same time.

Jackie grinned, pleased with himself.

"Okay, are you guys ready to rehearse?" I asked. "I think we should have our own practice before we go to Jamie's for the big practice." Our band had been rehearsing at the Newtons' because Mr. and Mrs. Newton had been nice enough to say that not only could our two piano players use their electric keyboard, but that we could set it up on their back porch, since it was easier for the band to play outdoors.

"Claudia?" said Jackie. "When we go to Jamie's, can we tell the other kids the name for our band?"

"Of course," I answered. "Except I don't think we should *tell* the kids. I think they should vote on it. Just to be democratic. Now, are you guys ready to rehearse?"

"We better warm up, first," said Archie.

The boys ran into the living room where I could see a tambourine sitting on the piano. Shea slid onto the piano bench, Archie grabbed the tambourine, and Jackie held up his kazoo.

"Scales!" ordered Shea. He placed his thumb on middle C and accompanied himself while he sang, "Do re mi fa sol la ti do."

Jackie played along, humming off-key.

Archie beat the tambourine in time to the piano.

"Fantastic!" proclaimed Shea when they had finished. "Okay, everybody. Get ready for 'Tomorrow.' Claudia, you sing."

"Me? Sing the *song*?" I asked, my voice squeaking.

"Yeah. It helps me keep my place. Besides, we're used to hearing Myriah and Gabbie and everyone sing while we play."

"But I *can't* sing. I have an awful voice." (Actually, my voice isn't all that bad, but I hadn't memorized the words to the song.)

"Oh, anyone can sing," said Shea.

"Not me."

"I'll sing then," said Archie.

Shea looked suspiciously at his youngest brother. "Are you sure you know the words?" he asked.

"Sure I'm sure. Let's start."

"Ready, guys? I'll count you off," I said. "One, two, three, four."

Shea's fingers hit the keys, Jackie blew seriously into his kazoo, and Archie beat the tambourine and sang, "The sun'll come out tomorrow. Bet your bell bottoms tomorrow there'll be — "

Shea stopped playing. "Excuse me?"

"What?" said Archie.

Jackie cracked up. "You said 'Bet your bell bottoms'!"

"All right, we won't have a singer," said Shea, sighing dramatically.

"Then can I have a tambourine solo?" Archie wanted to know.

"NO!" cried Shea.

He was clearly frustrated, but the rehearsal had to stop for awhile anyway when Jackie dropped his kazoo into the piano.

"You know what?" I said when the kazoo had been recovered. "It's time to go to Jamie's. Jackie, Archie, remember your instruments. Shea, remember your music."

The Rodowsky boys and I set out for the walk to the Newtons'. We could hear our band long before we could see it. From several houses away drifted toots and beeps and jingles and crashes and plinks and shouts and laughs and giggles.

69

"Hello, everybody!" called Jackie as we stepped through the gate in the Newtons' fence. "We have great news!"

"What is it?" asked Kristy and, one by one, heads turned toward us.

Jackie stepped forward. "I thought of a name for our band," he said. "I think we should call ourselves All the Children, because we are sort of like all the children of the world."

For just a moment I thought some of the kids, especially the older ones, might give him a hard time. But they just began to smile. I glanced at Kristy and she was smiling, too. So were the other members of the BSC. I put my arm around Jackie.

"I guess that's settled," said Kristy. "Okay. Who are we missing today?" She gazed around the yard.

We ran our rehearsals loosely. Anyone who was free was expected to show up. Anyone who wasn't free was simply supposed to try to show up at the next rehearsal. That afternoon, the Lowell kids were missing. So were the Barretts, Linny Papadakis, and David Michael Thomas. Even so, we were left with a fairly impressive band and three of our four singers.

"Okay, kids," I said. "Places!"

In the scramble that followed, Claire Pike

fell and bumped her knees, Archie managed to sit on his tambourine (without breaking it), Hannie Papadakis lost her harmonica, and two kids announced that they had shown up for rehearsal without their drums. So Mal soothed her sister, Mary Anne helped Archie and Hannie, and Kristy said, "How could you come to a *band* rehearsal without your *in*struments?"

The kids shrugged.

"Kristy?" said Jamie. "Mommy put some empty coffee cans in the garage. We could use them for drums today."

So we did.

Then, "Places, everyone!" I called again.

I turned to Marilyn Arnold and Shea at the keyboard. "One, two — "

"Hey!" We were interrupted by Karen Brewer, Kristy's sister, who looked extremely excited. "You know what our band needs now?" she cried. "Since we have a name, we need to paint our name on one of our big drums. All the best bands do that. We would look so awesome. A huge round drum that said ALL THE CHILDREN."

"But we don't have a huge round drum," pointed out Myriah. "Our drums are oatmeal cartons and coffee cans."

"Oh, yeah." Karen looked disappointed.

"I suppose," I said, "that we could write ALL THE CHILDREN on the lids of the oatmeal cartons, but no one would see that."

"I have an idea," spoke up Mary Anne. "How about if we make a banner with our name? We could make a really long one."

"Out of felt," I added. "We could cut out the letters and glue them onto a piece of background material."

"Pink and white!" cried Karen.

"Those are *girl* colors," said Nicky Pike. "How about blue and white?"

"*Boy* colors!" countered Karen.

"You guys, we need to re*hearse*," Kristy broke in.

"And then, when we have our banner, we should give a show," said Jackie. "For our families and friends."

"We really need — " began Kristy.

"A musical program!" said Becca Ramsey.

"With *lots* of songs," added Charlotte Johanssen.

"We haven't even learned one song," muttered Kristy.

"We could play all the songs from *Annie!*" exclaimed Myriah.

"Yeah. We know the words," said Gabbie.

"There's 'Maybe' and 'The Hard-Knock Life' and 'You're Never Fully Dressed Without a Smile' and 'Little Girls,' " said Myriah.

"I am not going to play a song called 'Little Girls,' " said Nicky.

"How about playing 'Tomorrow'?" asked Kristy loudly. "Right now."

The kids stopped and stared at her.

"Oh, yeah. Our rehearsal," said Jackie.

"Shea? Marilyn?" I said. "One, two, three, four."

"The sun'll come out tomorrow!"

CHAPTER 9

Thursday

I baby-sat at the Lowells' house, and my afternoon there was interesting (to be polite). I mean, basically everything was fine. The kids were good. I didn't have any trouble with them, Claud. In fact, it was just a regular, normal old baby-sitting job. But the experience was sort of like a rotten Easter egg. It looks pretty on the outside, but you sure don't want to find out what's under the shell.

When I first read Kristy's notebook entry I got all huffy. Okay. So Mary Anne had had no trouble with the Lowell kids, and Kristy had had no trouble with them, but I could barely handle them. What did that say about me? That I was all washed up as a baby-sitter? That I was as *talentless* on the job as I was in school?

That's what I thought at first. Then I calmed down and read on.

Kristy was not even supposed to baby-sit for the Lowells'. Mary Anne was scheduled for the Thursday afternoon job. But Kristy's curiosity about Mrs. Lowell finally got the better of her. She decided she *had* to know why Mrs. Lowell was so short with me, and why she turned Jessi away. So she asked Mary Anne if she'd mind giving up her job. She even offered Mary Anne the money she would earn.

"Oh, you don't have to do that, Kristy," said Mary Anne. "Go ahead and see if Mrs. Lowell minds if you and I switch. I want to know what's going on, too. Anyway, maybe I'll get another job for Thursday. We've been so busy lately."

So Kristy phoned Mrs. Lowell. "Hello," she said. "This is Kristy Thomas. I'm the president of the Baby-sitters Club. We've talked on the phone before. Um, Mrs. Lowell, Mary Anne won't be able to baby-sit for you on Thursday. Something came up." (This was not, technically, a lie. Something *had* come up. Kristy wanted to meet Mrs. Lowell, that was what.) "But if it's all right with you, I can take her place. I'm thirteen, like Mary Anne, and I'm a very responsible sitter. Everyone says so."

"We-ell," said Mrs. Lowell, "all right. I'll be in a bind if I don't have a sitter on Thursday, so I guess it will be okay."

A brief silence followed, and Kristy sensed that Mrs. Lowell wanted to say something more. When she didn't, Kristy said, "So . . . good-bye, Mrs. Lowell. See you on Thursday."

"Good-bye."

Ding-dong.

Thursday had arrived and Kristy was at the Lowells' front door. Her heart pounded as she waited for Mrs. Lowell to open it.

Kristy wasn't taking any chances. Like Jessi, she arrived *exactly* five minutes early; no more, no less. And she was wearing a skirt. For Kristy, this was a supreme sacrifice. Ordinarily, she wears dresses or skirts only for special occasions, or if her mother makes her. But to go to the Lowells', Kristy put on a Mary Anne type of outfit — skirt, blouse, knee socks, loafers, even a ribbon in her hair.

Sure enough, when Mrs. Lowell answered the door, she did just what she'd done to Mary Anne and Jessi and me. She eyed Kristy — just for a moment. Then she smiled and invited her inside.

Kristy got the nice treatment, the Mary Anne treatment. This was good because after Mrs. Lowell had shown Kristy the emergency numbers and given her special instructions, Kristy felt comfortable enough to say, "Mrs. Lowell, since you're a new client of the Babysitters Club, may I ask you a very important question? About the quality of our service?"

"Certainly." Mrs. Lowell smiled.

"Are you satisfied with us so far? Are we doing a good job?"

"Oh, I'm quite pleased."

"Pleased with Mary Anne Spier?"

"Definitely."

"Pleased with Claudia Kishi?"

"She did a perfectly adequate job."

"But you don't want her to sit for you again?"

Mrs. Lowell's voice came out in a croak: "It's just that the children simply adore Mary Anne."

"And Jessi — "

"Mackie!" Mrs. Lowell called suddenly. "Caitlin! Is that you?"

"Yup, it's me. Hi, Mommy!"

\

"Hi, Mom!" added Caitlin.

The kids ran into the kitchen and Mrs. Lowell focused her attention on them. Kristy didn't have another chance to ask her about Jessi. But that didn't stop her from asking the kids questions.

Later, when Celeste had awakened from her nap, and she and Caitlin and Mackie were eating a snack with their new baby-sitter, Kristy said, "Do you guys like being in the band?"

"Yup," said Caitlin and Mackie.

"I like playing my sticks," added Celeste. "I am good at that."

"Did you know the band has a name now?" asked Kristy.

"It does?" replied Mackie. "What?"

"All the Children."

Caitlin nodded. "Very nice."

"I wish you guys could come more often," said Kristy. (The Lowell kids missed more rehearsals than they attended.)

"Mommy says she wants to see what we do there," Caitlin informed Kristy. "She hasn't met the kids yet."

"What do you mean?"

"You know. She likes to know who we're playing with."

"Oh." Kristy nodded. That made sense. Her mom and Watson liked to get to know the

78

friends of her younger brothers and sisters.

"You're a nice baby-sitter," Mackie said a moment later.

"Thanks," replied Kristy. "I'm glad your mom calls our club. What do you think of your other sitters?"

"Mary Anne is fun!" said Caitlin. "She played games with us."

"I bet you liked Claudia, too. She's the one who helped you join the band. Remember? She took you to the Hobarts'."

"Oh, yeah," said Caitlin, and giggled. "She's the funny-looking one."

(Well, thanks a lot.)

For a moment, Kristy was confused. If I do say so myself, I am one of the more sophisticated kids at SMS. Everyone agrees. And one boy at school, Pete Black, has even said I'm awesome-looking. They say that about Stacey, too. It's pretty much accepted that both of us are way cool.

Which was why Kristy paused at the "funny-looking" comment. Then she thought about my clothes — and remembered why she herself was wearing a skirt that afternoon. That must be what Caitlin meant. My clothes and jewelry were too wild for the Lowells' taste.

"You know something weird?" Kristy went on. "Your mom hired another baby-sitter that

I don't think you guys even saw."

"Did she come really, really late at night?" Mackie wondered.

"Nope. She came in the afternoon."

"What does she look like?" asked Caitlin. "Maybe we did see her."

"Well, she's a dancer. She wears her hair pulled back. Her legs are really long. Um, she's African-American — "

Caitlin and Mackie were both drinking juice at that moment, and they nearly choked. "Well," said Caitlin scornfully, coughing, "I guess Mommy didn't like her." At least, that's what Kristy thought she said. But Caitlin was coughing so hard she might have said, "I guess that's why Mommy didn't like her."

Kristy couldn't stop thinking about the Lowells. She thought about them while her brother Charlie drove her home late that afternoon. And she thought about them during dinner.

"Kristy?" said her mother as they were clearing the table. "Are you all right? You're awfully quiet."

"Quiet for Kristy, or quiet for a normal person?" asked Sam.

Mrs. Brewer gave her son a Look.

Kristy barely heard him. "Mom, can we talk? Tonight?"

"Of course, honey. Girl talk?"

"No. Just serious talk. Can Nannie and Watson talk with us?"

"Whoa!" exclaimed Sam, and he whistled softly. "This must be *major*. What did you *do*?"

"Nothing."

"I'll find Nannie and Watson," said Kristy's mother.

"Are you flunking something?" asked Sam.

"Let's go in the living room, honey."

"Did you break something?" persisted Sam. "Steal something? Tell a lie?"

Kristy followed her mother into the living room. When Watson and her grandmother had joined them, she said, "What I'm going to say sounds awful, and I don't have any proof, but I *have* to talk to an adult. It's about the Lowells."

"Go ahead," said Mrs. Brewer.

"I think they're, um, racists."

"That's a pretty strong word," said Watson.

Kristy nodded. "I know. But Mrs. Lowell wouldn't let Jessi in their house, and the kids call Claudia 'the funny-looking one'. At first I thought they meant her clothes, but I have this horrible feeling they meant her — her face. Her eyes. They mean she's Asian." Kristy explained about our jobs with the Lowells.

When she finished speaking, she saw her mother and stepfather and grandmother looking worriedly at one another. Finally Nannie sighed and said, "With each generation I think it's going to be over. But it isn't even getting better. Maybe I'm just an old fool."

"The Lowells are the foolish ones, Nannie," said Kristy.

"Those poor children," murmured Mrs. Brewer. "They aren't even given the chance to make up their minds for themselves."

Watson nodded. "The sins of the fathers, et cetera."

"You know what?" said Kristy, her lower lip trembling. "I was hoping I was wrong. I was hoping you guys would tell me I was imagining things. Or being too dramatic or something."

"Oh, honey," said Mrs. Brewer. "I'd like to do that. Parents want to protect their children from everything that's bad. But they can't."

Kristy rested her head on her mother's shoulder. "Maybe I am wrong, though."

CHAPTER 10

"I guess," began Kristy, "that you guys are wondering what's going on."

I nodded.

"Yes," replied Jessi and Mal and Dawn.

"We need to talk about Mrs. Lowell," said Kristy.

I felt as if a block of ice had been dropped in my stomach. Something was very wrong. Kristy had been quiet at school that day, even during lunch. Now she was sitting in my director's chair, conducting a club meeting, but she'd forgotten to put on her presidential visor. And instead of sticking her pencil over her ear, she was toying nervously with it in her lap, twisting it in and out of her fingers.

Mrs. Lowell. Kristy had taken Mary Anne's sitting job at the Lowells' the day before. What had happened. What had Mrs. Lowell said? I was convinced I was in trouble.

Kristy bit her lip.

"What is it, Kristy?" asked Stacey. "What's wrong?"

Kristy looked so uncomfortable that I decided to save her from further torture. "I guess it's my fault. I blew my job at the Lowells and they've decided not to use the club anymore, right?" I said. "It's okay, Kristy. Just come out and say it."

Kristy couldn't look up. "That isn't exactly what's going on. But I guess I am trying to spare your feelings, Claud. Look, you guys. I think I made a horrible discovery. I talked about it with Mom and Watson and Nannie last night, and they think I might be right. The worst thing is, if I *am* right, we can't *do* anything."

"Kristy, please just tell me what — " Dawn began.

"The Lowells are prejudiced," said Kristy in a rush. "Claud, they didn't like you because you're Japanese. Jessi, Mrs. Lowell wouldn't even let you in her house because you're African-American."

My mouth dropped open. "But I'm a good baby-sitter!" I protested. I could feel my hands trembling and my cheeks burning. "That's — that's not fair! It really isn't fair." I looked at Jessi who was sitting cross-legged on the floor with Mallory. She wasn't saying anything.

84

"Jessi, aren't you mad?" I demanded. "At least Mrs. Lowell let me in the house. She closed her door to you."

"It's happened before," said Jessi quietly.

"Well, not to me!" I cried. For some reason I felt ashamed and I had the uncomfortable feeling that Kristy, Mary Anne, Mallory, Stacey, and Dawn felt ashamed *for* Jessi and me. "So — so what does being Asian have to do with being a good sitter?" I sputtered.

"Nothing," replied Jessi. "Prejudice doesn't make sense."

"It isn't rational or logical," added Mary Anne.

I was growing angry. The ice in my stomach had turned into a flame and now it was rising up, filling me, surrounding me. The problem was that I didn't know who to be angry at, since Mrs. Lowell wasn't in the room. Finally I got angry at my friends. "Will you guys at least *look* at me?" I shouted. "I am not dirt, you know. Nothing is *wrong* with me."

"Mrs. Lowell thinks we'll contaminate her children — and her house," said Jessi bitterly.

"Yeah, Mrs. *Low*ell thinks that," said Stacey pointedly.

"Sorry," I muttered.

"If it's any consolation," said Dawn, "I bet the Lowells don't like Jews or Indians or

85

Buddhists or Puerto Ricans or anyone who isn't white and just like their *perfect* family."

"Well, I'm not sure it's comforting to know I'm not the only one the Lowells hate — " I started to say.

"Claud, they don't hate you," spoke up Jessi. "They just don't understand you. That's the way my dad explained it to me once."

"What do they have to under*stand*?" I cried, still outraged. "I have two eyes, two ears, a nose, and a mouth, just like the Lowells. I live in a house like the Lowells' house. I have a family like the Lowells. My parents go to work and my sister and I go to school and when we get hungry we eat and when we get tired we sleep and we laugh and cry and fall in love. Just like the Lowells."

"Same here," said Jessi, "but my skin is black. And your eyes slant, Claud."

"So what?"

"That's why prejudice isn't rational."

"It must be hard to grow old," said Kristy.

I looked at her in confusion. "What?"

"Something Nannie said last night. She said she expected racism to decrease with each generation — or something like that — and that she's disappointed because things *aren't* getting better."

"Well, it does seem like things *used* to be worse," said Mallory hesitantly. "For hundreds of years African-Americans were kept as slaves. And during the Second World War the Nazis killed Jews and Catholics. But things are better now . . . aren't they?"

"Ever heard of the skinheads?" asked Stacey. "They beat up on people who are black or middle eastern or — or lots of things. And they live right here in the United States. Today. Same with the KKK."

"The what?" I frowned.

"The Ku Klux Klan," Jessi supplied. "They still exist. And not just in the south. In the north. In cities. In lots of places."

Mary Anne's eyes had filled with tears. "This is scary," she whispered. "I wonder if those skinheads could get *me* for anything. I think maybe some of my ancestors were Russian. I wonder if that's a problem."

"Ooh, now I understand what Nannie meant," said Mallory. "I guess as long as there's prejudice and misunderstanding, there's trouble. And innocent people worry and get hurt."

"Or killed," added Dawn.

Shame, anger, now fear. My feelings were jumbled up.

The phone rang then, and I jumped. I'd completely forgotten we were in a BSC meeting.

Jessi picked up the receiver. "Hello, Baby-sitters Club." She listened for a moment and her face became a mask. "Just a minute," she said coldly. "You can talk to Kristy." Jessi handed the phone across the room. "It's Mrs. Lowell," she said in a tone of voice I'd never heard her use. "I thought you might want to talk to her."

Kristy nodded. "Hello?" she said. And then, "I'll call you back."

"Why are you going to call her back?" I exploded as Kristy hung up the phone. "I was waiting for you to blow her off."

"So was I," replied Kristy, "but she took me by surprise. I couldn't think of what to say. Listen to this. Mrs. Lowell actually had the nerve just now to ask for the blonde-haired, blue-eyed baby-sitter she's heard about. Can you believe it? Who does she think we are? Who does she think I am? She knows I'm not blonde-haired and blue-eyed. Does she mean I'm not good enough to sit for her again?"

"See, Claudia?" spoke up Mary Anne. "I guess I wasn't such a hot baby-sitter after all. Mrs. Lowell isn't asking for me again either. Now you don't have to feel so bad."

Kristy was wearing a small smile. "You guys?" she said. "What are we going to do? When you think about it, this is sort of funny."

"Hysterical," I said.

Stacey, looking huffy, added, "I'm blonde-haired and blue-eyed and you wouldn't catch me dead sitting for the Lowells."

"Ditto," said Dawn.

By then, Kristy was grinning. "Perfect. Okay, watch this," she said. I couldn't help smiling a little myself. Kristy was up to something, and I knew it would be good.

Kristy phoned Mrs. Lowell back. "I'm sorry," she told her. "We're all out of blonde-haired, blue-eyed baby-sitters. And everyone else is busy. Oh, except for one of our associate members. His name is Logan." Kristy paused, apparently because she'd been cut off by Mrs. Lowell. Then I heard her repeat, "Boys don't baby-sit? Well, Logan does, but anyway, let me see. You know what, Mrs. Lowell? I *might* be able to sit after all. That is, if I'm not sitting for Emily Michelle. Did I tell you I have an adopted sister? She's Vietnamese. . . . What? You don't? . . . Yeah, well, I had a feeling. Later, Mrs. Lowell." Kristy hung up the phone. "We just lost a sitting job," she said.

"Good," I replied.

"She heard about Logan and Emily and suddenly — like magic — she didn't need a sitter anymore."

"What's wrong with *Logan*?" asked Mary Anne.

"He's a boy," said Kristy. "In Mrs. Lowell's world boys don't baby-sit. And *I* committed the crime of being a member of a family who adopted a Vietnamese child." Kristy's grin hadn't faded yet. "Hey, Dawn, Stacey, you blonde-haired, blue-eyed people — I bet you guys wouldn't have been good enough for Mrs. Lowell, either."

We were all starting to smile by then. "Why not?" asked Stacey.

"Because your parents are . . ." — Kristy dropped her voice to a whisper — ". . . *divorced.*"

"Ooh!" I cried. "I'm telling! I'm telling Mrs. Lowell."

"You know what?" said Mary Anne. "When you think about it, none of us would be good enough for the Lowells. Claud, you're Japanese. Jessi, you're African-American. Stacey, Dawn, and Kristy, your parents are divorced. *I* have a stepsister. Oh, and by the way, I made the mistake of mentioning that to the Lowell kids. And Mallory — "

"Yeah?"

"Your family is just too darn big. Caitlin thinks you're Catholic. You know what else?" Mary Anne went on. "I feel sort of sorry for Mrs. Lowell."

"How sorry?" I asked.

Mary Anne held her thumb an eighth of an

90

inch from her finger. "This sorry," she said, giggling.

Later that evening I was sitting in the kitchen with my father. He was making salad dressing. I was chopping vegetables. "Dad?" I said. "Did anybody ever hate you because you're Japanese?"

Dad's back had been facing me. Now he turned away from the counter. "Why do you ask that, honey?"

"I was just wondering."

"Did something happen?"

"There's this woman named Mrs. Lowell. She's a baby-sitting client. She doesn't want me to sit for her kids because I'm Asian. That's never happened to me before. I mean, I don't understand. What's wrong with being Japanese?"

"Nothing," Dad answered. "And I'm sorry anyone made you feel you had to ask that question."

"Did you know," said Janine, who apparently had been listening to our conversation from somewhere nearby, "that during World War Two thousands of Japanese were interned in concentration camps in the United States?"

"In the United States?" I repeated, aghast. "There were concentration camps here in America?" My voice had grown shrill. "I

91

thought the only concentration camps were the ones in Europe with those funny names. Treblinka and Dachau and — well, I don't remember any others, but we learned about them in school this year. Our teacher didn't tell us about death camps *here*, though, for Japanese people."

"They weren't death camps," said Janine. "But they were places where American Japanese were made to stay during the war."

"Because Japan and the U.S. were fighting on opposite sides?" I asked.

Janine nodded. "So Japanese-Americans weren't trusted, and they were pulled out of their homes, away from their jobs and lives, and made to stay locked up in camps."

"But they hadn't done anything wrong," I protested. And then I remembered what Mary Anne had said: Prejudice isn't rational. "How come people like Mrs. Lowell can't look underneath other people's skin? How come what's on the outside matters so much?" I asked.

"I don't know," Dad replied. "But I guess what's really important is that *you* can look underneath." My father smiled sadly at me.

CHAPTER 11

One Saturday, not long after Jackie had suggested putting on a show, we held a band rehearsal and nearly everyone came. All of us BSC members were there, and the kids just kept trickling into the Newtons' yard, clutching their instruments.

The Papadakis kids arrived with Karen, Andrew, and David Michael. Most of the kids from the neighborhood had shown up, as well as the younger brothers and sisters of the BSC members. I was standing in a noisy, happy crowd.

"Should we start the rehearseal now?" I asked Kristy.

"Let's wait a few more minutes," she answered. "If we do, maybe everybody will show up."

So we waited. Karen and her friends Nancy Dawes and Hannie Papadakis made up a dance to the "Little Girls" song. Then they surrounded Nicky Pike, hands on hips, singing, "Little girls! Little girls!" Nicky broke out of their circle and ran to David Michael. "Save me!" he cried.

The drum players — and there were quite a few of them — grouped together near the swing set, beating away happily.

Marilyn and Shea sat at the keyboard and played a duet.

"Claudia?" said Jackie, tapping my arm. "Can I make an announcement?"

"We're waiting for a few more kids to arrive," I told him.

"But I can't wait."

"He might as well go ahead," Dawn whispered to me. "I think the only kids who aren't here now are the Lowells."

I nodded. "Okay, Jackie. What's your announcement?"

"Shea, help me," said Jackie. "Help me get their attention."

Shea crashed out a chord on the keyboard. The kids gathered around him.

Jackie stood on an overturned plastic crate. "Everybody!" he said loudly. "I have an idea."

"Another one?" asked Vanessa Pike.

"Yup. It's about our show. I think we should play the songs from *Fiddler on the Roof*, not *Annie*."

"What's *Fiddler on the Roof?*" asked Becca Ramsey.

"I know!" cried Linny Papadakis. "We saw that show in Stamford."

It turned out that a lot of kids had. And many of them owned the music and were familiar with the songs. Still, not every kid knew what Jackie was talking about, so I said to him, "Tell them the story of *Fiddler on the Roof.*"

"Okay," answered Jackie, pleased to have been trusted with that task. "See, there's this family with all these girls — "

"More *girls?*" protested Nicky.

" — living in Russia a long time ago," Jackie continued. "And their father wants them to get married, only he wants this lady called a matchmaker to choose husbands for them. But the daughters fall in love with other men. Also, a war is coming, and the family is in trouble because they're Jewish . . ." Jackie trailed off and glanced over his shoulder at me. "I'm not sure why that got them in trouble. I mean, why the soldiers didn't like them. Well, anyway." Jackie turned back to the kids. "And the soldiers want to make the family — and all the Jewish people in town — leave the place where they've been living. It's called Anatevka. And they have to pack up their stuff and find another home and it's very sad. But the songs are good and Shea knows how to play some of them and I think our program should be called *Fiddler on the Roof* instead of *Annie*," Jackie finished up.

The kids who had seen *Fiddler on the Roof*, which was more than half of them, agreed. Our entire program had changed.

"Shea? What song do you and Jackie want to teach the kids first?" I asked.

Shea considered this. "How about 'Tradition'? I like that one. It has a good beat. And we know most of the words."

"Okay. Let's start."

Soon after we began, the Lowell kids showed up. Mrs. Lowell was with them.

"Tradishu-u-u-u-un! Tra*di*tion!" the singers were belting out.

I glanced at Mrs. Lowell, then down at the ground. "Hi," I said. I wondered what she saw when she looked at me. Slope-eyes? That was why I couldn't look at *her*.

"Hello," replied Mrs. Lowell. She was gazing around the yard at the kids, who'd stopped playing and singing. Then she approached Dawn.

Caitlin, Mackie, and Celeste ran to the children.

"Are you one of the baby-sitters?" Mrs. Lowell asked Dawn. (She ignored the rest of us. You'd never have known that Mary Anne and Kristy and I had taken care of her kids.)

"Yes," Dawn answered warily.

"Are you in charge here?"

"Actually," said Dawn, straightening her shoulders, "Claudia is in charge. The band was her idea."

"Oh." Mrs. Lowell looked at me, then back at Dawn. She cleared her throat. "There certainly is an assortment of children here."

"Oh, yeah," said Dawn. "All ages. The youngest one is — " Dawn stopped speaking. She realized that wasn't what Mrs. Lowell had meant. She also realized Mrs. Lowell was right. The children *were* "assorted." Becca is African-American. Linny and Hannie are Greek. Nancy Dawes is Jewish, but Dawn didn't see how Mrs. Lowell could tell *that* just by looking at her. The Hsu boys are Asian. And did Mrs. Lowell know that the Rodowskys are Polish? Frankly, Dawn didn't care. "I guess," she said.

"What songs are the children learning?" asked Mrs. Lowell.

"They're learning music from *Fiddler on the Roof*. They just — "

"*Fiddler on the Roof?*" Mrs. Lowell's jaw tightened. Her lips were pressed together so firmly they were turning white. "Caitlin? Celeste? Mackie? Come here, please. We're going home."

"But Mom — " said Mackie.

"I mean it. Right this instant."

"We want to *play*!" wailed Celeste, banging her sticks together.

"You can play at home."

Mrs. Lowell meant business. Reluctantly her children made their way to her. Celeste's lower lip was trembling. As they pushed past me, Mrs. Lowell made a face. It was the sort of face you'd make if you opened up a package of meat and discovered it was moldy.

Stacey put her arm around me.

I wanted to cry, but I looked at the grinning members of All the Children. They didn't know what had happened and they were ready to play again. Shea started at the beginning of "Tradition" and worked slowly through the song while the children tried to memorize the melody.

"What was *that* all about?" Mary Anne whispered to me.

My friends and I stepped away and clustered together at the edge of the yard. Kristy was fuming. Her face was beet red.

"I guess they didn't like our choice of musicals," said Jessi.

"Because it's about Russian Jews?" asked Mal.

"That's a bad combination for Mrs. Lowell,"

I said. "Foreigners *and* people of a different religion." I attempted a smile. Kristy just shook her head.

"Hey, come on. You were the one who was able to laugh before," I said to her.

"I didn't have to face Mrs. Lowell then," Kristy answered. "I couldn't *see* how much she dislikes me because my sister is from Vietnam. It's a little different when you're actually looking at her."

"What do you think we should do now?" asked Stacey.

"What do you mean?" replied Dawn.

"About our program."

"Go ahead with it."

"What if other parents don't approve of the idea?"

"What other parents? None of them is like Mrs. Lowell. And half of them have already taken their kids to see *Fiddler on the Roof.* We can't change the program because Mrs. Lowell doesn't like it."

"I guess," said Stacey. "But you know what? When you get right down to it, we're just kids. We might be good baby-sitters — "

"We *are* good baby-sitters," interrupted Dawn.

" — but we're still just kids. And *these* kids, the ones in the band, are other people's children. Not ours. Their parents think they know what's best for them. So we have to go along with that."

Stacey was right. Who were we to think we could change the world?

"Wait a sec, you guys!" said Dawn. "You are worrying about a problem we don't even have. As I just said, the rest of the parents are nothing like Mrs. Lowell. As far as we know, they love the band and they love the songs their children are playing. So Caitlin and Celeste and Mackie can't be part of the band anymore. That's too bad. It really is. But there are a couple of dozen other kids" — Dawn spread her arms, indicating the crowd of children in the yard — "who still want to make music. Right?"

"Right," agreed Stacey. "Okay, Shea. Take it away!"

CHAPTER 12

My friends and I tried very hard to be cheerful after that, especially when we were around the kids. Still, I don't know about the other BSC members, but when I was alone, I brooded. Not so much about the music our band was playing. It didn't take me long to realize that not *too* many people would find fault with performing music from a show as long-running and as popular as *Fiddler on the Roof*. No, I brooded about my awful revelation. (By the way, Janine was the one who told me about *revelations*. She says a revelation is like a discovery, only more dramatic.)

The thing is, I'd never thought of myself as different until I met Mrs. Lowell. I mean, everyone is unique. There is no other Claudia Lynn Kishi, no one who looks just like me, and loves art and junk food and is poor at school but good with kids, and so forth. I learned *that* when I was little enough to watch

Sesame Street. What I hadn't learned is that there are people — in my very own neighborhood — who don't value me or find me worthwhile, just because my ancestors happen to have come from a particular country.

Plus, the Lowells and my revelation were so tied up with the band that for awhile the band left a bad taste in my mouth. I didn't enjoy it anymore. I didn't look forward to rehearsals.

But Karen Brewer changed that.

One Saturday afternoon I went to Kristy's house to baby-sit for her little brothers and sisters — David Michael, Emily Michelle, Andrew, and Karen. As usual, the rest of Kristy's family had scattered. Her mother and Watson had gone off for an afternoon of peace. Nannie was at a meeting. Kristy was with Mary Anne at the library, working on a school project. Sam was at the high school for a dress rehearsal of the drama club's latest play (he had helped write the play). And Charlie had gone off in his car, the Junk Bucket. I wasn't sure where, but it didn't matter. (In case of an emergency I had decided to call my own parents. They're usually pretty easy to find.)

"Well," Karen said to me as soon as Charlie and the Junk Bucket had driven off. "That's the last of them."

"Last of who?" I was sitting on the front steps of Kristy's house. Andrew, Emily, and

David Michael were fooling around in the yard. But Karen had plopped down next to me.

"The last of the big people," replied Karen. "Now it's just us little guys and you. The fun can begin."

I smiled. "What do you feel like doing today?"

"Playing."

"Playing what?" I was thinking I could tolerate anything except hide-and-seek, which I had played all afternoon the day before with the three Barrett kids. I was all seeked out. All hidden out, too.

"Our songs," said Karen. "Let's rehearse. Hannie and Nancy could come over. And maybe Linny."

"Well . . . how about playing hide-and-seek?" I said, which just goes to show how I was feeling about the band that day.

"No!" cried Karen. "We *need* to rehearse. Please? I'll even let Emily play with us. I'll give her a pot and a spoon. She can pretend she's another drummer. That way she won't feel left out."

How could I argue with that? Before I knew it, Nancy and Hannie and Linny had come over and the kids were performing "Miracle of Miracles." The tune came from Karen who was playing her kazoo, and Hannie, playing her harmonica. The other kids were playing cymbals, sticks, oatmeal drums, and the pot and spoon.

When the children had run through the song one time, Karen said, "Let's pretend we have a big audience. Here. Claudia, you sit on the grass and be the big audience. We will play on the steps. The steps are our stage."

The kids arranged themselves on the steps. Then Karen came forward. "Welcome, ladies and — I mean, welcome lady. I'm very, very glad you could come to our show. My name is, um, Lucretia Marissa von Brewer and this is my band. I am your emcee this evening. Tonight, for your listening pleasure — "

"Excuse me!" spoke up David Michael. "Excuse me, Miss von Brewer. How come you get to lead things, like always?"

"Because this was my idea," Karen replied. "Now, as I was saying, tonight we will favor you with that ever-popular song 'Anatevka.' " Karen turned back to her band. "Places, everyone! . . . Emily, I said, places! That means you. Hey, are you in this band or not?"

"Are you in this band or not?" Emily repeated. She was wandering around the yard, filling her pot with sticks and fallen leaves and flower petals.

"Claudia!" Karen complained to me.

"Why don't you go ahead and play without her . . . Miss von Brewer?"

"Okay. Ready, guys?" said Karen to her band. "And a-one and a-two!" "Anatevka" rang across the yard, accompanied by exuberant drumming. When the song was over, Karen took charge again. "Not bad," she said. "Not bad." She frowned. "Well, not great." She eyed the group on the steps. "You know what we need?" she said.

Hannie and Nancy perked up. "What?"

"Uniforms! I bet we would play better with band uniforms."

I smiled. I thought of the movie *The Music Man*, about this traveling salesman guy who calls himself Professor Harold Hill (he's really a con artist) and breezes into this little town, River City, Iowa, and convinces the parents there that a band is just what their kids need. He gets everyone to buy these expensive instruments and fancy uniforms from him, so the band looks really terrific. But Professor Hill never bothers to tell anyone that he's not a musician, he can't play a note, and he can't teach the kids to *play* their instruments. It doesn't matter. The kids gain self-confidence from the way they look and everything, so in the end they can play after all (or something like that).

I could understand why Karen wanted uniforms for our band.

"Hey, yeah! Uniforms!" cried David Michael

unexpectedly. (He is not generally a fan of Karen's ideas.) "That would be way cool, right, Linny?"

"Yeah!"

"Okay," said Karen. "Then I will take charge. Allow me."

"You're in charge *again*?" cried Andrew.

"I have *lots* of ideas," said Karen haughtily. "Come on, Nancy. Come on, Hannie. I want you guys to help me."

Karen and her friends disappeared into the house. While we waited for them, Linny said, gazing into space, "I think blue uniforms would be good. With stripes up each leg. And blue hats."

"We'd look like policemen," protested David Michael.

"I think we should wear boots and spurs and chaps and ten-gallon hats and carry lassos," said Andrew.

"We want *u*niforms, not *co*stumes," David Michael replied.

"Oh. Well, what do band uniforms look like?"

The front door to the house burst open then. "They look like *this*!" cried Karen. She and Hannie and Nancy tiptoed between the boys and pranced onto the lawn.

I bit my lip to keep from laughing.

The girls were wearing long slips, clumpy

high-heeled shoes, and feather boas. Plus, Karen was wearing a straw hat, Hannie was wearing a motorcycle helmet, and Nancy was wearing a bride's veil.

"Dress ups!" cried Emily Michelle. She dropped her pot and ran to Karen. "I dress up! I dress up!"

David Michael, Linny, and Andrew stood on the steps, their mouths open. They couldn't speak. They could only stare.

"How do we look?" Karen asked me.

"You look . . . beautiful."

"Yeah, to Frankenstein," said Linny, recovering the power of speech.

"Do you really think those are *band* uniforms?" David Michael managed to ask. "Andrew's idea was better than this. He wanted everyone to dress as cowboys."

"What's wrong with these outfits?" asked Karen.

"You expect *boys* to wear slips and high heels?" answered Linny.

"No. I guess not. . . . But we couldn't find band uniforms," admitted Karen.

"Hey, I know!" exclaimed Nancy. "How about if all the band members just dress the same? We could wear, like, jeans and red shirts. I bet everyone has a pair of jeans and a red shirt."

David Michael opened his mouth, then

closed it. Apparently he could find nothing wrong with the idea.

"I have jeans!" exclaimed Andrew. "And a red sweat shirt."

"I have jeans and a red blouse," said Hannie.

"I have jeans and a red T-shirt," said Nancy. "The T-shirt says *'My parents went to Hawaii and all they brought me was this dumb shirt.'* "

We laughed. And Linny added, "Hey, maybe we could have red T-shirts made that say ALL THE CHILDREN on them. Then we would really look alike."

Even David Michael liked that idea.

"Well," I said, "I'll find out how much the shirts would cost. Maybe we could raise money to buy them."

"Or we could ask for donations at our first band concert," said Karen.

"You guys had better be *really* good then," I said.

"Don't worry. We will. Come on, let's rehearse, everybody!"

And the kids played "Anatevka" with new enthusiasm.

For awhile that afternoon I forgot about the Lowells.

CHAPTER 13

MEET

ALL THE CHILDREN

Come to our first band concert!

ENJOY THE MUSIC FROM

Fiddler on the Roof!

PLACE: The Newtons' backyard
DAY: Saturday the 6th
TIME: 2:00 p.m.
ADMISSION: Free — everyone is welcome!

★

DONATIONS ACCEPTED:
WE NEED BAND UNIFORMS!

★

"How are we doing?" I asked.

"One more stack," Jessi replied. "And it's a short one."

"Did we get rid of the fliers with those misspelled words?" Kristy wanted to know.

"*Yes*," I answered testily. The misspelled words had been my fault, of course. The first few fliers I had lettered had said things like "the Newtons bake yerd," and "every one is welcomb!" and "WE NEED BAD UNIFORMS!" Then Kristy had leaned over my shoulder and realized what I was doing. She'd given me a new job: decorating each flier. So what if I can't spell? Drawing little instruments and designs on the fliers was much more fun than lettering them.

It was a Friday evening. I had invited my friends to stay after our meeting and eat a pizza supper. Now we were sprawled around my room, preparing for the first band concert. It was going to be held in a week. We needed time to distribute our fliers. We were hoping lots of people would be free on Saturday at 2:00. Our kids were looking forward to a big audience.

My friends and I planned to post the fliers the next day and to hand them out to our neighbors. But we wanted the kids to be involved with inviting guests, too, so at our next

110

rehearsal we were going to hand each band member one invitation to give to someone special.

"Boy, I hope the kids are going to be ready for the concert," said Dawn.

"Oh, they will be," I assured her. "The ones who play the important instruments — not that the sticks and the oatmeal drums aren't important, but you know what I mean — the kids on the keyboard and the guitar and stuff have already learned the music. And the others follow along *well*. I think the concert is going to be great."

"So what's our schedule this week?" asked Stacey.

"Short rehearsals on Monday, Tuesday, and Wednesday," I replied, "dress rehearsals — or whatever they're called — on Thursday and Friday, and the performance on Saturday."

"I hope everyone can fit into the Newtons' yard," said Mary Anne.

"Oh, don't worry about that," I replied.

Mary Anne smiled. "What *should* I worry about?"

"Oh, things like whether Jackie will knock over the keyboard while Shea and Marilyn are playing it — "

"Or whether Claire will have a tantrum if she makes a mistake," said Mal.

"Or whether Karen will decide to perform

in her bathing suit or something," said Kristy. "You know, she likes our band uniforms, and she especially likes the idea of getting T-shirts, but she still wants to perform in an outfit that's a little, oh, flashier."

"Her *bath*ing suit?" I said.

"Well, you know, for instance, in her bathing suit with a crown and high heels so she could be Miss Kazoo."

"Oh, my lord. Miss Kazoo," I repeated, but I was giggling.

Six days later, on Thursday afternoon, not long after school had let out, the first dress rehearsal of All the Children got underway.

Everyone was nervous.

"Do you realize," began Stacey, edging closer to me, "that this time Saturday the concert will be over?"

"I wonder if everybody will be in one piece," said Dawn, who had overheard.

"We can only hope," I replied.

"At least," said Kristy, "the kids remembered to bring their instruments *and* wear their uniforms. That's a good sign."

She was right. It was a good sign. Then again, I thought I had once heard Janine say something like, "Good dress rehearsal, bad opening night." Maybe we didn't want the dress rehearsals to go too well after all. Not if that would jinx the concert.

I watched the kids enter the yard. Some filed in alone. Most arrived in pairs or in groups of three or four. All were wearing blue jeans with sneakers and red tops.

When everyone had arrived, Kristy tapped my shoulder. "Okay, Claud," she said. "Let's get started."

I clapped my hands and the kids gathered around me. "This is a dress rehearsal," I reminded the kids. "Remember what that means? It means we play every song, and we put on the program just the way we're going to put it on when we have an audience. We don't stop for mistakes because we won't be able to do that on Saturday. We keep on going no matter what. So now — you guys pretend that Stacey and Jessi and Kristy and Mal and Mary Anne and Dawn and I are your audience. In fact, we are your audience. And it's two o'clock on Saturday afternoon. Everyone has arrived and they're sitting patiently, waiting for the concert to begin. Jackie? Are you ready?"

Jackie stepped forward. Then he turned around and scrutinized the band. The children had arranged themselves as we had practiced — the kids playing "real" instruments in front, the kids playing kazoos and percussion grouped behind them, and the singers standing in a semicircle at one side. Jackie nodded to them. Then he faced his audience again.

"Welcome, parents and friends," he said loudly. He paused thoughtfully, then added, "And brothers and sisters and grandparents." Another pause. "Oh, and stepbrothers and . . . and, well, and stepfamilies." (He was covering all bases.) "And teachers . . ." (At this point I almost whispered, "Enough, Jackie!" but he was on his own.) "And aunts and uncles and cousins. Um, welcome," he said again. "Today I am proud to present All the Children. This is our new band and this is our first concert. We are playing music from . . . from . . ."

"From *Fiddler on the Roof!*" hissed Karen.

"I know *that!*" Jackie hissed back. "From that ever-popular musical, which my brothers and I have actually seen in Stamford, *Fiddler on the Roof.* And now for our first song, 'Anatevka.'" Jackie pointed to Shea and Marilyn. "Hit it, boys!" he called, and Marilyn flashed him an angry look. "I mean, um, hit it, kids!"

Jackie ran to the kazoo players, tripped over his untied shoelaces, fell over Mathew Hobart, the violin player, and lost his kazoo.

I closed my eyes briefly.

When I opened them again, the children had

sorted themselves out and Jackie had located his kazoo. At the keyboard, Shea and Marilyn glanced at each other. Then Shea nodded and the first chords of "Anatevka" danced across the lawn. One by one, the other kids joined in and soon everyone was singing or playing.

When the song ended, the members of the BSC clapped loudly.

All the Children performed two more songs.

During the fourth number, "Tradition," Claire lost her place. In a rest (that was supposed to be silent, of course) she banged on her oatmeal drum. Then she clapped her hand over her mouth.

"Uh-oh!" said Suzy Barrett loudly. "You did a boo-boo."

"I know it," replied Claire. Around her the music was starting up. But Claire's temper had taken over. "Quiet!" she yelled. "Quiet! . . . I said *quiet*! We have to go back!"

"Claire did a boo-boo," Suzy said again.

The band was confused. Some kids continued to play, others had stopped, several had lost their places.

"What should I do?" I whispered to Kristy.

"See if they can fix it themselves," she replied.

"If they can't, I'll take Claire aside," added Mal. "Maybe I should be prepared to do that on Saturday, too."

The band was nearly out of control when Jackie yelled, "START OVER! AND A-ONE AND A-TWO!"

Claire pouted for one entire verse, then joined in again.

"Whew," I said under my breath.

After one more song, Jackie announced, "And now it is time for a station break. . . . I mean, for intermission." He glanced at me, then added, "By the way, the band is trying to buy cool red T-shirts for our uniforms. If you would like to help us, we'd be glad to take your money. Remember — this concert is free. You did not have to pay to get into the Newtons' yard."

The kids relaxed for several moments, and I called Jackie over. Before I had opened my mouth he said, "I know we didn't rehearse that last part. It's new. I wrote it myself last night."

"And you did a good job," I told him, trying to be tactful, "but I don't think you need to say that. On Saturday we'll leave out baskets for donations. Please don't remind the audience that they didn't pay to see the show. I'm not sure they'll appreciate that."

"Okay, okay."

Jackie walked away and I stifled a laugh. I noticed Jessi and Stacey doing the same thing. Across the lawn, Mallory was having a talk

116

with Claire. When Mal joined us again, Jackie shouted, "Okay, everybody! That's the end of intermission. You can sit down now!"

"Is that how he's going to talk to the *audience* on Saturday?" said Mary Anne, sounding horrified.

"Maybe the grown-ups will think it's funny," whispered Jessi.

"Maybe. But I have a feeling I better talk to him before tomorrow's rehearsal. I don't want anyone to be offended," I said.

When the dress rehearsal ended I had another chat with Jackie. I tried to explain the meaning of the word *tact*. I'm not sure I did a very good job. "Be polite, Jackie," I said finally.

"Polite," he repeated seriously.

"Say things you'd like to hear if you were in the audience. Make the audience feel good. Flatter them."

"Flatter them."

"Just use good sense."

"Claudia?"

"Yeah?"

"I think maybe I was born without good sense."

CHAPTER 14

The time: 5:05 p.m.

The day: Friday.

Twenty-four hours from that moment the first public performance of All the Children would be over. I wasn't even going to be *in* the performance and I was nervous. I kept remembering Claire's temper tantrum and Jackie's guilt trip, which he hoped would bring in money for T-shirts.

"Oh, my lord," I muttered.

"What's the matter?"

I whirled around. "Geez, Kristy, don't sneak up on me!"

"I didn't sneak up on you," she replied indignantly. "I ran up the stairs like I always do. And I am not a quiet person."

"I know."

"Thanks a lot."

"Well, you said it." Kristy made a face at

me. "Oh, I'm sorry," I told her. "I'm nervous about the concert. I didn't mean to take it out on you."

"The rehearsal went really well today," said Kristy, flopping onto my bed. "You don't have to worry."

"Well, I'm worrying anyway. A little bit. I've been thinking about Claire's tantrum and Jackie's speech."

"But Claire didn't have a tantrum today. And Jackie's speech was much better than yesterday's. Shorter, too."

"You're right."

"Come on. Leave the worrying to Mary Anne. She's a professional worrier."

"I heard that!" exclaimed Mary Anne as she entered my room.

"Now *you're* sneaking around!" I accused her.

"What?" said Mary Anne. "And Kristy, I do *not* worry professionally."

Jessi ran into the room then, grinning. "I wish you guys could hear yourselves," she said. "My mother would say you are sniping and griping."

"Has anyone ever heard that saying about 'good dress rehearsal, bad opening night'?" I asked my friends.

"I have," Jessi answered.

"Do you believe it?"

Jessi shrugged. "I don't know. It's a superstition."

"Anyway, we can't do much about tomorrow now," said Kristy. "We've held millions of rehearsals. I think the kids are as good as they're going to get. We'll just hope for the best."

The rest of the members of the BSC trickled in, and by five-thirty Kristy was ready to begin the meeting.

"Any club business?" she asked after she'd called us to order.

"Yeah," I replied. "The Lowells."

Six heads turned slowly toward me. "The Lowells," Jessi repeated.

"I guess we could consider them unfinished business," said Kristy. "We haven't talked about them in awhile. Claud's right. We need to."

"Why?" asked Stacey, sounding whiny.

"What are you complaining about, O Blonde-Haired, Blue-Eyed One?" I asked. "They didn't say *you* were funny-looking."

"Exactly. How do you think I feel — being approved of by Mrs. Lowell? I don't want *her* approval. It's like, if *she* approves of me, then what's wrong with me? Something must be. See what I mean?"

"I understand," said Dawn, "but how come

you let Mrs. Lowell affect how you feel about yourself?"

Stacey paused. "I don't know," she said.

"Anyway, that isn't the point," said Kristy. "The point is — what if Mrs. Lowell calls the club again, wanting another sitter?"

"Do you really think she's going to?" asked Stacey.

Kristy shrugged. "Who knows? She might."

"Or what if the kids show up at a band rehearsal one day? That could happen, too," I said.

"Well, *I* think we need to teach the Lowells a lesson," Mal spoke up.

"How?" asked Dawn.

"I'm not sure. But I want to get back at them for the way they treated Claudia and Jessi. That was rude and mean and . . . and, well, dumb."

"How are we going to teach Mrs. Lowell a lesson?" asked Kristy. "We're just a bunch of kids."

"The next time she calls we should tell her we're not going to sit for her family anymore because we don't like bigots," I said hotly.

"Claudia. You know darn well we cannot say that," Kristy replied.

"Okay, we'll say we don't sit for blonde-haired, blue-eyed people."

"Claudia! Geez!" cried Dawn. "Stace and I

are blonde-haired, blue-eyed people. Besides, if we say anything like that then we're no better than the Lowells. That's bigoted, too."

"Isn't there a term for that?" said Stacey. "Reverse something-or-other?"

"Oh, who cares," I said.

"You know, we really ought to teach Caitlin and Mackie and Celeste a lesson," said Mal. "But not a mean one; just that most people are nice. If we don't do that and they grow up prejudiced, it'll be our fault."

"No, it won't," interrupted Jessi. "It'll be their parents' fault. It's already their parents' fault."

Ring, ring.

I dove for the phone. A split second before I picked it up, I remembered not to sound angry. I drew in a deep breath. "Hello, Baby-sitters Club."

"Hi . . . Claudee?"

"Hi, Jamie!" I said brightly. (Not too many people call me Claudee.)

"Hi-hi. Um, Mommy said I could telephone you. I was worrying about something. What if it rains tomorrow?"

I opened my eyes wide. Then I covered the mouthpiece of the phone and said to my friends, "Oh, my lord! What if it rains tomorrow? We never thought about that. The electric keyboard can't be on the porch if it rains. The

122

rain always blows in. This is a disaster!"

"Claud," said Kristy calmly, "it isn't a disaster yet. It isn't raining. And the weatherman is predicting sunshine for tomorrow."

"Well, what does he know?"

"If it rains, we'll figure something out. We'll set up the band in the garage so the kids won't get wet."

"But the audience can't fit in the garage, too."

Then we'll cancel," hissed Kristy. She waved wildly at the phone. "Talk to Jamie before he hangs up."

"Jamie?" I said sweetly. "Don't worry about it. See you tomorrow."

I hung up the phone.

"The Lowells — " Jessi began to say.

Ring, ring.

"I'll get it this time," said Kristy, eyeing me. "Hello, Baby-sitters Club." Pause. "Karen? What's the matter? . . . Your kazoo? Well, did you look *every*where in your room? . . . Okay, how about the car? . . . Are you sure you had it when you left rehearsal this afternoon? . . . What? You blasted it in Andrew's ear on the way home?" Kristy tried not to giggle. "Well, maybe Andrew has it. Maybe he doesn't want to be blasted at anymore. . . . Okay, put Andrew on. . . . Hi, Andrew. Listen, you don't know where Karen's kazoo is, do you? You know, she *needs* it for the concert. And if she can't find hers, then I'll lend her Sam's. . . . You just remembered where it is? Okay, why don't you go find it, and give the phone back to Karen." Kristy paused again and made a face. For a moment she held the phone away from her ear. Then she said, "Karen, what on earth is going on? . . . No, let Andrew get the kazoo himself. You don't have to see his hiding place."

Kristy stayed on the phone for over five minutes, straightening out the problems between Andrew and Karen. By the time she hung up, Andrew had produced the missing kazoo and Karen had apologized for nearly deafening him earlier. Kristy was laughing, but she quickly became sober. "Okay. The Lowells," she said to us. "We haven't made a decision yet."

"I have an idea," said Jessi. "I think if Mrs. Lowell calls the BSC again we should just tell her that no one can take the job. If that happens a few times, she'll stop calling."

"I guess," I replied with a sigh. "But then nobody has learned anything, except us. And we didn't need the lessons we learned."

"Maybe teaching the Lowells a lesson isn't our job," said Dawn.

"You know we *can* do one thing," said Jessi.

"What?" (The rest of us practically pounced on her.)

"We can be good examples for the kids we sit for. For *all* of them, whether they have prejudiced ideas or not."

"Yeah!" exclaimed Stacey. Then she added more seriously. "But we don't want to impose our ideas on them."

"No," agreed Jessi. "We can just show them how to be good neighbors."

Everyone was silent for a few moments. Then I said, "You know what? This may be hard to believe, but I can't hate the Lowells. I feel as though I *ought* to hate them, but I just can't."

"My parents," spoke up Mal, "say it's okay to hate some of the things people *do*, but it's not okay to hate the people who do them."

"Like Karen hating the fact that Andrew hid her kazoo, but not hating Andrew," said Kristy.

I frowned. "You guys? This is too much like school. Let's have a junk-food fest or something."

Mary Anne looked at her watch. "Too late. It's almost six. We don't have time. Anyway, let's be good girls and not spoil our appetites for dinner."

"But *we're* having liver," I objected.

"Then by all means scarf up a candy bar before you go downstairs," said Mallory. "Liver. Ew. Why not just serve up monkey or something?"

"Monkey!" exclaimed Kristy. "Hey — "

"Oh, please don't start," wailed Mary Anne. "Mal, why did you mention disgusting food? That's Kristy's favorite subject."

Kristy ignored her. "Six o'clock," she announced. "Meeting adjourned."

"Wait!" I cried. "Don't leave yet. The concert starts at two. Meet here at one o'clock tomorrow. Wear jeans and red shirts like the kids. Who's bringing those baskets for donations?"

"I am," said Mallory. "I found three."

"And who's bringing chairs?" (We had decided to provide a few folding chairs for older people in the audience. Everyone else would have to sit on the ground, like at any outdoor concert.)

"Me!" said Mary Anne, Dawn, Jessi, and Stacey.

Kristy looked at me. "Is that it, Claud?"

"I think so."

"Okay. See you guys tomorrow."

"And keep your fingers crossed for sunshine!" I added.

CHAPTER 15

I had nightmares about rain and thunderstorms. In one, All the Children were performing in Jamie's yard on a sunny, perfect day. Then, without warning, a storm blew in. It blew in so quickly that the children and the audience couldn't even run for cover before a bolt of lightning sliced down through the porch roof and struck the keyboard. The keyboard lit up like a neon sign, then crumbled into a little pile of ashes. Shea and Marilyn stood over it, their hands still poised to play, their mouths forming round O's of surprise.

In the dream, I screamed. (I hope I didn't *really* scream. That would be too, too embarrassing.) And then the storm blew away, and the concert began again, and Shea and Marilyn played air guitar instead of the keyboard. The audience thought the lightning had been a special effect, and they applauded loudly at the end of the concert and donated enough money for all the red T-shirts we needed.

Maybe that wasn't a nightmare after all.

At any rate, I was relieved to wake up on Saturday and see that the sun was shining. (Frankly, I was relieved just to wake up.) The sky was a deep, clear blue, without so much as a hint of a cloud. Still, I jumped out of bed, ran to my phone, and dialed W-E-A-T-H-E-R. "Good morning," said a tinny female voice. "Thank you for calling Weather. Here are today's readings and forecasts. Highs in the low seventies, lows tonight in the high fifties. The current temperature is a pleasant sixty-two degrees."

"Is it going to RAIN?" I shouted.

"Stay tuned for the remainder of the forecast following — "

I held the phone in front of me and said, "'What is this? The Telephone Company Variety Show?"

I listened for another minute and the weatherwoman assured me that the day would be "brilliantly sunny."

"Thank you," I said to her, and hung up.

That was at eight-fifteen. At one o'clock, when my friends began to arrive, the sun really was brilliant.

"Hey! What a great day!" called Kristy as she ran across the lawn.

I was sitting on the front stoop. "I know. We are *so* lucky."

Mallory showed up then with three wicker baskets, and soon the others arrived (in cars) with wooden and metal folding chairs, which their parents drove over to the Newtons'.

By one-thirty Jamie's yard looked like . . . well, it looked like a yard with a bunch of chairs in it.

Jamie dashed outside and tested every chair. "This one's good, this one's good," he kept saying.

Meanwhile, the members of the Baby-sitters Club ran an extension cord out of the Newtons' house and connected it to the keyboard. Someone set up three small tables and Mallory placed a basket on each one.

I propped up a sign by the garage. I had lettered it myself (but Stacey had given me a hand with the spelling). The sign said:

ALL THE CHILDREN
PREMIERE PERFORMANCE . . .
HERE . . . TODAY!
EVERYONE WELCOME
ADMISSION FREE
(DONATIONS ACCEPTED)

"We're here! We're here!" cried a small voice.

I looked away from the sign.

Running up Jamie's driveway, dressed in jeans and their red T-shirts, were Gabbie and Myriah Perkins.

"Are you ready?" I asked them, smiling.

"Very ready," said Gabbie seriously.

The members of All the Children began to arrive quickly after that. The ones who lived nearby walked to Jamie's on their own. Others showed up accompanied by their parents, and we had to separate the moms and dads from their kids so we could organize the band.

"Where's Jackie?" I asked at ten minutes to two. "We need our emcee. What are we going to do if he doesn't show up?"

"Claud!" exclaimed Kristy, exasperated. "You sound like Mary Anne again."

"And I heard that again," said Mary Anne. "Listen, you guys should be glad to have me around. I will personally do all your worrying for you. Claudia, you're not taking full advantage of me."

"Hello, everybody!" called a familiar voice.

"Jackie!" I replied, before I had even turned around. Then I ran to him and hugged him. "Oh, I'm *so* glad you're here!"

Jackie pulled away from me, pink-faced. "Do *not* hug me," he hissed. "You are a *girl!*" He searched the faces in the yard. "I hope Nicky didn't see that," he added nervously.

130

I grinned. "Oh, Jackie. Come on, let's get organized. The show will start in ten minutes. And look how big our audience is."

Jackie Rodowsky stood in front of the company of All the Children, who were arranged behind him in neat blue-jeaned, red-shirted groups. In front of him were grandparents and parents and children and neighbors and friends. Most of them were seated comfortably on blankets or beach towels. The others occupied the folding chairs.

The audience looked expectantly at Jackie as he said, "Welcome, Lysol and germs. You know, a funny thing happened to me on my way over to this backyard." Jackie glanced questioningly at me, and I waved my arms back and forth. I was sending him a gigantic NO signal.

(Next to me, Kristy had buried her head in her hands and was muttering, "I don't believe it. Who does he think he is? Johnny Carson?")

Luckily, Jackie got my message. He started over again. "Welcome, parents and friends, brothers and sisters, and grandparents and families," he said. (I heaved a sigh. Kristy unburied her face.) "Today I am proud to present All the Children. This is our new band and this is our first concert and actually this was all my idea."

131

"Jackie! Jackie!" called Claire Pike from the oatmeal drum section. "You aren't supposed to say that! You didn't say it before!"

Jackie ignored Claire. "We will be playing music from . . . from . . ."

"From *Fiddler on the Roof!*" supplied Karen, and several people laughed.

"From that ever-popular musical *Fiddler on the Roof*," said Jackie. "And now for our first song, 'Anatevka.' Hit it, Shea and Marilyn."

Jackie ran to the kazoo players (without tripping). He did drop his kazoo twice before getting a solid grip on it, but I don't think anyone noticed.

When "Anatevka" came to an end, the audience clapped. Kristy's big brothers even whistled. Then Shea and Marilyn played the opening notes of "If I Were a Rich Man." This was a difficult piece. We had arranged the number so that the keyboard and violin and guitar often played while the other instruments were at rest.

But Claire kept forgetting.

The third time she beat her drum out of turn, Archie nudged her.

The fourth time, Claire opened her mouth and —

"She's going to yell!" I whispered urgently to Mallory.

Mal looked calm. "I don't think so. I told

her that if she *had* to yell, she should do it inside her head."

Sure enough, Claire closed her mouth a few moments later.

The rest of the song, and the entire first portion of the concert, went quite well. Buddy Barrett sang once when everyone else was quiet, Charlotte forgot part of the music for "Tradition," and Jackie dropped his kazoo several more times, but nobody cared much.

Before the intermission, Jackie announced politely that there were three baskets for donations for the band T-shirts — but that was all he said. And when the concert ended he said, "Thank you for coming. I hope you enjoyed our show."

I wish someone had videotaped the concert. I really do. Especially the end. After Jackie thanked the audience, they clapped and clapped (and whistled) and clapped some more. Then a whole bunch of the parents stood up, ran to their kids, and hugged them and congratulated them.

"I'd say this was a success," I shouted to Stacey over the noise.

Stacey grinned. "Definitely!"

The yard seemed like a train station at rush hour; people running here and there, calling to one another. I looked from side to side, surveying the scene, and I saw two small figures sidling toward the gate in the Newtons' fence. Caitlin and Mackie Lowell.

Jessi was standing next to me and I elbowed her. "Look!" I exclaimed, pointing to the Lowell kids.

Jessi looked just in time to see them run through the gate and down the sidewalk toward their street. "I don't believe it," she murmured. "I bet their parents don't know they're here."

"Probably not. You know what? When I first noticed them they looked kind of sad." *Wistful* was the word I meant to use.

"I bet they wish they were playing today. I think they wanted to be in the concert," said Jessi.

"Even with *us* around? The funny-looking ones."

"I guess so."

"Jessi," I began thoughtfully, "do you think the Lowell kids *really* thought we were funny-looking or . . . or mean or stupid or whatever? Or were they just repeating things they heard their parents say?"

"I don't know."

"Because I was thinking. Right now Caitlin and Mackie and Celeste are pretty young. Maybe when they get older their opinions will change. Maybe they won't just automatically think what their parents think."

"You mean maybe they'll grow out of this?"

"It's possible. After all, they go to school. I don't know which school they go to, but there must be at least a *few* Asian kids and African-American kids and Jewish kids there."

"Yeah."

"And today they looked like they really wanted to be a part of this."

"Maybe we'll see them around the neighborhood sometimes."

"Maybe."

"Maybe one day they'll even be members of All the Children again."

"Maybe."

"Claudia! Claudia! How did I do?" cried Jackie, running to me.

I wanted to hug him, but instead I stood back and smiled. "Fantastic!"

"You should see the money everyone's giving us!"

"A lot?"

"Pretty much. . . . Did I really do a good job?"

"You really did."

"How good?"

I couldn't resist. I wrapped my arms around him in another hug. "Like I said, fantastic."

"Thank you," Jackie replied politely.

About the Author

ANN M. MARTIN did *a lot* of baby-sitting when she was growing up in Princeton, New Jersey. She is a former editor of books for children, and was graduated from Smith College.

Ms. Martin lives in New York City with her cats, Mouse and Rosie. She likes ice cream and *I Love Lucy*; and she hates to cook.

Ann Martin's Apple Paperbacks include *Yours Turly, Shirley; Ten Kids, No Pets; With You and Without You; Bummer Summer;* and all the other books in the Baby-sitters Club series.

Look for #57

DAWN SAVES THE PLANET

I could feel my voice growing louder with excitement as I said, "Do you realize how many items can be recycled? Newspapers, computer papers, plastic bottles, glass bottles, jars, aluminum foil." I pointed to Claud's wastebasket, where an empty Coke can lay. "That can. You could redeem it and get a nickle."

"Oops!" Claud giggled. "I guess I was just being lazy."

"Boy," Kristy said to Stacey under her breath. "Dawn's really gotten serious."

"You're right," I said, folding my arms across my chest. "This is very important to me, and it should be to all of you."

"It is," Mary Anne said gently. "I guess we're just not as upset about it as you are."

"Well, you should be." I pointed to Mary Anne's record book. "Look at the amount of paper you waste by just writing on one side of each sheet. Did you know that each of us uses 580 pounds of paper a year? And it takes 15 years for a tree to grow big enough to be made into paper. That's a lot of time and trees that are wasted."

Mary Anne stared down at the club record book, her cheeks now a deep red. "Next time I promise to write on both sides of the paper, Dawn."

I realized that I had embarrassed her and I felt bad about it. "Thanks, Mary Anne," I said, with an encouraging smile. "It means a lot to me.

The next fifteen minutes were filled with phone calls, so we couldn't talk about my project anymore. Just before the meeting ended, Claud announced, "I want everyone to come into the kitchen and see the new jewelry I've made. There's one for each of you. And," she raised one finger, "Dawn will be glad to hear that my jewelry is completely biodegradable."

Everyone giggled but me. I knew that I was really starting to sound like a grumpy old teacher, lecturing everyone, but I couldn't help it. If I couldn't convince the BSC of the importance of protecting our planet, how was I going to convince the town of Stoneybrook?

142

144

THE BABY-SITTERS CLUB®

by Ann M. Martin

More titles... ➤

The Baby-sitters Club titles continued...

Available wherever you buy books...or use this order form.

Scholastic Inc., P.O. Box 7502, 2931 E. McCarty Street, Jefferson City, MO 65102

Please send me the books I have checked above. I am enclosing $_____ (please add $2.00 to cover shipping and handling). Send check or money order - no cash or C.O.D.s please.

Name _____

Address _____

City_____ State/Zip _____

Please allow four to six weeks for delivery. Offer good in the U.S. only. Sorry, mail orders are not available to residents of Canada. Prices subject to change.

BSC1291

Enter **THE BABY-SITTERS CLUB**®

WIN A LOCKET CHARM BRACELET!

Super Special Trivia Giveaway

10 WINNERS

Take the Baby-sitters Club trivia challenge! Answer all the questions correctly and you have the chance to win a beautiful locket charm bracelet. Just fill in this entry page with the correct answers and return by November 30, 1992.

15 SECOND PRIZE WINNERS get Baby-sitters Club portable cassette players!
25 THIRD PRIZE WINNERS get Baby-sitters Club carry cassette players!

Fill in the blanks with the correct baby-sitter's name!

1. She has always lived on Bradford Court. _____
2. She is originally from New York City. _____
3. Baseball is her favorite sport. _____
4. She helped Jackie Rodowsky build a volcano for a science project. _____
5. She burns easily at the beach. _____
6. She has two pierced holes in each ear. _____
7. She would like to be an author. _____

Name_____ Age_____

Street_____

City_____ State_____ Zip_____

Where did you buy this *Baby-sitters Club* book?

☐ Bookstore   ☐ Drugstore   ☐ Supermarket   ☐ Library
☐ Book Club   ☐ Book Fair   ☐ Other_____ (specify)

BSC192

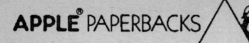

APPLE® PAPERBACKS

Pick an Apple and Polish Off Some Great Reading!

BEST-SELLING APPLE TITLES

❏ MT42975-2	**The Bullies and Me** Harriet Savitz	**$2.75**
❏ MT42709-1	**Christina's Ghost** Betty Ren Wright	**$2.75**
❏ MT41682-0	**Dear Dad, Love Laurie** Susan Beth Pfeffer	**$2.75**
❏ MT43461-6	**The Dollhouse Murders** Betty Ren Wright	**$2.75**
❏ MT42545-5	**Four Month Friend** Susan Clymer	**$2.75**
❏ MT43444-6	**Ghosts Beneath Our Feet** Betty Ren Wright	**$2.75**
❏ MT44351-8	**Help! I'm a Prisoner in the Library** Eth Clifford	**$2.75**
❏ MT43188-9	**The Latchkey Kids** Carol Anshaw	**$2.75**
❏ MT44567-7	**Leah's Song** Eth Clifford	**$2.75**
❏ MT43618-X	**Me and Katie (The Pest)** Ann M. Martin	**$2.75**
❏ MT41529-8	**My Sister, The Creep** Candice F. Ransom	**$2.75**
❏ MT42883-7	**Sixth Grade Can Really Kill You** Barthe DeClements	**$2.75**
❏ MT40409-1	**Sixth Grade Secrets** Louis Sachar	**$2.75**
❏ MT42882-9	**Sixth Grade Sleepover** Eve Bunting	**$2.75**
❏ MT41732-0	**Too Many Murphys** Colleen O'Shaughnessy McKenna	**$2.75**
❏ MT42326-6	**Veronica the Show-Off** Nancy K. Robinson	**$2.75**

Available wherever you buy books, or use this order form.

Scholastic Inc., P.O. Box 7502, 2931 East McCarty Street, Jefferson City, MO 65102

Please send me the books I have checked above. I am enclosing $_____ (please add $2.00 to cover shipping and handling). Send check or money order — no cash or C.O.D.s please.

Name _____

Address _____

City _____ State/Zip _____

Please allow four to six weeks for delivery. Offer good in the U.S.A. only. Sorry, mail orders are not available to residents of Canada. Prices subject to change.

APP1090